BOMBER'S MOON

This Large Print Book carries the
Seal of Approval of N.A.V.H.

A JOE GUNTHER NOVEL

BOMBER'S MOON

ARCHER MAYOR

THORNDIKE PRESS
A part of Gale, a Cengage Company

LIBRARY OF CONGRESS CIP DATA ON FILE.
CATALOGUING IN PUBLICATION FOR THIS BOOK
IS AVAILABLE FROM THE LIBRARY OF CONGRESS

ISBN-13: 978-1-4328-7682-1 (hardcover alk. paper)

Published in 2020 by arrangement with Macmillan Publishing Group, LLC/St. Martin's Publishing Group

Printed in Mexico
Print Number: 01   Print Year: 2020

ACKNOWLEDGMENTS

This is the thirtieth novel featuring Joe Gunther and his fellow investigators. Over their span, beginning in 1988, I have relied upon and benefited from the insight, intelligence, advice, experience, and guidance of hundreds of people. I thank them all again here, along with those listed below, who so ably assisted me in the writing of *Bomber's Moon*. I may take the credit for writing these stories, but the full credit belongs to many more. My gratitude extends to them. You have made me a better writer.

Peter Barton / Anita Bobee
Susan Randall
Rose Farley
Brian Cleveland
Randy Smith
Margot Mayor
The Barton Agency

Julie Lavorgna
John Martin
Dr. Walter F. Mangel
Jeremy Evans
Tracy Shriver
Windham Co. State's Attorney's Office

Richard Murphy
Bob Audette
Craig Cantwell
Scout Mayor
The Putney School
Castle Freeman, Jr.
Greg Kline
Ray Walker

VT Privateye
Greg Eaton
Brattleboro Police Dept.
Brattleboro Reformer
Southern Vermont Digital Forensics Laboratory

CHAPTER 1

It was cold, dark, and slightly breezy, causing a few dry snowflakes to scurry the length of Sally Kravitz's windshield. Across the street from her parked car was an example of some urban set designer's fantasy. Soaked in muted, indirect mood lighting and displayed, as on a theater stage, behind two enormous plate-glass windows was an awkwardly arranged tableau of British pub, Old West watering hole, and yuppie fern brew bar. The building housing it had been built long ago as a car dealership, however, and its windows intended not for picturesque intimacy, but to allow a full view of chrome-glazed behemoths within.

Sally shifted in her seat and adjusted her wool scarf, at once envying the contented patrons enjoying the warmth of a movie-prop-perfect cast-iron stove, while sensitive to how it must feel to have those two huge sheets of black glass reflecting back at them, ironically forbidding any view of the outdoors or, indeed, of her looking in.

She wasn't watching all of them, of course. Only Tom Morris, suspected of philandering by his wife — who'd hired Sally to "catch him in the act," as she'd quaintly put it.

That wasn't happening right now, however. Tom Morris was eating nuts at the bar, chatting with a male neighbor, and drinking a craft beer.

Sally gently let out a puff of air, away from the windshield, so as not to fog it up. There were private investigators who liked surveillance jobs — preferred them, in fact. She wasn't among them. But the wife in this situation was the mother of a friend, and from what Sally had been told, Tom — already an interloper because of being the stepfather — also wasn't deemed very smart, and therefore was expected to misstep sooner than later, thereby ending Sally's obligation.

She leveled her long-lens camera and took a picture of Tom and his companion, to have the latter on record. She'd been a PI for a few years only, but she already knew the value of keeping an open mind and collecting more than she might need. It was often the small, unexpected details that shifted the scales in a case's favor.

While it didn't apply to her, a large number of private eyes were retired police, given by their training to closing cases quickly, and with a prosecutorial outlook. Sally didn't fault their past training under demanding bosses, in dangerous work environments, and at low wages for creating a certain narrow-minded efficiency.

But she'd developed a different style. To be fair, she'd never routinely been in harm's way as had so many ex-cops. When things got dangerous for her, as they did occasionally, she could always take off. The freedom accompanying that option had encouraged a corresponding ability to frequently reflect and weigh her choices before acting.

Like now, watching Tom. He'd told his wife he'd be late getting home, as he'd be tied up in meetings. That much was a lie, although seemingly an innocent one, but where, to another investigator, the reason behind it might have suggested a quick drink before heading home, Sally held off jumping to that conclusion and stayed put, biding her time. Life had taught her early and often to be skeptical, if not cynical — a lesson too often refreshed by reality.

As if on cue, the source of her interest let out one last silent burst of laughter, drained his glass, and stood. He gave his drinking buddy a half-dismissive wave, laid his money on the bar, and headed for the door, donning his coat as he went.

Sally pursed her lips, her meditations interrupted by a sudden, if elusive notion, like a tune just beyond memory's recall. On the strength of it, the benign appearance of Mr. Morris's chosen activity — and that he'd lied about it — expanded in Sally's mind to something beyond a simple desire for some moments out on the town alone.

In the best of fictional private eye scenarios, given the hour, the snow, and the darkness, here is when some bit of action would have kicked in as Tom stepped outside — perhaps a kidnapping, a drive-by, or a long-anticipated clandestine meeting.

But this was Wilmington, Vermont, a tourist crossroads west of Brattleboro, south of several nearby ski resorts. It was a cluster of shops, restaurants, bars, and stores, heavily catering to flatlander travelers driving hormonal SUVs with sticker prices equaling those of many outlying local homes.

It was no place to encourage visions of *The Third Man* or an Alfred Hitchcock thriller.

Suitably, therefore, Tom Morris buttoned his designer-labeled coat across an increasingly expanding belly, pulled up his collar, and strolled along the sidewalk to the parking lot on Sally's side of the street. It was located behind her, which now made her position unwieldy, possibly requiring a U-turn. But she waited, studying her rearview mirror, trusting in her initial choice. Tom lived and worked in Brattleboro, and the shortest route there lay directly ahead, under the glaring red traffic light.

Sure enough, he fired up a BMW X5, ignited its blinding xenon headlights, and pulled past Sally's purposefully nondescript old Subaru to stop at the intersection, his blinker indicating an intended left-hand turn.

Sally waited until she knew he'd be checking both directions as he pulled forward, before mimicking his motions unnoticed and pulling into the road behind him.

From then on, it was smooth going, traveling Route 9 east, toward Bratt, as most locals called it, just two cars among a smattering of others.

Sally was happier being in motion. She was, if not a restless sort, certainly more given to action than to comforting predictability — or sitting for hours in a car. From youth, she'd been honed to this by a deeply eccentric single father, whom she only ever

11

called Dan, and who had a habit of breaking into high-end homes so he could absorb the illicit high, eat a small stolen snack, and slip away — after also tapping their electronic devices. Like a mountain climber leaving only footprints behind, he was happy to have met and conquered another challenge.

The fact that it was illegal, dangerous, and fundamentally weird had never seemed to weigh on him.

During daylight hours, Dan held off-the-radar, menial jobs, not for the negligible money, but to study the world around him, like a field anthropologist. His break-ins supplied him with access to information, rather than three-dimensional goods. He'd told Sally that her blue-blood education had been funded this way — investing in stocks using insider knowledge — but she suspected something a little less harmless might have also played a role. He'd certainly built a very sophisticated computerized data bank, filled with personal details far beyond a few good stock tips. And all of it was dynamic and self-perpetuating, since the "ears and eyes" viruses he'd installed on all those phones and computers allowed him to see and hear what was going on within them, as well as inside every device they subsequently contacted. If one of his victims texted or emailed somebody, the virus accompanied it, creating a new listening post for Dan. Over time, he had become a small-town, one-man National Security Agency.

It stood to reason that Dan had eventually begun training Sally in his tradecraft, if not his use of its results, bringing her along on some of his break-ins. And she'd enjoyed it, until the inevitable, near-lethal mishap, involving the wrong sort of people.

Everyone had survived that historic near miss, but Sally had taken its lesson to heart, and, to his credit, Dan had respected her decision to leave him to his own activities — to the point where they never even discussed them anymore. Dan, in fact, had helped in this self-effacement by stopping a peculiar trademark habit he'd practiced: In addition to eating something at every home he entered, he would leave a Post-it note greeting beside one of its sleeping occupants, a signature that had quickly earned him the nickname "Tag Man."

This he had stopped, either because he no longer practiced his "entries," as he called them — which Sally doubted — or out of respect for her.

Nevertheless, some of his inner drive must have worked its way into her soul. Which was in part why she'd ended up as a PI. It had been seductive, dropping into other people's lives. In an unusual mirroring of an actor's thirst for the identity of others, Sally had opted to observe people almost invisibly — to watch, listen, document, and learn from them. Either supportively, as when employed by a defense attorney to mitigate the prosecution's slanted portrait of an accused, or in opposition, as now, when a betrayed wife needed to cut her losses without sacrificing her rights to the silverware and a decent alimony.

And it was all legal.

That was Sally's particular code, as opposed to her father's more flexible outlook. Her brand of privacy intrusion had to be conducted by the book.

She could have become a cop. She had good and trusted friends in law enforcement, and no argument with their core mission. The structure of their world, however, was too constraining in its uniformity and single-mindedness. She liked the option of working on either side of an ethical debate, where she could choose to support either accuser or accused, based not on a prosecutor's appetite, but on her own interpretation of right and wrong. It appealed to her inner moral compass, constructed during a moth-

14

erless, vagabond life spent trailing a taciturn, if loving, father.

It made for occasionally uncertain ground, however, prone to shifts and error. She understood that. Take what she was doing tonight. Was Tom just trashing his vows out of lust and self-indulgence? Or was he a man seeking temporary harbor away from a demanding, unfair harridan?

Sally's internal jury was still out, waiting to find out if the first option had value, or if they both might.

To her surprise, the driver of the fancy car ahead of her suddenly hit his blinker again, now just a couple of miles shy of West Brattleboro.

"What're you up to, Tommy-Boy?" she said to herself, making sure to pass the motel's entrance before turning around and doubling back with her headlights off.

She waited by a plowed-up berm of old snow, and slumped in her seat to better steady her camera. Morris got out of his silver X5, registered at the desk, and then drove to a room halfway down a long row of doors. The motel was a battered-enough reminder of hopes long dashed to make his particular vehicle a standout.

As if it had been awaiting a stage manager's cue, a second car almost immediately swung off the road behind Sally and slowly entered the lot, like the tentative newcomer to a party of strangers.

With a small burst of energy, it seemingly recognized the Bimmer and scurried over to nestle beside it.

A heavily covered figure emerged into the camera's range finder, hat pulled low, crossed to the door of Morris's just-rented room, knocked, and briefly waited.

In the sudden pie-shaped light from the opening door, Sally saw Morris, in his T-shirt, smile, reach out, and remove the driver's hat.

Sally took a last photograph of Morris pulling his drinking buddy of twenty minutes earlier into the room and closing the door.

"You crafty devil," she said aloud, newly assessing this latest tidbit.

On one level, her impression of her target now actually climbed a couple of notches. More androgynous than frankly sexual herself, Sally had no strong stance on the merits of being gay or straight. That choice just didn't much matter to her. Life with Dan had bred a cautious and watchful distance from most people, along with a comfortable realization that sexuality might be a bother she could live without.

16

But that was a personal view, not em-braced by her client. Sally didn't see that it changed her assignment in any way, aside from probably making her report to the wife more awkward.

That clarity altered, however, in short order. Sally had decided to maintain her vigil, in part because she hadn't yet secured the "money shot" so desired by clients like hers: typically a photograph of the philan-derer dispensing a passionate farewell kiss in the morning. It was yet another feature of domestic surveillance cases that made them anathema to her. They generated money, to be sure, but they took too much time in mind-numbing isolation, immobil-ity, and discomfort.

Not here, though. To her surprise, Sally again saw the flash of Morris's door open-ing, this time to reveal the mysterious other man, stripped almost naked, his face cov-ered in blood from what appeared to be a broken nose.

"You son of a bitch," Sally growled, taking a picture as Morris, also undressed, ran out to drag his lover back inside, slamming the door.

Sally dialed 911 on her backup burner phone and dropped into one of the ever-ready chameleon roles she'd learned to instinctively employ since childhood, complete with accent.

"911. What's your emergency?"

"I'm at the Sleepytime Inn in West Brattleboro," she reported. "There're two guys fighting next door to me, in room twelve, and one of 'em's shouting for help. I heard something about a gun."

She hung up. The mention of a gun, she knew, would ramp things up. Nevertheless, to ensure a successful outcome, she also left her car, trotted across the parking lot in the anemic light of a single lamppost, and dragged a cinder block from near the Dumpster to behind one of the BMW's rear tires. She then stabbed both rear tires with a knife she always carried for extra measure.

After that, she repositioned her own car across the road, away from the scene, maintaining a good view of the entrance to Morris's door.

As planned, the police response was fast and efficient, if lacking in subtlety. Although no sirens were used, the entire parking lot pulsed with blue strobes as the first cruisers appeared, causing the door to room twelve to fly open once more as Tom Morris made a run for the BMW, again documented by Sally through her long lens.

There, with the car door ajar, he was surrounded by police with guns drawn, and forced to lie facedown on the ice-covered asphalt as his date, a towel held under his bloody nose, looked on from the doorway, also attended by cops.

Sally's shift was officially over. She eased the Subaru into gear and pulled into the road, unnoticed by anyone.

Hardly what she'd expected of an evening's work, but that was part of the job's appeal. Not to mention one satisfied, if soon to be startled, client, and one hapless, she hoped relieved — barhopping man, now due for a trip to the emergency room.

CHAPTER 2

"Alex B. Robbin' " was how he sometimes identified himself to his equally young and often reckless friends. His name was actually Alex Robin Hale. But the moniker was a pun. Robbing was his profession, or, technically, stealing, since he'd never, in fact, stuck anyone up. But "stealing" had no rhyme to it, no lighthearted Winnie-the-Pooh echo. And "burglarize" was even stuffier, although that was his specialty.

Which he was hoping to practice in a few moments.

He was fifty miles north of Brattleboro, his home base, in Windsor, whose only claim to fame, to his knowledge, was its boast of being the birthplace of the Republic of Vermont in 1777.

As far as Alex was concerned, that had to have been the place's high point.

Not that he was complaining. Currently, he was finding Windsor's threadbare reputation to be part of its appeal. He was parked inconspicuously in the Amtrak parking lot, which — because this was Windsor — wasn't, in fact, Amtrak's, but belonged to a restaurant that had bought the old station house and converted it, leaving passengers to be served by a bare, uncovered concrete slab running parallel to the tracks.

Alex's interest, however, wasn't the lack of amenities for railroad travelers. It was where they left their cars behind.

Alex was a prospector of sorts, or perhaps a dedicated bargain shopper. He had learned to read the geography, scan the landmarks, and look for opportunities. But he was more broad-minded than the average seeker of gold nuggets, both in terms of appetite and of how he could use, transform, secrete, fence, or otherwise channel his ill-gotten gains. And he was a lot more successful. Alex had an advantage over the run-of-the-mill thief, especially most Vermont versions: He wasn't an alcoholic or a drug user, which almost by definition meant he kept his mind clear, his actions organized, and his finances under control.

This hadn't always been so.

He'd begun conventionally, assuming the self-destructive habits he'd seen practiced by a dysfunctional family and by impulse-driven friends. Ironically, it was the very stanchions of society he now preyed upon who had saved him from most of that. He'd been forced by the state to undergo a substance rehabilitation program, and been reborn as a result.

Alex was a poster boy for reform, without the hoped-for end result authorities had intended.

What he'd heard loudest back then was how wasteful he'd been of his brains and potential. What he hadn't agreed with was how those assets should be applied to the pursuits of the average law-abiding citizen.

His was the soul of an entrepreneur, he'd discovered, not suited to the limitations of a nine-to-five routine. He could also hold his home life as a root cause for this, and that his attraction to nonconformity was born of a pathological dislike of authority. First his father and then his mother's subsequent string of boyfriends had all been heavy-handed bullies. He'd learned to skirt supreme rule and seek reward through independence.

Like a hunter, he'd once told a girl he was trying to impress, he'd found his best ground maneuvering unseen through the civilized underbrush, in search of prey. She hadn't understood a word of it, but a perfect example was now sitting before him, the analogy's equivalent of a ten-point buck, cluelessly munching the grass.

It was a brand-new, fully accessorized Cadillac Escalade that Alex had seen abandoned by its owners minutes earlier as the two of them had left it — hand in hand — in exchange for the southbound train.

Confident that he'd properly sighted his target, the self-perceived hunter started his truck and left the parking lot. He'd be back, long after dark. Passenger trains in this state were a once-a-day phenomenon, the Escalade's owners had been carrying luggage, wearing city-bound clothes, and the spot they'd left their ride was helpfully labeled long-term parking. Alex had time to work slowly and carefully.

"Reiling," the deep voice rumbled across the room.

Rachel looked up from her desktop computer. All the reporters had intercoms, texting, emails, even cell phones, if it came to that. Not that she faulted the timeworn tried-and-true approach — the newspaper's entire pressroom was the size of a generous four-car garage. And her boss preferred yelling. It reminded him of the old days.

That fit. With no hair except a snow-white

fringe around the edges and a grizzled beard, Stan Katz looked as old days to Rachel as her grandfather. That included his wardrobe, which apparently contained an endless and only slightly varying collection of corduroys, vests, and argyle socks.

She knew that was harsh, even at age twenty-four. Katz might have been getting on, but he was no candidate for an old folks' home. In fact, he still seemed capable of running circles around her and her few colleagues.

Rachel crossed the room to Katz's small office, whose desk seemed more tchotchkes museum than work space, festooned with memorabilia, knickknacks, old clippings, postcards, and piles of paperwork. His computer monitor resembled Custer surrounded by hostiles.

Katz propped one foot against the edge of the desk. "You happy here?" he asked as she stood eyeing his guest chair piled high with books and magazines.

"Are you happy with me?" she countered.

He smiled. "Sure."

"Then why the question?"

He shrugged. "People come and go. The *Brattleboro Reformer*'s the state's third-largest newspaper, but it's a way station or a springboard to most people your age.

That's neither here nor there to me. I used to care, but I don't anymore. I just live with it. But," he emphasized, dropping his foot and sitting forward, "I won't waste my time or enthusiasm on somebody who's gonna dump me at the altar."

She smiled back, aware that he'd been married for over four decades and had no true idea of the concept he'd just invoked. "That's some metaphor. Where're we going with that?"

He gestured to the chair, impressed as ever by her self-confidence. "Move that crap onto the floor."

She did so and sat as he continued. The pressroom beyond was empty. The *Reformer,* some 140 years old, had once filled the entire building. Now, perhaps reflecting modern trends, the police department was the majority tenant by a large margin, reducing the paper's footprint to one small section toward the back. There was more than old age encouraging Katz's fatalism.

"You know my history, right?" he asked.

"I know you were the editor here a long time ago," she said, about to add, "When the paper had some clout," but she stopped herself in time, finishing instead with "And that the new owners got you to return some-how."

He digested that before admitting, "Yeah, well . . . Once an old warhorse . . . The thing is," he resumed in a stronger tone, "we used to be a pretty big deal. I'd like to get that back, if not in the same way. Times have changed — I know that — along with how people access their news. But I and the people who hired me do want to aim for relevance again."

He straightened in his chair, his passion slowly fueling. "I love this town. Always have. And I like that this paper covers tiny house exhibitions and cow parades and whatever the hell else reflects who and what we are. People laugh at Brattleboro as being a left-wing haven for transplanted, tree-hugging trust funders. But that's nonsense. We care about what's important, and for each other, and in general, we think people should do more than just sit around and bitch. You know why I came back and gave up perfectly good money trying to teach corporate idiots how to communicate better, while they were busy staring at their iThingies?" he suddenly asked.

Rachel kept quiet, knowing the question to be rhetorical.

Katz held up a finger. "Because," he stated, "I think as journalists we can regain a little of the influence and purpose we used to have, and maybe bump up circulation in the bargain. I want us to be a paper whose phone call no politician or business leader will palm off on his press secretary. On that level, if nowhere else, I'd like us to get back to the old days."

"Okay," Rachel said quietly, still waiting.

Katz gave her a wide grin, which struck her as almost creepy, given how rarely she'd seen it. "Right," he said. "And who gives a rat's ass?" He became more serious, to her relief. "I'm hoping you do. That's why you're sitting there. You were hired as a photographer. You've done great work, as a shooter and writer, both. You dig, you bend the rules, you use what you've got to get what you're after. All good, as long as you don't get in trouble or break the law. That's why I've been asking you to write a few pieces, in addition to taking pictures. You been enjoying that?"

"Very much."

"Good. 'Cause I wanna ramp that up."

He extracted a small pad from the jumble before him and scribbled something down, still speaking. "Not too many people know this, Rachel, but I insisted on one condition when I came back: I told the owners I suspected the *Reformer* was part of a buy-one-take-all deal they didn't want when they purchased the flagship in Massachusetts, and that therefore this paper would pretty much have to fend for itself. They denied that, of course, and maybe I got it wrong. Nevertheless, I said I would wrestle and bicker and bargain with all the usual competing interests facing a typical small-town paper — advertising, obits, sports, the bottom line — as well as do everything from op-ed pieces to the calendar of events to answering the phones and fielding complaints. But," he emphasized, looking up from his writing, "I would do it only if they gave me a reasonably sized special fund that could never be lost inside the rest of the profit/loss mix. It was mine to spend. To their credit, they agreed.

"That money," he concluded, tearing off the top page of his pad and handing it over, "was to be used exclusively for whatever features and/or investigative articles might come our way, but which normal fiscal constraints wouldn't usually allow us to write. I've been in this post for over a year now, and I haven't used a penny yet. Partly because I wanted to make sure the owners were happy they'd brought me back, which they're proving by letting me hire a couple more people. Partly because I wanted you to gain your sea legs, which I think you have."

He pointed at what he'd just given her. "That's the name of a private investigator I know. Actually, I know her father better — have for years. Bit of a weirdo, but one of the most connected guys I ever met. Anyhow" — Katz pointed again at the piece of paper he'd just delivered — "since he's hard to reach, Sally's the next best thing."

Rachel read what he'd written: the woman's name, email, and phone number. "You want me to contact her?"

"Contact her, get friendly with her. Mostly, learn from her," he instructed. "I want you to take a shot at being that specially funded reporter." He waved toward his inward-facing office window at the pressroom. "You guys have smartphones and social media at your fingertips. Good stuff. I'm not saying otherwise. But there's a ton that won't show up there. Face-to-face chats, casual drop-bys, overheard conversations, old-fashioned dogging people's heels. Right now, we chase the news. We get a tweet, hear about a disaster, and off we go. That's okay. You've done well with that, and it works like a charm for a photographer, especially. You can't shoot what hasn't occurred. But if you're interested in doing more reporting — investigative reporting — you need to develop a nose for what's about to happen, or what's happening out of sight. That's why I want you and Sally to meet. Tell her that."

"She know I'm coming?" Rachel asked.

Katz stood up and looked around, the one-sided meeting over. "Nope," he said. "That's what I mean. Make it happen."

Alex Hale was back. The restaurant was closed, the parking lot dark, and the Escalade sitting where it had been left.

He was still in his pickup, kind of. In preparation for tonight, he'd taken his usual precautions. He'd altered his plates with black tape so they looked good at a glance, although no longer registered to him; placed a lightweight dummy cap over the truck's rear bed to change its profile; pinned a red tarp to the hood by slamming it in place, making it look like it had been primer-coated only; and, lastly, stuck magnetic signs onto the doors, advertising himself as a self-employed carpenter. All changes that could be reversed in minutes, distancing his vehicle from the details witnesses usually recall best.

He positioned the truck nearby but not too close, quietly got out, and began walking around — dressed completely in black — getting acquainted with the area. He looked for windows with lights on, checking for movement, the flickering of a TV screen. He tried determining any traffic rhythm at the end of the street, where it T-boned onto Main. He listened for voices, music, any barking dogs.

But the absence of most of that had been one of the attractions of this spot. The old station, typical of most railroad installations, was off the beaten path, on Depot Avenue, which, for all intents and purposes, didn't lead anywhere. There were no homes, no twenty-four-hour businesses, and no side-walks attracting midnight strollers.

It was also cold. It had snowed the night before, further encouraging people to stay indoors, keep their windows shut, and — just as important — their curtains closed against the chill.

On the other hand, there was a full moon, with nary a cloud in the sky, which, when combined with the fresh snow, lent a bright, almost pale blue boldness to the night, similar to the hue at the base of a gas flame. A bomber's moon, he'd heard an old juicer once call it, in mid-alcoholic stupor. A World War II term. Before lasers and radar and night vision were standard equipment on planes, night bombers ventured out over an enemy's monochrome landscape, using only their eyesight to seek out targets, much as Alex was doing now.

So far, so good, as the ancient drinker had commented, laughing. But beware what you wish for. "Whoever you target can target you in return," he'd said with unexpected eloquence. Apparently, many were the nights when the old man had barely survived the truth of that statement.

Alex had loved the allusion, being a nocturnal creature by instinct. He'd enjoyed its poetry and wisdom, and had certainly taken the latter to heart, which helped explain his covert appearance and the elaborate disguise of his truck.

But, too, he'd understood the warning, which had almost startled him with its all-encompassing relevance, especially in his dual hunter/prey identity.

Satisfied with his surveillance, he finally approached the oversize vehicle, as incongruous here with its chrome and gold accents as it might have looked on an African plain.

Using a small flashlight, he carefully checked it over, inside and out, without touching it, since it went without saying that it had an alarm. Whether it did or not, he made the assumption, if only so it wouldn't catch him by surprise.

On TV, the thief always disables any sensors, picks the door lock, hotwires the ignition, and drives away, all in under a minute.

In reality, Alex believed, his goal could be reached just as fast, if a little more crudely. After all, he wasn't, in fact, stealing the car. And his flashlight had already revealed what he was seeking.

He looked around one last time, withdrew a ball-peen hammer from inside his coat, and with practiced ease smacked the passenger's side window.

He'd mentally rehearsed his movements, planning on the yelping alarm to act as his starter pistol. He was therefore astonished not a single sound followed the sharp crack of the hammer.

"What the hell?" he wondered aloud, rooted in place for half a beat.

But instincts took over, regardless of good fortune. Hopping in through the high window, balancing his torso on its sill, he reached out with one gloved hand for the garage-door opener above the steering wheel, while simultaneously opening the glove compartment. Again, he was in luck. The car's registration lay right on top.

Within seconds, both items in his possession, Alex was back in his truck, heading toward Main Street. At no point had he seen a light go on, a voice ring out, or any blue strobes.

His adrenaline still pumping, he pulled to the side of the road several miles out of town and checked the address listed on the stolen registration, hoping it would be a street location and not a PO box. Again, he was rewarded.

Punching the location into his portable GPS, he pulled back onto the road in hopeful pursuit.

This was the process he lived for — the whole interconnected, fraught-with-peril smorgasbord of opportunity, chance, disappointment, surprise, and success. The rush he'd experienced using drugs as a teenager paled in comparison, and helped explain his evolution from that lifestyle to this. Here, he got all the spontaneity and excitement he craved, but with a payoff at the end, if everything worked out.

And that was an additional attraction. This high could last for days, what with planning, execution, and redistribution of goods — unlike when he'd indulged in pills or dope to take him away for a few hours only.

The house listed on the registration was on a dirt road, surprisingly almost sixty miles away from Windsor, south even of the Brattleboro station the car owners should have used to catch their train. It wasn't buried in the woods, but, like so many in the state, not crowded by neighbors, either. Encouraged by the lack of an alarm in the car, Alex nosed his truck into the driveway and killed his engine and lights for a moment, rolling down his windows to repeat the cautious, thought-out survey he'd taken at the railroad station.

As before, all was quiet and still. Through the trees, which also thankfully provided him cover from the moonlight, he could see a few distant house lights, left on for overnight security. Similarly, there was a light over the front door of this home, making it look both lived in and snug.

He restarted his engine but kept the headlights off, and turned the truck around, so it was facing the street. Then, with the motor idling, he donned a pair of surgical booties and left the truck to conduct a quick reconnaissance, waiting for dog barks, motion detectors, or even another dreaded alarm.

But reflecting the state's barely evolving concern about practitioners of Alex's vocation, nothing happened. He even knocked on the door and rang its doorbell to make sure.

He was now ready for his penultimate challenge. He reentered the truck, threw it into reverse, backed up to the attached garage, and hit the door opener. The door nearest to him trundled open, revealing a broad, empty space.

He continued inside, activated the remote once more, and watched as the door slid shut, closing him in.

Alex let out a breath, his brain on overload. Who might've seen him that he'd missed? How many silent alarms had he inadvertently tripped? Was there video footage of him now, wending its way across the internet to the homeowners or a security firm? And lastly — as he emerged into the garage, still lit from the overhead opener — was the connecting door to the house locked and/or wired?

He wouldn't be sure of some of these until much later, if he was lucky, but on the last topic at least, he was off the hook.

He placed his hand on the inner door's knob, twisted it, and stepped into the empty kitchen.

Time for Alex to be robbin'.

CHAPTER 3

Sammie Martens turned from the window, where she'd been watching Rachel Reiling photograph police officers by their vehicles, and glanced at her boss. Joe Gunther was, as usual, the motionless one in the group, his chin tucked, his expression thoughtful, his hands in his pockets. There was a dead man on the floor of this rickety, evil-smelling wreck of an ancient tenement, with a knife in his chest and a drying pool of blood encircling him like an undeserved halo. That explained the *Reformer* coverage. Crime-scene techs dressed all in white were moving about, documenting everything, gathering evidence, keeping busy. It was a homicide in Bellows Falls, probably drug-related, called in by someone not instinctively wary of the police. Who might've come in earlier, only to quietly retreat, was anyone's guess. "BF," as locals called it, was a town where you didn't volunteer much.

Information was a commodity, to be traded to authorities as barter.

Sam and Joe had been called in by the Bellows Falls PD, half as a courtesy and half as insurance. Their specialized agency, the Vermont Bureau of Investigation, or VBI, could be asked either to assist or to take over such time-intensive cases, especially if a ready solution appeared elusive. This one hadn't announced itself one way or the other yet — the detective/lieutenant in charge had people across town, checking on relatives, friends, and associates of the deceased. If they got lucky, VBI would know to fade away; if they didn't, Joe and his team would inherit a new case, bringing in more special agents from across the state.

Sam wouldn't mind either way. She was in a good place in life — her child, Emma, was thriving. Her partner, Willy Kunkle, was on the longest streak of near-normal, mostly predictable behavior that she'd witnessed in years. And this job was the plum opportunity in Vermont law enforcement — a pick-of-the-litter organization with a narrowly focused mandate and immunity from the tangles and politics of other red-taped, top-heavy agencies, many of which had lost their best investigators to the VBI anyhow.

And, finally, she got to work under Joe

Gunther, a legend in the business. Considerate, consistent, protective, and righteous, he was neither permissive nor controlling, but more like a tribal elder. He had his faults and weaknesses. He made mistakes. But his atoning for them, when they rarely occurred, only enhanced his stature. He'd made families of the squads he'd led, from the Brattleboro PD to the VBI, and he'd never let them down.

In fact, Gunther's present ranking was as statewide field commander of all VBI operations. However, instead of flying a desk at headquarters in Waterbury, alongside the agency's director, he'd insisted on also being agent in charge of the southeast office, one of five across Vermont. An unusual setup, it had been his only requirement for transferring to the VBI from the Brattleboro PD, where he'd been chief of detectives. He was among the longest-serving and most respected cops in Vermont. It hadn't been a big concession by the VBI brass.

The present scene Sam and Joe were occupying was looking at once sadly familiar, while missing a few pieces, which explained their still being held in limbo, despite having arrived an hour earlier. The rooming house was cheap, anonymous, and furnished — to Sam's eye — with what most people would have committed to the local dump. The facts gathered thus far mirrored the room's appearance: a drug deal gone bad, with one party, Lyall Johnson, wearing a cheap kitchen knife in his rib cage, and the other, Brandon Leggatt, having run for cover, probably within town limits. A nearby open drawer with a paltry collection of other utensils suggested the source of the knife and the spontaneous nature of its use.

That it had taken place in Bellows Falls was not a big surprise. An often hard-luck community at odds with its picturesque setting — complete with waterfall and mountains — BF had suffered the fate of so many long-retired New England industrial towns. But it was smaller, more compact, and with no backup employment options like a hospital or a prison — or even immediate proximity to an interstate exit to draw in drive-by spenders. It bravely fought the odds, and with increasing success lately. Still, the struggle seemed never-ending, with the scourge of easy drug money always lurking like a cancer.

It was not a source of comfort to town leaders that their hardship was matched by dozens of other afflicted communities statewide.

Vermont, for all its activism, beauty, and

romantic appeal, remained at its core hard-scrabble, tourist-dependent, thinly populated, and small in size. Which helped explain its frugality and historically fierce pride.

Joe looked up and saw Sam watching him. "What's up?" he asked.

She left her post by the window to join him by the body. "Rachel's outside, taking pictures."

"Wonder if she's heard something we haven't," he mused.

"You want to ask her, be my guest. I'm not doing it. She won't know squat and she'll bury me in questions." Sam had fallen prey to the conventional law enforcement attitude about newspeople, despite the fact that she and Rachel got along. Of course, most of that predated Rachel's recent employment at the *Reformer.*

Joe gazed back at the young man on the floor, whose dull, half-open eyes were staring up at the stained ceiling. "We and the press do tend to meet in the worst circumstances, expected to piece life stories back together, if for different reasons. Can't say I fault people being curious. I know I'd like to know more about him."

His voice regained its familiar, less philosophical edge as he continued. "There may be more than what's meeting the eye about Mr. Johnson, after all. We *think* we know what happened. We've got circumstances, past history, and even witnesses to lend it weight. But are we sure?"

He pivoted slightly so that he could point from the body to the apartment's doorway. "It could be supersimple: Brandon knifed Lyall over drugs. But why, when they were supposed to be pals? Did the knife come from the drawer, like it looks? Why no defense wounds? And why" — he pointed out a path to the front door — "does that part of the floor look cleaner than the rest, like someone wiped it up?"

He crossed to a half-opened dresser drawer and peered inside, adding, "And there's this: a bundle of standard wax paper heroin envelopes, all stamped with Pinocchio cartoons, and all empty. No heroin anywhere."

"Pinocchio was his brand," Sam said. "Not that he was anything but a middleman. He pretended to be a big shot, but he just repackaged the stuff. I'd guess he was waiting for a resupply or whoever whacked him stole what he had."

They were interrupted by an officer arriving at the doorway, holding up a cell phone. "They found Brandon. LT just called. He's holed up on North Oak."

The change in the room was immediate. Everyone looked up, like a herd of gazelles scenting danger, before training and procedure kicked in. The crime techs went back to work, the medical examiner's man advised, "Call me if you kill him," and the local cops filed out to render aid to their colleagues across town. Sam cautioned them as she and Joe followed. "Press is outside. Watch what you do and say."

Lyall and Brandon had been involved in the area's steady rhythm of minor crime for years — petty theft, vandalism, public disturbances, underage drinking — and, of course, doing their best to hawk Lyall's Pinocchio trademark product. Calling themselves "Batman and Robin" — the cops had dubbed them "Mutt and Jeff" — the duo had been seen entering Lyall's threadbare apartment last night, and were overheard arguing by neighbors between two and three in the morning. Now, it appeared, imitating a timeworn film noir, Brandon was possibly preparing for a showdown worthy of movie legend.

Except that Joe, for one, was going to do his best to see it didn't end that way. He didn't want theatrics interfering with what he hoped would be an enlightening conversation.

Almost everything in the tightly packed central village of Bellows Falls was no more than a thousand feet away from anything else, and in this case, even less. The address they'd been given was a two-story residence, cut up into several apartments but sharing a living room and kitchen — essentially a one-family home where each bedroom extracted rent. Not a rarity in this or other towns of its ilk.

When the small caravan of vehicles arrived without fanfare, the building had been unobtrusively surrounded, and Detective Lieutenant Marc Cote — the previously mentioned "LT" — was almost casually standing on the sidewalk, awaiting their arrival. The overall illusion of calm was maintained by several distant cruisers, which had sealed off an outer perimeter, making the area invisible against the incursions of gawkers or the likes of Rachel and her camera.

Cote directed a couple of his folks to the building in question before greeting his two colleagues from the VBI.

"You sure it's him?" Sam asked as they drew near.

"Oh yeah," he replied. "We were tipped

off by a resident who owes us a favor."

"We sure Brandon killed Lyall?" Joe asked more pointedly.

Cote caught his meaning. He barely ducked his chin, implying an ambivalence. "I don't have a confession," he stated. "It's likely, but circumstantial."

"Is he armed?" asked Sam, thinking tactically.

"Not that we know. But our CI couldn't swear to it."

Joe was looking over Cote's shoulder, getting a feel for the layout. "He know we're here?"

"No reason to think so. It sounded like he was negotiating with the residents about how long he could stay there, hiding out. I'm guessing he chose this place because he knows the people but doesn't hang with them much, making it somewhere we wouldn't normally check out."

"In other words, things could go blooey in a heartbeat," Sam said. "I'm gonna rig up." She broke away to fetch her ballistic vest and shotgun from the trunk of her car.

Joe, whose eagerness to enter combat had waned through the years, asked Cote what he thought was a reasonable question, given the mounting tension. "Has anyone considered just knocking on the door?"

Cote smiled — another pragmatist. "The old pizza delivery con?"

"Something like that. Why not?"

They both looked around. All their vehicles were safely out of sight. From inside the house, the residents shouldn't have known anything was amiss — unless cell phones and Facebook had told them otherwise.

It was Cote's decision. This was still his scene. He nodded and said, "I don't see the harm in giving it a try."

It wasn't to be. As they stood there, weighing how best to proceed, the front door to the house opened and a squat, pasty-faced young man stepped out onto the sagging porch.

"Shoot," Cote said. "That's him. So much for lying low. Maybe they threw him out."

To his credit, the cop instinctively overrode the reasonable norms practiced by more protocol-driven counterparts. He walked into the middle of the slushy, ice-clogged dirt driveway and waved to Leggatt.

"Hey, Brandon," he called out as he approached, a smile on his face. "You got a minute?"

Leggatt froze, looking around, no doubt convinced black helicopters would be next.

"What?" he said nervously, recognizing Cote.

It was more than one of the lieutenant's patrol officers could stand. Looking like a black-clad ninja, he stepped into view by the edge of the porch and screamed, *"Show me your hands!"*

Mercifully, rather than a shotgun, which procedure emphatically favored, the officer was holding a Taser in both hands. This turned out to be lucky, as, without further warning, he fired the device before Leggatt could respond.

The man dropped like a stone, the Taser's glinting twin wires delivering their fifty thousand volts, while the building's door-yard suddenly filled with cops from all angles, yelling simultaneously.

Leggatt remained oblivious, gasping like a fish during his five very long seconds of open-eyed agony. Taser shots are riveting that way, inflicting the worst pain imaginable, only to be followed by no lingering discomfort whatsoever.

Sure enough, Leggatt lay on the porch as the barbs were yanked from his body, blinking wonderingly at the memory. "Wow. Oh man. Wow." He seemed oblivious as his hands were pulled behind his back and quickly cuffed.

Cote and Gunther reached him, followed closely by Sam, as Leggatt was pulled into a sitting position, searched for weapons, and quickly Mirandized. Aside from a pack of cheap cigarettes, a lighter, a thin canvas wallet, and two small packets of heroin stamped with a muscleman ironically lifting a dumbbell, there was nothing.

Veterans like Joe and Marc Cote had developed an eye for the likes of Brandon Leggatt, who were not instinctively mean-spirited, despite their careless ways and worse choice in friends. They were often ignorant of kind and generous treatment, however, which could be helpful to experienced cops, especially after the rough-and-tumble just displayed.

As a result, after Brandon had been rendered safe, Cote quietly reassigned his crew, including sending a couple of them into the house to conduct interviews, while Joe settled in beside Leggatt, using the wall as a backrest. Miranda rights having been recited, Joe proceeded carefully.

"You warm enough?" he asked.

Brandon was thickset, dressed in an insulated, if worse for wear, hooded sweatshirt. "I guess," he said.

As Brandon sullenly watched the previously hidden cruisers making U-turns in the narrow street, Joe gently pushed him forward and released the handcuffs.

"That better?" Joe asked, resting his hand on the young man's shoulder to both push him back and give him a little friendly contact. Using a much-practiced show of replacing intimidation with empathy, Joe pulled out a pack of cigarettes that he, a nonsmoker, carried for such occasions and handed it over with a matchbook.

"Yeah." Brandon began the ritual of lighting up.

"First time for a tasing?"

"Yeah."

"Hurts, right?"

"No shit. Why'd you do that? I didn't do nothin'."

Joe chuckled as Cote returned and took a seat at the edge of the porch, a nonthreatening distance away. Sam had joined the two interviewers inside, in part to diminish any future claims of police bullying. But as this was still a Bellows Falls case, Cote was well advised to stay close by. "What d'ya think? We found Lyall."

Brandon turned his head sharply to stare at him wide-eyed. "You think I did that?"

"You were heard arguing."

"*Course* we were arguing. Fer Chrissake,

49

we *always* did that. Doesn't mean I killed him."

"But you know he's dead," Cote pointed out.

That stumped him, as if he'd been presented with a completely unexpected challenge.

"Yeah . . . ," he said slowly. "So?"

Joe bumped him lightly, shoulder to shoulder, as if they were sharing a joke. "See it through our eyes. You're with your best friend, you're both fighting, he winds up dead, and now we find you hiding out here. What are we supposed to think?"

Fortunately, Brandon didn't do the smart thing, which would have been to deny it. Instead, too well trained by a past of being caught, he simply shrugged. "I didn't come here to hide out. I got scared. It just seemed like a good idea."

"I understand that," Joe said sympathetically. "But it doesn't solve who killed him."

"It wasn't me."

"Then you don't have anything to worry about. Tell us what happened. It'll only help catch who did it."

Brandon nodded thoughtfully. "I guess."

"What were you fighting about?" Cote asked.

Brandon didn't hesitate. He looked over

at his meager possessions. "He wanted half that shit I bought," he said, referring to the heroin. "I told him I paid for it. He wasn't getting any 'less he laid out some cash. There wasn't enough anyhow, for two. He knew that. He was a cheap fuck."

Despite the words, both cops could hear the fondness for his friend in his voice. Joe was surprised, in fact, that the heroin hadn't been used for consolation by now, imagining that only the right opportunity and tools had maybe been lacking.

"He didn't have his own stuff?" Joe asked. "He sold Pinocchio brand, didn't he?"

"When he could, yeah. He was between deals."

"What happened next?" Joe prompted him.

"I left. I was pissed."

"But he was still alive?"

"Sure he was. It was after I went back that . . ."

"What?" Cote asked after the pause.

"I found him."

The two cops exchanged glances, this being the threshold they'd been seeking.

Joe spoke first. "Why did you go back?"

"I forgot my wallet."

"Where was it?"

Brandon looked confused. "What? On the

couch. It falls outta my pocket all the time."

"Meaning you had to step over your buddy to get it," Cote suggested.

"Yeah."

"You didn't think to call 911?" Joe asked.

Brandon's eyes popped wide in outrage. "And have all this shit happen? Yeah — right. I knew you'd pin it on me. Same ol', same ol'. Been there, done that. B'sides, I don't got a phone no more. Ran outta minutes."

"Okay, okay," Joe said, soothing him. "But tell us something. Really important. Roughly how much time was there between when you left and when you went back — after you noticed the wallet was missing?"

He didn't need to give it much thought. " 'Bout half an hour."

"You take Lyall's phone? You just said you don't have one."

"Nah." Brandon looked momentarily stumped before adding, "Didn't think of it."

"What's his number?" Joe asked, figuring they might be able to track his calls and texts later through his phone provider.

Brandon recited it.

"You know who he used as a carrier?"

"It was a burner. He got it at Walmart."

Joe moved on. "How 'bout the knife? You

52

notice it?"

"Hell yeah, I noticed it."

"You recognize it?" He pressed him.

Brandon blinked. "What? It wasn't mine."

"Not what I asked."

"It was Lyall's. He used it to cut things up, like to open packages for dinner."

Joe once more cast a look at his colleague, seeing confirmed in Cote's expression the feeling that, as self-preserving as Brandon might have been in response to his pal's death, he seemed to be telling the truth now. It had all been delivered directly and without evasive body language, and there were enough parts of it that would be too easy to check later by comparing them to the interviews taking place in the house right behind them.

Joe therefore shifted tack slightly, approaching Brandon more as a witness than a suspect. "You said earlier you were scared. Does that mean either of you saw something like this coming?" he asked.

"No," Brandon burst out. "Look at us, man. We're not like that. Maybe we mess around a little. Do stuff we're not supposed to. But nothin' that deserves killing."

"What've you been up to the last twenty-four hours?" Cote asked. "Either together or separately?"

"Nothin'. I scored that." He pointed to the two packets. "Before then, we messed around, down at Milly's, over to TJ's . . . like that." He shook his head sorrowfully. "There was *nothin'*, man. We didn't do squat. We were just hangin' out."

"But you scored your dope apart from Lyall," Joe said. "That's what you implied. What was he doing in the meantime?"

"Dunno. He said he had to meet somebody. Got a text message when we were eating dinner at Danni's. Didn't say who from. I even asked, but he blew me off, including after we hooked back up at the apartment later." Brandon looked from one cop to the other before asking, "You think that was it? That whoever it was came back and killed him after I left? Set me up?"

"We have no idea," Joe told him, but that was exactly what he was thinking. The notion was certainly supported by the fact that Lyall's cell phone had gone missing and wasn't among Brandon's possessions.

"One last question," Joe said. "When you went back to get your wallet, or even earlier, for that matter, did you wipe something off the floor, near the apartment's front door?"

Leggatt stared at him. "What? Wipe the floor? No."

Even Cote looked confused by that, so Joe rose to his feet, using Brandon's shoulder as a prop, and gestured the BF cop over for a private talk at the end of the porch.

"You as doubtful as I am that we got a slam dunk here?" he asked.

Cote took his meaning. "Do I smell a third person? Yep."

"Meaning VBI's probably going to inherit this," Joe mused.

"Christ, I hope so," Cote said.

"Then do me a favor, would you? While that's being put through formal channels, boss to boss, could you ask the crime lab to run two extra tests? I want a fluorescein analysis of the floor — from the body, out the door, and all the way to the building's exit — and a FARO shoot of the apartment and the hallway outside."

Cote raised his eyebrows. "Ah, you big-budget guys. Must be nice. What're you hoping to find? Whoever cleaned the floor?"

Joe looked noncommittal. "If someone was wiping blood up as they left, the fluorescein should catch any leftovers — meaning the techies can collect DNA. As for the 3-D FARO shoot? Let's just say I'd like that area visually available down the line. If it comes to it, the prosecution could present a jury with a virtual hologram of the crime scene."

Cote was agreeable. "If you got the toys, might as well use 'em."

Joe turned to address Brandon one last time. "You said you and Lyall met back at his apartment. Was that the usual?"

"Sure," Brandon answered slowly, looking confused.

"You sleep on Lyall's couch most of the time? I mean, you don't have a place of your own?"

"Not really."

"But you don't officially live together?"

Brandon tucked in his chin. "That makes it sound weird. Nah."

"After you scored your buy, were you the first one to get to the apartment, or was Lyall?"

"He was."

"And how long after you parted ways after dinner did you get back together?"

"I don't know. . . . Maybe an hour?"

Joe returned to Cote, who merely looked at him.

Joe answer the implied question. "Long time for things to go sideways."

CHAPTER 4

There are rules to conducting private investigations. People think that if the client just wants information, without intending to pursue any subsequent legal action, the PI can play a little fast and loose — maybe take a picture through the window of a private residence, or access a computer or phone without permission — in order to clinch a telling detail or two.

In fact, the client's motives don't drive the investigator's behavior, or shouldn't. At best, it's her own integrity and respect for the law that hold sway. At worst, it's the fear that breaching such boundaries could result in arrest, the loss of a license, or jail time.

Sally, however, wasn't working for a client. Not at the moment. This was strictly personal, and, she reasoned, born of self-preservation. As she stood alone in the darkness of Rachel Reiling's small, sparsely furnished, apparently rarely occupied apartment, she found herself less in the present, thinking more about when she used to break into people's homes with her benignly demented father.

The fact that she'd chosen to distance herself from his lifestyle, in exchange for a life of legal probity, didn't mean that she hadn't maintained the skills he'd passed along. She might have opted to break new ground, but his influential suspicion of others and inborn caution were more difficult to shed.

Plus, as she was the first to acknowledge, the thrill of trespassing was hard to deny. She began slowly analyzing her present surroundings, using a pair of night-vision goggles to avoid turning on lights, hoping to get a handle on who this woman was and what she might have in her background.

None of this was anything Sally had ever done on her own before. For that matter, once she'd stopped accompanying Dan, she'd vowed never to emulate him. In return, the two of them had agreed that he wouldn't even tell her about his outings, assuming he still indulged in them.

So why now? And why with this person she had yet to meet? In a word, Katz. Stan Katz had called her to say that he'd "sicced"

— his word — one of his reporters on her, the Rachel Reiling of this apartment. He had a fund to pay for investigative articles, if any came up, and he was hoping Sally might be helpful to a young and promising kindred spirit. Stressing that he hadn't told Reiling he'd be talking to Sally himself, he described her as a woman of Sally's approximate age — ambitious, creative, curious, hardworking, independent, and a good friend of Joe Gunther's.

That last part had encouraged Sally not to reject the whole notion out of hand. A key factor in her decision to forgo Dan's path was that their last escapade together would have resulted in their deaths had it not been for Gunther's quick intervention. On that very visceral level, Sally owed her life to the man.

She didn't need more friends, which was a category she managed carefully in any case. She sure as hell didn't need a trainee in her work. She didn't even want someone — a reporter, no less — being particularly knowledgeable of who she was and what she did. But whether he'd known it or not — and she guessed he had — Katz's invocation of Joe's name had pushed a closed door open, if just a crack.

That wasn't all, of course. As she examined Rachel's belongings, and through them glimpsed her personality, Sally learned about someone new to the area, too committed to her job to fully unpack, and whose interests in fashion, food, pastimes, and recreation echoed Sally's own in their paucity. From all appearances, Rachel was a dedicated workaholic — practical, focused, and, while sensitive enough to have a few family photos spread about, not so sentimental as to indulge in music CDs or have romantic pictures on the walls.

These positive discoveries notwithstanding, Sally wasn't going to take unnecessary risks meeting this girl without doing some research first. That's why she was here, invading Rachel's privacy. Sally had made a life for herself — a life almost terminated through her father's borderline recklessness. She didn't feel like threatening it again just because someone like Katz had hit the right emotional button in her. Once an outgoing and gregarious teenager, with friends aplenty, Sally had withdrawn considerably after her traumatic experience. She now lived alone, worked without partners, and interacted with friends only when she chose to.

She would agree to meet Rachel, but on her own terms, and as prearmed as imaginably possible.

Rachel, for her part, was ignoring a glass of wine poured for her in the kitchen of Angie Hogencamp, in a section of Brattleboro largely overlooked by most locals: a pleasant, peaceful, largely invisible middle-class neighborhood near the high school, and hemmed in by Clarke, Marlboro, and Mountain View Avenues. Encouraged by her conversation with Stan Katz to watch for stories of greater depth and significance than the usual day-to-day ones, she'd been chatting with a contact at the police department, and had been told to get ahold of Hogencamp. "She's got a good story," Rachel's source had told her, adding leadingly, "It might be a thread you could pull."

Hogencamp was plump, open-faced, good-natured, and chatty. She also liked her wine. "You're not drinking much," she commented, pushing over a plate of cheese and crackers. In the background, the muted drone of a television leaked in through the open living room door, where Mr. Hogencamp was watching sports.

Rachel obliged his wife with a slice of cheddar. "So, you were in the grocery store."

"Yes. The weekly chore, don't you know? Feed the tribe, not that they appreciate what

61

I get them. Still, if I didn't do it, they'd probably be found dead of starvation in front of the tube or plugged into their iPhones. I'm not sure my Frank has ever set foot in a grocery store."

"This was a major shopping trip, in other words," Rachel tried again.

"Well, the usual, you know? Between him and the kids, the shelves get pretty empty by the end of the week. God knows what they'd do if the supply chain broke, right?"

"Right. And you were robbed."

Hogencamp took a deep swallow from her glass. "Not *robbed* robbed. It wasn't like he had a gun or anything. I don't even know for sure it was a man, since I never saw anything."

"What happened?"

The older woman took a bite and continued speaking, mumbling slightly. "I'm embarrassed to say. When I told the police, I could tell the officer thought I was foolish — that I probably deserved what happened. He didn't say so, of course, but it was that look they give you, you know what I mean?"

Rachel nodded.

"Anyhow, it really was my fault. Not that people should steal your things; I'm not saying that. But you shouldn't make a target of yourself. It makes it too easy for people who don't have the will to resist."

Rachel was beginning to think that her police contact had sent her here as a hazing. "What did they steal?" she asked, although no longer sure she was that interested.

"Well, my purse," Hogencamp said. "I thought you knew that."

"Of course. I'm just looking for the whole story in your own words."

"Right, right. Well, I committed the classic mistake. Frank's already given me the what-for, so I might as well admit it. I left my cart with my purse in it to go down the aisle to get something. It wasn't more than a minute. It really wasn't. But when I got back, no purse."

"Oh," Rachel said sympathetically. "Everything?"

"Almost. My car keys were in the cart — I figured they fell out of the purse when he grabbed it. But whoever it was got everything else."

"But I heard it didn't end there."

"No," Hogencamp said with emphasis, followed by another deep swig of wine. "I wish it had. You'd think that was bad enough, to have your wallet and cards and money stolen. But that was the least of it."

"Do tell."

Hogencamp blinked at her. "What?"

"Sorry," Rachel said. "I mean, please go on. What happened?"

"Well, this was in the middle of the day, when the crowds are thinner. That's when I always do my shopping. I hate those long lines they have. They're the worst part, if you ask me."

"Right."

"So I went to the front and told them what'd happened. They said all the right things and called the police, and I waited around to talk to them. It all took a long time. Everyone was really nice and professional, but I was pretty upset and I wanted to call Frank."

"You couldn't do that?" Rachel interjected.

"No. My cell had been stolen, too. That's part of the story. Frank told me later I should've used the store's phone, but I didn't think of that. I've almost forgotten about real phones by now."

"But you did finally get home," Rachel suggested.

Hogencamp drank again. "Right. Frank says I ramble sometimes. Yes, I got home. Speaking of phones, ours was ringing right as I stepped inside, which it almost never does. I had to think where we'd put it. It struck me as a real coincidence in timing then, until the police told me why it happened that way."

Rachel scowled questioningly.

Hogencamp smiled. "I got you, didn't I? Okay, this is where it gets complicated. The person on the phone told me he was from the store and that he'd just found my purse near the Dumpsters, and asked if I'd come back. He had my cards, the wallet, even the cell. No cash, of course, but that made sense."

"Lucky," Rachel said, wondering again where this was heading.

"Hardly," Hogencamp said, pushing a hunk of cheese into her mouth, losing a small piece in her lap in her enthusiasm. For a victim of theft, Rachel thought, she seemed to be enjoying her moment of fame.

The other woman continued speaking. "I tried calling Frank, to tell him what had happened, but I had to leave a message, as usual. He never picks up at work. And then I drove back, all the way across town. I prefer Hannaford's. . . . I like their deli."

"Me, too," Rachel said, although it wasn't true. "Keep going. This is interesting."

"It is, isn't it? In a horrible kind of way. Anyhow, when I got back there, they had no idea what I was talking about. They hadn't found anything, and they hadn't called me at home. They didn't have the number, which I hadn't thought of till that moment. They were totally confused, and so was I, until I got back home the second time," she added with a flourish, taking another sip.

"What did you find?" Rachel asked.

"We'd been robbed," her hostess said brightly. "Jewelry, a laptop, two watches, a TV, a couple of Frank's guns . . . a bunch of stuff."

"The thief had sent you on a wild-goose chase so he could get inside?" Rachel asked, looking around as if he might still be there.

Hogencamp's eyebrows shot straight up. "*Worse.* The police told us he was probably in the house — or at least right nearby — when I got the fake call from the store. The way they described it, he stole my purse, came straight here, began collecting our things, and then called the house phone — *from inside* — to send me all the way back to the store. They figure that's why my car keys were in the cart. They didn't fall out like I'd thought. He left them there so I could drive around, which weirdly meant I gave him more time to rip us off."

"My God," Rachel commented. "That is amazing. It's like a movie plot."

Hogencamp finally looked a little rueful. "Well, if it is, it's not over yet."

"There's more?"

"Remember I told you Frank didn't answer my call? Well, he did later. The one thing he does do at work is answer texts, since that's how they communicate inside the office a lot. Of course, you can't text on the house phone here. He told me that in the middle of all this, he got a text from me. Not me, but the guy who stole my phone."

Rachel nodded. "Right, right. What did it say?"

"This is the 'insult to injury' part. It said, 'At the store. Need more cash. What's our bank PIN? I can't remember.' Can you believe that?"

Rachel was impressed, finally completely reassessing her police contact's recommendation. The logic, timing, planning, and boldness of this exceeded anything she'd ever heard outside of pure fiction. Thieves are driven by short-term needs — money, drugs, desperation. What Hogencamp had described had started with an average purse snatching and then evolved into a complex, completely thought-through strategic campaign.

"While I was running back and forth,"

Hogencamp continued, "this man was not only stealing our things, while I was probably just a few feet away, but he took time to drop by an ATM later and take out as much as he could from our account."

Without warning or further comment, Angie Hogencamp then bowed her head and burst into tears, her affable, cheery outer shell pushed beyond its limits. Rachel, coming around and rubbing her back, imagined that this same emotional cycle had run in circles enough times to make Frank step off the merry-go-round and resume his TV-viewing habits — assuming he'd shown Angie any sympathy to begin with.

Rachel was happy now to quash her earlier impatience. Despite Hogencamp's first appearing as a caricature hausfrau, her emotions had been worked over pretty thoroughly, and she'd fought hard to keep herself together.

That being said, she hadn't been hurt, Frank's current activity spoke of their finances as having survived, and time would heal what Rachel was trying to placate with a back rub. Staring over Angie's head at the kitchen wall, therefore, Rachel allowed herself a moment of triumph.

She'd been put onto this by a cop who'd mentioned that Hogencamp's tale of woe was at once predictable and unique, and clearly enacted by someone playful, ingenious, and wicked smart.

Which made the story exactly what Katz had been looking for.

"You think he did it?" Sam asked, accompanying her boss down the hallway toward their office. The VBI's Southeast Region office had been situated on the second floor of the Brattleboro municipal center several years ago as a temporary measure only, shortly after the Bureau's creation by a governor's pen stroke. At the time, Sam and Joe's former employer, the Brattleboro police, was housed downstairs, parking and location were convenient to downtown, and, although a tight fit, the one-room office had served its function. Now the PD had moved out, leaving the entire building with a disproportionately empty feeling, despite the ongoing presence of other municipal entities, like the record and town clerk's offices, and the board of selectmen. There were rumors that this VBI branch might be blended in with the state police up the interstate — indeed, overall, most VBI agents had migrated from that agency — but so far, nothing had happened, which suited Joe fine. He was happy staying independent.

Joe was removing his overcoat as he walked down the broad hallway. Built as a high school almost 150 years ago, the building — its initial role long since abandoned — nevertheless clung to its severe, if old-fashioned, institutional appearance.

"Brandon? He may have," Joe responded, shaking the last of the snow off his coat. A long-predicted storm was making its appearance, promising a night full of passing snowplows and some serious shoveling in the morning. It had begun during their drive back from Bellows Falls. "I'm not crazy about him for it, though. We'll have to double-check his version of events."

They reached the office and she held open the door. "The one about the stranger lurking in the shadows, waiting to frame him for Brandon's death?"

Joe smiled as he hung up the coat in their miniature vestibule. "You never know."

"Know what?" came a familiar voice from around the corner.

They stepped into the room, to see Willy Kunkle tucked in behind his corner desk, looking as if he'd prefer a stack of sandbags. Given his psychological makeup, situating his desk like he was the last man at the Alamo seemed a perfect fit for a retired military sniper from New York with PTSD, a past problem with alcohol, one permanently lame arm, and a reputation for ruthless honesty at the sacrifice of tact.

Sammie blew her partner a kiss. Baffling to most who knew them, the two had been a couple for years by now, sharing a house, a toddler, and, above all, a love Joe considered one of the true monuments to overcoming adversity and the prejudices of others. Theirs was a union built of trust, commitment, and sometimes brutal honesty.

"How was Emma, dropping her off?" Sam asked. "Given her hissy fit last night, I thought she'd want to join the French Foreign Legion this morning."

Willy lifted one shoulder in a half shrug. The two of them alternated preschool drop-off every morning, and hadn't seen each other all day. "You know her. It was like nothing had happened. That's not to say she hasn't killed somebody since and they don't know how to break the news. Louise texted me that she picked her up," he added, referring to their babysitter. "Didn't report any blood on her clothes."

His useless left arm — incongruous for a working cop — was mostly kept in place by burying his hand in his trouser pocket. The result of an on-duty bullet wound years ago, it had become an artifact no one much heeded within Vermont law enforcement anymore. Kunkle was a fixture, his lopsidedness as associated with him as a hooked nose or big ears might be on someone else. Whenever an outsider questioned the logic of having a disabled cop on anyone's payroll — much less the state's elite investigative service's — most knowledgeable respondents merely shrugged, explaining, "Hey, it's Vermont," as if eccentricity and independence were tenets of the region's DNA, which to some degree they were.

"Homicide on the home front?" came a question from behind them as the fourth and last member of their squad, Lester Spinney, entered, his fair crew cut glistening with melting snow. "How is the young ninja?"

"Like a United Nations interpreter," Willy said. "Goes a mile a minute, except that nothing's in English, at least most of the time, and most of it's said in a fury nowadays."

Lester, the only one of them not to have come from the Brattleboro PD, but, rather, the state police, was the father of two kids, both much older than Emma. In fact, the eldest was a rookie cop. "I remember those days," he said wistfully.

"I probably will, too," Willy said. "Right after she breaks the language barrier. Then all I'll hear is what a crummy father I am."

"Wrong," threw in Sammie, who actually considered Willy an exceptional father. "It's when *I* say that you'll have to worry." She studied Lester a moment as Joe continued to his desk by the room's one window. "You ought to wear a hat, Les," she said. "Where you been?"

"I don't like 'em," Lester said. "Interviewing Mr. Huntington for that bank case. Man's as dumb as a box of rocks." He looked at Joe. "We gonna inherit the BF homicide? I heard it on the scanner."

Willy shifted his attention to Joe, adding, "Good question. Lyall Johnson? I'm amazed he got that close to thirty — way beyond his life expectancy."

Joe glanced out the window as he draped his jacket across the back of his chair and sat down. It was dark by now, but the streetlight outside caught enough of the stormy weather to make it look like his image was being pelted with snow. Not a bad metaphor, given the news he was about to divulge.

He turned to face them. "The state's attorney and ours at the AG's office have to make the handover official, but it is now

73

our case. I've already got the crime techs ramped up doing extra tests, and I put in a request with the other VBI squad leaders to scramble five of our own to set up shop in BF and take over the groundwork from the locals."

"That's gotta be a relief for them," Willy said. "No way the BF cops want something that big. Is it a whodunit, to boot? Why's the lab being goosed up?"

Spinney had sat down and was perusing his emails. Willy's question made him look at Joe and ask, "Too early for you to fill us in?"

He leaned back expectantly in his chair. An extraordinarily tall and thin man — so evocative of a stork that he had jokey gift mementos of the bird all over his desk, and even one hanging from the ceiling above him — he was among the friendliest, most outgoing of people, in stark contrast to Kunkle, whom he considered a good friend. Joe saw him as living proof that police work could attract even the most unusual of candidates.

"Not much to it," Joe replied. "Perpetual bad boy Lyall Johnson was found dead this morning in his apartment, a knife in his chest. Witnesses claim they heard him shouting with his usual comrade in crime,

74

Brandon Leggatt, in the middle of the night. Brandon hightailed it across town and holed up at a friend's house, acting guilty as hell, even though he now claims he found the body after Lyall was killed and ran because he was scared of us."

"He's right to be," Willy said cheerfully. "I would love to use Lyall's death to work him over with a rubber hose — probably solve twenty open B and E's, robberies, and vandalisms."

Sam looked at him critically. "Focus, Willy. Focus. We don't do those anymore."

"What was the shouting about?" Lester asked.

"A pissant amount of dope," Sam replied. "Hardly the crown jewels."

"The PD do a canvass for witnesses?"

Joe didn't answer directly. "They started, but we'll want to go back over it — and put interviews into Brandon's and Lyall's past associates and family. And, to do it right, we're going to have to pretend like Brandon's a choirboy and telling the truth, until proven otherwise."

"Making like somebody had it in for Lyall," Willy suggested. "That should be easy."

"Brandon told us that when he parted ways to buy his dope," Joe said, "Lyall took off to meet someone. Brandon didn't know who. But if that person then followed Lyall back to his place, and hid until Brandon left after their argument, you may be right. The flies in the ointment right now are that Lyall's phone is missing — and Brandon seems legitimately clueless about its whereabouts — and it looks like somebody wiped the floor as they backed out of the apartment, maybe cleaning up blood. I asked for that path to be checked for DNA."

"Ah," Willy said softly, "so we're off to the races."

CHAPTER 5

Sally sat in what had become an alternate home, her car, complete with almost everything a tiny house might need. From running water, replaced here with bottles, to bathroom facilities, less happily substituted for with more bottles, she otherwise had food, extra clothing, flashlights, a toothbrush, even makeup and a dress, in case she needed a quick identity change.

She was gazing ahead at the young woman standing by the curb on Brattleboro's Main Street, looking up and down, her eyes blinking against the driving snow and her body held tight against the wind. The world had closed in overnight, reducing visibility with a swirling, nebulous, claustrophobic mantle of white.

Such environmental shifts were as normal and expected for Sally as sea changes to a mariner, which still never dulled her wonder at their effects. Her father had said how he enjoyed living in an environment that threatened to kill him six months out of every year, and she was hard put to disagree. Like him, she believed it was a good influence on building stamina, inventiveness, and character — all lauded regional traits.

Rachel Reiling was homegrown, too, although a Burlington brat, and thus — in parochial terms — a city dweller. Sally had learned that from her clandestine mining of the girl's apartment, which had been useful in other ways, too, as in detailing that not only was Rachel's mother, Beverly Hillstrom, the state's medical examiner and Joe Gunther's companion but also that her divorced father was a high-priced Burlington lawyer who maintained affectionate ties with his daughter.

Sally had read about Rachel before, as had anybody who heeded the news. Not once but twice, the girl had been subjected to death and violence, where Gunther and his investigators had also been involved — once, when Rachel's roommate had been murdered in their Burlington apartment, and just recently, when, while on one of her first assignments for the paper, albeit in Colchester, one man had killed another right in front of her.

Given the odds of that happening to any

one person in a lifetime, this poor girl could've easily been labeled a bad-news bear.

However, as a result, Sally had discovered that several people she knew well — best of all, Willy Kunkle and Samantha Martens — were friends of Rachel's, which supported the biggest piece of intel Sally had acquired last night pertaining to Rachel's character.

Evolving from a wannabe star reporter, Rachel had expanded in Sally's estimation into someone of substance, who had suffered loss and endured pain, been helpful and bold when called to action by the police, and displayed a readiness to take risks for the greater good. Additionally, she'd obviously been an asset to Joe and company, implying that despite her current occupation, she knew how to keep a confidence.

Sally put the car into gear and pulled up opposite her person of interest. She rolled down the window as Rachel bent at the waist to see who was driving.

"Get in," Sally told her.

"You Sally?" Rachel asked, pulling open the passenger door.

Not an auspicious start, Sally thought, ignoring the question.

They pulled out into the sparse traffic, or

what little they could see of it through the falling snow. Visibility had been cut to barely fifty feet.

"Thanks for doing this," Rachel said. "Katz asked me to say hi for him."

"He still acting like he should be chomping a cigar and calling women 'babe'?" Sally asked, heading north up Brattleboro's Main Street, toward Putney Road beyond.

Rachel laughed. "That's what everybody asks me. He must've been something, in the day. He's kinda gruff, but he's not that bad. I almost see him as an old hippie, full of left-wing idealism sometimes, and increasingly depressed by the modern world. He's never called me 'babe.' How long have you known him?"

Sally wasn't getting into that. Unlike her passenger, who, despite all past trauma, seemed lighthearted and optimistic, Sally was made of darker, more brooding stuff. She occupied common turf with Rachel, having experienced violence firsthand, but her upbringing with Dan had been the more formative experience. A kindhearted and generous man, he'd nevertheless stamped her with his unusual views, not the least of which was that people were not to be trusted until they'd truly and utterly proven their mettle. And even then . . .

What Sally knew of Rachel had been promising, as far as it went; that didn't mean she was going to open up to her at first blush. Or, for that matter, work to put her at ease, which explained why she'd orchestrated this initial meeting the way she had.

"What did he say?" she therefore countered.

"What? Oh. Nothing, really. He just spoke highly of you. I guess the implication was you two went back, but he didn't really say."

Sally was grateful for that. The value she put on being inquisitive about people didn't work both ways. The less anyone knew about her, the better.

Sally eased by the courthouse on their left and engaged the Putney Road, Brattleboro's version of a miracle mile — not that many of its commercial landmarks were evident in this weather. Instead, the nearest of them loomed up on both sides, passed by, and faded, like snow-clad icebergs, silent and lifeless.

"Well," she told Rachel, conceding only this much, "it's out of respect for him that you're in my car. Why is he playing matchmaker?"

Rachel nodded, gathering her thoughts and looking straight ahead as she prepared

81

to answer. Despite the fact that she and Sally were contemporaries, she felt in the company of someone far older and more experienced. She knew little about her companion. Katz had told her almost nothing, the internet even less. And perhaps because of it, she felt Sally to be a source that could vanish at the first misstep, leaving Rachel by the side of the road, only dreaming she'd even been in the car.

Whether it was Sally's intention or not when she'd agreed to this meeting, most of its aspects so far were reminding Rachel of Alice's famous journey down the rabbit hole. The weather didn't help. Nor did this disorienting drive to who knew where.

"He told me one thing when he suggested we talk," Rachel said slowly, "but I think that he had some other things up his sleeve, as well."

"Okay," Sally said noncommittally.

"In order to get Katz back on staff, the new owners had to agree to his assigning some more time-intensive pieces. Supposedly, that was his only requirement, although I don't doubt he held out for a decent salary, too. Anyhow, he asked me to be the one to write those pieces whenever they came up."

Sally remained silent, leaving the Putney

Road for a huge lot designed to service a now barely visible grocery store. Rachel was left to imagine being parked on the deck of an otherwise-empty aircraft carrier. For Sally's part, the location had been carefully considered — for its privacy, yes, but more for its aura of discomfiting alienation.

"He knows that I'm pretty new to the area," Rachel said, forging on. "So he recommended that I reach out to you, mostly so we could get to know each other, in case I ever need help with contacts, or if you hear of something that could lead to a good article."

She finished, her words sounding as lame to her as she was convinced they did to Sally, who'd pulled to a stop facing the road, far from any other cars.

She left the engine running but killed the windshield wipers before asking, "And I'm supposed to get what out of it?"

Rachel was ready for this. She'd asked herself the same question, without much satisfaction at the time, and only hoped it would sound better now. "I could be help-ful to you, too. Katz told me that you do a lot of defendant mitigation work, where you dig up good news about the person in trouble so their lawyers can present it at sentencing or before, and maybe make the judge or prosecutor more lenient. I thought there might be times when a well-timed article about such a person could help you out."

Sally turned from staring at the snow settling on the windshield to give her a look. "So much for journalistic integrity."

"No, no," Rachel protested. "The papers are full of feel-good pieces about people in a jam. That's all I'm saying. Since we'd be looking for that kind of stuff anyhow, you'd be a source I'd pay extra close attention to. And it would be on a case-by-case basis, so each one would make sense to both of us."

"Sounds cozy," Sally remarked, going back to studying the snow.

"Plus, we could hire you now and then," Rachel added, having been authorized to make no such offer.

Sally returned her gaze. "Really." It wasn't a question.

"Sure. You know how to do this. You're way more experienced than I am. If I catch a good lead, maybe you could suggest how I might develop it — professionally, I mean. You've got resources I can only dream about, I bet."

"Who told you that?"

Sally's unblinking blue eyes almost made Rachel squirm in her seat. She was tanking here, and feeling like she was being dragged back into childhood. "No one. I mean, Katz implied it. I figured you'd had a lot of training."

Sally surprised her then by smiling thinly and commenting, "Well, that's not wrong." Rachel had no idea how much of her time was indeed apportioned to defense work, fighting to alleviate and weaken the bad reputations that prosecutors routinely used against defendants. The work was a natural fit for her solitary lifestyle, but, more important, it supported the training she'd received from her father concerning the plight of the less advantaged.

In the ensuing awkward silence, Rachel asked, almost timidly, "I'm sorry, I don't know that much about you. You from around here?"

Sally kept looking straight ahead, observing how the snow had so quickly become a slushy, melting shield two feet from her face. By this point, the car was like a warm and dimly translucent igloo. She considered their contrasting positions, this insecure, upper-middle-class, recent college graduate, on her first full-time job, living — as Sally knew now — in the second apartment she'd ever laid claim to, and Sally, who at best would have flummoxed most career counsel-

85

ors and shrinks, both.

They'd each suffered personal upheavals, but while Rachel's had been random and exceptional, Sally's entire youth had been spent with a father so remote and self-contained — while good-natured — that her everyday life had been a tightrope walk over an emotional void. For reasons Dan Kravitz had never laid out, the two of them had never stopped moving, even within Brattleboro's tight orbit, often living for months in spare rooms or on people's couches, and always on the outer fringes of society. Shielded only by Dan's protection and her own sense of survival, Sally had witnessed daily the mishaps that populated the newspaper's police log. Families beset by financial insecurity, mental abuse, addiction, and the undertow of chronic depression had been a steady diet throughout her youth. She and Dan, cocooned by his steady, if muted, watchfulness, had been like the only immune riders on a communal train wreck that cops, courts, and social workers routinely got to disentangle.

And then, at the end of it, either by chance or because of some never-shared parental grand plan, he'd paid full tuition to send her to an elite prep school, purportedly so she could partake of the cultural flip side, as well as acquire a first-class education. It was no doubt a credit to her own levelheadedness, as well as the paternal hand of an utterly enigmatic man, that she hadn't gone off the rails herself.

Nor had she ever had the option to blend into any world of her own choosing. Dan's real-life anthropological experiment might have been revolutionary and enlightening, but it had created in his daughter a permanently floating observer, a cultural chameleon forever slated to see everything around her from a distance.

A loner.

How was she now to respond to polite conversation comparing backgrounds?

Nevertheless, Sally had been struck by something in Rachel's pitch. Rachel had a manner to her, a youthful eagerness that bespoke an open mind. Perhaps influenced by her lawyer father and scientific mother, Rachel had benefited from an ability to stay balanced, a drive to seek things out, and to keep at it until she'd gotten results. Sally didn't know her well enough to determine if she'd be any good at this new job, but she appeared to be of a character to bring honor to her efforts.

And Sally had seen enough of people to heed such distinctions.

Still, she ignored Rachel's question about her family circumstances, asking instead, "Are you actually working on anything right now, or is this purely a meet and greet?"

Rachel's relief filled the tight space, shoving aside Sally's stillness like the boisterous guest at a party. "It *was* supposed to be that. But I have just stumbled over something I think might have potential. And, like usual, I suppose, it's something I sure never saw coming."

Sally smiled. "Right."

Rachel allowed for a rueful half smile herself. "It's hardly *All the President's Men*. I know that. But I think there's somebody out there — a thief — who's pulling off jobs almost like an artist, full of complexity and invention, as if he were doing it as much for the entertainment and challenge as the cash."

Sally was instantly struck by the similarity between this and her father's style. When Dan had been making his mark as the Tag Man, leaving Post-it notes saying "You're it" in his wake, some had painted him just as Rachel was describing her mystery thief now.

Sally's interest was stirred — and additionally laced with suspicions about Dan's possible involvement.

Rachel was still speaking. "A police contact of mine told me about a woman who'd had her purse stolen in the grocery store. Turns out that was just the beginning. Whoever it was also used her cell phone to get the bank's ATM PIN by sending a phony text to her husband, and then robbed their house by sending the poor woman all over town on a wild-goose chase. And get this: In order to make it work, he made sure to leave her car keys in the grocery cart, so she could do all that driving. When've you heard about that kind of preplanning for a purse grab?"

Sally nodded absentmindedly. Maybe not for a purse grab, but she certainly knew of a brain capable of such thinking.

"After I interviewed this woman," Rachel went on, "I went back to my contact, as a follow-up. He had nothing more to offer, since so far the guy's gotten clean away, but he mentioned that what happened wasn't unique — that there'd been a law enforcement bulletin issued to watch for other convoluted schemes like that. Supposedly, there've been a minor rash of them."

Sally considered all this for a moment, her thoughts moving beyond the merits of an alliance with this increasingly appealing reporter to a place far more personal and complex.

In a world like hers, built on an intricacy of borrowed bits and pieces, along a life journey where discretion and playacting frequently jostled, her only companion had been Dan. Predictably, she loved him, trusted him, and saw him as the one constant who knew her better than anyone else.

But those feelings were not equilateral. Just as in so many parent-child interactions, significant information was less available to one party than to the other. Sally had lived with Dan, been trained by him, and finally invited into his secret chosen profession. Which didn't mean she understood him, or even knew much of his past history. Love and devotion, in her case, had not equaled insight.

With Rachel's description of the arcane, illegal activities of an intelligent, unusual, only vaguely familiar individual, she felt the urge for a little father-daughter catching up.

"Okay," she finally said, switching on the windshield wipers to reveal a thin line of traffic groping along the Putney Road. "I'm not shaking hands on this deal, but I promise to consider it. Will that work for the time being?"

Rachel was elated. "Oh, sure. Totally understandable. And much appreciated. I can't thank you enough."

Sally began heading toward the parking lot's exit, thinking ahead to her next conversation, and content to let this one lapse into a long and awkward silence.

CHAPTER 6

As with so much he witnessed, Willy was ambivalent about Bellows Falls. It was a pretty town, beautifully situated, and well suited for the resorts that had made it attractive to city dwellers in the mid-1800s. They'd headed out in droves from their often pestilent home bases, leaving behind industrial smog and complaints of stifling heat and polluted water. But the allure of a pristine Connecticut River, a picturesque cascade, and surrounding hills of verdant forest soon collapsed against what became a miniature version of what those very people had once fled. Already the site of the very first canal dug in the United States, BF didn't stop at appealing to the idle rich, but subsequently wooed less nature-loving industrialists, resulting in yet another mill town of now past glory, its once unspoiled landscape populated by hollowed, abandoned brick buildings sitting on foundations of time-glaciated, hazardous muck.

That being said, Willy admired the town, and drew parallels between its condition and his own — and beyond that, all of humanity's. Bellows Falls, and he, never quit struggling against the odds. He had his disabilities and addictions, while BF was saddled with a poor reputation of low-income stressors, including drugs. But they both persevered — he by putting his faith in the love of a woman and the child they'd created; the town by stubbornly reinvesting in itself and adapting to a reality it had never anticipated.

Of course, he thought as he looked around after locking his car, some days things looked better than others.

"Thinking of investing in a little property?" asked Marc Cote as he exited the warmth of the car parked just ahead of Willy's.

"Don't think I'd last long here," Willy said. "Someone would burn my house down."

"You might be surprised. I live here," Cote countered. "Everybody knows everybody, and I'm impressed by the respect for boundaries. It's like an unwritten law: You can tangle on the streets, but leave families and homes alone."

"Like the Old West with rules?"

Willy's tone told Cote he wasn't remotely convinced. "Well," the latter therefore gracefully segued, "the real estate gold rush days here are over anyhow. Have been for a while. We're running the risk of becoming respectable."

Willy surveyed the neighborhood again. "Yeah. That'll keep me awake at night." The street they were on was one of the rougher assemblages of old worker housing, since converted into run-down, low-income tenements — nicknamed "beehives" — mostly owned by out-of-town landlords.

Willy decided to skip any remaining small talk. "Why're you here?" he asked Marc. "We already got guys going door-to-door, retracing Lyall's last hours. I thought you'd been happy to wash your hands of this."

Cote nodded, used to Kunkle's manner. "I am. But I thought I'd introduce you to Danni Boyce, at least, since she's a perfect place to start. That's why I texted you. Brandon mentioned he and Lyall had dinner at her place before they split up that night. Plus, I haven't seen your charming face in way too long. I needed a fix."

"Girlfriend?" Willy stepped carefully from the street, over a mound of frozen snow and slush, and onto the roughly cleared side-walk.

"That and more," Cote said, joining him and pointing to the nearest of the beehives, a classic wooden triple-decker with sagging balconies and a zigzagging exterior staircase serving as a fire escape in name only, since snow, stacked firewood, and personal clutter rendered its role impossible. "Of her four kids, at least one is his."

"You're not sure?"

Cote dismissed it nonjudgmentally. "I don't know if they are. The timing was iffy, since he was in jail for most of it. She's on the ground floor."

"What shape's she in?" Willy asked as they climbed gingerly up the porch stairs to the front door, avoiding more snow and several toys strewn across the melted ice.

"She's good. You know. Life goes on. But that's partly why I'm here. She's used to me. You'd be meeting her sooner or later, but I figured my hanging around might help."

Willy cast him a look. "You dying of cancer? So nice all of a sudden."

Cote laughed. "Ah, Willy — such a classy guy."

Life's going on was certainly confirmed as they entered the lobby into a virtual cloud of overheated, fetid, uncirculated air, all telling of too many unwashed bodies inhabiting the same space. Ahead was a battered stairway, and scarred apartment doors to each side and beyond the stairs.

Marc gestured toward the rear. "Number three."

"Did Lyall live here at all?" Willy asked, recalling that Johnson's apartment had been listed under his name.

"No more than anyone else, except Danni," Marc explained. "The others come and go."

It took a while for their knock to stimulate a response. When the door opened, it revealed a tired-looking woman wearing sweatpants and a man's untucked red-and-black-plaid wool shirt, suitable for disguising any number of physical excesses.

She took in their identities at a glance. "What do *you* want?" she asked, blocking the entrance with her body.

"You remember me, Danni?"

"Duh."

"This is Willy Kunkle, of the VBI. We'd like to talk to you about Lyall."

"I don't know nothin' about that."

Willy turned on his most personable expression, which Marc admired in mute surprise.

"Danni," Willy told her, "I'm real sorry to bother you, but I gotta find out what happened."

"Who cares?" she responded. "He's dead."

"I know," Willy agreed. "And I can't do anything for your loss, or how you're going to break the news to the kids. You haven't done that yet, have you?" He paused before adding, "They're not here now, are they?"

She dropped her voice, thrown off by his solicitous tone. "Just the baby. The rest're in school."

Her eyes had drifted away and he now stooped slightly to catch her gaze. "I care, Danni," he said gently. "No one should die at the hands of another. It's not right, and the grief spreads everywhere. I knew Lyall. Not well, but we got along. I'll miss him."

Her face softened. "He could be such a pain."

He smiled, having never actually met the man. "He had his moments."

Danni Boyce sighed. "You could say that."

Willy tried his luck. "Can we come in for a minute?"

She stood back and widened the door gap. The two men sidestepped into a smelly, tempest-tossed, ramshackle cave of an apartment, variously appointed with discarded heaps of clothes, toys, magazines,

97

pizza boxes and paper plates, and several odd and unappealing thick smears on the bare floor that even Danni stepped around as she led them through a disgusting kitchen and into a dark and virtually unusable living room.

She waved at a heaped-upon couch as she sat heavily on what might have been an armchair under a pile of sheets, towels, and clothes. "Have a seat."

Cote passed on the offer, leaning instead against the room's doorframe. But Willy shoved a few of the more innocent-looking items aside and perched on the edge of the sofa, facing her at her own level. By nature, he was a surprisingly fastidious man, whose home would have looked almost sterile were it not for the efforts of Sam and Emma. But he never commented upon, or seemed to mind, the often rank environments this job took him to.

"When did you last see Lyall?" he asked, hoping to ride the momentum he'd set at the door.

"The day before," she replied dully.

"Before he died?" he asked.

"Yeah."

"He came over?"

"Yeah. He liked the kids. We had dinner."

"He alone?"

She looked up, stirred by the question. "You mean was that asshole Brandon with him? Course he was. Fucking Siamese twins."

"You don't get along?"

"No, I don't get along. That loser did more than anyone to ruin Lyall's life, but he couldn't get enough of him."

"Lyall couldn't," Willy clarified.

"Yeah. I used to tell him that since he wouldn't marry me, he should just get it over with and tie the knot with Brandon. Come out of the closet."

"They were gay?"

She gave him a pitying sneer. "No, they weren't gay. I was givin' him shit. Worked, too. Used to piss him off. But I could handle Brandon."

"Meaning what?"

"Well, like that night. I made him eat in here alone, while we stayed in the kitchen, to put him in his place."

Willy didn't say Brandon might have gotten the better deal, instead asking, "Just to be sure, that was the same night Lyall died?"

Her gaze returned to the floor. "Yeah."

"Did he talk about what he was planning to do after dinner?"

She shook her head. "He never did. He kept his distance, like I hadn't got the message about us."

"Did he seem different than usual?"

"Nah. He was having fun with the kids, like usual, and jokin' with me, like he did. Then he left, Brandon following like a dog."

Perhaps by instinct only, based on the smallest catch in her voice, Willy thought to ask, "Why did Lyall leave?"

"It was time. It's what he did, like I said, kept his distance. Plus, he got a call."

"What was that?"

She looked uninterested. "Not a call. A text. That seemed to do it."

"Who from?"

Her voice regained a bit of its earlier edge. "How'm I supposed to know? Some other stupid cow, probably. God knows how many more kids he had around town."

Willy worked to keep her on point. "It was a woman?"

"That's what he said. He read the text, said, 'Gotta go see a woman about a horse.' Then he laughed, like it was a joke, and he left, Brandon in tow."

" 'About a horse,' " Willy echoed, familiar with how the old expression about needing to see a man about a horse traditionally meant, *I have to go, but I'm not saying why.* "No doubt about that?"

"Nope. My hearing's fine."

"But he gave no clue what it meant?"

Something snapped within her. She heaved herself free of the chair's grip and said angrily, "No, I got no fucking clue. That's your job, and I'm tired of talking about it. Leave me alone. Now."

Willy rose without comment and walked toward the kitchen and the front door. Once there, he said, "Danni, I know you're pissed and hurt and feeling bad, and I'm sorry we added to that. But thanks for your help."

He reached into his coat pocket and gave her a business card, which she reluctantly took. He had no doubts it would instantly join the trash underfoot. "That's who I am and how to reach me, if you feel the urge. For any reason at all, okay?"

She held it as if suddenly frozen in place. Her other hand was poised on the edge of the open door. Marc Cote was waiting, by the staircase in the lobby.

"What happens now?" she asked, looking dazed.

Willy hesitated on the edge of a platitude before admitting, "I'm the wrong person to ask, Danni. Focus on what your kids need. That'll help you through. It has me."

Sally had left her car parked under cover in Brattleboro's municipal parking garage. A good idea with an only marginally appealing look, it was one of those structures everyone had clamored for at the time, only to complain about later.

It was convenient to Arch Street, however, located on the other side of Main, where limited parking was only exacerbated by the snowbanks.

Arch Street was not well known. Shaped a bit like a fishhook, it dropped off of Main at a steep angle, turned a corner at the railroad tracks that paralleled the Connecticut River, and ran to a dead end a few hundred yards north. It was increasingly narrow, unpaved, often overlooked by the road crew, and invisible to all but a few.

That made it perfect for Sally's father, Dan Kravitz, who had an almost hermetically sealed office near its end.

She walked down the middle of the street's uneven surface, between the twin railroad tracks to her right — and the gray frozen river beyond them — and a towering wall of rear windows belonging to the buildings facing Main Street. It was a view of urban Brattleboro that made her think of post–World War II photos she'd seen of Europe — blighted, starved, and barely hanging on. The solid wall of bland buildings, stained by the ages and signed by graffiti artists, suggested neglect, which the winter lighting rendered in the monochrome hues of an old newsreel. It was an illusion, of course. The street-facing side of this was scrubbed and historically photogenic; it was only this back view that had been left to fend for itself.

In its day, Arch Street had been a scene of high industry, when the trains — and before them, river barges — used to off-load product onto the loading docks feeding retail businesses on Main, one flight up. But that was ancient history, like so much else giving New England its identity. Now building owners were hard put to find a purpose for these nether reaches and their industrially sized portals, platforms, and freight elevators. A few, like Dan's landlord, rented out space — for storage, workrooms, or even an apartment or two, where the grim view, the odd knife fight between bums, and the occasional explosive clatter of a passing train weren't a concern.

Sally climbed a set of chipped concrete steps without a handrail, looked up and down the street to check for other pedestrians, and, seeing none, brought her right eye up to a rough hole in one of the old bricks surrounding the thick steel door before her. There was a soft whirring sound, a gentle light that scanned her retina, and a noticeable click from the door, which sprang open an inch.

"Hey, Dan," she said to the microphone she knew to be listening, amused as always by her father's fondness for gadgets. She pushed her way into a completely bare white-painted hallway that led to a second door some fifteen feet away.

She didn't have to repeat her performance there. As she approached it, the door opened instead, revealing a near-emaciated man of medium height, whose most distinguishing characteristic was that he seemed as clean and expressionless as a cutout paper doll. Sally had years ago run an unscientific experiment, asking a few friends to describe her father. No one, including some who'd known him for a long time, even knew where to start — at least not after beginning with "Well, he's the cleanest guy I've ever met." After that, there'd been nothing offered to separate Dan Kravitz from any one of a thousand nondescript, beardless, short-haired, slim white males.

Which she knew fit his overall social design. His ambition as a human being exceeded being seen as doing good deeds. He'd sought to act out his altruism while staying virtually invisible. Obviously, not during his antics as the Tag Man. That was separate, and kept from her until she was deemed of age. As a result, what had left the biggest impression on Sally during their wanderings throughout the Brattleboro of her youth was his goal to expose her to life's miscarriages on one hand while also demonstrating how kindness, support, encouragement, and, crucially, the lack of self-aggrandizement should outweigh any financial benefits.

Sally put her arms around his neck and gave him a hug, to which he responded with two gentle taps of one hand on her back — a sign of unrestrained exuberance for him.

"Hey, sweetheart," he said, smiling down at her. "It lightens my heart to see you."

She laughed and allowed him to close the door behind them, sealing them into an immaculate windowless white room equipped with a couple of tables, wall-to-wall shelves, and as many computer screens and monitors as the average air-defense control center.

The irony surrounding Dan, to Sally, who'd been the only person ever allowed in here, was how much warmth and kindness he could show, regardless of the setting. Part of his charm, and much of her adoration for him — despite his eccentricities — stemmed from that devotion to the underdog, his anthropological obsession with finding out what made humanity function, and the truly odd way he had of switching between being the best of friends and a complete ghost.

"You made me a proud father," he said now, pulling out a chair for her and moving to a corner counter to prepare her favorite blend of cocoa. "How you ensured that Mr. Morris did not get away after brutalizing that poor man at the motel was quick thinking."

She smiled at both the compliment and the implication that he was keeping a paternal eye on her. Thankfully, she'd never resented this latter practice, ever since they'd hammered out how and when he could put it to use. She knew he occasionally trespassed, as most caring parents will, but he'd almost never acted on his knowledge as a result, and so had honored her privacy, at least in name.

There was an additional reason for her forbearance: Living her life as she was for the moment, alone and without companions or intimate contacts, it was nice to know that somewhere, somehow, Dan was out there, watching like the Shadow from the rooftops. Not for the first time, she hoped that regardless of what lay ahead for each of them, it would never involve a shrink asking how they'd made their peculiar relationship work.

"Have you been enjoying your private-eye duties?" he asked her from his corner.

"Mostly," she told him candidly. "The one you just referred to notwithstanding."

"I can see that," he commented. "Love turned into hate or betrayal. Hard to watch."

"And hard to listen to," she said. "Domestic clients in general go on and on about the other guy, when all you need is the basic information. They pay the bills, but if I never had to do another one, I'd be fine."

He finished his preparations and crossed to her with a steaming mug in hand, along with a paper napkin. She gratefully accepted the ritual offering as he settled onto one of his desks, his hands on its edge and his feet dangling above the floor.

"But the work for defense lawyers is still rewarding?"

"It's interesting," she replied, speaking between careful sips. "I don't know if 'rewarding' would be the exact word. It has worth."

He lifted his chin agreeably. "I take your meaning."

She enjoyed hearing his voice, especially since she knew she was among a very select few to get more than a grunt or a head nod from him.

That had been much truer recently. Dan used to be more publicly visible as the out-of-focus worker in the backgrounds of local gas stations, truck depots, machine yards, and the like, moving accumulated debris around or cleaning out rarely visited storage rooms. He'd been the ubiquitous but unnamed gofer hired by owners of places mired in trash and industrial detritus. It had been, she imagined, his way of being at once involved in and apart from the people around him — the real-life equivalent of that actor you recognize in the movies but can never actually name.

Enhancing his obscurity, in addition to being someone others rarely focused on, he was also virtually mute, to the point where Willy Kunkle, upon first meeting him years earlier, had been astonished when Dan had finally dropped his "Yup"/"Nope" dialogue, to speak in the manner that Sally was enjoying now: eloquent, learned, and thoughtful.

It went a long way to explaining how Dan had so easily traveled the circles he had with his growing daughter in tow, among the dispossessed, the emotionally fractured, and the despairing in general. He had a knack for putting people at ease.

"I love your company, as you know," he

said now, giving her a considered look of appreciation. "But I'm sensing an element of mission in you. Did you come for cocoa, or something with a bit more substance?"

"Both." She smiled, weighing her approach. "But I want to start by thanking you again for letting me choose my own career path, after we were grabbed by that crazy dude and almost killed. You could've gotten all weird and protective, or guilty about putting me in that position, and you did neither. I rarely tell you how much I appreciated that."

"You did through your actions," he responded. "I was never so grateful. I felt terrible at the time. In many ways, that won't ever stop. But your not blaming me was a lifeline."

"I'm glad," she told him, having suspected as much. "Still, I do have kind of an awkward question to ask."

He chuckled. "Our friend Kunkle would say, 'Ask me no questions and I'll tell you no lies.' But that would be where he and I part ways."

She laughed, having never warmed to the brusque, acerbic cop. "I think you're safe there, Dan. Nobody I know would ever confuse you two."

He tilted his head. "Be that as it may."

In the following pause, he suggested presciently, "You'd like to know if I still visit people's homes now and then."

But she surprised him. "Not exactly. I'd like to know if you've started something new, if you've mixed up the formula and are now taking more than just information and data."

He paused before replying, his gaze resting unflinchingly on her face. She could sense that he was searching for the appropriate response. Not seeking the best lie. Not that. But possibly trying to veil how her question had struck him.

However, it was his style never to make anyone a target of his own agitation. When he spoke, he did so carefully. "I know you're looking for safe ground here — not to hear anything you might be forced to repeat under oath. I think I understand what you're after. If I'm right, the answer is no. I am up to nothing new or unusual. But the question implies that someone else's activities are making you think so."

Her relief was physical. She felt her grip on the mug relax enough that she could risk another sip before saying, "Sorry if I hit a sore spot."

He was already pushing that away. "You didn't, sweetheart. I took it as an inquiry, not an accusation. Was I accurate?"

"Well, there was an inkling of fear, followed by curiosity. Not too surprisingly, you were the first and only one I thought of to ask, even as I told myself you couldn't have been the one responsible."

"Of what, exactly?"

"Let me back up and explain," she proposed.

Cradling her mug in her lap, she detailed what Rachel had told her of what she'd come to nickname in her mind the "Mythical Thief," since he sounded almost too good to be true.

Dan chuckled at the label. "I like that. The Mythical Thief. He is that."

Her eyes widened. "So, you know him?"

"I believe so. If I'm right, he's almost a kindred spirit, although with less convoluted motives than mine, and certainly fewer scruples. Despite his young age, I'd actually call him old-fashioned, even a romantic, in the style of Arsène Lupin, let's say."

Sally laughed. "Right. Let's say. Who the hell is that?"

Dan looked slightly embarrassed. "That was a little snooty, but I couldn't think of anyone else. Arsène Lupin was the fictional hero of a Frenchman named Maurice Leblanc. Lupin was a so-called gentleman

111

thief. A very popular character at the time, like A. J. Raffles in *Raffles: The Amateur Cracksman,* but without the staying power."

"Easy for you to say. Meaning the guy we're talking about wears a top hat and carries a cane?" Sally asked incredulously.

"Okay. I shouldn't have mentioned him. But you shouldn't have named him the Mythical Thief. The actual guy is all too real — less a gentleman than a conceited brat who thinks he's too smart to work an honest job. He is charming, to be fair, and I'm probably not one to call the kettle black. His name is Alexander Robin Hale, and, keeping with the literary allusions, he likes to call himself Alex B. Robbin'. I suppose it makes him think he's referencing a slightly dark fairy tale."

CHAPTER 7

Arriving after dark, Joe was now grateful Beverly had hired someone to plow the driveway. He'd once offered his services for the price of a snowblower, like the one he used at his place in Brattleboro. But after the season's third snowstorm, he was happy she'd merely cocked a doubting eyebrow at him before making the requisite phone call.

She'd been right on multiple levels, of course. This second house of hers was in Windsor, near her extra, part-time job as an associate professor at the Geisel School of Medicine in Hanover, New Hampshire. But it was a fair stretch for him from Brattleboro whenever he wanted to drive up and enjoy some time with her. His volunteering to clear snow had been a blatantly romantic impulse, which the always pragmatic medical examiner had dismissed out of hand.

He was happy for another reason, as well. Beverly's car was parked near the door, and the lights were on inside her picture-book-pretty home.

The house represented an experiment for them both. He, a decades-long widower, and she, divorced many years ago, had just recently begun spending weekends and the odd night here, using her new job as the excuse to try out "a little light housekeeping," as Beverly had put it.

So far, it seemed to be working. Although Joe had enjoyed past relationships, some of them lasting years, none had brought him so close to the first, instinctive love he'd felt for his late wife, taken by cancer at a young age. And yet, against all expectation, here he was again, feeling connected to another as if by natural design.

The smell of a meal cooking and the warmth of a woodstove greeted him as he closed the front door. Beverly, entering from the kitchen in a thick cable-knit cardigan, wrapped her arms around his neck before he could remove his coat, then gave him a long and suggestive kiss.

"We've got one hour," she said into his ear.

He pulled back enough to look at her, feigning cluelessness. "For what?"

She kissed him again. "Rachel's coming for dinner and I don't want to wait until

114

she leaves."

He reached up, unbuttoned the top of her blouse, and said, "Lead the way, Doctor. The clock's ticking."

Beverly later lifted her head from his bare chest and checked the bedroom clock on the night table.

"How're we doing?" he asked, his eyes still closed, enjoying the weight of her body on his. Sex with this woman had become a haven he'd never thought possible anymore, to the point where it sometimes scared him. He was no stranger to losing people he loved most in life, and the fact that both of their professions circled around grief and sorrow made such pessimism feel reasonable. At times, he wondered if she felt the same, but Beverly was more restrained about voicing emotions, letting her actions speak for her — such as buying this house so the two of them could enjoy it.

"Time to become presentable," she said, rising and allowing him a nice view of her body. "The girl's always late unless she's on a deadline. Nevertheless, I wouldn't want this to be the first time she's on time."

He smiled as he joined her, getting dressed and neatening the bed. One of Beverly's many charms was her belief in old-fashioned tenets.

As it turned out, she'd been prophetic, as Rachel drove up only five minutes behind schedule. Windsor, located partway between Burlington and Brattleboro, had turned into an unforeseen oasis for the three now gathering around its weathered country kitchen table. Where once Joe and Beverly had faced five-hour round trips to see each other, and Rachel hadn't featured much at all, this Windsor base had presented a much-improved chance for more frequent, less stressful encounters.

But the warmth, comfort, and even the aroma of a home-cooked meal still did little to quell the underlying tensions between Rachel's job and Joe's, as became evident when she said to him between bites of her mother's from-scratch chili, "I saw you in Bellows Falls, at that stabbing. You think Brandon Leggatt did it?"

Beverly shot her daughter a warning look, which the latter avoided. Joe, on the other hand, honored the girl's dedication to duty over politesse, if unhelpfully. "Don't you wish," he commented, smiling.

Now she glanced at her mother. "Did you do the autopsy, Mom?"

Beverly picked up Joe's example, speaking

languorously. "Dahhling, why evah would you ask me such a thang?"

"Cute," Rachel said. "Do you two rehearse this stuff?"

Joe cut her a little slack. "Off the record?"

Her face brightened. "Sure."

"We're still investigating."

After a pause, Rachel scowled. "That's it?"

Joe answered seriously. Having no children of his own, he nevertheless felt a surprising affection for her. "It's not always a line. And it is what we're supposed to do: be thorough, balanced, careful, and accurate."

She accepted that with a nod.

"What about you?" Joe asked. "Anything hot on your plate? Beverly told me Katz had made you an offer."

Rachel cheered up. "He did. You're speaking to the new, under-the-counter, rural version of Spider-Man — ace photojournalist, on the hunt for front-page fodder."

Joe laughed. "My God, such a cynic at such a tender age. Have you been hanging out with Kunkle?"

"And have you found any fodder?" her mother wanted to know.

Rachel kept her eyes on Joe. "Maybe. You ever heard of someone named Alex Hale?"

"Doesn't ring a bell," he admitted. "In what context?"

"Burglaries," Rachel answered. "But really complicated ones, as if done by someone who's either showing off or seriously into puzzles. Or both."

Joe frowned. "Nothing comes to mind. Speaking of Willy, though, he'd be the one to ask. Or a local cop. Does Hale operate only in Bratt? They might know him."

"Someone at the PD did give me the idea, without the name." Rachel looked slightly embarrassed. "Which I'm hoping to keep to myself for a while, since I'm just poking around for now. I don't want to cause anyone any trouble until I know more."

"How did you get a name, then?" Joe asked.

"A source," she replied coyly, in part as payback, in part to compensate for having said too much already. In fact, Sally had just called her an hour earlier with Hale's identity, and, while Rachel had wanted to accept her mother's invitation to dinner, she'd been torn by a strong desire to start chasing this lead immediately. She rationalized now that asking Joe about Hale made this a work-related meal.

"Fair enough," he said as Beverly laughed. "If he is restricted to Brattleboro, and just starting out, I don't guess we *would* know anything about him. Not on our major crimes radar."

"He travels outside town limits," Rachel said almost defensively. "And I don't know how long he's been working."

Joe was looking interested. "Without giving anything away, what did you mean by 'really complicated'?"

Rachel considered how to answer that. For once, however, she had little to be guarded about, since her initial source had been the Brattleboro police. As Joe and her mother absorbed every detail, she therefore gave them the condensed version of Angie Hogencamp's story.

When she'd finished, Beverly said, "You weren't kidding. It sounds more like a novelist's concoction than reality."

Joe didn't comment, which prompted Rachel to ask, "What? Does this remind you of something?"

"Someone," he told her. "A guy I used to know. It's not his style, and he's not a burglar per se. Plus, I hope he's retired. But the flair of it sounded familiar."

"Maybe he knows Hale," Rachel suggested. "I could ask him, if you think that would be okay."

Joe considered the suggestion. His fondness for Rachel had prompted him to be helpful in the past. Apart from her connection to Beverly, Joe found her to be a young woman of character and integrity who honored her beliefs and commitments. None of those were traits he wanted her to think he took lightly.

"He does owe me a favor," he finally said. "I mention that because, without using my name, I doubt he'd talk to you. Still, it'll be his choice to cooperate, not mine."

Joe pulled out his smartphone and opened his contacts list, transferring what he was seeking onto a piece of paper from his note-pad as Beverly brought a large bowl of salad to the table.

"He's actually Kunkle's informant," he said as he was writing. "But Willy wouldn't play ball with you. Asking him about Hale is one thing, but this other guy's special. Willy treats him like private property. He'd be pissed if he knew I was doing this, so you might want to keep that in mind. Still, like I said, I think he's been out of the game for years."

He slid the piece of paper across the tabletop to Rachel, adding, "That's not to say, by the way, that he hasn't reinvented himself and is now calling himself Hale. That kind of convolution would fit him. I know him as Dan Kravitz. Back in the day, there wasn't much he didn't know about who was doing what to whom. He's the person I'd ask about Alex Hale, unless they are one and the same."

Rachel stared at him, stunned into momentary silence, her mind racing back to when Stan Katz had first broached the subject of her new job description, and told her of the Kravitzes.

"Does he have a daughter?" she asked, fighting to keep her voice neutral. "The last name sounds familiar."

"Yeah. Sally. She's a PI nowadays. You might've seen her ad. Don't know how much she has to do with her old man, though."

Sally had several cell phones, none of which contained any personal information pertaining to her, and most of which were without GPS chips and turned off. They were tools to her, similar to plastic pens, and disposed of as easily and readily.

One was the exception, however. That served as her office phone. It only took calls, was never used to place them, and its number was released judiciously, meaning that in most cases, she recognized the caller's ID at a glance. As she did when it began buzzing late that night.

"Mr. Marotti," she answered. "Long time.

How may I help you?"

Brattleboro, Vermont, was not renowned for headliner bigwigs. It was, however, an area commercial hub, the state's seventh-largest community, and in 2008, its voters had approved a measure calling on its police force to arrest the president and vice president of the United States, were they ever to drop by. Such peculiarities aside, it was as entitled as any town to its fair share of millionaires.

Jonathan Marotti was certainly one of those, possibly the foremost among them. Beyond that, he was an activist-businessman, a political godfather, a committed philanthropist, as well as a man whose name appeared on a dozen of the area's boards of trustees and directors. He had employed Sally in times past to conduct background checks on people, review the financial records of organizations, or simply to research individuals or businesses about which he was curious. He paid well, promptly, and had never once left Sally with the somewhat creepy feeling that so many superrich clients give to private investigators.

Perhaps passing that highest of hurdles, however, the man had also earned Dan's approval; he'd once told his daughter that he considered Marotti "one of the good guys" — a phrase he reserved for precious few. She'd never asked, nor wanted to know, how Dan had reached that conclusion, but she doubted it had much to do with her father's reading the social pages.

Marotti began in an uncharacteristically hesitant manner, "For the first time, Sally, I'm asking for your advice in a matter of some delicacy. Do you know Thorndike Academy?"

"I've heard of it, of course," she replied. Who hasn't? she thought. Located below Brattleboro, in Vernon, near the Massachusetts border, it was a small, very expensive and elitist prep school, chartered by a group in the 1930s as an homage to a branch of the Boston-based Thorndike family, which itself may have actually played no part, leaving behind an endowment disproportionate to the school's size. No one knew for sure.

"I'm on the board of trustees there," Marotti continued. "Have been for over ten years. One of my grandchildren attended, and I got involved as a result."

"Good school, from what I've heard," Sally said conversationally. In fact, she knew little about it.

"It is," he agreed. "At least for the most part. That's why I'm calling."

123

"You have concerns?"

"Yes and no," Marotti said. "I'm considering a large donation — the cost of a combination auditorium/black box theater/basketball arena. It would be in excess of fifteen million dollars. But as you and I have done in the past, I'd like a reconnaissance done before I commit."

"Sounds straightforward enough," Sally said, running through her options and available resources, not to mention the amount of time such an audit might take.

"Well, that's where things get delicate, as I said," Marotti unknowingly interrupted her. "There are a couple of complications to consider."

"Okay," she said leadingly, shifting in her armchair to get more comfortable.

"I don't want to sound coy," he explained. "But I'll address those afterward, if I still think them relevant. If you'll consider the job, I'd like you to go in unprejudiced by me first, to see what you root out on your own, if anything. Of course, I can tell you what's on my mind eventually, but I'm thinking this approach might be more open-minded. On my part, of course. I trust your judgment completely. Is this all too odd?"

"Unusual," she said, "but not off-the-wall. It'll take more time, without a specific target identified."

"That's understood, of course. Another part of my reasoning, just so you know, is that this will encourage an overall health check, rather than simply a strategic strike against a particular problem."

"Okay. I think I've got it. How would you like me to approach this?"

"As discretion personified," he told her. "I'd prefer you to go in undercover, as an office temp. There's a shortage of one clerical assistant right now. The staff's small enough that they're feeling the stress. The school's administration operates from a single central office, with a lot of shared personnel. You'd be in there as a kind of generalist, available to all but primarily responsible to the CEO."

"How's that going to happen?" she asked. "There's got to be a regular hiring procedure."

"There is. But we have an ally in this enterprise. The head of school is aware of my plan."

"Doesn't that border on suicide?" she asked, surprised. "I thought the head was an employee of the board. Aren't you afraid he or she might want to cover their backside? They get caught holding out on your fellow board members, they're gone."

She caught the hint of a chuckle in his voice, which she took as a sign that he was feeling good about having called her. "It is a she, and there is some risk to her. But I am dangling fifteen million dollars before her — a big feather in her cap — and she also shares my concern that there may be something rotten going on."

"Is anyone else in on the secret?"

"No," he reassured her. "Only she and I know about it. That includes my interest in building an auditorium."

A silence stretched between them as Marotti gave Sally time to ponder his offer. It wasn't an impossible assignment. She could work her other cases during the time she wasn't pretending to be a secretary. It wasn't as if office staffers had to live on campus, which the faculty did. It might take considerable time to complete, however, especially without any specified end result. But, she finally reasoned, however long it took, it would generate a great deal of money. She knew this man as generous and considerate. Sally could end up pretty comfortable by the end of it.

"Okay," she told him. "We'll have to hammer out the details, as usual, but you've got my interest. When do you want me to start?"

She could hear his relief and pleasure

through the phone. "You have put an old man's concerns at ease. Drop by my office tomorrow, if that's convenient, and we'll write up a contract. I cannot thank you enough, Sally."

Alex Hale sat back from the stolen laptop and pursed his lips thoughtfully. Of the many things he enjoyed about his lifestyle, from the planning to the adrenaline to the satisfaction of collecting a good haul, the rewards of an unrushed and methodical inventory afterward ranked near the top. The process reminded him of a Christmas present-opening frenzy.

Especially computers. They represented an attraction wrapped twice over, once when stolen, for their intrinsic value, and again when opened and their contents perused. Computers had become people's diaries, ledger books, communications devices, photo albums, and Rolodexes, all in one. Taking one's time to explore them usually paid off in unexpected ways.

All of which was certainly true with this one.

It had come to him as a result of the SUV smash and grab he'd committed in Windsor — the one that had subsequently led him to a house below Brattleboro and a treasure trove of swag.

The whole gig, as he called his escapades, had interested him, starting from when he'd punched the address of the car owner's home into the GPS and discovered that the guy had parked two train stations north of his most reasonable option. Not to mention that he'd then headed south, toward Massachusetts, Connecticut, and New York City.

At the time, Alex had figured it had something to do with cost or security. Normally, a resident of Vernon would drive into Brattleboro and park, or reduce the cost of his ticket by driving to Springfield, Massachusetts, and grabbing a ride from there, where trains were more plentiful than in Vermont, had better scheduling options, and more secure parking. Departing from Windsor only made sense if you were adverse to urban parking, which was certainly practical, or because you'd had something else planned before or after the train trip, making Windsor a more logical choice.

But Alex had a devious way of thinking, and he'd smelled a rat. The contents of the computer now fed that suspicion.

Stolen computers generally presented four avenues to the likes of Alex Hale. They opened easily without a password; offered a weak challenge, overcome by typing "1234" or "password"; proved impenetrable with an unbreakable code; or solved the last problem by having that very code written on the computer in some inconspicuous spot.

He'd gotten lucky with the last scenario, locating the password on the machine's bottom, scribbled in minute lettering near the battery's access panel, as if the owner had hoped that being tiny, his secret would pass unnoticed, like a child hiding behind an undersize bit of shrubbery.

Now, over two hours later, Alex pushed the laptop away as he might a clean plate after a full meal, and contemplated his options.

For all his much-loved Byzantine planning, he'd remained a young man with simple goals. He liked to steal stuff, fence it for a decent return, enjoy the financial proceeds, and start over again. Pretty straightforward.

Also a little dull. Although not yet thirty, he was beginning to feel stale. And, as he saw his contemporaries die of overdoses, become saddled with families and debt, and/or get carted off to jail, he was becoming aware that the shelf life of his chosen career might be nearing expiration. Sooner or later, something was going to go wrong, and he'd end up with little to nothing to show for all his self-perceived cleverness.

That had been tickling his subconscious lately. His ego not only drove his actions but also helped secure him from self-destruction via drugs or alcohol. If, at the end of it all, he was still to end up at the same dead end as the people he viewed so contemptuously, then what was the point?

He pursed his lips and considered the glowing laptop before him — the unexpected and possible solution to all those concerns.

Might it be a serendipitous sign? An arrow by the side of the road, indicating a new vocation at just the right time? What was running through his brain right now was no longer burglary or fencing stolen goods. It was potentially just as complex and convoluted as some of his past schemes, but it involved blackmail, extortion, maybe fraud, and who knew what else.

Based on what he'd read so far, skimming through documents and photographs, it certainly suggested access to more money than Alex had ever hitherto imagined, and with it a choice of lifestyles he'd never considered possible.

All he needed to do was head down to

Vernon and carefully examine the workings
of Thorndike Academy.

CHAPTER 8

There had once been a farcical challenge issued, stating that whoever located a normally proportioned room anywhere in the three-story fire/police building in Bellows Falls would win a free case of beer. Nicknamed by some "the House of the Seven Gables," the bifurcated home of these agencies was indeed pretty unusual, both inside and out.

Certainly the room where Joe and Willy met with five other VBI agents from across the state would not have won the prize. High and narrow, with asymmetrical sloping ceilings and windows too high to see from, it was at least out of the way of the building's usual inhabitants, on the third floor, and relatively quiet, until or unless the fire siren went off.

" 'Meet a woman about a horse'?" one of the attendees asked Willy after the latter had informed them of his conversation with

Danni Boyce. "Was that just a line, or was he serious?"

Willy waggled his hand from side to side. "Danni didn't seem to understand the question when I asked her, but I doubt Lyall would've known a metaphor if it bit him in the ass. Maybe he was speaking literally."

"So what did he mean?"

Willy was ready to move on. "Not sure. Probably he was meeting a woman about some horse — heroin. Old-fashioned word."

"It'll probably make sense later," Joe commented, adding, "if we're lucky." He turned to an oversized map of the village and pointed out the apartment building where Lyall Johnson had been found dead. "I know it's early," he went on, "and that you guys have been pretty much thrown into the deep end, canvassing an area where we're only hoping Lyall was spotted on his last day. But we were curious about what you'd heard so far. Especially" — here he moved his finger to Danni Boyce's apartment several blocks from Lyall's — "between these two locations. The man hasn't been dead a full forty-eight hours yet. With any luck, seeing him wandering around might still be fresh in people's minds."

Willy pointed to one of the agents, a thickset veteran of Middlebury's police department. "Scott, kick us off."

"I was told to start from Danni's place," Scott Baitz began. "Like you said, it's early on, even though it's Bellows Falls, where a lot of people are at home during the day, but I'd say I've been batting about seventy percent on who'll talk to me. Of those, two claimed they saw him around the time Danni said he left, after dinner. The second told me he was alone, walking toward downtown and his apartment beyond. The first said he saw him and Brandon part ways almost as soon as they left Danni's driveway."

"Was he on his phone?" Joe asked. "As in reading or writing a text? Brandon said he got that weird message from a woman at dinner."

Scott shook his head. "I asked. He was just walking. Course I'll be going back to the people I missed and asking them, too, but so far, that's it. I'm holding out for someone named Nelson, who lives barely a block over. He's supposed to be the neighborhood peeper. Sits at his window all day, sometimes with binoculars. He's wheelchair-bound. Lyall should've walked right in front of his place."

"Lester asked Brandon for more details about the mysterious text Lyall got," Willy told his boss. "He could only confirm the wording about the horse — no details."

"How 'bout concerning Lyall beyond that?" Joe pursued. "You ask any of your witnesses if they knew him generally?"

"Yup. A few did. A couple said he was okay; others that he was a waste of time. Nobody I met so far had anything concrete. What did the fluorescein show?"

"I just heard back about that," Joe told them all. "They got some hits. They're still analyzing the results, but the fluorescein revealed several drops of something, starting at Lyall's body, running out the door, and stopping at the top of the stairs. Any of you seen this stuff at work?" he suddenly asked.

"On the tube," one of them named Al answered. "Never in the field."

"You spray it on a surface," Joe explained, "kill the lights, hit the area with a special light, and it glows orange when it contacts the iron and enzymes in blood. You can photograph it, swab it, whatever. The bad news is that those two molecules are in animal and human pee, too, along with bleach, some types of metals, and probably a few other things. But we're hoping this is human blood."

"No hit on whose yet?"

"Come on," Willy groused, scowling. "Like we wouldn't tell you. Al, what did you find out?"

And so it went. In turn, they each reported on the last journey through town of a man who was generally poorly regarded, had been seen in casual conversation with at least a couple of other locals, neither of them a woman, and whose overall direction had been toward home, in a roundabout way. The survey included one agent who'd interviewed most of Lyall's apartment building neighbors, largely confirming what had already been gleaned about Brandon's regularly being a guest, along with the fact that the two men routinely argued.

Assignments were then made to chase down all of Lyall's seemingly unplanned encounters, and encouragement offered by Joe to continue the canvass until everyone possible had been interviewed. Hopes were high that later in the day, at about the same time Lyall had gone through town, potential witnesses would be back where they'd been at that hour, willing to talk about whatever they might have seen.

After the meeting, alone and surrounded by carelessly parked chairs, which Willy compulsively and unconsciously began squaring up to the table edges, he and Joe

136

compared notes before he went to join the others out canvassing and Joe returned to Brattleboro.

"What did Hillstrom say about Lyall?" Willy wanted to know, moving about the oddly shaped room and enjoying the chance to compare notes with his boss. Not that he ever admitted it, even to Sam, but Willy's respect for Joe and his Socratic problem solving was an unexpected bonus to a man usually given to keeping his own counsel.

"What you'd expect. The tox results'll take the usual few weeks, but she said the knife did the trick, regardless of what he might've had in his system."

"The photographs I saw showed a big knife shoved in deep," Willy said. "If we are after a woman, did Hillstrom think that fit the profile?"

"I asked her the same thing," Joe admitted. " 'The answer's predictably in the details,' to quote her. Had the knife encountered ribs, entering perpendicular, you might've needed some muscle behind it, but Beverly said that, for whatever reason, it went in between two ribs, without catching either one, and straight through some major vessels connecting the heart to the lungs. Maybe not the easiest thing to do, but apparently not a huge challenge for any adult, man or woman."

Willy took that in before asking, "Did Brandon confirm the knife was Lyall's?"

"Yeah. Supposedly, it came from the drawer near the hot plate. Cote told me that before we inherited this case, he interviewed a couple of people who'd been to the apartment before. One of them confirmed the knife's usual place."

"So," Willy surmised, "maybe we've got a woman, either very careful or very lucky not to have been seen, spontaneously grabbing a weapon and knocking this guy off, for no reason we know."

"That's it," Joe said cheerfully. "We wouldn't get these cases if they were easy."

"It is interesting, though," Willy said, unusually thoughtful for him. "The first half of that hints at careful planning, the second half at an act of passion. Not the usual mix."

Joe was struck by the comment, and yet again impressed by his colleague's often surprising insight. "You make anything from that?"

Willy made a face before rising to his feet to leave. "Only that something else is definitely going on. Like the wiped-up drops, going out the door. Brandon didn't have a scratch on him. Could be our stabber got sliced during the stabbing."

■ ■ ■ ■

Rachel angled her camera to capture the chef, the cutting board, and the open brick oven mounted on the far wall, all in the same frame. She was in downtown Brattleboro, covering a restaurateur who cooked pro bono meals for charitable events. Internally, however, she was on autopilot, circling the man as he chatted away, trusting his press release to supply what would appear in the caption.

Joe's comment the night before, referencing Sally's father in the same breath as Alex Hale, was haunting her, at once infusing self-doubt about her own possible credulity, and suspicions about being somehow manipulated. The fact that Sally had said nothing about her father when Rachel had described Hale's style — especially after Joe had gone straight to that connection — certainly implied a covert game on Sally's part. But to what end?

Rachel kept shooting, occasionally indicating to the chef how she wanted him to pose.

She didn't think she was being paranoid. She had good reason to be wary of the world and its rough intentions, being no stranger to that universe. She'd seen it up close, thanks in part to being associated with her mother and Joe. Not to mention that ever since reaching maturity, she'd developed a knack for being in the thick of the action, intentionally or otherwise. It hadn't made her hard-bitten, but she sure as hell had become more aware of life's ability to deliver bad news unexpectedly. Sally wasn't the only one who could be guarded.

So what *was* the story with her? Rachel had been flattered and pleased by Sally's careful acceptance of her pitch to work together. But had this friendliness been prompted by the mention of Hale's name? Was Sally shielding him because he and Dan were one and the same? Or was there another connection? Could Hale be an associate of Dan's? Another protégé, for instance?

To answer these questions and more, Rachel reasoned further, she needed to become a little less transparent, and perhaps not so overly reliant on Sally.

Two hours later, her photo shoot long over, Rachel straightened in her chair, raised both hands high above her head, and gave her back a long and welcome stretch. Now she was on the municipal building's ground floor, having pored over marriage, property, and tax records in pursuit of all mentions of Alex Robin Hale.

She hadn't found an address yet. Truthfully, she hadn't expected to. There was something about Hale's style that suggested that even a background search — much less obtaining a current residential listing — was going to be an ordeal.

But she believed she'd lucked out anyhow. It had taken some help from the town clerk, but Rachel had wound up with a name on a birth certificate, Carol Wilcox, who appeared to be Alex's mother.

And Rachel did have Carol's address. After checking her watch and ever-present smartphone, she headed off across town to the town within a town that was West Brattleboro's Mountain Home trailer park.

Mountain Home is the reality that doesn't fit its cliché. In the public's imagination, so often mirrored in movies, books, and on television, trailer parks are squalid retreats, just shy of the shelter provided by living under a bridge.

In fact, in the majority, they are the saving grace for millions of people who cannot afford conventional stick-built houses and choose not to lose their savings living in rental units. In one instance after another, from coast to coast, they cluster together in neat, well-run communities decorated with flower beds and gardens and happily used playgrounds.

In Rachel's experience, they made a lie of their rarer but more frequently portrayed counterparts — decrepit trailer parks filled with humanity's criminal backfill. The more standard models are too tame and bland to be fodder for popular fiction, and thus all but vanish in plain sight, situated on the edges of virtually every large town in the country.

In West Brattleboro, beyond downtown and Interstate 91, Mountain Home trailer park lives on the south-facing slope of a forested hill overlooking Route 9. Rachel received directions from the town clerk before setting out to locate Mrs. Wilcox.

Upon entering one of the park's two major access roads, she was also quickly disabused of another truism — that all such communities are rigidly laid out like Lego villages. Twisting and turning her way up and along a confusing series of quaintly named streets, lanes, roads, and avenues — all crowded in by piled-up snowbanks — Rachel began wondering if she'd ever find her way out. Her GPS was undaunted, however, and as the sun began to set, she eventually found herself squeezing into the narrow, short driveway of a modest, well-tended single-wide, still featuring a Christmas wreath across its front door.

She hadn't called ahead. Whether it was the desire for a clear answer or the latent fear that all her homework would be for naught, she'd wanted to show up face-to-face instead of relying, as usual, on her phone.

Rewarding such old-fashioned thinking, the door opened on the first ring, revealing a middle-aged woman who looked poised to deal with any eventuality, and resigned to it not panning out.

"Yes?" she asked in a downcast voice.

"Are you Carol Wilcox?" Rachel inquired.

"Who are you?"

"My name's Rachel Reiling. I was hoping to speak with Alex. Is he here?"

She was aiming for her most ingenuous look. She failed.

"Why?" Wilcox's affect was not encouraging. She also kept barring entry, despite the cold air entering her house.

Rachel kept smiling. "I just wanted to pick his brains about something."

"What's that?"

The young reporter tried to look embarrassed. "I'm not sure I should say. It might be wrong, but he's the only one who can set me straight, so I don't want to start anything that could be off base."

Wilcox's expression settled on a look of contempt. "You're full of crap," she said. "Nobody named Alex lives here."

She closed the door.

Rachel waited a moment, as if studying the wreath, before softly saying, "Cool." She slid her business card under the door and retreated to her car.

Back in the village of Bellows Falls, the handicap transport van pulled up opposite a peeling, sagging, snow-burdened house, smaller, older, and more set back from the road than its industrial-era, working-class neighbors. Two overweight men in blue uniforms emerged like twin bears and lumbered over the slippery, uneven ground to the vehicle's side door, sliding it open to reveal an older man wearing a nasal cannula, sitting in a wheelchair at the edge of a hydraulic lift.

One of the attendants climbed up behind the chair as the other readied the lift. They then worked together to extract and lower their charge to the ground, wrestling the chair's wheel free of the ramp and toward the icy, narrow pathway to the small house's front door.

"There you go, Mr. Nelson," one of them said. "Back home in two hours, just like we promised. Was that as bad as you were saying?"

Nelson grunted in a tone somewhere between agreement and resignation.

"You didn't say no," the other man said, laughing. "That can't be all bad. Hey, you didn't even have to wait ten minutes before the doc saw you this time. That qualifies as a miracle, right?"

"Everything takes a miracle nowadays," Nelson growled.

They'd reached the steps leading up to the door and were calculating their safest approach when a man wearing dark glasses and a balaclava against the cold spotted them from the sidewalk.

"Let me help you," he called out, jogging through the snow by the side of the path to reach them. "You got the key?" he asked, jumping up onto the top step.

"It ain't locked," Nelson said. "Never is. No point. Who're you?"

The man twisted the doorknob as one of the attendants replied, "You kidding? In that getup? That's Spider-Man, Mr. Nelson. Don't you watch TV?"

Having thrown the door open behind him, the new arrival seized hold of the wheelchair's front end as the others each grabbed a handle toward the back. Between them, they made short and easy work of their project, delivering Nelson into the house and rolling him down the hall and into the small living room facing the street.

The two from the van service then went about settling in their charge, removing his hat and coat, and situating him in his favorite place by the window, complete with binoculars and an older bound notebook in which he religiously took notes about the outside world. During this process, one of them looked around and asked, "Where'd Spidey go?"

Nelson followed his lead. "Who?"

"The guy who helped us," the other said, straightening.

"Musta figured we were set and left," the first one guessed, adding, "Last of the Good Samaritans."

Five minutes later, they were gone themselves, off to their next charge, a woman who needed delivering to her physical therapist in nearby Springfield.

Nelson continued making himself comfortable, making sure the equipment and supplies that accompanied him everywhere — the tangle of oxygen tubing, the insulin pump he kept clipped to the chair, the panic button he was supposed to wear but kept on the table beside him, and his dizzying array of pills — were all accounted for and where he liked them.

He was reaching for his low-power binoculars and pad when a vaguely familiar voice inquired from behind him, "You all squared away?"

Startled, he looked around, trying to locate the voice's source. Out of the corner of his eye, he saw a gloved hand appear and take his panic button.

He twisted in his seat to see better, recognizing the man in the balaclava. "What . . . ," he began.

"Surprised you, didn't I?" the man said affably, his hands still moving faster than Nelson could track, rearranging the carefully ordered setup that Nelson had just accounted for. Confused and frightened, the elderly invalid watched as if frozen, not understanding what was happening.

He tried again. "Who . . ."

The man let out a muffled laugh. "Didn't you hear? I'm Spider-Man, the Good Samaritan. You could call me the Sandman, too, if you'd like, 'cause I'm really here to help you sleep. You're a little pooped out after your doctor's visit, aren't you?"

Nelson was about to try answering that,

147

to say it wasn't true, but the man had already disappeared, stepping out of the room quickly and without a sound.

Or maybe he hadn't. Nelson couldn't actually see the whole room, not being able to turn around. His hands grappled with the chair's wheels unsuccessfully, even reaching for the locks and trying to free them, his notebook sliding onto the floor in the process. But he began to realize that his immobility was due to something else. The wheels had been chocked with wadded-up towels and carpeting.

"Goddamn it," he muttered, beginning to gasp with the effort.

That's when he noticed that his breathing was impaired. No airflow was coming through his cannula. Panicking a little, he stopped trying to move and visually traced the tubing that snaked across the floor to his oxygen machine. It wasn't where it belonged anymore, but had mysteriously been moved far beyond his reach.

It was also completely silent. Turned off.

"What the hell?"

He now groped for the panic button, remembering having seen it, before abruptly stopping, the image of the gloved hand grasping it fresh in his mind.

"Hey," he called out feebly. "Hey? I need help."

The room didn't answer. In fact, without the perpetual and comforting sound of the oxygen generator, it was starting to sound like the inside of a tomb.

He felt his thoughts becoming vague and disorganized. Now shifting more violently in the chair, he tried to focus on helping himself. The visiting nurse was scheduled to come by, as she did every day, morning and evening. When was she due? He shook his head. Was that her, wearing dark glasses and a hood? Why did he suddenly feel so disoriented?

Sleepily, panting for air, he again looked around, blinking several times at another anomaly before finally registering its import. His insulin pump was missing. His fingers numb, he tried locating where its leads attached to his midriff. Was it gone? But he found it at last, although he could barely feel it.

Confused, scared, and now at his wit's end, Nelson felt his mind tugging him to a familiar place of comfort, unexpected in the midst of such panic. But having no alternatives, he yielded to it nevertheless.

He fell asleep.

Minutes went by in silence. The occasional

sound of pedestrians chatting just reached the window by Nelson's unmoving shape. Once, the sound of a passing car came and went as it moved slowly down the street.

Eventually, the hooded man reappeared by the side of the wheelchair. He removed a glove and checked Nelson's carotid pulse. Finding nothing, he carefully replaced the panic button and the pump where he'd found them, making sure to reset the latter's controls as they'd been. He also turned the oxygen generator back on, bringing its gentle hum back to life, if not its user. He retrieved the dropped notebook and briefly checked its contents before putting it into one of his coat's oversize pockets, and, finally, freed the chair's wheels.

At last, checking everything twice, he backed out of the room, moved down the short hallway, and, after very carefully looking out for any other devoted watchers — as Nelson had once been — took his leave.

CHAPTER 9

Sally liked Mary Mroczek immediately as she circled her desk to welcome Sally "on board" to Thorndike Academy's staff. The head's stride was self-confident, her eye contact direct, and her handshake firm.

The impression was further enhanced after the receptionist had left the room, closing the heavy office door behind her, and Mroczek burst out laughing, gesturing to Sally to sit in one of the two leather armchairs facing the elaborately ornate antique oak desk. "Hey," she said, sitting in the other chair, "at least I didn't say 'Welcome to Team Thorndike.' I hear one of my predecessors was big on that one."

"No, no," Sally reassured her, looking around at their high-ceilinged, baronial surroundings, heavy on dark wood, Oriental rugs, leaded windows, and brass light fixtures. "It was rah-rah without being too manly."

The head of school rubbed her forehead. "Oy. Tell me about it. You should see me at a board meeting. It's all I can do not to hand out cigars."

"Old-school, huh?"

Mroczek's expressive face opened up. "But that's the problem, isn't it? We're not. The school's not even a hundred years old, not that you could tell from all this." She waved her hand around at the decor. "Plus, we're in Vermont. Windham County, no less. One of the hot seats of liberalism in a state already nicknamed a 'socialist republic.' Having Thorndike Academy here feels like plonking Windsor Castle in the middle of a commune."

"That bad?" Sally asked.

But Mary's response was typical of her, as Sally was beginning to sense. "No. That *good.* This place is ripe to bursting for a shake-up. And the funny thing is, most people I approach with new ideas are delighted with them."

"The operative word being 'most,' " Sally ventured.

Mary raised an eyebrow. "Well, that's always true, but you're right. It can get a little political."

"Does that explain my being here?" Sally

asked, not big on avoiding direct questions herself.

"That one's tricky," the head replied. "I'm not absolutely sure why you're here, and if I were, I'm under instructions not to say. Jonathan made that crystal clear: You're to ferret out what's wrong on your own."

Sally let a moment elapse before saying, "You know how crazy that sounds."

"Yes and no," Mary said. "Yes, it's inefficient and expensive. I have no idea what you're charging him, but I bet it's not cheap. And I can only hope you're as ethical and honest as you present and won't give him the fleecing of a lifetime. I really like the guy, and I want my collaboration with him to be the start of the best era this school's ever known. But no, it's not that crazy when you consider that both of us really do feel that something's not right around here."

Sally pressed her. "In what way? Can you give me that much? Is it financial, drugs, sex-related?"

Mroczek laughed again, despite the subject matter. "Ah yes. Lust, love, lucre, or loathing. I've read my P. D. James. The four corners of murder." She paused before adding, "Not sure where drugs fit. I guess those weren't as big in her experience."

153

"Maybe lunacy," Sally suggested.

Mary nodded. "Good point. Okay, in answer to your question, I think Jonathan's own apparent madness has more than enough method to it. Let me put it to you another way. In your world, you usually respond to an assignment: Catch this embezzler, get the pictures of that cheating spouse. This isn't like that. Jonathan's been here awhile. His grandchild came here. He's got a sense of the place, including an understanding of the appeal of all this ancient England crap, even to those who pooh-pooh it."

She rose again, restless by nature, and began pacing the room as she spoke. "I'm a newcomer. A California leftie whose parents met at a protest, no less. But my Ph.D.'s in education business management, and my degree's from Harvard. So I know that world, too."

She stopped in her tracks to look closely at Sally, who'd already taken in the framed degrees on the wall. "Haven't you ever entered a room and wondered what the hell was going on? People are talking, laughing, dipping their chips in salsa, and behaving themselves. But there's something off. You've been there, haven't you? You just can't put your finger on it. It's like a revealing conversation stopped just before you arrived, and everyone's struggling to act normal."

"Okay," Sally conceded. "Sure."

Mary resumed pacing. "That's what Jonathan and I are feeling. And what we want you to check out. It may be one of those letter *L*'s; for all I know, it may be all of them. Not murder, of course. But it could be something crooked. The conversations I alluded to just now, I've run into them when I've walked into someone's office and they've suddenly put their hand on the phone, or they've obviously switched off what they were looking at on the computer. Is that because I'm just the newcomer and they're having trouble adapting to me? Could be. Is it because there's something going on that more than one person doesn't want Jonathan or me to know about? Could be that, too. Is it simply paranoia on our parts, because we've got all these new ideas and we're running afoul of a bunch too set in their ways?"

She walked up to her chair and placed both hands on its back, leaning forward to look at Sally pointedly. She didn't bother answering that last rhetorical question. "He told me you thought I was putting my backside in a sling by agreeing to this little conspiracy, given that the board would fire me like that if they caught wind of it." She snapped her fingers. "But that's the risk I'm willing to take." She waved her hand as she had earlier. "All its *My Fair Lady* trappings aside, this is a good school, and board members like Jonathan Marotti are the reason why. But we're at a crossroads where we can either peter out as a platitude or become one of the great legacies of second-ary education. I won't beat around the bush with you. Jonathan and I are highly invested in making the latter vision come about, but not if it's built on something rotten. If you find out in the end that the two of us are catering to paranoia, then that'll be an end to it."

She straightened and relaxed a bit. "That answer your question? Sort of?"

Sally couldn't resist smiling at the perfor-mance. "Next time, I'll try to phrase it as a yup-or-nope choice."

They both laughed before Sally then asked, "You must've come up with a cover story for me, beyond my being a short-haul Kelly girl."

"I have," Mary said brightly, crossing to sit on the sill before one of the ten-foot-tall leaded windows decorated with a sprinkling of stained-glass panes. "I haven't been shy about my hopes for Thorndike, and one of the things I said I wanted done was a form of efficiency study — an in-depth analysis of the school's systems. People are usually twitchy about such things, assuming it's code for 'You're all being fired,' so I took pains to stress that my reasons for it were based on plans for eventual expansion. That's where Jonathan's multipurpose building comes in, not that anyone knows about that yet — or any other projects he'd like to follow it, if everything works out. In any case, that's your cover. You're part of the admin staff; you are, in fact, filling an empty slot. That's all true. But you are also an actor in this analysis, which gives you complete run of the premises and direct access to me."

"How legit do you want me to be?" Sally asked.

"Totally," Mary replied. "Assuming you can do two things at once, which Jonathan seems to think you can. I'd like you to actually do the job. For real. Or at least start it until you figure out what's making us both uneasy." She smiled broadly suddenly, tacking on, "I might as well get what I can, since he's footing the bill anyway."

Sally read her new boss's tone of voice and rose, this meeting concluded. She did reasonably ask one last question, however. "You mentioned interrupted phone calls and the like. You wouldn't like to give me some names to go with them, would you?"

Mary walked her to the door across the vast, thick rug, her hand lightly on Sally's shoulder. "I would if it were up to me," she conceded, "but Jonathan already told me his terms with you. Good hunting."

Across the broad snow-covered lawn from Mary Mroczek's office window, Alex Hale stood hidden among the winter-stripped hardwoods, a pair of binoculars trained on the woman's profile. She was speaking with someone out of sight and not looking in his direction. He therefore continued his preliminary survey of the school property, comparing what he could see with what he'd learned from his research online.

Thorndike Academy was a transplant from a *Masterpiece Theatre* docudrama — crenellations, slate roofs, evergreen box hedges, and church-ready, ancient-looking windows. What it lacked was any imposing central citadel, instead offering a spired union hall at the head of a herd of lesser buildings grouped around a large rectangular central commons that looked suitable for the queen's own foot guards. Around the outer periphery, strung like pearls, were athletic fields, tennis courts, a track, and more — along with an incongruously humble, if nicely painted, New England farmhouse.

This is going to be interesting, he mused, continuing his careful survey. Appearances notwithstanding, the place only looked like a stronghold, while in fact offering more open entry points than Alex knew what to do with.

But that would have to wait until later, even days into the future. For the moment, he would keep circling the place, acquiring an inventory of daily routines and a sense of the target's overall rhythm. Alex was a patient man when necessary, and from what he'd been reading in that stolen laptop, patience would be amply rewarded.

Scott Baitz had joined the Middlebury police straight out of the military, and had signed up with the marines on the day he'd graduated from high school. A local boy, he had never been tempted by a huge number of professional options. His father, also a vet, had run a machine shop on the edge of town, and with the sense of predestination that guides so many others, Scott had seen nothing wrong in emulating the old man.

The marines had given him a taste for order and discipline, however, that the machine shop lacked. Not to mention that when Scott finished his hitch, his father was still working, and couldn't afford a full-time assistant. So he'd done the next best thing, as he'd seen it, by buying a small house down the road from his family and knocking on the PD's door.

That had been fifteen years back — years patrolling the same patch, often arresting the same people, and arguing with the occasional entitled college student who loved to assume an attitude with the police. By the time Scott had reached the pinnacle available to him, the senior of three sergeants and responsible for most of the tough investigations, he was yearning for broader horizons.

The VBI had supplied that, and Scott had been a happy member of the organization ever since, working out of their Burlington office — the largest in the state. He loved the lean organizational structure, the autonomy of being responsible for his own caseload and hours, and the challenge of dealing solely with major cases. He also thoroughly enjoyed, as now, working far from his squad room, on the state's opposite border, getting to know a community he'd never visited before. It was a distant cry from his old days in Middlebury.

Regardless of such changes, however, Scott Baitz remained a man of deliberate habits and unhurried demeanor. He practiced a slow and steady philosophy, which suited his bearlike physique, and was exhibiting that style now as he repeated the canvass he'd conducted earlier, hoping to add to the witnesses he'd already interviewed.

It wasn't going too badly. He was catching more people in their residences than before, although the results were still proving a disappointment.

This was viscerally driven home when he climbed the snow-clotted steps of one address he'd been anticipating with high hopes and got nothing in response when he rang the doorbell.

"Can I help you?" said a voice from behind him.

He turned and saw a woman getting out of an older car, opposite the house's walkway.

He opened his coat so she could see the badge on his belt. "Police, ma'am," he said. "I was hoping to see Mr. Nelson."

"I'm afraid you're out of luck, if what you mean is to talk to him. He died."

Baitz was stunned. "When? How?"

"I don't know the when, exactly," she told him, unloading a box from her backseat and placing it on the car's roof. "I just got the call that they'd found him dead and I was supposed to pick up our supplies." She looked at his blank expression and added, "My service provided him with most of his equipment. He was in pretty bad shape. Oxygen, insulin pump, CPAP mask, walker, wheelchair, shower stool . . . bunch of stuff. Costs money if you have to get it without people like us."

Scott had gingerly walked back down the icy path and was helping her with her cartons and bags. "How did it get called in?" he asked. "He live with somebody?"

"No," she replied. "He has a daughter in town — Louise. We always dealt with her. But it was his visiting nurse who found him. He was a real character. Sat in that window for years, watching what happened out here. People got used to it. Used to wave to him. Some of the kids did naughty things, like drop their pants, to get him worked up, but he was harmless. I liked him."

Scott followed her back to the house, his arms full. "Did they call the cops? Was there an investigation?"

"They called the cops unofficially, but it

162

was ruled an attended death," she said. "He'd seen his physician that same morning, so when the police contacted the doc, he said he'd sign the death certificate, no problem."

She paused with her hand on the doorknob and looked back at him. "Why? Do you think something bad happened? You said you were police."

Scott didn't want rumors to start flying. "No, no. I just wanted to ask him something."

She opened the door and led him into the hallway. "Come on in and look around, if you want. He never locked up, so you can come back later, too, if you want. I doubt Louise'll mind."

Scott didn't see much point to that, so he helped her spread out her various containers and took his leave, wishing her well and thanking her for the update.

Back outside, feeling cheated of an encounter he'd been anticipating, he pulled out his notebook and studied its contents, a list of potential and already-interviewed witnesses, before heading toward his next address of interest.

This turned out to be at the end of the same block, another worse-for-wear, subdivided, hundred-year-old, working-class building, as found in old factory towns everywhere.

The person he was seeking was Shelly Ayotte, who, he'd been told by a neighbor during his first drop-by, worked as a night custodian at a business north of town. That also was supposed to explain why he'd missed her earlier.

Scott was more hopeful about his luck this time. It was later in the day, which should have allowed her to return, catch some sleep, maybe eat a little, and start thinking about returning to work.

As it turned out, unlike with the late Mr. Nelson, he got a hit. A woman, possibly in her early thirties, although with a face stamped by years of hard living, opened the second-story door on his first knock.

She was dressed in a T-shirt and tight jeans, both suitable for what turned out to be an overheated, cramped, messy apartment, decorated with posters of rock stars and sheer colored scarves draped atop the window rods and across several lamps.

"Who're you?" she asked directly but without hostility, as if open to possibilities.

He decided to play it safe from the start. "I'm a cop," he answered her. "Doing a neighborhood canvass."

"I heard about that," she said. "The guy

that got whacked a few blocks from here."

"Right," he acknowledged. "Did you know him?"

Ayotte stood back from the door slightly. "I don't even know his name. I just heard about it a coupla hours ago. Wanna come in?"

He hesitated until she smiled and added, "Leave the door open, if it helps."

"It would, actually."

She laughed and stepped back, widening the door completely and retreating to a nearby sofa. "These're weird times — I bet especially for you guys."

Scott couldn't argue with that, and he carefully chose a chair across from her. She watched him with clear amusement as she lit a cigarette, inhaled deeply, and asked, "So, how can I help you?"

"You've probably seen from TV how we do this," he began. "We spread out from a crime scene, going door-to-door, try to re-create people's actions, and see if we can corroborate what we find with witness accounts."

"Okay," she said. "What'm I supposed to have seen?"

He pointed to the window near her. "Well, I noticed you've got three windows that look out on the sidewalk we're thinking this man

165

used. What I'm hoping is that you saw him."

He pulled out a fairly recent mug shot of Lyall Johnson, which they'd chosen because he was both alive and didn't look too moronic, and handed it to her.

Ayotte surprised him by merely glancing at it and saying, "Yeah. That the dead guy?"

Scott couldn't suppress a smile. "You saw him?"

"That's what you asked, wasn't it?"

"Yup." He pulled out a small recorder and waved it before her, asking, "Mind if I get this down? Make it part of the record?"

"Knock yourself out."

He hit the Record button and balanced the machine on his knee. "When was this?"

"Day before yesterday. I was leaving for work. Modified graveyard shift, eight P.M. to four A.M."

"Tell me the circumstances," he urged, his disappointment over missing Nelson gone.

"Like I said, I was getting set to leave. Outside already, walking to my car." She gestured toward the street. "I park on that side of the building. I just happened to see him approaching the corner."

"He was alone?"

"Yeah. Well, he was then."

"He met someone?"

"That's what made me notice him," she

166

explained. "I probably wouldn't have other-wise — just a guy in a hoodie, you know? On a cold night? Who pays attention?"

"So what happened to change that?"

"A woman yelled at him. She was pissed. It caught my attention. Not that I did anything. In fact, I made sure to get in my car quicker than I might've. Doesn't pay to stick around when people get into a fight around here."

Scott waved at her with his fingertips. "Let's back up a little. You didn't really see him until after the woman called out?"

She pursed her lips. "I did and I didn't. I mean, I was vaguely aware of him, like you are of everything when you hit the street and you're watching your back, but I didn't focus on him. He wasn't that close, you know? He was just coming up from the end of the street. Then, after she yelled out, that made me pay attention more."

"Okay," Scott replied. "Got it. Where was this woman?"

"Far side of the street, walking toward the crosswalk from her car, as if she might've wanted to go in the direction he'd come from, if she hadn't seen him first."

"And what did she say?"

"I think she just called out his name."

"What was that?"

"I don't know. It was more a noise at that point. I wasn't listening. Maybe she just said, 'Hey, you.' I don't really know. I thought it was a name, but I can't swear to it."

"That's all right," he said. "Keep going. What did he say or do?"

"He crossed the street to her. I didn't hear him say anything. No, I mean, I heard him talk, but I couldn't understand. He was going away from me by then. And what with the hoodie and my wanting to leave, I didn't catch any of it."

"Did he look tensed up?" Scott asked. "Ready for a fight?"

"Not particularly," Shelly said. "She looked like the one ready for a fight."

"Could you see her hands?"

Shelly laughed. "Was she holding a baseball bat? Yeah, right. No, it was her voice I'm talking about — not that she was waving a gun around or anything. I told you: She was pissed."

"What did you see next?" Scott asked, pressing her.

"They met on the sidewalk and I drove away."

"They hug or shake hands or exchange any gesture at all?"

Shelly hesitated, thinking back. "Trying to

remember. I don't think so. He kept his hands in his pockets and she was moving her arms around a little. Not like a crazy person, but, you know, worked up."

Scott sat forward, resting his forearms on his knees. "This part's pretty important, as you can guess. What did she look like?"

But Shelly was already shaking her head. "I knew you'd ask. She was just a woman. Maybe my height. Had a hat on, a coat. What can you really tell? Especially from a distance. Everybody's bundled up this time of year. I don't even know what her hair color was."

"Pants?" Scott asked. "Dress? What was she wearing? Was the hat colorful?"

"Nope. I got nothin'. It was a knit watch cap–type thing, the kind that covers damn near everything. She was wearing pants, but it was all dark, and there's no streetlight on that corner — not that works anyway. I think the coat was short and puffy — one of those down things — but I wasn't look-ing for stuff like that."

Scott nodded, sitting back. "Okay. Take a second and rethink the moment, try to bring it all back in your mind, and tell me if you can recall anything else."

Ayotte looked as if she was casting back, but whether she was or not, she still ended

169

by frowning and saying, "Nope. That's it. After that, I took off."

He wasn't surprised, not after having interviewed a few thousand people over the years. The more you pressed them for details, he'd found, the fewer they had to tell.

He retrieved the recorder from his knee, asked her to swear to the accuracy of her statement, under penalty of law, and turned it off.

He then rose to his feet, exchanged a business card for the mug shot, and headed for the open door. "All right, Shelly. If you do remember anything, that's how to reach me."

At the door, however, he did think of something else: "By the way, you mentioned at the beginning that you saw this woman approaching the corner from her car. What kind of car was that?"

Ayotte's eyes widened. "Easy. It was one of those older VW hippie vans. Really stuck out."

Scott was heartened. "You see the license plate?"

But that was too much. "No," she said. "Too —"

"Dark," he said, interrupting her, still pleased to have partially identified the VW.

"I know. I figured it couldn't hurt to ask."

She smiled up at him, coquettishly curled up on the incongruously threadbare couch, her cigarette posed just so. "Yeah. You think of anything else you'd like, come back."

Scott looked at her, hiding his surprise. "Right."

CHAPTER 10

It was near midnight, Rachel was tired, and merely glancing at the dishes in her kitchen sink quelled whatever appetite she might have been harboring.

She knew she wasn't making much sense of late. Working too much, eating too little, not exercising at all, and her social life had vaporized. Curiously, given her workload, her interesting and challenging job, and her overall ambition, she found herself on the edge of depression.

This wasn't new. She'd struggled with it since her late teens. She'd first written it off as a reaction to her parents' divorce, but, in fact, that had been unusually well handled, especially by two people who'd been more than ready to call it quits and instead become friends. Certainly Rachel and her older sister, Anne, talking between themselves, had seen no real downside, at the time or thereafter.

She'd questioned whether the source of her melancholy might be more fundamental. There, she believed she was onto something, a genetic disposition, perhaps, that she could imagine in her father, if not so easily in her more stoic mother.

Look at their jobs, after all. Each wealthy and successful, well known and respected, but one defended the sort of people in court that most of society found contemptible, and the other cut up corpses, rooting out what had killed them.

As psychologies went, this couple had been an interesting match. Why wouldn't they have produced a kid with a tendency to see things on the dark side?

And then, there was Rachel's own recent history of violence and mayhem, seeing not one but two people killed, and being involved — via Joe Gunther — as a videographer, while still in college, in a couple of other cases where human nature had hardly been showcased for its good cheer and optimism.

Rachel stood at the window, resting her forehead against the cool glass, her warm breath fogging the pane.

But she knew it was something more. She was used to all of the foregoing, including the killings. If anything, in Rachel's opinion, her parents' DNA had even helped there, making her more insightful about others and the world in general.

What she suspected was that she was melancholy because of Sally Kravitz, along with the odd and enduring disappointment at having been misled.

She didn't blame Sally. She was now more up to speed about some of the poor girl's background, and understood why she might be a little self-protective.

But Rachel had admired her upon their first meeting. Although roughly Rachel's age, Sally displayed self-confidence beyond her years — wisdom, even — which gave her a natural bearing Rachel envied.

It hurt to consider that the same woman had possibly seen her simply as a pawn, or dismissed her altogether. Rachel was just starting out. That her first encounter with a hoped-for kindred spirit might have been laced with deception was saddening. Rachel felt she didn't need more life experiences as much as a new friend she could count on.

Her phone, always within reach, buzzed for attention on the counter nearby. The screen read PRIVATE CALLER.

By instinct, she wasn't inclined to answer such calls, which routinely disguised tele-marketers. But given the company she'd

174

begun keeping, and her recent mixed emotions about Sally, she wasn't about to ignore this.

"Hello?"

"Hey, there. This is the man of your dreams."

She seriously doubted it, but she was also pretty sure this wasn't a crank call.

She thought quickly enough to respond, "Maybe it is; maybe it's not."

The man laughed. "It better be, 'cause you're the one chasing me. I'd hate to think you were that dumb."

She put the connections together, along with the memory of leaving her business card with Carol Wilcox. "I guess this means you and your mom talk more than she let on."

He didn't address that, saying instead, "I don't do phone. You want to talk, it's face-to-face. My terms."

"Fine," she replied without pause, her earlier blues forgotten.

He gave her directions to Flat Street, in Brattleboro, paralleling Whetstone Brook, near downtown, but notoriously empty of foot traffic at this time of night. Again, she didn't hesitate — youthful invulnerability overtaking caution — instinctively grabbed her camera, and headed for the door.

Fifteen minutes later, having walked to the rendezvous site from her upper Main Street apartment — a location she assumed he knew about before calling — she found herself at a loss in the middle of two parking lots, a closed machine shop, darkened businesses, and the town's multistory garage. Aside from an occasional passing car and a single couple walking by, she was alone.

Her phone came alive in her hand. "Yes?"

"Keep the phone to your ear. Walk toward Elm. I'll tell you where to go."

He did so, directing her to the back of another parking lot, along a short alleyway, and almost to the stream bank — or as far as the frozen snow allowed. She was grateful she'd worn her boots.

"Jesus," she finally protested. "Am I supposed to start swimming now?"

He chuckled. "Not quite. See the door to your right?"

"Yes."

"It's unlocked."

He left it there, letting her fill in the rest on her own. This she did, with as much apprehension as enthusiasm. By now, her situation had begun dawning on her, and with it the realization that no one knew of her whereabouts.

The door led into a cavernous space, cluttered with abandoned machinery and heavy equipment, most of it in rusty heaps. It was a place she'd never imagined existed, given the warehouse's bland exterior.

She was using her phone screen as a light, held up near her ear, and therefore only marginally effective.

"You see well enough?" he asked.

"Kind of," she replied, fighting to sound calm.

"Take your time. Follow the aisle between the two piles ahead of you and stop in the middle of the room."

She discovered a clearing the size of a tent site, with a small card table in its middle. On the table was a hinged box.

The phone went dead in her hand as a voice came out of the surrounding gloom, "Nice job. You can put the phone and camera in the box."

She did as ordered, killing her light source in the process. The box was heavy and thick-walled, as if lined with absorbent material. Its lid closed with an authoritative snap. She thought it was probably a so-called Faraday box, designed to seal off electronic signals.

The resulting darkness from losing the phone wasn't absolute. There were distant windows overlooking Elm Street. They were

177

filthy with grime and allowed but a glimmer from the lumberyard lights across the road. More important, the fact that she was now in the actual presence of her caller, even if not face-to-face, had incongruously steadied her nerves a little.

She heard more than saw a figure approaching, still speaking, "Sorry about the hocus-pocus, but I have no clue what this is about. Can't be too careful."

He was standing two feet away, close enough that she could hear his breathing. The faint light let her see that he was wearing a balaclava over his head. His build seemed athletic, and his voice young, self-confident, and curiously kind.

"Are you Alex?" she asked.

"You Rachel Reiling?" he asked, ignoring the question.

"Yes." She liked that voice. It was also soft-spoken and reassuring. She found herself steadied by the notion that a man with such a voice couldn't truly wish her harm.

This was a good thing, considering what he said next.

"Okay. This is the awkward part, and if you don't want to do it, I'll completely understand and you can just go on your way. But I'll need to search you."

She stiffened. "Why?"

"You know exactly why," he replied patiently, adding, "And I know this is creepy. I will keep it as unthreatening and clinical as possible, and the choice is yours, even after I start, but right now I have to insist that this conversation remains strictly between you and me. Should I start, or not? You want me not to do this, just say the word and I'm outta here."

This time, she did hesitate. During her pursuit of this man, she'd gone without thought of consequence. It was a story, an opportunity, maybe a career move. It had not involved standing alone in a dark place with a man she didn't know who'd just announced he was going to run his hands all over her.

She felt like an idiot. Nevertheless, she'd come this far, and there was that voice.

"Okay," she said without conviction.

He began slowly and respectfully, having her remove her coat so he could examine it. The building was unheated, so he draped it over her shoulders when he was done, which helped diminish her misgivings, if only slightly.

He then knelt before her and carefully palpated her legs, working up to her hips and waist, using the back of his hand alone

179

to brush between her legs. He spoke throughout, explaining, "I am sorry for this. Recording devices have become ridiculously small, not to mention guns. In the day, this was no big deal — like they show in old movies. But now? The movies don't have enough time to show this being done properly."

He was standing by now, running his hands up her back, under the coat. His businesslike approach couldn't mask the sensations of what he was doing, and indeed, his gentleness and calming banter increased the sensual undercurrent, making her experience a disturbing commingling of apprehension and pleasure. He then slid around to her front, apologized yet again, and rubbed the backs of his hands across her breasts.

He stopped, his eyes inches from hers, his breath smelling faintly of peppermint, and tapped one knuckle against the side of her breast, hitting something hard. "You could've told me about that, but I would've searched you anyhow, so I won't hold it against you. You want to take that out? I'd prefer not to do it myself."

"Okay," she said, her red face invisible but her voice quaking. She reached up under her sweater and removed the recorder from where she'd secreted it in her bra, handing it to him. He dropped it into the Faraday box without a glance.

He finished by reaching up to her armpits, running down her arms, and finally lifting her wool cap to check its interior, finding nothing more.

He stepped back. "Okay, take a breather. You all right?"

She did find herself taking a deep breath. As promised, despite what she'd anticipated, it hadn't been too bad, and his discovery of the recorder certainly removed any sense of outrage to which she might have laid claim.

Not to mention that he'd thought to eat a mint before their meeting. That, she never would have expected.

"Yes," she said, adding impulsively and with regret an instant later, "Sorry."

He let her off the hook. "Don't be. You're a reporter. And better than most. You tried, as I expected you would. That's to your credit. Stay standing there for a sec."

He abruptly vanished into the darkness. She heard him clattering about as she put her coat back on; then he reappeared with two unstable rolling office chairs, which he arranged by the table.

"Sit," he invited her, taking up his own invitation in the other chair, saying, "But watch yourself. They were left behind as trash for good reason. Wobbly."

Moving cautiously, she followed his example, until they looked like two people at a closed, condemned café.

The image was somehow apt, if a little absurd. By now, reassured by his manner and the fresh memory of his touch, Rachel couldn't deny the smallest feelings of attraction for this man, as she might have at the start of a first date.

"There," he said contentedly. "Now, what do you want?"

She'd thought about this, while not in this setting: cornering her quarry at last, asking him about why he did what he did; using him as a conduit into a lifestyle that most people considered unacceptable, if they even bothered to think about it.

But now that they were facing each other, and in part confused by his courtesy, she found herself at loose ends. She therefore began by saying, "Let me turn the tables on you. Why did you agree to meet? You don't know me, and I wasn't having any luck finding you. You could've left it like that."

"Not in my world," he explained. "You find out somebody's tailing you, you double back and check 'em out. It's insurance."

"Sounds military," she said. "That where

you learned it?"

She could almost hear him smile in the shadows. "I learned it watching old Westerns, right up with headin' them off at the pass, which is what I'm doing now."

He paused to let silence substitute for a repeat of his earlier question.

"You're like no thief I've ever heard about," she began. "Like a fictional character everyone knows couldn't really exist. My boss told me to go out and find stories you can't read anywhere else, especially in a small-town newspaper operating on a shoestring. They can be investigative pieces, or features, or anything at all, but they have to be good enough for his bosses to sit up and take notice."

"If you build it, they won't put you out of business?" he paraphrased.

"Something like that," she agreed, impressed by his ready grasp of her meaning. "It's a double threat to him. They wooed him back to the job on the premise he could revive the paper's past glory and increase circulation, but he's worried they wouldn't mind him failing, so they can then cut their losses. Meaning he'd love to succeed *and* shove it up their noses. He's using me to prove that newspapers aren't dinosaurs."

"You think I can do that?" he asked scornfully. "Sell more papers *and* give you another rung up the ladder?"

"Honestly? Sure," she admitted. "Where's the harm, if I also shield your identity?"

"How's that work?" he asked incredulously. "Even if you keep my name out of it, or change me into a girl, or pretend I'm eighty years old, the cat'll be out of the bag. The cops'll be so embarrassed and pissed off, they'll be hunting for me like I was public enemy number one."

"You've already done that yourself," she countered. "Who do you think told me about you? But," she then said, seizing hold of a tactic she hoped might be persuasive, "that was the point from the start, wasn't it? Any moron can break into a car or rob a house with a brick, some luck, and a good pair of running shoes. You've always seen this differently, like Picasso saw how to paint portraits. You're an artist.

"Be straight with me: Do you do this just for the money? Or is it the challenge? The flair? The feeling of doing something better and smarter than anybody else? I can see us collaborating on an article dealing with all that and more. People are constantly asking why and how artists do what they do. This would be your answer to that, and from an incredible perspective. I mean, think of it —

a man whose creative outlet is stealing stuff. Have you ever heard of that outside the movies? You're the real deal."

Alex was laughing by now. "Damn, girl. I can see why you got hired."

He stood up and moved around a bit, perhaps stretching his legs, although she hoped her enticement was a factor. Not that she could truly see anything. Her eyes had adjusted well enough that she could glimpse his outline, but only as the complete lack of any light at all, like a black hole.

"I still don't see an upside to talking with you," he said, to her disappointment. "If what you say is true, then my reasons for doing capers should be for my own personal pleasure. If I get an audience, I get attention; I get attention, I do jail time. On the other hand, if I keep my mouth shut, I'm in more control. That makes sense, doesn't it?"

"Sure," she agreed. "Except that nobody gets to see and appreciate your art, other than a few cops. Picasso didn't paint for himself. You're smart; you're creative; you've got ambition, like I do. If you want to maintain control in this collaboration, I can make sure you're in the driver's seat. You can check what I write, edit what I put in or omit."

Running the risk she knew it carried, she

then played her trump card. "Otherwise, I'll just do it without you. The secret's already out, Alex." She shrugged. "I can put something together by myself that'll impress 'em. But you'll read it later and think, 'Shit, she got it all wrong. She missed the whole point.' *That's* what I'm trying to avoid. I don't want to increase the pressure on you; I want to give you the scope you deserve. And by working with me, together we can better preserve your identity. Even without meaning to, I could mess things up there."

She stopped and waited, her hands in her lap, her energy spent. She'd laid it out, to the point of possibly pissing him off and endangering herself. Only now did it cross her mind that while her approach had been collegial, based on little more than his tone of voice, in fact, Alex Hale was a criminal. It was wholly within the realm of possibility that he could solve the problem she represented by simply knocking her on the head.

Still, it was out. She'd done her best, given the circumstances. On a more hopeful note, he could now just walk out the door, since, hearing the echo of her own pitch in her head, Rachel was left utterly unconvinced. Her only real ally against at least being dumped, and at worst, attacked, was the man's ego.

The reason he'd committed these crimes with such style spoke to a possible hunger for recognition. Anonymity has its place, certainly in ducking the law, but it runs counter to any personality so eager for attention that he arranges a clandestine meeting with a reporter.

That's where she was counting on personal desire overruling logic, or even self-preservation.

"You know," he said slowly, as if collecting his thoughts. "I don't just steal things. I find out about people, too, and what they're up to."

"Meaning what?"

"Phones, computers. You wouldn't believe what people put in them that they used to lock up in banks. All these things" — he gestured toward Rachel's locked-up cell phone — "are open to anyone with the know-how to get into them, and those crooks are a dime a dozen — government types, hackers, blackmailers, you name it. It's not that hard, especially if you have the training and tools."

"Which I'm assuming you have," she prompted him, encouraged. "Where're you going with this?"

His enthusiasm was building, as she'd barely dared to hope. "You're suggesting an article partly about security, where I could offer advice based on what I know. How 'bout I do you one better? We could ramp it up. I mean, we could still do security — God knows it would be helpful, since folks are so dumb about it — but we could go for more: talk about the deeper layers that're on everybody's computers and phones. That runs to a different kind of security, see? More personal. More embarrassing."

"Okay," Rachel said slowly, unsure of his direction, and certainly not interested in writing a how-to about cybersecurity. "Do you have examples of all that?"

His demeanor became almost playful. "Maybe. You'd be surprised by the things I know."

She took a stab at filling in the implication, suddenly thoughtful of what he might not be quite saying. "You've discovered something recently. Something important," she ventured, taking an intuitive guess.

He turned coy. "Let's say that if you like the idea, I got more to talk about than inventing a good password. And there's poetic justice to it, too, like when what people're protecting is older than the computers and cell phones they use to hide it — to where they *should've* stuck with a wall safe. Tried-and-true is undone by newfangled high tech."

She had no clue what he was talking about. Her proposal had shape-shifted into something only he could see. But the bottom line was that he was now on board. They could sort out their differing visions of the project later on.

"How would you want the logistics to work?" he asked, almost eager by now. "How and when do we meet? Things like that?"

It was her turn to smile, her earlier fear dissolved. Regardless of how she answered, she knew she had him.

CHAPTER 11

Joe and Gilbert eyeballed each other from four inches apart, steadily, without a word, Gilbert's expression utterly impassive.

"Don't say much, do you?" Joe challenged him quietly.

The cat, resting on Joe's chest as he lay on the couch, blinked in slow motion, purring softly.

Gilbert had come to Joe as cats often do, unexpectedly. But they'd hit it off, despite Joe's never having had a cat before. Gilbert gave him something to talk to during Beverly's absences, which were most of the time, and, typical of the species, he was low-maintenance and forgiving of Joe's human shortcomings, such as the latter's fondness for making loud noises in his woodworking shop.

Or the ceaselessly buzzing cell phone, which went off just now for the fiftieth time today. Gilbert all but rolled his eyes and

190

lazily abandoned his host's chest as Joe reached for the phone on the coffee table.

"Gunther."

"No shit," said Willy, continuing without pause. "D'you hear what Scott dug up in BF?"

"What?" Joe asked, inured to his colleague's lack of etiquette, on and off the phone.

"He found a witness who saw Lyall meeting a woman on the street, between when he left Danni's and when he ended up with Brandon again at the apartment."

"He was alone with her?"

"Yeah. Must've been after Brandon left to score his dope. It's sounding like this is maybe the 'woman about a horse' Lyall mentioned he had to meet after dinner, except that from what Scott was told, it's more like the woman may've been an unhappy customer."

"Oh?"

"Yeah, supposedly, she was ticked off about something. The witness —" Joe suddenly heard a child speaking loudly in the background.

"Hang on," Willy said, putting the phone down.

Joe could hear him speaking to his daughter, Emma. He was impressed by Willy's

191

calm and reassuring tone, even though he couldn't make out the actual discussion. Around adults, Willy displayed two moods, dour and dismissive, although he could fake nice during an interview. But Joe had never seen him be anything but thoughtful, caring, and patient with his child, regardless of what demon was chewing on his soul simultaneously. At times, it was like watching a highly disciplined split personality at work, and almost as disturbing, except that it happened every time, without exception, proof of Willy's having taken a pledge he wouldn't betray shy of death.

Sammie had recognized this part of his core early on, when she'd committed to living with him. While most onlookers figured she'd gone nuts at the time, Joe put his faith in them both, and was only rewarded at moments like this.

Willy resumed speaking as if nothing had interrupted them. "The witness told Scott the woman was waving her arms and yelling as Lyall crossed the street, giving weight to her being angry. But then the witness got into her car and left for work, and that was that."

"So, no description, nothing overheard, and nothing beyond a little arm waving," Joe summed up, disappointed.

"Nope," Willy confirmed. "And no horse, either."

Joe waited, sensing the man's unusual sense of humor lurking.

"There was a vehicle, though," Willy threw in. "An old-time VW hippie bus, no less. The witness saw the woman get out of it."

"Can't be too many of those still on the road," Joe commented.

"Not even in groovy Windham County," Willy agreed. "I got DMV searching for every VW bus registered in the state. Keep in mind, though, that Scott's source didn't get a plate — just that it was an old-time love bus. Could've been from Massachusetts — or Texas, for that matter."

Gilbert had returned and was settling back onto Joe's chest, watching his actions suspiciously. He was well advised. Joe gave him a gentle shove to the floor before sitting up and swinging his feet off the sofa, still speaking to Willy.

"Anything else from the canvass?"

"No. Scott was bummed because a possible good source died of natural causes before they could meet — a prehistoric and famous neighborhood rubbernecker, apparently — but that's it so far. He's still pounding on doors, set on finding whatever happened between the woman and Lyall."

"Did anybody double-check on Brandon's version of that night?"

"Yeah. The PD helped with that, as did Brandon himself, since he knows what's hanging over him. So far, so good. He left Lyall, like he said, beat feet across town, made his buy, and retreated to Lyall's. We got three unhappy people corroborating it, including the seller."

Joe was silent for several seconds.

Willy asked, "What d'you want to do with the canvassers? They're good keeping at it, but I know a couple of spousal units are complaining, and all the squad bosses are getting antsy to get 'em back."

Joe, being such a boss himself, was unimpressed by that second comment. "They'll survive," he said. "Keep the canvass going another twenty-four hours. I want that VW added to the list, along with the woman. Could be she was seen around town before disappearing."

"While dangling a bloody knife out the driver's window, just to be helpful?" Willy said.

Joe smiled. "Why not?"

"This JungleJim?" Alex asked.

The man at the other end of the line stayed silent, recognizing with a shock the chat room identifier he used on a porn site.

"Who's this?" he finally asked.

"Need to know, JungleBoy. You hung like Tarzan, like you wrote, or is that wishful thinking? I'm thinking we both know the answer there."

The man didn't respond. Alex could feel his animosity radiating through the phone like heat. It made him doubly happy the call was untraceable.

"Yeah, okay. Don't wanna talk about it. Understandable. Other things on your mind by now, right? Like I must be the guy who got your laptop."

"What do you want?"

"Good question. This is where it gets tricky, don't it? 'Cause I do want something. And you won't want to give it to me. Interesting things, other people's laptops. You ever taken hours and hours to really go through one that didn't belong to you? It's amazing what you can learn, especially when the owner is as sloppy with passwords as you are. Not that I'm complaining."

"You going to just talk me to death?"

"Impatient?" Alex taunted him. "And, I bet, used to getting results. Big boss in charge. That's okay. I can do that. Here's the deal: I'll sell you the computer back for two hundred and fifty grand. Enough to hurt; not enough to cripple."

JungleJim was dismissive. "Sure, and I'm to drop it into the knothole of some tree? On good faith you'll do the honorable thing, no questions asked? I don't think so."

Alex was unperturbed, having expected as much. "Who's talking about knotholes, Jim? No, no, we'll do this reasonably, considering you think I'm a bad guy, and I know sure as shit you are. There's an element of risk to each of us here. That's just reality — can't do anything about it. I've gotta think you'll try everything possible to cheat me, beat me, maybe even kill me; and you've gotta believe I downloaded the laptop onto a drive and I might be back for more later. We both have to live with that.

"Something to keep in mind, though," Alex warned. "I know all about your connections to the school, and what the place means to you. You might want to remember how I could really mess that up — even if I'm dead — considering what I learned. Is a measly quarter million worth that kind of hassle to you?"

He finally stopped, allowing Jim to ask after a moment's pause, "You finished?"

Alex was disconcerted by the man's coolness. He had never tried anything like this before. He was a hardware guy — breaking and entering, moving around product for cash. Negotiating for high stakes wasn't in his comfort zone.

But for this kind of money?

"Yeah," he said, waiting.

"You have something to write with?"

Alex hesitated before repeating more doubtfully, "Yeah."

"Good," said the man in a businesslike tone. "Take down this address. It's a restaurant. Should be lots of people there. You know what I look like? You should."

"I do."

"Good." The man gave him a time for the following day and a few more directions, then hung up without further comment, leaving Alex holding on to his phone, unsure of what had just occurred.

The paradox of the bomber's moon had slipped from his mind.

Between the exhaustion of a long day and the adrenaline drop-off following her encounter with Alex Hale, Rachel was as worn out as she could remember since her college-era all-nighters.

She was therefore ill disposed toward guests when she heard a knock on her apartment door at midnight. And even more so when she opened the door and saw Sally

Kravitz standing there.

"Hi," Sally said. "I saw your lights on."

"Not for long," Rachel replied flatly, not inviting her in.

Sally gave her a split second's analytical look before pretending she hadn't picked up on Rachel's mood. "How did that lead about Hale check out? He your guy?"

It was an interesting opening gambit, to Rachel's way of thinking, confronting her nagging suspicions with an open and frank lack of guile. And truthfully, while Rachel had initially questioned Sally's honesty concerning Hale and Dan Kravitz possibly being the same person, now that she'd met Alex — kind of — she knew absolutely that he couldn't be Sally's father.

That didn't preclude the possibility of other cross-connections between the two men, but it certainly lessened the sting Rachel had felt upon hearing Joe describe their similar styles.

Relenting, she stepped back and said, "Maybe. Probably. Come on in. I can make tea."

"That okay?" Sally countered. "It is late. I just wanted to follow up. But I can tell my timing's off."

"No, no," Rachel said, feeling better already. "Please, come in. I got Earl Grey and English breakfast. Slim pickings. Sorry."

"English breakfast is fine."

Using her offer of tea as an excuse to resettle herself, Rachel crossed to her kitchenette counter and began preparing to boil water, while her guest pretended to take in her surroundings for the first time.

"How long have you lived here?" Sally asked, looking around at what was a toss-up between an apartment and a storage facility. The walls were bare aside from a calendar and a clock, and cardboard boxes were the dominant furniture.

Rachel glanced over her shoulder. "That a variation of 'Love what you've done to the place'? I know it's a dump, and looks like I'm still unpacking. I've actually been here for months. I just can't seem to get my head around decorating when I get off work."

Sally laughed. "Tell me about it. And I bet you've only seen the place in daylight maybe twice."

"Sunrises," Rachel said. "I see those."

Sally plopped down into a beanbag next to a box doubling as a side table, complete with a wobbly IKEA lamp. She was feeling the aftereffects of a long day herself, having started at Thorndike Academy, pretending to be an outgoing, upbeat team player, and maybe just a little dumb — none of which was a natural fit. "When I was a kid, my dad and I moved around so often, I sometimes had no idea where I was when I woke up. Home was a suitcase, some favorite books, and a small stuffed animal I called Bearmouse."

"Your father sounds like a character," Rachel commented.

Sally's response appeared unguarded and spontaneous. "You heard about him, huh? Yup. Pretty unusual. Good guy, though," she added after a pause.

Whether it was exhaustion, conflicted emotions, or simply ingrained curiosity, Rachel turned around fully, propped her elbows on the counter, and came straight to the point. "I thought at first he and Hale might be the same person. According to Katz and Gunther, their styles are similar."

Sally startled her by replying, "I did, too, so I asked him. Turns out, none of us was far wrong. Dan's been keeping tabs on Hale for a while, in an admiring sort of way. Sees him as a kind of kindred spirit, I guess, although without my father's moral code."

Sally laid her head against the back of the beanbag to look straight up at the ceiling before saying, "Creeped me out at first, when you mentioned how Alex operated. I may have buttoned up because of it. Sorry.

I just wanted to ask Dan directly before going any further with you. Nothing personal."

"I did wonder," Rachel told her. "I thought you might be covering for him."

Sally chuckled. "Nothing that conspiratorial. Most of the time, I have no clue what he's up to. *Could* be robbing banks, but I doubt it. The man is part Knight of the Round Table, King Arthur himself, and Merlin, all wrapped up in one weird package."

She straightened enough to look at her hostess again. "As he sees it, he has a strict ethical belief system. It's just not one the rest of us could even pretend to figure out."

Rachel nodded, satisfied and relieved, and returned to her preparations, the water now boiling. "Well, in answer to your question at the door, then," she said, "the lead did pan out, and I have met with Alex Hale. At least I think it was him. He was dressed as a ninja. What we finally hammered out was an article about security, based on his successes at breaching it. That's his plan, in any case, which I'll try to make more personal to him. We'll see how it goes. The trick will be to get him to open up. I chased down his mom," she added, as an afterthought. "After I felt you were playing games with me."

"You did?" Sally responded, clearly impressed. "Despite his efforts to duck the limelight? How'd you do that?"

"Old-fashioned document search. A birth record, finally. Not that it came to much, since she shut me out when we met, but it proved to me that he's left a trail, despite his obsession with privacy and spycraft."

"Flaky, is he?" Sally asked, accepting the mug that Rachel handed her.

"I'm not sure what he is," Rachel said. "We met in an abandoned warehouse on Flat Street, just a while ago. No lights, no heat. He searched me for any listening or tracking devices, and put my phone in what I assume was a signal-blocking box. It was like interviewing Batman."

"He searched you?" Sally burst out. "I would've kicked him in the nuts."

Rachel laughed. "I bet you would. He was actually really polite about it. Thorough but weirdly prudish, like he was more embarrassed than I was. And given that, I didn't want to slam the door in his face prematurely."

"Still . . . ," Sally muttered.

"Anyway," Rachel continued, "the whole encounter was bizarre, especially the end, when he hinted he was in the middle of something that would expand the scope of our project. He talked about cybersecurity, and how people keep things they shouldn't, on platforms they think are secure, until they're not."

"That's hardly late-breaking news."

"I know," Rachel mused, thinking back. "But I couldn't shake the feeling that it was all somehow topical, and therefore relevant to me and this series. He's a small-town boy, after all. And he was acting like a cat in front of a fresh can of tuna. It was almost funny, how excited he was, working out logistics on how and where we should meet in the future. He was obviously in the middle of something he could barely resist telling me about."

"Ah, boys . . . ," Sally said, sounding world-weary.

Charlestown, New Hampshire, police officer Travis Monroe eased his cruiser down Lower Landing Road, toward the town's boat ramp, respectful of the slippery surface under his tires. He was on routine patrol, the light was fading fast, and the temperature had fallen sharply during the day. This winter had been tough, even on natives like himself, who used to scoff at how old-timers waxed on about the brutality of previous winters.

There hadn't been much reminiscing like that this year.

Monroe didn't come here often during the off-season. Indeed, the only reason it was even plowed was for ice-water rescue crews to gain access to the Connecticut River.

But there'd been a call. Someone claiming to have seen a car down here — probably already long gone.

If it had even existed.

Monroe grunted as the landing appeared in his headlights and he saw a vehicle positioned near the bottom of the summertime parking area. "Okay," he said to himself, calling it in to Dispatch as he drew near.

He got out of the cruiser slowly, looking around, his tactical senses sharpened. The driver's door was ajar, its window partly rolled down.

He rested his hand on his holstered weapon, ready to move fast. Better safe than sorry.

"Police!" he shouted, his voice quickly absorbed by the surrounding open space and the ominous rush of nearby water. He scanned the snow for telltale signs with his flashlight, but while there were footprints, it was hard to tell their source or direction. This was a popular spot for local misbehav-

ior in warmer weather, which in part was why he was familiar with it.

No one answered him. Watching his step, his eyes on his surroundings, as well as on the car's interior, Travis slowly circled his objective, trying to take note of everything.

The car was a slightly rusting truck, still holding its own, with a heavy diamond plate toolbox bolted to its bed. About par for the average vehicle on northern New England roads. Its license plate was from Vermont, which he passed along to Dispatch over his portable.

"Hello?" he called out more quietly, increasingly confident that he was alone. He reached the passenger door and pulled it open with a gloved hand, taking note of the shattered window glass at his feet. That told him the force of impact had come from inside.

Dispatch came back to him as he checked the narrow storage space behind the truck's seats, finding little of interest.

"Repeat the owner's name," he requested, his attention having been abruptly distracted.

"Alexander Hale."

He keyed the mic again. "Better send a supervisor," he said. "I think we've got something here."

He leaned forward carefully, making sure not to touch anything, despite his gloved hands, in order to confirm what he'd thought he'd seen on the driver's seat cushion.

"Swell," he said regretfully.

It was blood.

CHAPTER 12

Joe got the news first from Rachel, who called him at the office.

"What is the fucking deal?" she demanded. "Do bad things have to happen to *everyone* I know?"

"What's going on, Rachel?" he asked her calmly. "Where are you right now?"

"In my car."

"Where, sweetheart? I'll come to you."

There was a pause. "I don't know. I mean, the district courthouse parking lot."

"I'm right across the street."

Joe was moving to the coatrack as he hung up, and announced to his colleagues, "Be right back."

"What's going on?" Lester asked from his desk.

"Rachel. I'm guessing a friend got into a jam of some kind. She's right across the street."

"Got it. Good luck."

Joe cautiously jogged down the inclined driveway toward the street separating the municipal building from the courthouse, watching for any black ice, and headed over to Rachel's dark green car.

Without ceremony, he opened the passenger door and slid in beside her, moving her camera bag to the backseat. The engine was still running and the heater on, for which he was grateful, not having buttoned his coat on the way out.

Rachel looked at him, clearly upset. Her smartphone was in her hand.

He placed the back of his hand against her cheek. "I'm sorry, kiddo. What happened?"

"I didn't know who to call. I was hoping you'd be in. It's probably nothing, but I just have this horrible feeling."

"It's fine. I'm glad I was nearby."

She gestured weakly with the phone, its screen glowing. "I got a heads-up from a service I use — a text-messaging version of an old-fashioned scanner."

"Okay."

"They found Alex Hale's car by the river in Charlestown, empty."

Joe thought quickly to recall Alex Hale's name. "Your master thief. You mentioned him at dinner the other night."

"I met him," she told him. "He was like I was hoping, all full of energy and mischief. I mean, you knew he'd get his butt in a jam sooner or later. But . . ." She stopped and let out a shuddering sigh. "It's all so fucking familiar, you know? I'm just so sure he's in big-time trouble."

Joe kept silent, Rachel's past history sharp in his memory. She was made of sturdy stuff emotionally, like her mother, a fact he'd witnessed firsthand while observing her through more than one tumultuous event. But her outburst on the phone had been well founded: How much misery was one young woman destined to attract, through no fault of her own? He suspected that her reaction now was less pinned to the disappearance of one young man and more the result of a dammed-up reservoir of grief.

He pulled out his own cell and punched in the office number.

"Lester," he said, "get hold of the Charlestown PD and see what they've got by the river. Maybe a car registered to an Alexander Hale." He spelled out the last name.

He disconnected and said to Rachel, "A convoluted thinker like that, it could be he just stashed his car out of the way to hitch a ride with somebody else," although he was no less convinced than she that Hale might have come to a bad end. "Did your source say where the car was found?"

"The boat ramp," she answered, her voice partly muffled as she blew her nose.

That didn't sound promising.

His phone vibrated in his hand. "Yeah, Les."

"You alone?"

Joe glanced at Rachel. "I can be. Hang on."

He got back out of the car, promising, "I'll just be a minute," slammed the door, and put the phone on its roof so he could button his coat. The sun had set, and the already-frigid air was diving fast into the single digits.

"Speak," he ordered.

"You know the chief over there?" Lester asked. "Bob Vogel?"

"Sure. We've met."

"He'd like you to call him direct. He's at the scene." Lester gave Joe the number, adding afterward, "When you're done, call me back. They told me something that's looking like a crossover to what we're doing."

"Got it."

Regretting that he'd now placed himself beyond both his office and the warm car, Joe entered the number, put on his gloves, and began pacing the parking lot.

"Bob," he replied to the other man's greeting. "Joe Gunther."

"Hey," Vogel said. "Long time. You been okay?"

"Landed a new one in Bellows Falls you probably heard about," Joe said. "Still sorting it out. What're you looking at?"

"Nothing good. The name Alex Hale mean anything to you? He's supposed to be from Brattleboro."

"Yeah. Suspected of a bunch of high-profile local burglaries in and around town."

"Ever connected to anything violent?"

"Not that I heard. Supposedly, he worked alone and had a flashy style — liked things complicated. A show-off, I guess. Never knew him personally."

"Okay," Vogel said thoughtfully. "Well, he may've pushed somebody's button. His pickup was found by the boat ramp. Door still open, blood on the driver's seat, blown-out window, and from what we're putting together, there're indications that he was likely dragged to the water's edge and dumped."

"Great," Joe said. He glanced at Rachel's car. Once more, he was going to have to escort this poor girl through another grieving process, as he'd suspected when she called him. Reading her body language right now, she looked like she was using her own phone — he hoped to talk with her mother. Good move, if accurate — for all her outward cool professionalism, Beverly was great in times of stress.

"We've already contacted the state dive team," Vogel was saying. "They won't be doing anything till daylight, since it'll take 'em a couple of hours even to get here. And unless you say otherwise, I don't have any reason to tell them to step it up."

"Nope," Joe replied. "I don't. I heard he's been active lately, but not for anything that warranted being killed. Did you find anything in the truck that'll help?"

"Yeah. That's why I asked your guy to have you call me direct," Vogel said. "And thanks for cluing me in on what Hale did for a living — makes more sense with what we found."

"What's that?"

"Appears to be research, once we managed to get at it. That part was weird. We found it all in the toolbox behind the cab, but we had to force our way in. The key wasn't on the key ring, or anywhere else. It's like Hale customized an extra layer of security. And that may've been smart — there were signs somebody had tried to jimmy their way in. Maybe the same guy who bushwhacked him, if that's how this turns out. When we get the crime people to really turn the truck inside out, we'll likely find the key tucked away somewhere tricky.

"It does look like he ran his office out of the pickup, what with a computer, binoculars, a camera, burglary tools, and such. Maybe it was so if he ever got stopped by law enforcement, no one could gain access and bust him. I don't know. Anyhow, we found pictures, hand-drawn maps, notes. Pretty organized. If he was a thief, like you say, it might be he was casing a job just south of you. You know Thorndike Academy?"

"By name," Joe replied. "Not our kind of venue, normally. It's a high-end prep school. He was looking at that?"

Vogel reacted to the incredulity in Joe's voice. "I know. Doesn't make sense to me, either, but he was clearly spending a lot of time sniffing around the place."

People talking in the background suddenly distracted him. "Hang on," he said, and Joe imagined him cupping the phone in his hand.

Vogel returned a minute later and said, "Look, I don't have much more than that right now. We gotta get all this back to the office and go through it where it's warm and we have better control. Call me first thing tomorrow morning, and we'll see where we stand. Work for you?"

"Sure, Bob. Later."

"You got it."

Joe followed up on Lester's request to call him back. "What's up?" he asked when Les answered.

"Vogel fill you in?"

"More or less. We're supposed to talk in the A.M."

"He mention the school?"

"Yeah. That sounded a little random, from what I know about Alex Hale. I thought he did cars and purses and empty homes."

"You're right," Lester confirmed. "Willy and I have been running his background over here. Thorndike Academy is way off his normal radar."

Again, Joe cast a look at Rachel's car. He didn't want to leave her alone for too long. "Why did you want me to call back?" he asked.

"It's the school," Lester said. "Remember we'd asked DMV to cross-reference any older VW buses, possibly with female owners, just to see if we got lucky with the one Scott told us about from BF?"

"Sure." Joe's focus on the conversation abruptly sharpened.

214

"There were several hits, like you'd expect in crunchy Vermont, all of which have been accounted for. The only standout, as luck would have it, is in Windham County. Male owner — Frederick Dougle. And here's the kicker: He lives at Thorndike Academy. We're checking him out now."

"Damn," Joe said softly.

"I know, right?" Lester agreed. "Makes ya think."

"That it does," Joe agreed, before hanging up and returning to the car.

He felt bad for Rachel. Although possessing similar resilience to her mother, the girl had been through enough. In the emergency services world, people like her were politely called "black clouds," or less daintily, "shit magnets." If bad things happened, they regularly did so when such people were on duty, on call, or just standing around clothed in bad karma. It wasn't fair, and statistically, it could probably be proven untrue, but for the person so involved, it could feel like perpetually reliving Job's travails.

Joe climbed back into the warm car and slammed the door. Rachel was staring ahead, her phone in her hand.

"I'm sorry you got caught up in another one of these," Joe said.

"That's what Mom just said," Rachel replied, gesturing weakly with her phone.

"I hoped you were talking with her."

"Yeah," Rachel said, with no bitterness he could discern. "She is the one to call when somebody dies. Weird, but there you have it."

Joe considered adding his own variation on what Beverly must have told her daughter, but thought better of it. Rachel was right. Her mother was the pro.

"You were saying you met him?" he asked instead. "When was that?"

"Night before last. It was straight out of a spy movie. Silly, really, but he seemed to have a flair for it. I've been thinking about him a lot, because of the article, and one thing I wanted to ask him was whether a theory I was developing made any sense."

"What's that?"

She sighed. "Doesn't make much difference now."

"Maybe not," Joe agreed. "But who says the article's past history? Let's find out what happened — or didn't happen, if it turns out he's fine. Could be that what you write'll still have real merit. Tell me what you were thinking."

She looked at him at last and gave him a sad smile. "Thanks, Joe. You're really nice."

216

"Go on," he urged.

She gave a barely perceptible nod. "Okay. I wanted to see if he was the kind of person who was smarter than his circumstances implied." She suddenly showed more enthusiasm, adding, "I know you can say that for tons of people, especially in their own minds, but that's the catch: what you think of yourself versus what's reality. I mean, consider it: Circumstances have put you in a social stratum; people tell you your options are limited; they even prove it through their own choices. But deep inside, you know otherwise. So how do you work through that? Show them they were wrong? Or maybe just show yourself that. Can you overcome your own history? He seemed a natural candidate for that kind of question. To me, he was even an artist of sorts, if that's not too over the top."

She twisted in her seat, her sorrow momentarily diminished. "I was going to talk to his family, friends, classmates, teachers, you name it. Find out what made him tick, if there were any watershed moments in his life, or people who inspired him or threw him off-balance. We do all these feature pieces about celebrities with no talent. What about a kid from the other side of the tracks who turns stealing into a creative act?"

She caught herself in mid-sentence, paused, settled back into her seat, and added, "At least that was the plan."

He tried encouraging her. "It still can be."

"What did you find out?" she asked then, indicating the phone in his hand.

"The locals have called in the dive team for tomorrow morning. We'll let them do their thing while we interview those who knew him, along with the usual things we do." Joe reached out and took hold of Rachel's right hand. "Most of the time, we figure it all out. And I'll do my best to keep you in the loop, given the professional barriers between us, as usual."

She was already nodding in agreement. "I know, I know. I appreciate it, Joe. Thanks."

He broke off to pull his wallet from his back pocket, then scrounged around inside it for a moment before revealing a dog-eared business card, which he handed over.

"You may not want to act on this," he explained. "Your choice entirely. But that's the name of a shrink I use now and then, off the record. He's a neat guy. A German, originally, and an expert at grief counseling. You'd like his office, if nothing else. It's like a set from an old black-and-white British movie — *Goodbye, Mr. Chips,* or something. Makes you feel totally at home. His name's

Eberhard Dziobek, and if you want to see him, you'll never find a nicer human being. I wouldn't recommend him otherwise."

Rachel's expression didn't betray her reaction to Dziobek one way or the other, but the look in her eyes was openly appreciative.

"Think about it," Joe said quickly, so she didn't have to speak herself. "If you do end up calling him, use my name. Over the years, we've become good friends, but secret ones. I've never told anyone that we meet now and then. I got my John Wayne reputation to maintain."

That, at least, got a laugh from her.

With Willy still in Bellows Falls, wrapping up the last of the canvass, it fell to Lester and Sammie Martens to drive to the Thorndike Academy campus in Vernon and check out the details concerning the older-model Volkswagen bus.

This was an uncommon treat for Lester, who only occasionally got partnered with Sam for an outing. There was no standing protocol covering who rode with whom on a call, but as he reflected on the matter, sitting in the passenger seat, he realized that he teamed up with her least of all. One of those odd bits of mathematical happenstance, he figured.

"How's Emma doing?" he asked.

"She's good," Sam replied, watching the car ahead of them warily. It was pure mythology that northern New England drivers were as comfortable as sled dogs on the snow. Unlike the average Texan, perhaps, they knew what snow was, but their prowess navigating its challenges left much to be desired.

"Willy thinks she's got all the makings of a back-alley knife fighter, but I like the way she stands up for herself. I don't think she's unreasonable when she puts up a fuss, most of the time. I do think her father and she are too much alike when it comes to being stubborn. I don't know how you and Sue did it with your two kids."

Lester was typically self-effacing. "Oh hell. That was all Sue. I just ran out on a call when things got tough."

Sam knew the truth to that. Sue was a nurse, often worked nights in past years, and so left the parenting to Lester far more than he was letting on.

"Besides," he added, "Wendy was like a kid cut out of a picture book: respectful, tidy, hardworking, funny, and good at school. And her brother wasn't much worse. I had it easy."

Left unacknowledged between them was that the same son, David Spinney — perhaps ironically now beginning a career in law enforcement — had almost landed in jail for running with a rough bunch while a teenager. Lester had risked his job sorting it out. Sammie would keep that footnote for another day, however, when Emma had reached the same age and was maybe facing the same bad choices.

"Wendy's out of high school by now, isn't she?" Sam asked.

"Yup. First year at Northern Vermont U., in Johnson. Likes it so far. Pretty much over being homesick."

"Would you have sent her here if you'd had the cash?" Sam asked as the car nosed between twin square stone columns supporting an open ironwork sign reading THORNDIKE ACADEMY.

"Nah. I think prep schools are an elitist waste of money and just one reflection of a screwed-up educational system. I can't argue with the quality of teaching that probably goes on here, but I don't think I'd like the company she'd keep. Just a local woodchuck's stupid prejudice, no doubt."

"Hey," Sammie said. "You're allowed." But the exchange made her wonder, considering her obligations to her own kid. Her ambitions for Emma were like any responsible parent's, she hoped, and a good education played a major role. Her own childhood had lacked many hallmarks of a decent upbringing, including good schooling, and she certainly aspired to better for Emma. Beverly Hillstrom had become a true, trusted, and valued friend over time, and Sam knew that she'd attended this kind of place, along with the type of college usually associated with such schools. Wouldn't Sam want such a fate for her child?

She made a mental note to call Beverly sometime soon to ask her opinion.

"Damn," Lester said, half to himself, as the car crested the top of the long driveway and came into view of the campus, clustered artfully in a shallow valley before them like the setting of a Jane Austen novel.

Sammie seconded his reaction. "Wow. Feels weird to be in a car instead of a carriage."

The time of year helped, capping all the faux-Victorian structures with crowns of fresh snow, but neither one of them thought that the effect would be any less come spring. It was, all partisanship aside, spectacular.

It turned out that what they'd come upon was the centerpiece only, consisting of the

222

administration building, the dining hall, a farmhouse, and the gym, which hinted disingenuously at having once been a barn. Upon consulting a decorously designed map mounted by the side of the road, they discovered that a separate core of less imposing dorms, class buildings, and maintenance shops was located behind a low rise ahead, tucked away to preserve the fantasy that had greeted them.

Indeed, the illusion was not perpetuated by the campus's lesser half. It was equally large and imposing, and clearly expensively built, but it was no Downton Abbey look-alike.

"You think we should check in with Admin first?" Lester asked as Sammie continued driving.

"Fuck 'em," she said, sounding like Willy, which she often did lately. "No reason to grant them more authority than they have. We're just here for a vehicle check, when you get down to it."

She did slow down for a small coed group of students who were walking between two buildings, and rolled down the window as she drew abreast.

"Hey," she said in a friendly tone. "Any of you know where we can find Fred Dougle? I lost the directions he gave us."

"Sure," one of them offered, pointing to a structure in the near distance. "He's master of Percival. That one. His door's on the right side. You can park opposite it."

"Thanks," she said cheerily, moving ahead and saying to Les, "Percival. I should've known. Why not Wadsworth-Harrington?" She glanced at him. "And did you see the skirt on that girl?"

"Yeah," Spinney acknowledged, smiling. "I did."

"It's frigging winter. She's gonna have frostbite on her ass, for Christ's sake." Sam took them around a small traffic circle and off onto a tangent that ended where they'd been directed, across from a door helpfully labeled DOUGLE. Next to it was an older-model Volkswagen bus, colorfully painted with stars, flowers, and rainbows in true ancient hippie fashion, if considerably faded by age and wear.

"That takes the challenge out of it," Lester said as he swung out of the car into the cold air.

"The fat lady hasn't sung yet," Sam told him, again emulating Willy and his standard lack of optimism. The comment made Lester think, not for the first time, how often it was that people sought out versions of themselves with whom to form a union,

224

as he had done with Sue. Nevertheless, despite such similarities, Lester remained impressed that the Sam–Willy odd coupling worked as well as it did.

Sam got to the door first and pressed the buzzer, which was answered a minute later by a pleasant, athletically built woman, perhaps in her mid-thirties. "Hi. What's up?"

Both cops revealed their badges. "We're from the VBI, ma'am," Lester began. "Looking for Frederick Dougle."

The woman looked vaguely concerned. "The police? Is he okay? I'm his wife, Jill."

"He's fine, ma'am," Sam told her. "This is strictly routine, but since you brought it up, is there any reason you think he might be in trouble?"

The woman's expression became one of convincing incredulity. "What else am I supposed to say to two armed cops? And from the VBI, no less. That's major crimes." She placed one hand protectively along the edge of the door. "What exactly do you want?"

Lester made a show of his best aw-shucks imitation, smiling broadly and bowing slightly. "Whoa. We forget the effect those initials have on people. No, no. My colleague wasn't kidding. This is really no big deal." He jerked his thumb over his shoulder. "We heard your van was seen in Bellows Falls a few days ago, and we're just here to confirm it. But that's all. It wasn't used for a bank robbery or anything. Identifying such details is just part of what we do."

"It sometimes helps us find witnesses," Sam threw in, already impressed that their challenger knew their status within law enforcement. Even at this late date in its existence, the initials VBI still drew blanks from most people.

Almost curiously, Jill seemed to relax, saying, "No clue about the bus. You want to come in? It's cold. I've got some fresh coffee on."

They followed her down a hallway lined with winter clothing hanging from hooks, careful not to disturb the row of ice skates and snowshoes along the wall, designed for feet ranging from adult sizes to small children's.

"You have kids?" Sam asked the woman's back.

"Three. They're all out right now. Day care and school, depending. That's one thing you can say about this place. Terrific for people with little ones."

They reached a kitchen, bright and modern, with large windows overlooking a white field behind the building. Both cops sat where indicated, at the room's island counter, while Jill went about pouring cups of coffee, as promised.

Lester took out a pad. "Do we call you Mrs. Dougle?" he asked. "Or do you go by something else?"

Jill raised an eyebrow. "Very hip, Detective. No, the van notwithstanding, we're pretty traditional. Dougle's my name, too, and you can call me Jill. You never gave me your names."

Properly chastised, they introduced themselves while accepting the steaming cups. Jill sat on the other side of the island.

"Is it fun, being a cop?" she asked.

Sam was too surprised to respond immediately. "More interesting than fun," Lester replied, taking a sip of the best coffee he'd enjoyed in years. Right now, he was thinking maybe prep school life had perks he'd never imagined.

"What did you mean by 'No clue about the bus,' Mrs. Dougle? I mean Jill," Sam asked.

"Just that we wouldn't necessarily know where it had been or who'd taken it," Jill said. "In that way, it's less ours than the whole community's." She paused to take a sip from her cup before continuing. "Call it an adapted bike-share program. It was Fred's idea. I'll give him that, but I warned him at the time that it would come back to bite us."

She put her cup down to explain. "None of us drives much around here. Room and board is part of the deal, and the food's outstanding, in order to appeal to our precious charges. Add to that the crazy schedules and how everything gets purchased over the internet nowadays anyhow, and you end up asking, Why have a car at all?

"Well, the answer's obvious, of course, but the point remains that few of us really need transportation that often. So Fred came up with turning our bus into a community thing. Originally, I made sure it had a checkout sheet, and people had to ask us for the keys, but that fell apart pretty fast. Now the keys are just left in it, and it comes and goes as if it were a remote-control drone."

She laughed suddenly. "Not really a drone, given its age. Fred calls it 'A Horse with No Name,' after the song by America."

The idea of a communal car was appalling to Sam's sense of paranoid propriety, but the reference to a horse overrode her attention. She exchanged a look with Lester.

He smoothly kept the conversation going. "Cool," he said. "I can see your concern, though. It really could be used to rob a bank, except for your preselected population."

"That's the thing, right?" Jill Dougle agreed. "We've had this going for a couple of years, and not a single problem. People have even chipped in for repairs and maintenance." She lowered her voice slightly. "We've spared telling our insurance company any of this, of course, and the administration doesn't know about it, either, officially. That probably would get awkward. But there're a lot of things like that where management winks a collective eye." She then laughed. "Like sex. This place is a hotbed."

Both her guests joined in. "Really?" Sam said. "I would've thought they'd mix saltpeter with the morning cereal, or whatever it is."

"No, no," Jill went on. "I'm sure they'd love to, if they could get away with it. Instead, they offer counseling and try to stay vigilant. But you know teenagers. Not that the adults are much better, although I'm exaggerating a little there. Still, the kids are like rabbits. The school nurse can even dispense birth control and morning-after pills, with parental consent."

Lester shook his head. "Okay, back to the bus, or the horse. Do you think Fred might have a better idea of its comings and goings? Or anyone else, for that matter?"

"I don't think so," she said. "Neither one of us pays much attention to it, since we have a car of our own. You can ask him, but I wouldn't put money on it. He can be a little absentminded about things like that."

"How 'bout people who use it more than the others?" Sammie asked. "Have you picked up on that, maybe?"

Jill gave it a moment's contemplation. "Can't say I have."

"Women versus men?" Lester prompted.

But her response remained the same. "As I said, it's become an entity unto itself."

"Where is Fred?" Lester asked casually.

"Teaching. U.S. History." Jill checked her sports watch. "He should be done in another half hour, but then I think there's a faculty meeting. I could call him and yank him out of that, if you'd like, but he won't be happy, now that I know what the gist is. He's pretty gung ho, and being interrupted to talk about the VW won't go over well. Unless you've got something you want to ask him that you don't want me to know about."

Sam liked that. "Smart," she said. "Wrong, but it's a good way to think about us."

Lester laughed. "Great. Tell her all our secrets. No, that was it, and we'll leave him alone for a later visit, maybe."

The two of them stood, preparing to leave, when Jill asked, "What was this all about anyhow? You never did explain why the VBI is checking into our car usage."

The cops were putting their coats back on and already heading down the short hallway. "Not to sound ungrateful," Lester said as he went, "especially given how helpful you've been, but we're pretty much under orders to keep a lid on that for the time being."

She exited the building with them, stopping halfway to Sammie's car. Her warm breath created a small fog around her head as she said, "BF. That's where you said it was seen." She indicated the old bus.

"Yeah," Lester replied. "Something occur to you?"

"Not what you're thinking," Jill told him, her expression rueful. "I remembered reading about the killing up there a few days ago. That's why you're here. The paper said the VBI was investigating that."

"Thanks again, Jill," Lester said, hoping

his friendly expression would offset his evasion. "You serve one mean cup of coffee."

CHAPTER 13

Scuba diving in freezing New England rivers is even more difficult than it sounds. Documentaries abound featuring divers floating in proximity of glowing blue icebergs, the water's clarity as sharp as the surrounding temperature, giving the whole scene a brittleness akin to glass breaking on concrete. The imagery is stunning, beautiful, and memorable.

Winter river diving is just like that — with a trash bag stuck over your head.

Rich Werner had been a member of the New Hampshire Fish and Game dive team for more years than he cared to remember. Like most emergency responders, however — firefighters, EMTs, police officers, or rescue divers — when he saw a calming, weightless portrait like the iceberg image, all he could think of were the chances of a mishap, as in a huge chunk calving from overhead and punching into the water to squash that happy diver like a soft-shelled crab.

The equipment his team used, the training they received year-round, the situations that called for their services, all had a single common denominator. It wasn't pleasure or bonding — although each member enjoyed the job and its purpose — it was the peril they faced in every single case. Similar to mountain climbers and sky jumpers, rescue and recovery divers could be killed in a snap if they didn't heed every detail, every time.

Murky, ice-choked, fast-flowing river water only made that truer.

Rich sat in the warmth of the unit's command vehicle, parked by the Connecticut River on the Charlestown boat ramp, a Styrofoam cup of hot coffee in his cold hands, looking out the window at the rest of this operation's participants. He was colder than he'd admitted to his handlers when he'd finally escaped the river's embrace, but not so much as to have hindered his abilities. There were standards they all agreed with — of time and exposure and circumstances encountered — that governed acceptable levels of risk.

But there was no standard for the adrenaline, stubbornness, or even hubris that could fudge the margins of allowable behavior.

And Rich, now safe, dry, and warming up, could concede that maybe he'd pushed the envelope a little this time.

It wasn't a huge deal. They all did it to a degree. When Rich had been hauled back on board the unit's airboat, his line tender had even assessed him with a knowing smile and whispered in his ear as he'd helped him remove his scuba tank, "Pushed it a little, didn't ya, bucko?"

So why had he done it? So he could be the guy who brought home the results, so his team could look good to the people who'd sent for them, and so the older investigator from Vermont's VBI — the famous Joe Gunther, who was now standing by the water, watching his part of all this being addressed — would be impressed.

Childish on some level, perhaps, but part of the same chemistry that fueled all type A units like the dive team, and pushed them to consider danger as a challenge to be calculated and methodically defeated, in the name of public service. Rich Werner was not a mindless booster for New Hampshire Fish and Game. But he was proud of their calling and work product, and happy to think that today his actions had helped Joe Gunther move toward a resolution.

So there you had it: a successful conclusion, arrived at in a timely fashion against less than ideal circumstances.

But it hadn't been easy, luck had played its usual role, and Rich could now privately admit that he was happy it was over.

They'd arrived at first light. The day was forecast to be somber and possibly snowy later on. The river ice was either thick or absent, depending on its location, the current beneath it, and the effects of wind and sun.

One saving grace had been the airboat, a new addition to their armory. Small but nimble, it made short work of the river's obstacles, unlike the Zodiacs of yore. They had only the one statewide, but Rich and his group had gotten lucky this time.

That had turned out to be more than a perk. When they'd launched and begun surveying the site, complications had arrived in droves. The river was colder, faster, deeper, and more dangerous than reported. Fallen trees, snags, and upstream debris had chosen this stretch to create an obstacle course of barriers. And finally, there was the visibility below — or lack thereof.

This is where river diving earned its special place among challenges. To everyone with that picture of the iceberg diver in their heads, imagine an environment where seeing five feet ahead was a bonus, and where an endless stream of sludge, twigs, vegetable matter, the odd fish, and sometimes a log or branch came at you with the numbing regularity of baseball-size snowflakes hitting a car's windshield.

Then reduce those five feet to half that or less.

There are tricks to the exotic practice of body recovery. Grappling hooks, water-scent cadaver dogs, sonar devices. There are also the physics of an inert body in water: how far it travels, how fast it sinks, how much it weighs given its buoyancy below the surface. There are dozens of calculations to be made, local fishermen to interview, past history, if any, to consult. Rich had once described the process as being similar to planning a mountain assault for climbers.

But in the end, more often than not, it came down to someone getting into the water.

And there, despite the ropes attached to human line tenders above, or the presence of a boat with backup divers ready to assist, the person in the freezing, murky, fast-moving, surprisingly noisy darkness was all alone, battling the elements, fighting to conduct an organized search despite the buffeting current, and hoping like hell that those above were keeping their eyes open for any submarine-like submerged log that might be aiming for a head shot.

Luckily, in cold water, dead bodies tend to sink predictably, and stay at the bottom until bloating reverses the process. That wasn't a factor here. The man they were seeking had been missing a short time, and the implications were that he hadn't been fighting the water or trying to swim when he'd gone under. It had been deemed a good bet that, although no sonar readings had given any clear-cut guarantees, their guy was most likely still in the neighborhood of the boat ramp.

Rich took another swallow of his coffee, reminiscing. But, man, this had been a bitch. Pushing the boundaries as he had, being less than entirely truthful over the radio mounted in his helmet, he'd been almost too numbed to see his discovery when it appeared.

Fortunately — although not for the startled people above who'd heard him shout in surprise on the radio — circumstances and that element of luck had combined at just the right moment. Swimming inches above the riverbed, studying the buried trees and rocks and occasional discarded shopping cart, Rich had actually been scanning to the right when a white lifeless hand had fluttered up from behind a formless, muddy hummock to the left and smacked him in the mask.

He could smile at his reaction now, but it had damn near given him a heart attack.

He continued watching Joe Gunther as the remains of Alex Hale were tagged, bagged, and shifted into the back of a hearse for transport to the New Hampshire medical examiner's office.

The depth of that fright would stay his own secret. Rich had already been ribbed for simply yelling as he had — not his best Mr. Cool moment, to be sure. But he'd done his job.

Now it was up to the man from Vermont.

At the time he'd mentioned it, Rachel hadn't fully grasped Joe's allusion to *Goodbye, Mr. Chips.* But now that she was sitting in Eberhard Dziobek's office, it was hard to miss. From the worn carpeting to the dusty framed prints to the messy floor-to-ceiling bookshelves, the room looked like a rarely visited, small-town museum, including a dusty stuffed bird standing forgotten on a small table in one of the dark corners.

The man responsible for it seemed also perfectly in context, to the point where Rachel imagined he'd look like an escaped time traveler if he so much as stepped outside the building. He was all tweeds and waistcoats and wool argyles and wrinkly, slightly threadbare cotton.

But, as advertised, he was, in addition, gentle, thoughtful, and of great help. Over the past forty-five minutes, he had carefully guided her through a recitation of her background, family, experiences, and, most important, her recent spate of emotional turmoil.

She had just finished telling him how isolated it was making her feel, especially being in a new town, at a new job, fresh from the protection of a nurturing academic environment. Even the once-comforting proximity of Joe and her mother had developed an edge, since her profession so often ran at odds with theirs. She'd seen that in the courthouse parking lot when, giving her Dziobek's name, Joe had obviously avoided passing along what he was learning on his phone as they were speaking.

"I don't speak of other patients as a rule," Dziobek informed her, "but Joe told me to mention him if I thought it might be useful. Are you aware of his background at all?"

"No," she said, genuinely curious about a subject she'd considered but never pursued out of shyness.

"You may find it useful," the therapist continued, his softly accented voice soothing in itself. "I believe what you've been telling me puts the two of you in unusual proximity, given what you've both gone through, and how you've dealt with it."

"I know he had a girlfriend who was killed," Rachel said, expressing a young person's eagerness to display her knowledge.

"And a wife he lost to cancer as a young man," Dziobek added. "Causing a degree of trauma from which he's never fully recovered. I believe it's why he never remarried, despite two long-term and devoted relationships."

"Oh," Rachel said, surprised she'd never heard about the wife, and interested about where this was heading.

"It is that second loss I'd like to explain," Dziobek said. "What do you know about it, so I can skip over traveled ground?"

"Just that a sniper shot her as a way to get at Joe — make him suffer the kind of loss the killer had undergone."

"That's perfectly correct," he confirmed in his carefully paced manner, "as far as it goes. In fact, the young lady was leaving a building, side by side with Joe's previous companion of many years, who was now considered a good friend. Lynn — that was the new girlfriend — had gone to meet that older woman, in part to discuss where she stood with Joe. By the way, given how Joe felt about them, there was little doubt that the sniper would have attained his goal regardless of which one he'd killed.

"But his aim," he went on, "was particularly accurate, since Joe later blamed himself for Lynn's death. In retrospect, he felt that if he hadn't been so remote with her, so unreachable emotionally, she wouldn't have made that journey and ended up in the shooter's rifle scope."

Dziobek had been sitting across from Rachel in a large and ancient leather armchair, and now he paused to remove his glasses and wipe them on his tie, which she seriously doubted would help much. "I am telling you all this, as I said, because Joe specifically thought it might help you. His point in so doing, however, was that you may be carrying around a similar burden concerning your friend Jayla, whom you'd invited to be your roommate in Burlington, and who died at the hand of that man you were telling me about."

Rachel opened her mouth to protest but was stilled by the older man raising his hand to stop her. "One moment. I understand you bear no responsibility for the troubles that Jayla brought with her, but I would argue that you, like Joe, do think you could have done something to prevent the demise of someone close. And," he threw in, "that this parallels the feelings you harbor concerning the death of the individual who was killed at your feet a few months ago in Colchester, when you were in pursuit of your newspaper story."

Rachel was stopped by his comment.

"What I am suggesting," Dziobek concluded, "is the death now of Alex Hale — as unlikely as it is that it resulted from any action by you — nevertheless strikes you as your fault, as well." He replaced his glasses and asked, "Can you see what I'm saying? How people like you and Joe, while blameless, in fact, are inclined to take on such burdens, in part because no one else will — and you both feel the need for someone to say, 'I am accountable.' "

He leaned forward for emphasis. "Rachel, both you and Joe are virtually driven to be responsible. That is commendable in spirit, but it can be self-destructive. Often, life — especially active, committed lives like you've both chosen — dishes up situations where terrible things simply happen."

He lapsed into silence, watching her

absorb what he'd said, and settled back into his chair.

"Was that helpful at all?" he asked.

She got the subtle hint, checked her watch, and rose. She crossed to him as he did to her and shook his hand. "It really was. Not to be disrespectful, but it's not like any of it was so mysterious. I mean, all the pieces were there. I guess they usually are in your business. But I really appreciate your lining them up like you did, mentioning Joe. It not only helps me, but gives me a better angle on what makes him tick. I'm glad my mom and he found each other."

Dziobek smiled and patted her arm as he escorted her to the door. "He is, too."

"I sure didn't see this coming," Joe said.

Beverly gave him a smile before donning her surgical mask. "Well, I am now associated with Dartmouth-Hitchcock, I am the ME in Vermont, and my New Hampshire colleague in Concord did ask if I would assist, because she's got enough cases lined up for her table as it is. I won't deny that it's a funny commingling of circumstances, but here we are, and I couldn't be more pleased."

He laughed at her usual precise syntax. "So am I."

Dartmouth-Hitchcock Medical Center, in Lebanon, New Hampshire, was the site of Beverly's new part-time employment, and while her contract technically involved teaching only, a door had been left open for the occasional professional reinforcement, should the need and opportunity arise. The medical center's autopsy suite, located amid the facility's truly vast pathology wing, was already available to the New Hampshire medical examiner's office for local cases, so, especially with Beverly's being at hand, it had worked out perfectly to transport Alex Hale here instead of the extra distance to Concord, where he would have been put on hold.

This was Joe's first visit to the DHMC lab, however. It had been built only within the last couple of years, and the contrast to Vermont's far humbler and more disjointed arrangement was impressive. Some three hundred people worked in the same area, relying on a system of pneumatic tubes from around the huge campus that delivered pathology samples with the efficiency of a modern metropolitan parcel service — a FedEx for human tissue. Receiving staff opened the cylinders at a central location, logged in the contents, and assigned them to the appropriate pathologist for examination and analysis.

It was sprawling, free-flowing, well lighted, and oozed efficiency. Even the autopsy room was airy, uncluttered, and had fourth-floor windows for natural light, although they'd been thoughtfully frosted over.

That was in stark contrast to the room's primary occupant. Alex Hale had not rested underwater without mishap. He was wrinkled, almost white, cut and dented by debris, and had a hole in his forehead of impressive dimensions. Almost jarring, given this damage, was how clean he was, having been washed and scrubbed by the river, and subsequently the lab assistant.

"Looks more like a wax museum reject than a cadaver," Joe commented, as always enjoying seeing Beverly, even in these surroundings.

"True," Beverly agreed, beginning her well-practiced routine.

It took a little over an hour, not counting the preliminaries and cleanup. Joe and Beverly were accompanied by two New Hampshire cops, the DHMC diener, or assistant, and a couple of techs. The conversation was terse and pointed, directed solely to the processing of Mr. Hale as evidence. The involvement of two separate law enforcement agencies from two different states kept the usual casualness to a minimum, and aided the procedure's speed.

By the time Beverly straightened and stepped away from the table, everyone in the room knew what they had: a homicide victim, dead of a through-and-through gunshot wound to the head, whose lungs suggested, though did not prove, that he'd been dead when dumped into the river by a party or parties unknown.

Joe turned to his New Hampshire counterpart toward the end of all this — a man not from the Charlestown PD, which had ceded jurisdiction to the state police — and asked, "No luck finding that bullet, I'm guessing?"

The man shook his head. "Not a chance. We ran a couple of likely trajectory plots, given the car, the blood's location, and the drag marks in the snow — not to mention the blown-out exit hole in the passenger-side window — and every time, the laser dot ended up either in the river or the Vermont countryside on the opposite bank."

"He was sitting at the wheel when it happened?"

"Looks that way. He either knew the guy and didn't suspect him or never saw him coming. He did have his driver's-side window rolled down, though. There was one interesting detail related to all that: the shooter's footprints. Our lab guys are saying that he must've planned ahead. It looks like he wrapped his shoes in garbage bags or something. For all intents and purposes, there are no tracks. And you already know we didn't find fingerprints. Nor did we find extra tire marks that would fit with a second car in the same location. Could be he parked up the road and hiked in."

Joe sighed quietly. "No footprints, no bullet, no latents, and a remote location with no cameras. Somebody thought this through."

The man smiled sympathetically. "Better you than me on this one. I'm glad our prosecutors wanna kick this to you. Best of luck."

Joe had already returned to sadly staring at Alex Hale's mute remains, recalling how the young man's enthusiasm had so infectiously charmed Rachel. "Thanks," he said. "We're gonna need it."

CHAPTER 14

Rachel was sitting in her own passenger seat, where she could work on her laptop, unhindered by the steering wheel. She was uploading her latest assignment from Living Memorial Park in Brattleboro: photos of families happily riding inner tubes and sleds downhill after school. She did this often, editing and forwarding her shots to the paper and her website from the scene. It pleased people like Katz, who had her results before he thought to ask for them, and made it easier for Rachel to proceed to the next assignment without having its predecessor gnawing at her conscience.

Fortunately, in this instance, there was no next assignment pending.

The knock on her window made her almost dump her computer onto the floor. *"Jesus."*

Sally Kravitz was inches away from her, a small smile on her face.

Rachel rolled down the window. "You could walk up to the car, where I could see you coming," she complained.

"And ruin that reaction? No way. The driver's door unlocked?"

Curious, Rachel nodded. "Sure. Feel free," she said, shifting her camera, an equipment bag, her cell, and a notebook off the seat to the floor by her feet.

Sally circled around and slipped in behind the wheel. The engine was running, the heater working. Sally reached out and killed the softly playing radio, however.

"You like meeting in cars?" Rachel asked, noticing that under her jacket, Sally looked professionally attired, in slacks and a button-down shirt, reminiscent of an office administrator perhaps. Her hair, tied back, had been arranged to match.

"Good as anywhere. Too bad what happened to Alex."

Straight to the point, Rachel thought. One of the reasons she liked Sally. "Yeah. I'm still working through that."

"Really?" Sally asked. "You had nothing to do with it."

"It happened right after he agreed to work with me."

Sally chuckled. "That spy movie imitation in the warehouse? He was such a drama

250

queen. That had nothing to do with why he was killed."

"You know that for a fact?" Rachel challenged her, now a little put off by her tough manner.

"As good as," Sally replied. "I'm not knocking your being upset, but he was the one flying low and taking chances. His death is not your fault. You told me he was like a cat closing in on a can of tuna."

Rachel studied her a moment, again struck by the maturity of the comment. For all the exoticism and questionable wisdom behind Sally's upbringing, no one could say it had shorted the girl on worldly knowledge.

"So why was he killed?" Rachel asked.

Sally took her eyes off the hill sliders across the parking lot and looked at Rachel in surprise. "I have no clue. But people like him and my dad don't endear themselves to others." She paused a second to glance over Rachel's shoulder and went on: "Speaking of which, I was talking with Dan about all this, and he agreed to see if he could help."

Without further ado, the car's back door opened and a dark figure climbed in. "Hey there," it said.

Rachel burst out in surprise, "God. You guys." She turned around and saw the ultimate average male, dressed modestly in the latest from Goodwill. He had short hair and glasses, and an almost shy expression on his face.

He peeled off a glove and wiggled his fingers at her in greeting, "Hi. Dan Kravitz," he said, introducing himself.

"Hi yourself," she said. "It's a pleasure to meet a legend, at last."

"Oh," he protested. "Hardly that. I am glad to meet you, though. My daughter's been singing your praises."

Rachel was astonished.

"Dan," Sally corrected him, "you make it sound like a girl crush. I said I thought she was okay people — maybe."

That made Rachel laugh again. "I'll take his version."

"Anyway," Sally said, as if interrupted in mid-sentence, "I was thinking Dan might be able to lend a small helping hand."

"Really?" Rachel asked him. "You know why Alex was killed?"

Dan went through a noticeable transformation, his face getting serious and his tone direct. "Rules of engagement first," he said. "I'm not in this car, you and I have never met, and I'll leave it to your imagination to figure what will happen to you if you ever quote me. I am here because of Sally, and in the interests of abetting a process that *might* — and I stress that word — result in the righting of a great wrong. Is all that clear and understood?"

"Absolutely," she told him, recalling her first conversation with Sally, out in the middle of nowhere in a snowstorm. Father and daughter apparently had a genetic fondness for covertness.

He loosened up a little. "Good. Then the answer is no, I have no idea why he was killed or by whom."

"Buzzkill, Dan," his daughter said.

"Perhaps, but accurate."

"What *can* you tell me, then?" Rachel asked, disappointed.

Dan returned to being circumspect. "I'm not sure what Sally has told you about some of my habits."

Rachel told him. "That you saw Alex as a form of kindred spirit, and there was a chance you kept an eye on him because of it — more or less. At least that's my interpretation."

"That's helpful," he replied. "All right, then, to that point, I do have an idea of what his next target was going to be, and it caused both Sally and me some discomfort."

He stopped there, Rachel was unsure why, until she considered that she might be part of the discomfort referred to.

She tried addressing the impasse by asking a potentially self-sabotaging question. "I'm starting to get this. Neither one of you is a social butterfly, and you sure as hell don't cozy up to the press. But here we are sitting in one another's laps. Something made that happen. What're you trying to tell me without telling me?"

"Alex was targeting Thorndike Academy," Sally said flatly, breaking the logjam. "Why, we don't know."

Rachel looked from one to the other. "That's it? That's what he was casing out?"

"Yes," Dan said.

"Who cares?" Rachel asked. "It's bizarre. I'll give you that. But he had to be targeting somebody. It's what he did."

"I'm working there undercover," Sally explained reluctantly. "I knew you'd be chasing the story — that you'd find out what he'd been up to eventually, and I didn't want you blowing my cover story."

Rachel felt her confusion dissipate like smoke in a breeze. "Your father gave you the heads-up when he saw what Alex was doing. I thought you guys didn't keep in close touch."

"We do and we don't," Sally said. "It depends."

"What she's not saying," Dan added, "is that I keep up with what's happening in town, and certainly with my own daughter. Whether she tells me what she's doing or not, I often have a pretty good idea, so when I noticed she was spending entire workdays at the school, and that Alex was circling it like a buzzard, I had to let her know."

"Which meant you both had to let me know, whether you wanted to or not," Rachel said.

"Bingo," Sally replied.

"Are the two related?" Rachel asked.

"Alex and me?" Sally said. "I seriously doubt it. I think I'm looking at something he'd have no interest in, but who knows? Funnily enough, that's more your business than mine, assuming you're going to keep doing what you were before he got himself killed. I'm not sure I see the point myself. Like you said, he was probably just planning a new rip-off."

"Which got him ambushed and executed," Rachel said. "Hell yeah, I'm gonna keep at it."

"Where do we stand, boss?" Lester asked Joe.

The two of them were sitting with Willy and Sammie in their office.

"With our thumbs up our butts," Willy suggested.

"Wow," Sammie said just audibly. "Nice."

"But not entirely inaccurate," Joe said, "which is why we're here. We need to figure out what we've got."

"We got lucky, for one thing," Willy commented. "Alex being whacked in New Hampshire has cut us a little slack with the media. I don't think they figured out yet we inherited it."

"Small favors," Lester agreed, passing around a bag of doughnuts he'd brought in. "But I'll take what we can."

"It won't last," Joe told them, thinking of Rachel. "And we can't do much about it anyhow. Not to mention" — he pointed at his phone — "that headquarters has already called me in a panic about getting a lid on this PDQ. So, with that in mind, let's break what we've got into component parts, starting with the late Lyall Johnson."

Sam and Lester vied as the squad's best computer operators, with Willy close behind. Joe didn't even feature in the contest, being of a less receptive disposition to technology. It was Lester who turned to his laptop now, projecting the image on its screen onto the wall-mounted display dominating most of one wall in the small space.

"This is a first for me personally. I've only seen this used in vehicle crash reconstructions, but the crime lab forwarded their FARO data of the crime scene."

What appeared was a ghostly three-dimensional image of the crime scene in Bellows Falls, as if seen through the eyes of a bug perched high in a corner of the room.

FARO was a company specializing in 3-D measurement technology, originally invented for the medical field but here applied to accident and crime-scene reconstruction. For the latter application, a 3-D camera was set up on a tripod in multiple strategic positions, and scans were taken in 360-degree sweeps. The collected imagery was then crunched by a computer and turned into what the squad was seeing: a virtual reconstruction of the scene, complete with dead body and furniture, but including much smaller and more subtle details also. At Lester's keyboard commands, the view rotated and tilted, emulating that metaphorical bug flying about and peering into every nook and cranny that had been recorded by the camera's eye. It was an effective and useful way of revisiting old ground, including being able to turn corners, look up and down, and examine an area from unconventional angles.

It was a far cry from any small collection of old-fashioned static Polaroid snapshots — where invariably the one item of most interest was always the one not photographed at the time.

Lester was speaking as he manipulated the view. "At first glance, pretty straightforward. Body's roughly in the middle of the room, a drawer containing other, shorter knives not far away, where Brandon said Lyall kept the larger blade he ended up wearing, and as Joe noticed when you were there — and FARO managed to catch — a weird kind of sweeping pattern going from the dead man to the door, as if the killer cleaned up as he retreated."

He swapped images, showing the same scene, but as if a black light had been turned on, which in a sense it had. Now, where the virtual hologram had showed a dirty floor only, there were glowing yellowish patterns covering it in a darkened room.

"The fluorescein dye under special lighting," he narrated. "They killed the lights and partially blocked the windows, misted the floor and other surfaces, and shot again, with only a few minutes before it all faded. But they got it. It ain't perfect, not like the shot we just had, but it gives you the idea."

"Somebody was bleeding as they headed

out the door," Willy commented dryly.

"Which we knew," Lester went on unimpeded, "but not for sure. Now, because of this" — the display switched to two DNA readouts side by side — "we also know that the genetic identity of the drops heading away from Lyall and Lyall's own are different."

"Wild guess," Sammie ventured, "we didn't get a hit on the stranger DNA."

"Nope," Lester confirmed.

"Go back to the original FARO image," Joe requested.

The four of them studied the familiar, if ghostly, apartment.

"What can we tell from the layout, the body's position, or anything else?" he asked.

"He was stabbed inside, not standing at the door," Sam volunteered.

"Does that suggest anything?"

"Multiple things," Willy said. "He may have known his killer and let him in. But the door might've been open already, and the killer just walked in. For that matter, Lyall might've gotten home and found whoever was already there. We've learned that the door was never locked."

"But Brandon said he left Lyall at the apartment and then went back a half hour later, to find him dead."

"True," Willy agreed. "Which doesn't guarantee Lyall didn't leave, too, and go back during those thirty minutes. He could've been lured out by a phone call or text, just so his attacker could slip inside and ambush him. But not only do we not have Lyall's phone; the warrant to his carrier got us zilch. He used a burn phone they couldn't trace, because his IP address was clustered, or 'netted,' with about five hundred others. I don't know enough about it, but suffice it to say it's a dead end, according to them. So — we have no clue what he was doing that night, at least after dinner at Danni's and then meeting that woman near the VW, who may or may not have been part of this."

"Speaking of which, did the lab at least get a gender for that stranger DNA?" Joe asked Lester.

"Yeah," Lester said, sounding doleful. "It was male."

"Cool," Willy murmured. "Boy–girl hit team?"

"Or boy–girl sequence with no connection between them," Sam counterproposed.

Willy silently nodded his acknowledgment. As an investigator, he was always open to having his mind changed or adapted, in contrast to a personality that suggested otherwise.

"But with the boy pretty seriously wounded, whatever the case," Joe said.

"Maybe, maybe not," Lester argued. "I asked the techies about that. They wouldn't commit. Said it depended too much on where the guy'd been cut. Plus, I was told that the amount of blood found at the scene wasn't as much as you might think — not like an arterial bleed, or what came out of Lyall."

"I doubt it was too bad," Sam hypothesized. "Amateur or not, he had the presence of mind to clean up after himself — or try to."

"Why and how did he get cut in the first place?" Joe asked.

"First thought," Sammie said, "his hand slid off the handle onto the blade. That's the standard. You don't realize how hard it is to stab somebody."

"No stranger DNA on the blade they pulled out of the body," Lester reported, reading the data off his computer.

"Don't know about you," Sammie countered, "but when I've cut myself in the kitchen, a lot of times the bleeding doesn't start for a second or two."

"How did our mystery man choose when to step up and shove the knife in?" Willy asked. "They have a fight first? Yell at each other? No neighbors mentioned it, if they did. All they talked about was Brandon and Lyall mouthing off."

Joe crossed to the 3-D picture of the apartment, which Lester was slowly turning on its axis so they could visualize being in the actual space, looking around.

Joe reached out and tapped on a spot. Lester froze the image. "There. That closet, with the shoved-aside bedsheet serving as a door. Look at what you can see of the shoes and clothes and crap on the floor. Why's that space clear when the rest of it's covered wall-to-wall?"

Lester saw what he meant. "Looks like it was to make room for something."

"You always do that, so you can look at your clothes and not step on your shoes," Sam observed.

" 'Cept that the clothes on the hangers have also been moved to either side," Willy pointed out, "allowing for someone to stand there and peek out or just eavesdrop when the sheet's been pulled closed."

"Which suggests he prepped the site and hid behind the sheet when no one else was there," Joe commented.

"Do we have a time line for who arrived at the apartment when?" Willy asked. "Brandon said he went to score some dope when Lyall disappeared on his 'woman about a horse' mission, and that he returned to the apartment about an hour later and found Lyall already there. But how long between then and when Brandon stormed off in a huff?"

Sammie picked it up. "And we need to figure out if the killing was even related to Lyall's meeting with the mystery woman. They might've had nothing to do with each other."

"Maybe," her boss allowed. "But let's not think along those lines too soon."

"Okay," Lester said. "If we are thinking the woman with the VW might be tied to Lyall's death, and the minibus lives at Thorndike Academy, then do we connect the murder to the school?"

Willy shrugged, unconvinced as yet. "Maybe," he said, "if nothing else, it'll give us more to chase than we got now."

"All right," Joe said. "Keep it going. Could be the school's also mixed up with Alex Hale's death. It's no more unlikely than linking Lyall to them."

There was a pause as they considered this new angle.

"That suddenly makes Thorndike a common denominator," Lester said. "Is there anything else tying Hale to Lyall or Brandon, or anyone in Bellows Falls, for that matter? Is there any connection between them besides the school?"

"The person who killed Alex and Lyall, both," Willy proposed.

"Nice," Joe said to keep things moving. "Why?"

"Why do people usually kill other people?" Willy retorted.

Lester took the question literally. "Drugs. That was Lyall's business."

"But not Alex's," Sammie clarified. "How 'bout money? Or sex, like jealousy?"

"The woman near the VW bus?" Willy pondered out loud.

"If you're talking motivations in general," Joe suggested. "Along with sex and drugs, there's hatred, ambition, and, often, something to do with money. That school's rolling in dough, Alex was stalking it, and kids with cash love drugs. Was Lyall a middleman who stepped out of line somehow?"

They were exchanging looks, realizing this wasn't advancing them far, despite the pleasure each received from the process.

Willy put it into words: "None of which fits what we actually know."

"Which is what, exactly?"

"Fair enough," Willy continued. "Back to

basics: the knife. You plan to kill, you take along what you need."

"So the guy was standing in the closet, not sure how things would end?" Lester proposed.

"And he cut himself," Sammie added, "not just because he was unfamiliar with that knife but also because he hadn't been intending to use one in the first place. It was an impulse killing."

"So he heard something said between Lyall and Brandon?" Lester asked. "And it pushed him over the edge?"

"Or Lyall and someone else," Joe suggested. "Brandon told us they didn't fight about anything unusual. That could be where Alex Hale comes in. And what did Lyall meet the woman about? Under normal circumstances, we'd be thinking it was her in the closet, except for the DNA gender portrait saying otherwise. There's a wild card in here somehow."

He suddenly interrupted himself to say, "We need to nail down Alex's last few days, hour by hour, if possible. And interview everyone he had contact with. Somebody must know what he was up to. We still have his apartment sealed? The address we found through Motor Vehicles? That still current?"

"Yeah, boss," Lester said. "And under the

sheriff's twenty-four-hour guard."

Joe returned to a prior thought by asking, "I'm assuming we got no other sighting of the minibus in BF, is that right?"

"Nope," Willy confirmed. "Which strikes me as weird. It's a nosy town. Everybody watching everybody. That bus is hard to miss."

"Which makes having seen it in the first place all the more credible," Sammie said. "Why make something like that up?"

"Turn it around," Willy suggested. "Ask yourself if it *was* made up just to throw us off, maybe as a red herring connection to the school. And speaking of red herrings, like I said before, don't forget that 'horse' is another word for heroin."

Joe rubbed his temples in frustration before looking at Lester, who still had his computer before him. "What was the name of the witness who saw Lyall meet the VW lady?"

"Shelly Ayotte."

"We know anything about her?"

"I looked her up in CAD," Willy replied. "Nothing jumped out. I could take another run at her."

"Wouldn't hurt," Joe agreed. "At some point, at least. Right now, I figure Thorndike Academy's earned a little more of our focus, mostly because of Alex's interest in it. Call me crazy, but I think there's something hinky going on there."

He took them all in as he issued instructions. "Time to divide and conquer. I'll swing by the dead kid's apartment and see if I can locate any of his family or friends. Willy, go after Ayotte and any other BF leads that make sense. Lester and Sam, start delicately knocking on doors at the school, like you did with the Dougles. We may meet again like this, or, if push comes to shove, do a conference call. Throughout, make sure you update the case file online so we're all kept posted in real time. I want to make sure that when the boss calls me again, bitching about how the press and *his* handlers are breathing all over him, I got something to tell him. We good?"

Sam nodded sharply; Lester said, "Got it." Willy, of course, ignored him.

CHAPTER 15

"Hey, Joe. You taking over?"

Gunther nodded to the gray-haired sheriff's deputy standing outside Alex Hale's apartment. "You're officially off detail, Vern. Thanks for keeping a lid on the place."

"Don't know if it wasn't too little too late," Vern said, gathering up his thermos and magazines from the folding chair the landlord had supplied. "I can't say who might've come and gone before I got here."

"I know," Joe acknowledged. "You do the best you can sometimes."

They were on the fourth floor of one of the old redbrick buildings on Brattleboro's Main Street, a virtually unknown universe of low-cost, minimally maintained, small and dark apartments, home of fringe inhabitants the rest of the townspeople — window-shopping on the sidewalks just below — knew little about.

Vern shook hands. He was another old cop

who, even if he hadn't seen it all, had stopped being surprised by much. "Take care of yourself, Joe. See ya at the next one."

"You, too, Vern. I'll let your dispatch know if and when we need more help. I'll probably be here a couple of hours."

"No problem. I'm heading for a beer."

Joe watched with true fondness as Vern shambled down the dim hallway. There were hundreds like him out there, warhorses fighting complete retirement by finding part-time work as deputies, constables, or auxiliaries for a state agency. In truth, Joe often wondered what he'd end up doing whenever the VBI decided it no longer wanted his services.

He used the door key they'd located on Alex's key ring and stepped into the apartment beyond, taking comfort in the thought that, as old as he might feel, he was livelier than the young man he was investigating.

As a norm, entering a deceased person's home is like seeing the everyday from another realm, as if the visitor and not the owner were the ghost. It is at once disorienting, intrusive, embarrassing, and even touched by guilt, one irrational thought being that some spectral figure might throw open the door and demand an explanation.

On this occasion, however, that unlikely

concern was immediately offset by what Joe saw confronting him from the opposite wall: a large poster of the 1943 movie *Bomber's Moon*.

Curiosity trumping reflection, he crossed the room to better study it. A fan of older movies, especially ones concerning World War II, he was dimly aware of this one, if only for its lack of impact on cinematic history. George Montgomery and a French starlet named Annabella. Joe was hard-pressed to remember what else they might have been in. And yet the poster, though old, was mounted and framed, and displayed where it could be enjoyed from every angle of the room. A valued icon.

Joe turned from the poster to take in his surroundings, half-hoping they would complement the vintage poster. But there were no plane models or memorabilia or other nods to the movies or the war. On that level, the room was mundane and secular — a cluttered and messy collection of the usual modern artifacts, including the predictable flat-screen TV, a rumpled mattress on the floor, scattered CDs, clothing in heaps, and a few dishes piled in the sink of a small kitchen. It amounted to the sketch of a young life, starting out, in motion, and with no inclination or time to accumulate the deeply ingrained detritus that so often clogs the closets, attics, garages, and corners of older, more settled lives.

But that was at first glance. As he toured the small room, bathroom, and one closet, Joe began to archaeologically exchange his first impressions for a deeper, more nuanced insight. His discoveries expanded beyond what a young Vermont male might typically have on hand, to include a more unusual sampling of material objects. Some were expensive — clothes, kitchenware, audio equipment, artwork, jewelry — that better reflected the taste of women, older folks, and others who didn't fit Alex's known persona. Furthermore, several of them were piled up, rather than being available for daily use. There were crystal ashtrays, stacked DVD players, and silver picture frames displaying children or pets or fat men posing beside large fish.

They looked like the proceeds from a fire sale, or — as better fit the profile here — the unrecycled backwash from multiple burglaries. The discovery made Joe rueful, reminding him of a youngster grabbing items in part for their value but also because they were shiny, unusual, and attractive.

There was also a slowly emerging telltale gap within this clutter, as apparent, finally, as a missing tooth in a portrait: Nowhere was there a computer, a tablet, a smart-phone, or even a thumb drive, despite the generous supply of chargers and wires lying about. The implication echoed the comment made by Vern, that someone might have been here already, cleaning house of pre-cisely what Joe had hoped to collect.

There was a quiet knock on the door, fol-lowed by a tentative female voice. "Hello?"

Surprised, Joe crossed the room and opened up, to see Rachel's equally startled expression.

"Oh," she stammered. "Hi."

Joe smiled, if guardedly. Unlike when they met socially or in Windsor with her mother, there was no missing Rachel's official role as she stood before him with camera in hand.

"Hi yourself," he replied neutrally, pur-posefully not putting her at ease, despite what he normally would have done.

"I didn't know anyone would be here," she said.

He didn't respond, a natural paternal instinct conflicting with professional self-protectiveness.

That left her at a loss.

"But here you are," she added lamely. "You find anything?"

Joe was holding the door open only about six inches. "Really?" he asked pleasantly.

"You won't let me take a peek?" she blurted out, transparently doubtful.

Joe didn't disappoint her. "Nope."

"I know. Dumb," she said, almost in the same breath.

Taking pity at last, Joe sidestepped into the hallway and closed the door behind him, ending his own internal debate. "How're you holding up?" he asked her quietly, keeping his voice low to frustrate any neighbors who might be listening at their doors.

Almost relieved, it seemed to him, she replied, "Better. I went to see your guy, Eberhard. He was a real sweetheart, like you said."

"And helpful?"

"Yeah," she admitted, looking at him with the psychologist's words fresh in her memory. "He said you'd given him permission to mention what had happened to you. That was really nice. Thank you. That did a lot."

"Good. It was his choice to use it, if he needed to." He turned slightly to lean against the flaking, dingy wall and asked, genuinely curious, "Why did you come here?"

Her response had the ring of truth. "I don't know. I feel guilty about what happened. I didn't actually think there'd be anything to see, but I didn't know. Maybe I just wanted to know where he lived."

"You've never been here?"

She looked up and down the hall. "No. It's drearier than I thought it would be."

"How'd you get the address?"

She smiled thinly. "I have my sources."

"I'm going to risk being condescending, Rachel," he said, addressing the glaring obstacle between them, "and remind you that we're not on a level playing field here. You and I may want the same things, but our reasons for that are in direct conflict. I won't help you possibly undermine my case, and I won't play favorites if I find out you've done anything illegal to gain an edge."

She took it well, he thought, without sounding defensive or offended. "I know."

They were quiet for a moment, and then she said, "I also know I should keep my mouth shut and observe that line between us, but I have learned something I think you should hear."

He was impressed by her making such an offer, when she could have simply walked off in a huff. "Okay."

"I got something besides this address."

He didn't say anything, seeing how she was struggling — a neophyte journalist working through the pros and cons of any conversation involving the police.

"I don't want to tell you how I got this," she began hesitantly.

"I understand," he replied.

Steadied by that, she went on. "But I think it's reliable. You know how Alex seemed to do his homework? At least as far as we know?"

Joe nodded.

"Well, it looked like he was scouting out Thorndike Academy."

Joe didn't betray his surprise at hearing that name again, especially in connection to Alex. "The whole school?" he asked instead. "Or a specific aspect or person?"

"I don't know," she admitted, glancing down at the floor. "It doesn't make much sense to me. It is a wealthy place, of course, with a lot of art and equipment and electronics. The one time I met with Alex, when I was trying to get him interested in my piece about him, I could tell he was excited about something, like a project he might be working on, but the school never came up."

"What did he say?"

"It was supergeneral. He talked about how much people put on their phones and computers without considering how insecure that is. Something about when the stuff they're protecting is older than the electronics they use to hide it — to the point where they should've left it in a wall safe. It sounded a little crazy, and made me think he was avoiding telling me more. Now I can't get it out of my mind that it also got him killed."

Joe wasn't going to argue the point. He also wasn't about to tell her just how perfectly her piece had just dropped into the growing puzzle before him.

Sally took in the heavyset man standing before her desk, a frustrated look on his face. His gleaming white shirt and straining buttons met her at eye level.

"You know anything about computers?" he asked.

She glanced at the desktop unit between them, on which she'd just been working. "Some," she replied. "You need help?"

He stuck out a pudgy hand for a shake. "Sally, right? Barry Rice. I know we met when they gave you the tour, but that was kind of 'Hi' from the door."

"Sally Moore," she offered, taking his hand without pleasure, anticipating it would be soft and a little moist. She wasn't disappointed. "Need some help?"

He stood back and gestured down the

hall. "It's my laptop. Emily usually helps me, but she's away from her desk. I'm trying to format something I'm writing and it won't cooperate. It's driving me nuts."

Sally stood and circled her desk, which was situated along one side of the broad hallway. "Lead the way," she said.

Rice was Thorndike's CFO, with a corner office, a handsome salary, and a reputation for knowing his job. That was a good thing, given the size of the school's operating budget and its endowment, which was reported to be well over $400 million. Tuitions here ran to $60,000, Sally had learned, and this man easily authorized from ten to fifteen thousand checks a year to keep things running.

He led her into his office and waved a hand at the misbehaving laptop, saying, "I'm good at what I know, but that's numbers and spreadsheets, not Microsoft Word or writing."

Sally sat in the oversized chair at the desk, both matched to his considerable bulk, feeling like a kid at the grown-ups' table. She studied the screen for a moment. A professional secretary, she guessed, would have trained herself to focus solely on the problem at hand and not read the document's contents. She, of course, was no secretary.

Unfortunately, it didn't matter. It was a memo based on an earlier meeting, discussing long-term scholarship strategies. She expanded the document's control tabs and addressed Rice's spacing problem, standing up a minute later.

"That ought to do it, Mr. Rice," she reported.

"Barry," he immediately replied, a broad smile covering his round face. "No formalities. Please. And I can't thank you enough."

They conducted a little dance, exchanging places as he settled comfortably into his chair like the admiral in his stateroom. For all his physical ungainliness walking around, Sally thought he did look like a man in his element here.

"My pleasure," she said as she headed out the door, "and nice meeting you officially."

But he was already lost in his own prose, and merely held up a hand and waved, his eyes back on the screen. "Yup. Thanks again."

Outside, his secretary, Emily, was returning from the bathroom, and she smiled as Sally stepped away from the door.

"Microsoft Word?" Emily asked quietly, looking conspiratorial.

"Happens a lot?" Sally replied.

In response, Emily raised her eyes toward

the ceiling. "Thanks for coming to the rescue," she said, sitting at her desk, which, like Sally's down the hall, was out in the open. "He's a genius with numbers but a kid with that stuff, and a terrible writer. I tried to train him once, but it's not worth the effort. Simpler just to fix his problems yourself, no matter how easy they are. His writing style? He's on his own. I'm no English teacher."

Sally saw an opportunity. "I am, or at least I'm a good writer. I'd be happy to help. Is he a nice guy?" she asked.

Emily and she were two of only three so-called executive assistants, the third of whom worked for the head, Mary Mroczek, although they were all expected to share duties as needed. It was a purposefully lean group, reflecting a long-standing tradition of conservative, almost austere leadership practices. That was the first thing Sally had picked up upon arriving, in fact: that Mroczek's recent hiring — because of her gender and progressive outlook — was causing some serious, not readily apparent crosscurrents amid the school's supposedly placid waters. Despite having barely arrived on board, Sally had already identified a couple of talkative and knowledgeable sources, Emily among them.

"Very," Emily now said. "And generous. He really pulled strings to get a scholarship for an employee's kid a few years ago, and rumor has it some of the money came out of his own pocket, although nobody knows that for sure. I do know he pays for little extras all the time for us: more beer at staff social events, pizza for the office people now and then. Stuff like that. Never wants to be thanked or even acknowledged. He is super-scrupulous, though, and demands that every dime be accounted for." Emily dropped her voice. "That can be a pain in the ass sometimes. He's a stickler."

"Wife?" Sally asked. "Family?"

Emily lowered her voice to a whisper. "Used to have. I heard it was a real nasty divorce. She got the kids — three of them."

Sally prentended to match her companion's enthusiasm for the subject. "She clean him out?"

"I don't know about that. I'm guessing he pays a ton for their upkeep." She touched her chest. "It was a heartbreak, though. He misses them big-time, from how he talks about them."

"What happened?"

"Don't know. I never asked, and no one ever told me."

"You think he cheated on her?"

Emily looked slightly scandalized. "Barry? I don't *think* so. You want somebody who's into that, check out Norm Ketcham, the COO. You met him yet? You'd be his type — blond and pretty. And you have a pulse, of course. He insists on that."

Sally smiled as she shook her head. "Just heard the name. I didn't see his office up here."

"It's not. He prefers being near 'the guys,' as he calls them. Grounds have a separate building where they keep all their junk. Norm's got an office there. He comes by all the time, though. He'll find you soon enough."

"Same thing, with his wife and family?" Sally asked. "Divorced?"

Emily's eyes widened. "Ketcham? Oh no. Barry's the only one I know who's divorced. It's like a thing around here — they want their people hitched, even if they're miserable. They made an exception with Barry because he's so good at his job. Norm's married and has a kid. He just plays the field like he isn't."

Sally glanced around, making sure they were still alone. "Jeez, Emily. Sounds like a breeding ground."

Emily laughed. "Don't I wish. That would be more fun. No, Norm's the only one I know about, and he's at least smart enough to keep it under wraps. I just got an inside source. His poor wife is a basket case — isolated, lonely, drinks too much. Not that I blame her. Course, we in Admin are pretty isolated from the others. You should meet some of the teachers." She lowered her voice conspiratorially. "Now, the students . . . *There*, you're talking. Incredibly horny bunch. They're always having to discipline somebody for fooling around. Talk to Cindy Puza, Dr. Klein's nurse. She'll fill you in. Tell her I sent you."

Sally was absorbing the fact that the school's medical professional was a gossip, when Barry Rice reappeared from his office, a sheet of paper in his hand.

"Thanks so much, Emily," Sally said quickly, pretending to be on a mission. "Lot to learn."

Her newfound chatty friend had turned to her boss, extending her hand for the document, her manner instantly transformed. "I was telling Sally how a good writer would be handy around here, since you and I have our challenges there. She said she'd be happy to help. Says she's a champion editor."

Sally burst out laughing as Barry fixed her with a pleased and welcoming expression.

She interrupted his "Really?" with "Hardly a champion, but I've always loved playing with words and cleaning up other people's writing."

"You've got a deal," Barry said, turning back toward his office. "I can't write to save my life. Thanks."

Emily gave her a wink and a thumbs-up as Barry disappeared.

If Emily is any indication, Sally thought as she returned to her desk, getting people to open up is going to be easier than I'd imagined.

CHAPTER 16

It was snowing when Joe pulled into the trailer's tight, short excuse for a driveway, careful not to hit the old Toyota ahead of him. He didn't want to explain having his agency-issued car's rear bumper sideswiped by a plow truck.

He was at the high end of Mountain Home trailer park, which always made him think someone had used an M. C. Escher print as a blueprint for the project's layout — an impression heightened by reduced visibility and snowbank-narrowed access.

He picked his way carefully alongside both cars, walked over to the narrow steps leading to the front door, and rang the bell beside the Christmas wreath still heralding a season past, if not forgotten by the weather.

The woman who answered was short, solidly built, dressed in slacks and a blouse, and wearing a neat dark blue sweater. Her expression bordered on angry.

"Yes?"

"I'm sorry to intrude," he said, displaying his credentials, which he rarely bothered doing. "My name is Joe Gunther. Are you Alex Hale's mom, Carol Wilcox?"

The woman facing him shrank slightly at the words, as if some vital energy had just drained from her.

"Yes."

"I believe you've already heard about your son. I'm sorry that didn't happen in person. I was told someone phoned you?"

"Yes."

"That shouldn't be. It's hard-enough news to get without then being left alone with your thoughts."

She blinked, looking surprised. "What's your name again?"

"Joe," he told her.

She stepped back. "Come in. I'm sorry. I should have offered."

He accepted, removing the ancient fishing hat he wore in bad weather. "You had no idea who I was."

She looked him over as the home's warmth settled around them. "I knew you were a cop. God knows I've seen enough of you people. I guess that'll stop now."

He slipped out of his coat and removed

his boots. The snow covering them was already melting into a thick pad she'd laid in front of the door.

"That may be true," he replied. "But at too high a price. Alex and I may have lived in opposite camps, but he was a real pro in his way, smart, well organized, and highly motivated."

Her brow furrowed. "You knew him?"

"Nope. Never met," Joe said. "But I knew his work. He stood out."

That brought a smile as his mother's glance strayed to the floor between them. "He did that, even as a toddler."

He let her reminisce for a few seconds, hoping his silence and sympathy would work to his advantage. He was here for a reason, after all — the sad but reasonable motivation behind most visits by cops.

She looked up again. "You want coffee? I just made some."

"Thank you. That'd be great."

They didn't have far to go. Where they stood was the living/dining room. The partial kitchen was to the rear, behind a half counter that served as a food-prep area and room divider.

"Sit." She indicated a barstool as she entered the kitchen, filled a cup from a cof-feemaker near the stove, and placed it before him. She didn't offer cream or sugar, and although he took both, he didn't ask. She moved her own cup from where she'd left it by the sink when he'd rung the bell, then sat across from him, her eyes settling on the falling snow drifting by the living room window past his shoulder.

"It's hard," he said, "even if they no longer live at home. That part's kind of unexpected."

She switched to looking at him. "The emptiness?"

"Yeah."

"You, too?" she asked.

The question flooded his mind for a moment. He'd never had children to lose, but certainly two much-loved women.

"Yeah."

She sipped from her cup in silent response.

"A lot of kids become distant as they get older," he said.

"Not Alex."

"That must've felt good."

She pursed her lips. "Yes and no. It meant I had to deal with your type more than I should've — coming around to find him."

He was a little surprised. "Often?"

"Not in the last few years. But early on? When he was starting out? I got to know a few of the local cops personally. Whether he'd done anything or not, Alex was always on their list."

"Did you know what he was up to?" Joe asked.

"Sometimes," she admitted. "As a kid, he'd be so full of himself, he couldn't *not* tell me. Everybody needs an audience when they think they hit a home run. Otherwise, what's the point? Later, though, he got better at protecting me, so I didn't have to lie anymore."

"He began to appreciate his work for himself."

"Or he got a better audience," she suggested.

He let her see his interest in that. "You know that for a fact? We were wondering if he had a significant other."

She frowned at the reference. "I wouldn't go that far. He had friends, and girlfriends, but nobody special."

"You meet any of them?"

"Saw one. In his car once when he dropped by. About a year ago, or not quite. I guess it was spring. The weather was nice. I remember because she looked out of whack in the sunshine and warm air. She was a Goth girl, all pale and spiky, with something shiny through her lip. I'll never get that. It made me think of vampires, caught out in the daylight."

"Did you get a name?"

She nodded. "Stella. Who could forget? Like I said, we didn't meet, but I asked him who was in the car."

"No last name?"

"No. And I don't know who she was, really."

Joe made a mental note of the name, and the telling description. It was unlikely that at least one of the Brattleboro patrol officers didn't know something about Stella.

"The reason I ask is because I really want to know what happened," Joe explained. "No one deserves this, but Alex especially didn't seem to be running that kind of risk."

Carol scratched an eyebrow with her fingertip — a deliberate and thoughtful gesture — before asking, as if against her better judgment, "What did happen? They just told me somebody killed him near the river."

Instinctively, Joe trusted her enough to be honest. "We can only go by what we've put together so far, but it looks like he was lured to an isolated spot on the New Hampshire side of the Connecticut. He probably thought he was going to some kind of meeting."

"And they drowned him?" she asked incredulously, her voice cracking for the first time.

"We think they just put him in the water," Joe said, "afterward."

Her eyes returned to the window behind him, seemingly transfixed with the continual blur of white streaks. Joe had often done the same — stared at a fire, breaking waves, or snow falling without a sound. The latter remained the most wondrous to him personally, possibly because it was so readily available half of the year.

"Did he suffer any?" she finally asked.

"No," he replied unequivocally. "It looked to us like he never saw it coming."

This may not have been true, but there was value in occasionally being less than completely honest.

"Good," she said quietly. "That's something."

"What does have us wondering," he said now, touching on an earlier theme, "is what he was doing to make someone so angry."

He paused, allowing her time to formulate a suggestion. He was hoping not to influence her response by saying too much. All cops have their own interview style. Joe's was quiet and patient.

"He was excited about something lately,"

she said vaguely, probably sorting through the images Joe had only hinted at. "Enough that he said something."

He gave her a moment before barely pressing. "Oh?"

"He called it a 'major score.' A 'game changer.' Still, I didn't pay much attention. I didn't want to encourage him. I always worried about what he might get into. We didn't fight about it anymore, but I still worried." She again fixed him with a stare. "It made me mad, he was so stubborn."

"I bet," Joe replied, hesitating. Interviews like this were heavily influenced by instinct, on both sides.

"Anyhow, I didn't ask him on purpose," she continued. "I could tell it pissed him off, since he wanted me to cheer him on. That's when he said the payoff would change my life, too, and that it was something he'd never tried before, that it just fell in his lap."

"Okay," Joe said, spurring her on.

"Well, that's it, isn't it?" she asked enigmatically. "I told him I didn't want any money he made that way, and he left angry. That's the last I saw him. Next thing I knew, some girl showed up at the door, wanting to talk to him. That was a first, and it made me really wonder what the hell he was getting into."

Joe looked at her sharply. "What girl?"

"A reporter. Said she wanted to ask him something but wouldn't say what. I closed the door in her face. Said I didn't know anyone named Alex Hale."

"When was this?"

"A few days ago. I don't remember. It's not one of the things I do well."

"You remember her name?"

Carol shook her head. "No."

She then got a lost look on her face, as if trying to recall something long ago forgotten. "Hang on," she said, getting up, circling the counter, and walking to the front door.

There was a small table there, to catch gloves, mail, keys, and whatever else one entered holding. After a moment's scrounging, she returned and handed him a business card.

"Here. She left this. Slid it under the door."

Joe read it with conflicting emotions. As cards went, it was of the cheaper variety, printed off a laser printer rather than a quality offset press — fitting the organization on its face.

Printed under the *Brattleboro Reformer* logo and over the word "Reporter" was the name Rachel Reiling.

■ ■ ■ ■

Rachel was back in Stan Katz's untidy office, wondering what her eccentric boss might be after now, and wishing she were outside — falling snow notwithstanding — so she could do her job.

"How're things going?" he asked from his usual slouch behind the desk.

"Fine."

"That sounds cautious. What're you not telling me?"

"I don't know if I've got anything yet, and I don't want to stick my neck out."

Katz dropped his foot from the edge of the desk and landed with a thump. He put his forearms onto the paperwork before him and fixed her with an intense look. "Sticking your neck out is what I ask you to do. Risk of failure is secondary to taking the risk in the first place. What d'ya got?"

"That's just it," she protested. "Nothing solid yet. I found out about a thief named Alex Hale, interviewed him for a piece about what he was doing, how, and why, to maybe put it against a bigger social backdrop, depending on what he gave me."

"The same Alex Hale they pulled out of the river, the one we ran a story about on page one?" Katz asked.

"That's what I'm saying."

"I have no idea what you're saying, Rachel. You *are* chasing this, aren't you?"

"Yes," she said nervously.

He sat back again. "Well, thank God for that."

"You want me to write about a murder as an investigative piece?" she asked. "I wasn't sure. I thought maybe the *Reformer* would find it suitable as straight news only."

"The old *Reformer* would," he agreed. "I'm not saying we'll make a habit out of it, but if you really think you've got something interesting by the tail, that's exactly the kind of piece that attracts a Pulitzer — not to mention new readers. The story behind the story. What better way to win respect and breathing room if not with one of those? To my mind, from what we know so far, it almost sounds like a mob hit, in li'l ol' Podunk."

Rachel stared at him, her mouth slightly open. "A Pulitzer," she said with difficulty.

He grinned. "Whatever. I can dream, can't I? Don't let that get in your way. Just do the best you can, and, for Christ's sake, give me updates. If I feel you're wasting my money, I'll let you know."

"Okay," she said without conviction.

"Fine. Fill me in on what you got so far."

Feeling increasingly less confident as she went, Rachel described her progress, concluding with the information she'd received about Alex hovering around Thorndike Academy, without mentioning Sally and her dad.

"No shit," Katz responded. "Thorndike. Vernon's own little oasis of upper-class pretenses. You have no idea what he was after?"

"Not yet. I was thinking I'd dig into the school's past, since I'll need that anyhow if I do write anything. I've already been warned by the police not to get in their way, when I dropped by Hale's apartment, so I thought for the time being I'd try to figure out what would make the school so attractive to a thief."

Katz was rubbing his chin, his eyes on where the wall met the ceiling. "That's good, although I wouldn't pay much attention to any warnings from the cops. What do you know about Thorndike?"

"Almost nothing."

"Larger than average endowment — in the hundreds of millions — especially given the enrollment, which is between two and three hundred. Founded around World War Two but looks like a British public school rip-off from the Middle Ages, complete with fortress architecture, gargoyles, slate roofs. A Hogwarts look-alike. What the hell it's doing in Vermont is beyond me, but it's always had friends in the right places, supplying money and elitist children."

"What friends?" Rachel asked, telling herself she shouldn't have been surprised that this man would know all about Thorndike Academy.

"Jonathan Marotti, first and foremost," Katz replied without hesitation. "You know him?"

Rachel's blank stare kept him going.

"Maybe worth a billion by now. A flatlander transplant, but decades ago, managed his own investment firm. Decided a long time ago to get out of the Wall Street rat race, although in his case it was Boston, but apparently he can't avoid making money wherever he is, poor bastard. That being said, he's a known soft touch locally, handing out more cash than even the old nuke plant used to do before it shut down. He's on every board you can name, like they all are, including Thorndike's. Had some relative or another go there. That part I can't remember. Anyhow, he's their biggest whale. The others, you'll have to look up."

"Has there ever been anything unusual

that we've covered out there?"

He dropped his gaze to her. "The school? For some reason — maybe the isolation — they let some of their seniors drive. That's resulted in a violation now and then — DUI or a crash. They're coed, as of a few years ago, which the starchy elder alums blame on the new head of school, a woman named Mary Mroczek, although that ball was rolling before she arrived. Probably Marotti's fault, if you ask me. If you consider it a fault," he added quickly. "Which I don't. Let's see . . . Nope. Oh, there was a guy they arrested for pilfering from the grounds crew. He was stealing odds and ends for drug money. Speaking of which, there's a problem that's most likely bigger than anyone will admit."

He suddenly looked more animated. "Check that out, come to think of it. I bet the cops won't be all over it yet. If Thorndike's anything like most of its sort, it tries to police its own. You know and I know there're evil doin's going on there we're clueless about. And I bet drugs are high on the list."

She nodded. "Okay."

The phone rang beside him. He grabbed it and said, "Hang on" before covering its mouthpiece and addressing her again.

297

"Everything else going okay? You meeting all your deadlines with this on your plate, too?"

"Yup. I just cut out more sleep."

He smiled. "Join the crowd, and don't expect to get paid for it. We'll make you one of us sooner than later."

He went back to the phone and let her find her way out.

In Bellows Falls, Willy stepped back from fruitlessly ringing the doorbell by the mail slot, returned to the sidewalk, and looked up at the second-floor windows belonging to Shelly Ayotte, careful not to slip on the fresh snow covering the pavement.

"Landlord won't hire anybody to shovel out front," a male voice told him from a cracked-open window on his right. "Told us if we had a problem, fix it ourselves. What d'ya think about that?"

Willy didn't bother looking at the window. "Not much. Shelly around?"

"Nah. She took off."

Now Willy addressed the window. All he could see was a small sliver of an old man's face. "Took off where?"

"How'm I supposed to know?"

" 'Cause I figure you know pretty much everything that happens in this dump."

The man laughed. "You got that right. I try to, anyway."

"So?"

"The way she told it, a rich relative left her a bundle, enough to take off for a month and stretch her legs."

"What about her job?"

"Not that kind of job. Per diem. It'll be there when she gets back."

If she gets back, Willy thought, then asked, "Where're the sights she's seeing?"

"I asked. She said, 'Nowhere you'll ever go, old man.' How's that for respect?"

"Not much," Willy said again.

And not much for putting the squeeze on Shelly Ayotte about her purported sighting of the mysterious woman and the VW van.

This small development most definitely ramped up Willy's suspicions.

CHAPTER 17

Sally made herself comfortable in her father's antiseptic inner sanctum — the one place in a crowded world where she knew he almost felt relaxed. In part, she wondered if the glowing computer screens, the non-stop hum of servers and air-conditioning also helped him to emulate a sociological air traffic controller, keeping him above the fray.

As always, his face was bathed in happiness at the sight of her. "How're things out there, sweetheart?"

"You know how they are. Weren't you at your job an hour ago, or something? What is your job nowadays, by the way? I don't think I know."

He chuckled. "Good point. I sweep and clean the auto-collision place near where the landfill used to be. Nice people."

She took that in without comment. That was the flip side to this room's remoteness and sterility: the ever-changing bottom-rung jobs that he also pursued to "keep a finger on society's pulse," as he'd once put it.

"Is your undercover job proceeding the way you'd hoped?" he asked, proud of how she'd used his influence and training to create an open and legal living.

"That's why I dropped by," she told him. "Since Jonathan Marotti wants me to find out what's bothering him without giving me directions, I was wondering if you could tell me what you know about a few people I'm looking into at the school — the entire board of trustees and the executive management team, to name two. I don't want to waste a lot of time chasing people you think are in the clear, if at the same time there're some others you know are crooks."

He hesitated before replying. "You've never asked for a favor like that before, even when I've offered. You said it would taint the legal integrity of your cases."

"Doesn't apply," she said. "I called Marotti before coming here and asked him what happens if I find something criminal. He said it would depend but that probably he would just blow the whistle and withhold that gift I told you about. He's less interested in bringing anyone down than in safeguarding his millions from going to an outfit that's one step away from self-destruction."

"He's that worried?" Dan asked.

She looked noncommittal. "More cautious than worried. He's careful about his money. Makes sense."

"What happens if you find they're running a sex-slave operation?"

"Call me goofy, Dan," she replied with a smile. "But I'm guessing you'd have already let the right people know about something like that, if you'd fallen over it. Just as I would've. I'm only asking for your gut reaction. Not to do any homework for me. And since we're dancing right up to the edge of propriety, I'll ask you not to give me specific details, just impressions. Kind of the way Deep Throat told Robert Redford to follow the money, rather than flat out giving him the goods."

He nodded thoughtfully. "Well, you know I'm delighted to help. But there's a caveat: I've accessed hundreds of devices, directly and by proxy, as you know. But data can change, get lost, or become corrupted or updated, and devices are swapped out. I'm not as universally knowledgeable as you think I am."

He was purposefully being modest, she knew. But she also took his point. Fiction forever portrayed the NSA and its sister agencies as all-seeing and all-hearing. Realists knew that the human factor would always make a mess of that robot-perfect nightmare. Intelligence gathering — which essentially was what her father did — had always been an approximate and interpretive art.

Nevertheless, Dan Kravitz had access to reams of information, and Sally suspected that between the high-paid leadership of the school and its millionaire trustees, he'd have something to offer her concerning at least a few of them.

Stella Franklin worked at the Brattleboro Food Co-op, where her choice of clothes, tattoos, hairstyle, and piercings appeared comfortably in context — or at least not jarringly out of place.

Joe found her in the employee break room, nursing a cup of tea at a table, staring at the wall opposite, and surrounded by safety advisories, sign-up sheets, a Velcro dartboard, and a couple of supposedly inspirational framed posters. What he saw in her demeanor, despite the distraction of layers of trendy urban camouflage, was a young woman in distress.

He quietly sat across from her, which she

barely acknowledged.

"Stella?" he asked.

She shifted her attention to him without answering.

"I'm Joe," he said. "I'm a cop, and I'm looking into what happened to Alex. How're you holding up?"

She returned to studying the wall.

He reached into his jacket pocket, sorted through several business cards he kept for such occasions, and slipped one toward her, explaining, "That's a grief counselor I like people to know about. Depending on how you're doing, I can either leave things there and we can talk later, or I can keep going. What would you like?"

That took her by surprise, which he'd hoped it might. He'd located her through one of the statewide police databases, and thus knew of her sometimes less than collegial relationship with law enforcement. When approaching people with histories like hers, he knew that often the best way to break through was to avoid traditional openers.

Her eyes narrowed and she glanced at the business card, even rotating it between her glittered fingertips to better read it.

"You ever hear of her?" he asked.

"No."

It wasn't much, he knew, but at least she'd said something.

"I used her once myself," he went on, not quite truthfully. "It helped, although I didn't think it would. You know, the whole male ego thing."

Her brow furrowed. "You think you got a big ego?"

He smiled. "Not awful, I hope. But that's what most of us are accused of. Probably a holdover from when we were told as kids to shove a cork in it."

"Tell me about it," she muttered.

"Feels lousy, right?" he asked, propping his chin on his hand, encouraged by what he hoped was progress.

She sighed and sat back, dropping the pretense of drinking her tea. "Yeah, it does."

"It's not right what happened to Alex, either," he tried, hoping he wasn't moving too fast.

Her mouth tightened before she said, "He never hurt anybody."

"I don't disagree," Joe said, not at all sure about that, "but he clearly pissed off someone."

She scowled. "People are so crummy."

"Did Alex give you any idea that he'd stepped on some toes?"

Her expression turned pitying. "How

305

'bout everyone he ever ripped off?"

"You get angry if your silverware's stolen. You don't ambush and kill the thief," Joe argued.

For the first time, he felt he got a genuine, spontaneous show of interest.

"What do you want?" she asked.

"Your help. Anything you can give me."

"*I* don't know who did it." Her tone verged on being sulky.

"I'm not saying you do. But you might've seen something, heard something even, that seemed unrelated at the time."

"Okay," she said doubtfully.

"So," he began, encouraged, "one of the things we do is try to rebuild what was going on right up to the end. When did you last see Alex?"

"Just before he disappeared. We spent the night at my place. He was all excited about the new project — that's what he called them. And we texted a couple times after that. Then, everything went quiet. I wrote a bunch more, but that was it." She paused, adding quietly, "Till I heard what happened."

"How did you hear?"

She tapped a nail on the facedown iPhone beside her tea. "People were full of it," she said. "Then I saw it in the paper."

Those phones, Joe wondered, having missed the boat when it came to embracing the things. He understood their function, even their usefulness in some instances, but not the dependence associated with them. He had one, but kept it in his pocket, and his colleagues often had to remind him to either recharge it or turn it on.

Nevertheless, he was pleased about where this conversation was heading.

"This is good, Stella," he told her. "Really helpful. What was he headed off to do when you last saw him?"

"A meeting. He said it was going to lead to a big payoff. A 'game changer,' he called it. Guess he got that right," she added bitterly.

"Who with?"

But here, she shook her head. "He wouldn't say. He said it might be dangerous if anybody knew. Can you believe that? He could be such a fucking moron sometimes."

Joe gave her a moment to work through her outburst, during which she wiped her nose angrily with the back of her hand.

He chose his next words carefully, so he couldn't later be accused of planting ideas in her head. "Had Alex been up to something recently that suggested what this big deal was about?"

His reward was instantaneous. "That stupid school," she said. "He was like a dog circling a hydrant, for Christ's sake. I couldn't figure out what the hell he was doing."

"What school?" Joe asked innocently.

"That stuck-up place — Thorndike."

"And the meeting Alex went to was somehow connected to Thorndike?"

"Well, *duh*. He's sniffing around it, he goes off to meet somebody, and he gets dead. You figure it out."

"He said that?" Joe persisted. "That the meeting and the school were connected?"

That drew her up short. He worried for a moment that she might lash out at him. Instead, she reflected before conceding, "No. He didn't. I just think that's what happened."

"Did he say if he was meeting with a man or a woman?" Joe asked.

"A woman?" Stella seemed startled by the thought. "No . . . I mean . . . No. I don't think so. I'm not sure. I *thought* it was a man."

"Okay," he said agreeably. "Fair enough. How 'bout the nature of the payoff? Did he mention an amount?"

"Just that it was huge. He said 'ginormous.' "

"You said you both texted," Joe reminded her. "What did you say?"

She picked up her phone, manipulated it effortlessly, and spun it around on the table, faceup, so Joe could see the screen. "There," she said. "That was it. 'Late.' That's all he wrote."

Joe took the phone and ran his finger along its surface, scrolling up through the messages. He read one from Stella, who was inquiring, "It happen yet?" and Alex's response, "Nope," before his final comment.

Joe also discovered where there'd obviously been a change of venues for this supposed meeting. A few messages earlier, he found where Alex had written, "No show," with a frowny face, immediately followed by "OK — meeting moved. Good to go." Stella had inquired "Where RU?" and received back "Restaurant. Noisy!"

Joe was relieved that the texts were still there to be read. "I'd like a copy of these," he told her. "All right if I send them to my own phone, just so I can have them on hand?"

She shrugged in response but didn't reach out to demand her phone back. Well trained by Lester, Joe executed the necessary procedure and returned the device, at the same time continuing the conversation. "He say where he was after he left the restaurant?"

"No. That was part of the secret."

The timing between the restaurant and the "Late" message was forty-three minutes. It was no great leap to imagine that his killer had used Alex's greed to lure him away from the noisy but safe restaurant to where he'd ended up at the boat ramp.

Joe let a moment slide by before asking, "Let's go back to his interest in the school. What started that? Did something happen?"

During their conversation, he'd seen her mood shift from despondency to something more engaged. She continued in that mode, stating, "We didn't live together. We had separate lives, so I didn't always know what he was doing. I even saw other people sometimes. He didn't care."

Joe was struck by how people, including the young and hip, so often fell back onto corny euphemisms. "Did *he* see anyone else?" he asked, using her vernacular.

"I don't think so. He was too much into his projects. Plus, he was pretty paranoid about people getting too close."

"So, no guy friends, either?"

"Not really."

"Okay. Back to the school. How did you first become aware of it?"

"He showed me pictures he took. All

excited, showing me old buildings and stuff, like I cared."

"What triggered his interest?" Joe asked, pressing her. "He never said what he was after, or mention anyone's name?"

"Only the buildings. He went on about the age of some of them — like they were people. 'This is the oldest,' or 'This was the first one.' Junk like that. I thought it was crazy. It was like he was going to steal one of *them,* instead of just break in, like usual."

"How 'bout what got him started in the first place?" Joe repeated. "He never did anything like this before, did he? Wasn't he always focused on cars or homes?"

"That's what I'm saying," she said, frustrated. "Aren't you listening? I don't *know.* He showed me his stupid pictures, talked about hitting the big time, and got himself killed. I don't *know* what the fuck it was all about."

She checked the clock on the wall, adding, "Look, I gotta go. I'm past my break time. I don't need for these assholes to fire me, on top of everything else."

"Of course," Joe replied, rising with her and placing his business card alongside the other one for the grief counselor. "I really appreciate your help, Stella. Call me if you think of anything else."

311

Stella scooped up the cards along with her phone. Joe imagined she was only being polite; he seriously doubted he'd ever hear from her.

They walked together toward the door, Joe saying, "I am sorry we had to meet this way. It's a terrible thing to lose a friend, especially like that."

Stella stared at him on the threshold, her expression back to its protective hardness. "Whatever. He was a douche."

Joe was back in his car in the snowy co-op parking lot when his phone began vibrating in his pocket. Reading its screen, he was happy to answer this time.

"Is this my favorite medical examiner?" he asked.

Beverly laughed at the other end. "Good Lord. I hope it's your only medical examiner. How many do you want or need?"

"Point taken," he replied. "To what do I owe the pleasure? You rarely call me in the middle of the day."

"I wouldn't be now," she admitted, "except that I always like to hear your voice. You can thank my field investigator for this, though."

"Oh?" Joe asked, intrigued. The ME's death investigators were dispersed across the state, functioning as Beverly's eyes and ears concerning the hows and whys surrounding Vermont's recently deceased. They were traffic cops in a sense, directing which cases became autopsies, waivers, or some category in between. In the most obvious situations, like overt homicides, the police called for the so-called assistant medical examiner, or AME; in other, more elusive instances, it could be the reverse, with the suspicious investigator notifying law enforcement.

"I am gaming the system a bit," Beverly explained. "As you know, this office reviews every death certificate written in the state. We received one from Bellows Falls yesterday, and it was straightforward enough that on first reading, we gave it the thumbs-up. Homer Nelson was his name," she added, supplying his date of birth and address. "That should have been the end of it. As a result, I'm now sad to say, Mr. Nelson was therefore cremated. Only subsequently did I flag it to be researched by our Windham County AME."

"Why?" Joe asked, knowing as he did that he was rushing her — always a misstep.

Beverly paused, preferring to proceed sequentially, as her scientific background had taught her. "It was purely instinctual.

The man was frail, elderly, and suffering from life-threatening ailments, so his physician quite properly completed the death certificate. What caught my eye, Joe, was that Mr. Nelson's date of death was so shortly after Mr. Johnson's, and in the same general neighborhood. I thought you might find that interesting."

"What were his complaints?" Joe asked, hoping for more of an "aha" revelation.

"Nothing out of the ordinary for the modern American of a certain age," she said, disappointing him. "Diabetes, smoking-related COPD, obesity, atrial fibrillation, atherosclerotic cardiovascular disease. The catch is that when he was later interviewed, Mr. Nelson's physician said that he was surprised to hear of this turn of events; that despite the list I just gave you, Nelson was faithful about taking his medications, observant of medical advice, and had just that day had a checkup, which showed him much improved over his previous visit."

Joe was stumped. The coincidence of an old man dying of natural causes on the heels of a young drug dealer getting stabbed was hardly a showstopper. He kept quiet, however, trusting her instincts.

"None of that was enough for me to contact you at first," Beverly went on. He now sensed she was enjoying herself a little. "Not until the physician imparted one piece of nonmedical information. Wasn't that address I just gave you one of the streets you were canvassing for Lyall Johnson's last movements?"

"Yes," Joe said, smiling and dragging out the word in anticipation.

"It turns out," Beverly concluded, "that Mr. Nelson spent every day at his window, with a pair of binoculars, noting the comings and goings of all his neighbors."

"Aha," Joe said quietly, Scott Baitz's earlier discovery finally finding the right place to roost. "I'll let Willy know. That *is* interesting."

Beverly laughed. "I was hoping it might be."

Joe smiled, amused by her pleasure, and delighted to witness her brains at work yet again.

CHAPTER 18

Rachel looked up at the door, to see a tall, balding man wearing half-glasses enter. They were in the local history room of the Brattleboro town library — actually, two adjoining glass-fronted cubicles on the mezzanine overlooking the building's main reading room. Rachel was sitting at one end of a short conference table, hemmed in by framed documents, display cases of artifacts, and several rows of bookcases. Multiple open volumes were spread before her.

"Hello," the man said. "Are you finding everything you're after?"

"Yes and no," she replied.

"Need some help?" he asked, extending his hand. "I'm the librarian assigned to this room, which supposedly makes me knowledgeable in all things historical. Christopher Pluff's my name. But call me Topher. Everyone does."

"Rachel Reiling," she said. "I work for the

Reformer."

His smile expanded with recognition. "Oh. I know you. You take all those wonderful photographs. You write, too?"

"They like us to be jacks-of-all-trades."

"Just like around here." He waved a hand. "I also help out upstairs and with special events. So what're you looking for?"

"A history of Thorndike Academy."

Pluff pulled out a chair catty-corner to her own and crossed his long legs. "No such animal, probably with good reason. It may look like it's been around since George Washington was in shorts, but it was really founded around World War Two, close to the same time Marlboro College came into existence, although that's where the comparison ends. The college was a form of academic commune in the early days. Thorndike always struck me as a wannabe Eton or Harrow — I hope minus the canings and hazing."

Rachel looked surprised. "Really? Sounds like something out of Dickens. In Vermont?"

Topher chuckled and apologized. "I shouldn't have said that, especially to a reporter. Please forget it. There've never been reports of anything like that, at least not that I know. I just meant that it's a very conventional, traditional American prep

317

school in the old mold, unlike, say, the Putney School, which is much more counter-
cultural, as is Marlboro, let's say. Call it a
Windham County prejudice on my part —
all liberal, all progressive, all the time, you
know? I take it you weren't brought up
around here."

"No. Burlington," she told him.

"Ah. The big city, such as it is. To us, that's
a foreign land. Anyhow, back to your research. I'm afraid you won't find much, unless you pore through all your own newspaper archives. But even there, you'll mostly
find articles about campus activities, sports
events, famous people visiting to give
speeches. Things like that. Of course, if you
go back far enough, there may be something
about the founding. Still, it would most
likely be just a small business news item.
You know, 'Property changes hands with
plans to create school,' and so on."

"What do you recommend, then?" Rachel
asked. "I did find a basic organizational flow
chart: headmaster, trustees, officers, enrollment, and the rest, but those're just lists. I
was hoping to find something with a little
more meat on it. Something interpretive."

Topher crossed his arms comfortably and
smiled. "Fire away. You never know what I
might remember."

"Really?" She laughed. "Okay. If you don't mind."

"Mind? It's my job, sort of."

"Right. I guess it is. Well, let's start at the beginning, then. I've got most of the current stuff, like I said — at least the stats. How did it come into being?"

"People forget," Topher began, "that before the war, this country was very much in the pits. The Depression had been dragging on for years, Roosevelt's programs were trying to keep people busy, but the USA was far from the powerhouse we take it to be now. There were bad memories about the First World War, and resentment about Woodrow Wilson's getting us involved internationally."

Rachel stole a glance at her watch, wondering what she might've gotten herself into.

Topher caught the gesture and held up his hand. "That's the background. Just to set the stage. The founders of Thorndike were the exception to all that — a small minority no one talks about now. They were the people who did just fine during the Depression, having gotten rich in the twenties and converted their holdings to cash before the market collapsed. To them, purchasing opportunities littered the ground. They therefore became hell-bent on creating a school that would prepare young, elitist men to enter the premier colleges, trained to rule the new world they suspected was coming. It was a very highfalutin vision."

"But wasn't New England already covered with fancy prep schools doing the same thing?" Rachel asked.

Topher waved that away. "You know how competitive people get. Sure there were, but I guess these people thought they had a better mousetrap. Even back then, Vermont appealed to the rich and famous — witness *White Christmas* and Bing Crosby in the early fifties — plus, at first, not too many famous people went to Thorndike back then. It takes time to establish snob appeal.

"Honestly? I remember hearing that in those days, the place was a dumping ground for loaded losers. Makes sense, when you think about it. If your young prince had any brains, you put him in Deerfield or St. Paul's or Exeter; if he didn't, then Thorndike looked pretty good. It was still a prep school, after all, and it didn't take that long before it upped its standards. Nowadays, it's solidly in the middle of the pack, according to what I've read. Not bad for a place that's under a century old."

"Why Vernon?" Rachel asked.

Topher's eyes gleamed as he held up a

finger. "Ah! That's where the topic becomes interesting, to me at least, since I'm a local genealogy buff. Now, like I said, there's no definitive documentation for much of this. It's mostly bits and pieces I've put together after a lifetime of reading, traveling around Windham County, and conducting interviews for the library archives, of which I've done two hundred, easy. So please don't quote me, okay?"

"Understood," Rachel said.

"Not to mention," he added, "that some of it could be construed as libelous, or at least rude, and I'd hate to be caught in that wringer."

"Got it," she repeated.

"All right. Well, I think the whole deal with the school's location had as much to do with lobbying and influence peddling as with choosing the best spot. I can't swear when the whole process began, or who got the ball rolling, but it was early on when the organizers of the school — mostly people out of Boston and Hartford, Connecticut — started hanging out with an interesting Vernon family named Dunning."

Rachel looked up, the reference familiar to her from having seen Thorndike's current board of trustees, one of them being Willard Dunning.

"Rings a bell, I see," Topher observed. "And you're right. Willard Dunning is a direct descendant. It was his grandfather who moved heaven and earth — and from what I heard maybe more than that — to catch the eye of the school's founders."

"What's that mean?"

Topher tilted his open hand back and forth. "Hard to say. There were rumors that not all his neighbors were as crazy about the idea as he was, and that maybe he twisted a few arms to get his way. At the bottom of it all, it was basically the old land-rich, cash-poor story all over again. The Dunnings had the first in spades, which is why the school does, too, in the here and now. Well over two hundred acres. But Arvid Dunning wanted money something fierce, and supposedly was a man who got what he went after."

Topher laughed. "Anyhow. Water under the bridge. The deal went through, money changed hands, and the school broke ground. The rest is history."

"And Dunning?" she asked.

"He and his clan did well. Arvid died. The money from the sale grew. Willard's father, Peter, was smart and canny, and increased the pile a lot, but he died young of cancer, handing the financial reins to young Willard.

322

That's when things got wobbly. The 2008 financial crisis made a pretty good dent, from what I was told by people who also said Willard had been cruising for a bruising anyhow. I would be the last to understand any of it, but supposedly he's no wizard of Wall Street.

"Still, you've seen his name on the board of trustees. So, he wasn't wiped out. And another small throwback I love about the story is that it's stated in the sales contract that, forever after, at least one male Dunning per generation would be allowed to attend the school, at no cost to the family. Course, that was the old days, and the school was originally all male. I always wondered if the phrasing there would've been the same had it originally been co-ed. Never sounded to me like old man Dunning was terribly enlightened."

Rachel asked, "Does that mean Willard attended?"

"Yup," Topher said. "Before going on to Trinity College in Hartford. I know I said he took a clobbering on Wall Street, after inheriting from Peter, but before you burst into tears, keep in mind that it's all a matter of scale with these folks. Another board member is Jonathan Marotti, arguably the richest man in Vermont; Vincent Clemente, of Clemente Lumber, is another. He owns huge amounts of the state's timberland. And the list goes on, including a couple of rich flatlanders who don't have anything to do with Vermont but have ties to the school. Dunning may have taken a shellacking, but it only brought him down to his last ten million or so. Hardly anything to dump him into the street."

Rachel tried narrowing the scope of the interview slightly, returning to a question she'd asked earlier of Stan Katz. "Have there been any scandals or controversies associated with Thorndike over the years?"

That made him pause. He studied the tabletop thoughtfully for a moment before replying, much like Katz before him, "Not that jump out. Nothing big enough to deserve a headline. There may've been a theft or some vandalism or a tax dispute with the town that got a mention, but nothing like what you're suggesting. On that score, Thorndike's a little like the Putney School or Vermont Academy in Saxtons River, if a bunch richer. They either mind their manners or they're really good at keeping out of the news."

Rachel tried a different angle. "What about Mary Mroczek, the new head? Any local reports about her?"

"People associate the school going co-ed with her," Pluff said. "I don't think that's technically correct. But a female head of this kind of recently all-male bastion is probably pretty rare. It's got to cause grumbling. I've never met the woman. I wouldn't guess she gets off campus much. You have to keep in mind that all of these places, colleges, private schools, you name it, they're like islands. They might as well have moats around them."

All of which left Rachel still wondering not only what Alex Hale had been circling but what Sally Kravitz's undercover assignment might be.

She checked her watch and began gathering her belongings, including her ever-present camera, explaining, "I gotta go. The fire department's having a ceremony I need to cover. I can't thank you enough, Mr. Pluff. You've been a great help."

"Topher," he said, correcting her. Standing up as well, he added, "And I'm delighted to have been of use."

"Oh, you were," she reassured him, thinking that Topher Pluff might have been more on target than he'd intended, invoking moats. In the process, he'd unwittingly shaken loose a memory of something Alex Hale had said the one time they'd met.

"Believe me," she emphasized.

She was now even more determined to find a way across Thorndike's drawbridge.

Willard Dunning studied his boy's face. "Rugby?" he asked. "It looks more like you were the ball. And you promise me you're all right. How long ago did this happen?"

"Dad," the young man complained. "I knew you'd do this. That's why I didn't tell you, and why I didn't see you last weekend. It was a week ago, maybe more. I don't know. The infirmary checked me out; they even took X-rays. I'm fine."

"I want to talk to the coach. This is not okay."

James Dunning reached out and grabbed his father's arm. "Dad. Stop. It had nothing to do with coaches. It was a pickup game, in the snow, after hours. Kind of a dare."

Willard started pacing his son's dorm room. It was a single, which was unusual. But James was a senior, a school leader, and — most important — a Dunning. Special privileges for special people, for which neither man made excuses. They were proud of their heritage, and their role in the school's creation.

It didn't mean, however, that Willard didn't also regard the room as little better than a monk's cell. One of the advantages of being rich, in his view, was that he rarely had to expose himself to such environs. It was parental showmanship that had brought him here now, mostly to compete in his son's eyes with his ex-wife — a woman he'd married upon getting her pregnant, never loved, and spent time with only in the company of others, until they'd divorced. She made an issue of never visiting the state, much less the campus or this room, making these Willard's prime years to exert his influence.

"Who were the other boys?" he asked.

"I'm not telling you," James said defiantly. "You wouldn't tell me, if our roles were reversed. You went here. You gonna tell me crap like this didn't happen in your day?"

He had his father there. Especially back in the all-male days, excessively hormonal activities were commonplace, and James had no problem imagining his father in the thick of it.

"No," the elder Dunning conceded, inventorying his only child's almost feminine features, bruised and scratched. His eyes drifted down to James's hands, also battered. The right was swathed in a bandage. "How bad is it?" he asked.

James held up the hand. "This? Not horrible. Got mangled in somebody's cleats. I think some sharp ice came into it, too. Bled like a stuck pig, but no lasting damage." He touched his swollen nose, which had produced bilateral bruises beneath both eyes. "This was worse. You ever have something punch you in the nose?"

Willard chuckled at the memory. "Hurt like hell. Made my eyes run for fifteen minutes. Everyone thought I was crying, which didn't help." He paused. The conversation brought him back to Tiffany, his ex-wife, who lived in New York, at vast expense to him. "When do you next see your mother?" he asked cautiously.

James laughed. "She'd love this. No, I think we're both covered there. I don't plan to go to New York for a couple of months, at the soonest, and there's no way she's coming here."

"Don't I know it," his father said.

James cocked his head. "Why are you here, Dad? I don't usually see you midweek."

Willard waved it away. "Routine trustees thing. Not even a full board meeting. Just some housekeeping that needs a quorum." He hesitated before admitting, "Plus, I like hanging out with you." He laughed again, "Although not necessarily when you're looking like that."

James touched his damaged nose again self-consciously. As father and son, they weren't overly affectionate, but the love was surprisingly there, and strongly felt. Since the divorce years ago, the two had experienced some rough times, especially as Tiffany had roiled things up with her complaints about Willard. James, just coming into his own as a young man and still living with his mother, had been easily influenced by that, along with her lavish spoiling of him. His arrival into Willard's domain at fourteen — enrolling in the school and therefore living in Vermont — had initially been rocky. Resentment, isolation, loss of old friends, Tiffany's stream of invective, now delivered via Skype and texts, had played interference with Willard's attempts to win his son's affection.

They'd come quite a way, Willard thought. The boy had matured, hardened, become more independent. The lesions and contusions he was sporting now spoke to some of that; it wasn't so long ago that the younger James would never have exposed himself to such peril.

He remained spoiled. Willard saw that. Tiffany's obsession with status and upward mobility was like candy to the kid. And sadly, it wasn't completely at odds with the school's training and Willard's own appreciation for the same benchmarks. Tiffany saw them as God-given rights, Willard as rewards for battles well fought. But both outlooks and influences had combined in James to perhaps an unhealthy degree. Willard had to concede that his son, while bright, athletic, good-looking, and ambitious, probably wasn't a terribly nice guy, and was certainly a snob.

But then, so was Willard, when it came to honest self-appraisal.

The older man suddenly reached out and touched his son's cheek, much to the latter's surprise. James pulled back instinctively, although smiling, if quizzically.

"I'm sorry you got smacked, James. Proud, but sorry."

James laughed awkwardly. "Hell, Dad. No big deal."

"I know, I know. I just love you a lot, and hate it when you get hurt."

"Hey," the subject of all this responded with manly brio, "you should see some of the other guys. Talk about a mugging."

They smiled at each other, each with his own thoughts veiled. In James's case, he hoped his father would never see the others involved in that little spontaneous rugby

game. Not one of them had suffered a
scratch.

CHAPTER 19

Sally looked up from her computer screen. "Hey, Barry."

The Thorndike CFO was standing before her desk, looking as benevolent and kindly as always. "Hi, Sally. I was just wondering if you were able to proof that memo I gave you."

Sally feigned forgetfulness. "Oh, jeez. I'm sorry. Yup, all done. It's also formatted and on a letterhead." She extended her hand, holding a thumb drive. "I put it on this. All you have to do is shove it into your computer and hit Print, unless you want to read it one last time. I did make a couple of changes for clarity and grammar, so that might be a good idea. Sorry I didn't run it down the hallway for you. Mary gave me a rush job to do."

He'd already taken the drive and was backing away, saying, "No, no. The deadline's not for a day yet, so I was actually jumping the gun. Not to worry."

Sally smiled, waved, and returned to work as he retired to his distant office. That's the last of them, she thought to herself. One by one, she'd pulled variations on the same trick she'd just used on Barry — including the COO and the directors of development, summer programs, food services, admissions, and financial aid. She'd even done it to Mary Mroczek, so as not to play favorites. According to her research, this included everyone with any access to discretionary funds that might cause Marotti concern — or anyone else who cared about the school's welfare.

Via thumb drive, her own laptop, or by accessing the person's computer herself, Sally had traveled the campus and collected each target's IP address, using a variety of secretarial ploys. Now, through a specialized snooping program supplied by Dan, all she had to do was sit back and pore over the contents of all those computers.

This was plan B. Plan A — why she'd dropped in on her father earlier — had turned out to be less than fruitful. Together, they'd scrutinized the school's list of trustees, nine in all, and hadn't found enough to work with. Dan had "visited," as he'd put it, four of them over the years, including

Marotti, Dunning, and two other locals, but the rest didn't live nearby and therefore hadn't been available for Dan's particular form of attention. Of the locals, none except Marotti had received a visit recently enough to truly be relevant; and concerning Marotti, nothing had surfaced of an incriminating nature. Mirroring the man's public persona, he was as good as he presented, in Dan's book.

As for the school's administrative staff, they had all escaped Dan's interest, not fitting the profile he favored for his targets.

Therefore the snooping program. There was no guarantee that it would supply the smoking gun Sally was seeking, but it would certainly give her more insight into Thorndike's cash flow than she had now.

Outside Bellows Falls, Willy looked admiringly at the building housing the handicap transport service. Although a Vermont resident for decades by now, his eye was still trained to expect businesses to look the role, especially one dedicated to running large vehicles in and out on health care–related calls every day. Ramps, concrete truck yards, rolling doors, large-windowed dispatcher booths, an area reserved for washing and maintenance — all of it would have been predictable in an urban environment.

But in these remote northern hinterlands, making do was less a reflection of tough times than a statement of can-do pragmatism.

He was outside the village proper, in front of what might have been a farmhouse 150 years ago, and which had since grown to include a collection of buildings, some wooden, others cinder block, one even made of unfinished plywood, and all of it rough, peeling, swaybacked, and awful to look at. Past uses had included the housing of livestock, perhaps a machine shop or garage, light manufacturing, and more. The dooryard he gingerly traversed, grateful that he was wearing boots against the mud, slush, and melting snow, had never been paved, and most likely was a quagmire during the region's dreaded mud season.

It seemed, from what he could decipher, that the main house was the office, and the other buildings a series of irregularly shaped burrows for the vans and buses, the grilles of which he could see just barely poking their noses out into the cold weather.

"Goddamned woodchucks," Willy said to himself, nearing the office, which he could now see was advertised by a handwritten cardboard sign.

He pushed open the door, disturbing a small metal bell above his head, and entered an office with three desks, one with a dusty and ancient computer, a few photographs, a calendar, a clock, a coffeemaker, and a flat-screen plasma TV set suitably sized for the Boston Celtics home court, opposite a large and disreputable sofa that looked stolen from a Dumpster.

Two impressively girthed men in blue uniforms were decorating the couch, watching a ball game with the sound all but off. An equally ample woman was staring glumly at the computer screen.

"Yes?" she asked, not breaking her fixed gaze.

"Police," he replied, waiting for what effect that might have.

It wasn't earthshaking, but he did get all of them to look at him.

"Waz-up?" asked the nearer of the men.

Willy decided to follow the flow, bypassing all introductions or casual references to medical confidentiality — if they even applied. "You folks used to transport Homer Nelson to and from his doc's office, didn't you?"

"Yeah," the woman answered. "Nice old gentleman. A regular. Sorry to see him go."

"What d'he do?" the far man asked. "He like Whitey Bulger? The sweet old guy who turns out to be a serial killer?"

"Was he a sweet old guy?" Willy asked.

"We didn't complain," the first man said. "Mostly 'cause he didn't, either. Some of them? You can't do nothin' right. Homer was okay. Why you wanna know? Somebody bitchin', now he's dead?"

"Not that I heard," Willy told them. "I'm just here to reconstruct his last day."

The Whitey Bulger fan let out a short laugh. "Here it comes. Somebody's screamin' foul play." He reached over and pushed his colleague's well-padded shoulder. "I wondered about that guy. Remember? I told you that was weird."

"What guy?" Willy inquired.

"Don't know," the man said. "We were working Homer up his walk, dealin' with the snow and ice. His dooryard was worse than some of them. That's when this guy shows up, offers to help. Outta the blue."

"You called him 'Spider-Man,' " the first man said, " 'cause of the outfit."

"Yeah. He had on one of those bank robber masks."

"A balaclava?"

"I guess. With holes cut out for his eyes and mouth. It had red stitching. And he had dark glasses, too. We appreciated the help, but I sure never saw him coming, and I didn't see him leave, neither. He was just there one second, helping out, and gone the next."

"Without ever taking the glasses or mask off," the other one added. "Just like Spidey."

"He say anything?" Willy asked.

They exchanged glances.

"Not much," said one.

"No more than 'Wanna hand?' or something. It was superquick. Like I said, we all got Homer in, and Spidey was gone. Like that." He tried to snap his fingers but failed.

"You think he left the building?" Willy asked. "Did you hear the door slam or anything?"

"Nope, but it wouldn't have mattered anyhow. Homer never locked up, and he didn't have anything worth stealing anyhow. Cut down on his messing with answering the door. We always just walked right in when we were called."

Implying the man in the mask might not have known that, Willy thought.

"What did he look like otherwise? Tall, short, fat, thin?"

"Average," said one, while his companion nodded.

Perfect.

"You catch if he was white or black? You see around the mouth hole, or his wrists? Maybe a tattoo?"

They both shook their heads, one saying, "Sorry."

Willy paused, thinking. "Okay," he said. "What about next of kin, power of attorney, anyone like that? Homer have anybody?"

"His daughter," the woman said. "Louise. Same last name." She rattled off a local address.

"You know her?" Willy asked.

"We attend the same church. She's nice."

Louise Nelson lived in an offshoot of Bellows Falls accessed by a single narrow street called Griswold Drive. A relatively modern development of some fifty to sixty houses, established over two hundred years after the founding of downtown, the remote hillside neighborhood was neither fancy nor threadbare, like the patchwork of the village, but, rather, an exemplar of middle-class stolidity. Some of the houses had swimming pools and meticulously tended lawns — now buried under snow — others needed paint and the infusion of a little home-improvement funding, but by and large, over the decades, Griswold Drive had

339

resisted much of the anthropological corrosion of its mother ship at the bottom of the hill.

Willy pulled over shy of Louise's driveway, parking against a snowbank disguising an unidentifiable curb. At this time of year, parking was a hit-or-miss affair, based on opportunity or memories of buried landmarks. Idle chat in Vermont was always punctuated by discussions of mud season, mosquito plagues, heat waves, dry spells, snowstorms, black ice, and countless other attributes of a muscular, quirky seasonal parade of weather-related iconography. Every time Willy thought he'd pegged the one he hated the most, like struggling right now to find his footing upon leaving his car, another came up that made him curse more.

Why he lived here, worked here, and wouldn't do so anyplace else proved to him how much brain damage he'd suffered from PTSD.

Finally reaching the modest house's front porch, he straightened, stamped his feet clear of snow, and was about to knock on the door, when it opened, exposing a small, spare woman with white hair, a worn face, and a smile, it seemed to Willy, of utter resignation.

"Louise Nelson?" he asked, identifying himself.

"Yes," she replied pleasantly, stepping back. "Come in out of the cold."

Willy didn't refuse, but he also didn't proceed farther into the warm and tidy home, indicating his feet. "I don't want to mess up your floor."

"Oh, that doesn't matter," she said. "If it bothers you, take off your shoes. I can get you some slippers."

It was feasible, of course, but not convenient with his crippled arm. In general, he tried to avoid such practices aside from the start and end of every day. Also, truthfully, he didn't want to spend more time in the midst of such sadness than he had to. It was an occupational hazard he tried avoiding if he could.

"I'm good, thanks," he told her. "I won't be taking too much of your time."

Louise looked quizzical. "All right. If you're sure. What is this about?"

"Your dad," Willy told her. "I know it's standard fare for people like me to say 'Sorry for your loss,' in the same way others say 'Have a nice day,' but I am truly sorry to be meeting you under these circumstances. From what I'm piecing together, he seemed like a nice man. If a bit of a neigh-

341

borhood snoop," he added with a smile.

Louise laughed and shook her head mournfully. "He was that, God bless him."

"I also heard from his doc," Willy went on, "that while Homer wasn't in the best shape, no one was expecting him to die so suddenly. Was that your understanding?"

She processed the question before agreeing. "I guess so, yes. He'd been doing well lately."

"How did he spend his days?" Willy asked. "I don't guess he got out much, and it doesn't seem he had many visitors."

She was already waving that away. "No, no, no. That's true. Like you said, he spent all his time at the window, happy as a clam. He lived for it. I would try to get him to eat at the VFW or the Elks, but he never wanted to miss his 'parade.' That's what he called it."

Willy was smiling and had opened his coat against the warmth. "Did he ever talk about what he saw?"

She laughed softly. "All the time. I heard more about people I didn't know or care about than I can say. The one thing I did enjoy was how much he got out of it. And he knew so much, unless he was making it up. But I doubt it. He really knew who was related to who, who was in or out with someone else, who was sneaking around behind somebody's back. It was like keeping track of a real-life soap opera. He even kept notes."

"Oh?" Willy stopped her. "Why?"

"He was in the Army Signal Corps for twenty years, listening to radio transmissions. It wasn't anything very secret, as far as I know — not like James Bond — but it got to be a habit. After he got disabled, he bought one of those bound cardboard notebooks with the black-and-white cover, like we all had in school. Wrote in it every day. He kept it by the window, right next to his binoculars. I think it helped bring back the old days."

"You have that?" he asked her. "I'd love to see it."

She looked surprised. "Oh, no. It's missing. I thought it might've been one of you. After he was removed and taken to the funeral home, I went in to collect his papers and notify the gas and utility people, and settle things with Medicare and all that. But the notebook was gone. I wanted it as a keepsake, but somehow I guess it got lost." Her voice trailed off, as if in memory of the notebook.

Willy seriously doubted that. "Louise, take me through the sequence of events, the day

Homer died. How did you find out?"

"His caregiver called me. Betty Du-Champs. She's a visiting nurse. Been tending to him for years. She came in when she was supposed to, found him, called me first, and then offered to phone the doctor and funeral home. I asked her about the book later. She knew what I was talking about, of course, since he was always at it, but she had no idea. She told me she thought I had it."

Willy let it go. "So he had a DNR? No one called 911?"

"No. We had all the paperwork. There wasn't to be any fuss when it happened, and there wasn't." Her eyes narrowed slightly and she leaned toward him. "Is all this because something bad happened?" she asked. "I heard about the murder."

"We have nothing telling us that," Willy replied diplomatically. "I'm just here because I was hoping he'd seen something I'm interested in."

"What's that?" she asked reasonably.

He put his good hand on the doorknob, preparing to leave. "It's nothing, really. If I do come across that notebook, though, I'll let you know."

After I put its last page under the proverbial microscope, he thought as he retreated into the cold.

CHAPTER 20

"Huh," Lester murmured, studying his iPhone.

"What?" Sam asked him.

"Willy just updated the case file from Bellows Falls. Homer Nelson, who died of natural causes in his home right after Lyall, kept a notebook of everybody and everything that passed before his window, like a log. Now it's gone missing and your better half's shit radar is going nuts."

"What's he think the guy saw?" Sam asked, pulling into Thorndike Academy's magisterial entrance drive, immaculately plowed down to the tarmac.

"Something he shouldn't have?" Lester guessed.

"Interesting," she commented. "He gonna order an autopsy? Find out if he was escorted to the far side?"

"Nope. Too late. Cremated. One additional detail," Lester added, reading to the end. "The late Homer Nelson's viewing perch had a bird's-eye view of the street and corner where Lyall supposedly met the mysterious lady of the Horse with No Name."

"Just like Shelly Ayotte."

"Right. She who's vanished like the wind after receiving a bundle of cash from parts or persons unknown."

"Damn," Sammie said. "This case is gettin' complexer and complexer, eh?"

Lester laughed. "Easy for you to say."

"Anything from the boss?" Sam asked.

Lester shut off the phone and returned it to his pocket. "He met with Alex's girlfriend, who confirmed Thorndike was his target, but she had nothing specific."

Sammie sighed. "What the hell is it about this place?"

Les looked at her. "Last time we were here, I never asked you if you'd consider putting Emma here."

They'd driven by the imposing central courtyard by now and were sweeping around to the campus's back end, toward the dorms and other, more modern buildings.

"No," Sam said. "I'm not as down on it as you are. I can see the advantages. And I know the education is probably prime-A.

But even if we had the money, I don't think I'd be comfortable sending Emma here. This is like a foreign country to people like us. I'd be afraid we'd lose her."

She didn't add that, having been bullied as a child, and rendered insecure forever after, she was wary of subjecting her daughter to an environment that certainly implied wealth and class could be used as blunt objects.

Sam aimed the car at the far end of what looked like an administrative building, and a parking lot located before its front door.

"Okay, hotshot," she said. "Let's find out if your brainstorm is storm or brain."

Lester held up two crossed fingers as she killed the engine. Earlier, at the office, calculating how best to "delicately knock on doors at the school," he'd proposed that if they did actually believe Lyall's death and the school were somehow connected, then the infirmary might be worth a visit, based on the blood found at Lyall's apartment.

It was a long shot, and fraught with legal stumbling blocks. While cooking up this approach, Lester had even phoned the unit's legal counsel, Deputy Attorney General Tausha Greenblott. She had briefed him on the highs and lows of getting around HIPAA, including a mouthful called

FERPA, a federal law that interfered with cops' gaining access to school records and data. She'd finally delivered her own recommendation, which was to invent a different wheel entirely, since — without a court order — "private schools and colleges around here don't tell us nothin' about nothin'."

That had encouraged Lester to switch approaches. If the system wasn't going to work, he figured, a more parochial angle might. As he'd told Tausha, he was hoping he'd found a possible loophole along such lines. Her recommendation: "Knock your socks off, but keep it legal."

The sign on the door said INFIRMARY, but upon entering, all they found was an empty waiting room populated with magazines, a few comfortable chairs and side tables, and a watercooler. There was a closed door on the far wall, which almost immediately opened, revealing a nurse in pale blue scrubs, her hair tied back and a smile on her face.

"Oh," she greeted them. "Grown-ups."

"Worse," Sam replied. "Cops."

That only widened the woman's smile. "Ooh. Cool." At that, she did a small double take and studied Lester more carefully, much to his satisfaction. "Hang on. I know you, don't I?"

"Lester Spinney," he said. "And you're Jamie Duncan's niece, Cindy Sue Puza, right? Talk about a small world."

He extended his hand in greeting, which she brushed aside for a hug. Sam gave him a congratulatory look over the nurse's shoulder. His brainstorm was paying off.

Afterward, Lester draped an arm across Cindy's shoulders and, avoiding mention that this happy discovery had been triggered by finding her name among the school's employees, said, "I used to torture Cindy Sue as a kid. Her uncle Jamie was the inspiration for my getting into law enforcement."

"In Springfield?" Sammie asked, playing along.

"Yes," Cindy replied, poking Lester with her elbow. "I go by just Cindy now; sounds more professional than Cindy Sue. And he's typically talking nonsense about torturing me." She looked up at Lester happily.

"You were my guardian angel, always coming to the rescue when I got in trouble. You were a really nice guy."

"What happened, Les?" Sam challenged him mockingly, making all three of them laugh.

Lester squeezed her shoulder. "It's super-good to see you again. I had no idea you'd ended up here. I heard you'd become a nurse. I'll have to tell Sue I bumped into you."

Cindy's face glowed. "Oh, please do. I always loved her. She still working in Springfield?"

"Different place," he replied. "UVSC, up the river a bit. It's smaller, more specialized, better pay. She loves it."

"Good for her," Cindy said. "I did kind of the same thing, coming here from Brattleboro Memorial. I don't have the years Sue has in, of course, but this is a good gig. Dr. Klein's a decent boss, most of the kids are okay, if a little snotty, and the workload and pay are really decent. One of these years, maybe I'll have had enough of it — gotten bored or something — but it's good so far."

"That's great," Lester said. "I'm really happy to hear it."

Cindy gave Lester a pat on the back and asked, "So. Enough of that. What can I do for you? I'd heard the police were on campus, asking questions, but it's been very hush-hush."

The two visitors looked around. "You got somewhere we can talk?" Lester asked.

"Sure do," Cindy said, gesturing toward the far door.

She led them into the back, along a short

350

hallway with several examination rooms, and into an office at the far end.

"Sit," she offered, indicating two seats, as she spun her office chair around to face them. "We're all alone for the moment. Dr. Klein's not even scheduled for today, so we should be good."

Lester spoke first, folding his coat and resting it on his knees. "This is a long shot. We have reason to believe that someone associated with this school may have been cut by a knife, badly enough to need medical attention."

"Wow," Puza said. "What part of the anatomy?"

"Best guess is the hand," Sammie said.

The nurse considered the idea for a moment before replying, "I have dealt with knife cuts in the past: kitchen staff, theater crew, art student — a linoleum knife that slipped. But not in a while. When did this happen?"

"Let's say in the last week," Lester said.

Cindy Puza shook her head. "Nope. Not a one. Sorry."

Lester pursed his lips in disappointment. Long shots have hope built into them, despite their usual success rate.

"Of course," Cindy then added, causing both cops to stop in mid-motion from rising to leave, "I can only go by what they tell me. We just treat and document. We have no real way of knowing what's truthful."

Lester settled back down. "You got something?"

She tilted her head. "Maybe. But I have to watch my step. Unless you have a warrant or something, I could get in real trouble. Probably fired."

Once again, Lester rose, saying, "Say no more. I wouldn't want that on my conscience."

Not sure of his game plan, Sam also got up, more slowly.

Cindy was now looking distressed. "I'm really sorry, Les."

His posturing aside, Les had not, in fact, moved toward the door. "Nah, Cindy, we put you in a tough spot. That's on us. It is too bad, considering what's at stake, but it is what it is."

She actually fell for it, Sam thought as Cindy asked, "What?"

"That killing in BF," Lester said casually. "That's what we're working on. Just promise not to tell anyone."

Cindy's eyes widened. "And you're looking around here for that?" She held up both hands suddenly. "Oh, jeez. Don't tell me. It's gotta be drugs. Every time."

Les now returned to his seat and leaned toward her conspiratorially, his voice low. Unnoticed, Sam also sat back down.

"We're in a bind, Cindy," he said. "I won't lie to you. We'd have a warrant if we could get one, but we don't have enough. That could be good news for you, though, come to think of it. We're not asking for access to any records; hell, we don't even have a name. We just think that maybe — if there's a God and we're lucky — that this fishing expedition will net us something."

Cindy Puza looked at him long and thoughtfully before asking, "And you didn't hear it from me?"

"Nope. That's what I meant: We're not even here."

Across campus, at roughly the same time, Sally Kravitz was in Mary Mroczek's office with Jonathan Marotti. Mroczek was looking unhappily from one to the other.

"I'm not going to like this, am I?" she posited.

Sally didn't respond. Marotti smiled as he said, "Yes and no, Mary. I hope you will in the long run."

As was her habit, Mroczek rose to stand before the tall leaded windows overlooking the school's campus. "Meaning the slippery slope I'm on just got steeper." She turned to face the older man. "Jonathan, I'd be less than honest not admitting I've lost some serious sleep over all this."

She returned to her desk, sat down, placed both hands flat on its surface, and said, "All right. Let's have it."

Sally took over. "Barry Rice has been skimming from contracts for the past fourteen months, embezzling close to three-quarters of a million dollars."

Mroczek's mouth opened. "Good Lord. You can prove this?"

"Yes. Without his knowledge, I found a way into his computer. It took work to defeat his passwords, but I traced the money from the contracts through his accounting, all the way to his own bank accounts. I then used that to go online into his bank, made sure their records and his agreed, and tracked what he's been doing with the money."

"And that was all legal?" Mary asked doubtfully, already recovered from her shock and back in damage-control mode.

"Not to sound too much like Mr. Marotti," Sally said, "but yes and no. It was the school's computer, which you authorized me to access. As for the bank, arguments could be made, either way. That," she added pointedly, "is assuming you want to go public with any of this."

"Which I wouldn't recommend," Marotti contributed.

Mroczek was already a believer, holding up both palms. "I know, I know. I'll talk with Barry, retrieve as much of our cash as he has left, and make the rest of it — and him — disappear." She ran her fingers through her hair. "Damn."

She looked at Marotti then. "Jonathan, you were the one who got this ball rolling. What tipped you off?"

He shrugged with one shoulder. "Instinct. I can't say. Perhaps I've developed an ear for the inner workings of capitalist enterprises, like a mechanic has for engine noises. I am extremely pleased with Sally's quick and surgical efficiency, though."

"Yes, yes," Mary agreed. "Of course. This is actually nothing but good news. I was just working out in my head how our lawyer's going to explain it all."

Sally laughed. "Not my department, thank God."

"Speaking of that," Marotti said, "I'd like to ask a favor, since we're all here."

Mary watched him carefully. "Okay."

"I'm hoping you'll let Sally stay on awhile longer."

Both women stared at him.

"I'm not suggesting a specific purpose," he continued. "It's just that if she found what she did so quickly, why not keep her on so she can finish a complete physical of the place? Surely that would be prudent, and I'll continue paying her bill."

Mary frowned. "Jonathan, I know you mean well, and I can't dispute the value of what she uncovered, but to keep her on bothers me on two fronts, if I can be blunt."

"Please," he said, encouraging her.

"No offense, Sally, but it's a minor miracle none of this sneaking around has come to light, costing me my job and possibly resulting in a lawsuit from some random pissed-off parent, alum, or benefactor. I know I agreed with Sally's mission, but letting her now extend it makes me very uncomfortable."

He tried to mollify her. "My request is not a threat, Mary. If you wish, I could even broach the subject of Sally's employment with the other trustees, stating that given Barry's so-called accidental exposure, it might be good business practice to hire an investigator to make sure there aren't other rats on the ship."

"Pretend that hiring her is a brand-new idea," replied Mary, clarifying.

She sighed, rose once more, and returned to her view of the outdoors, as if wishing herself wings.

"Fine," she said, not turning to face them. "Keep her on, but let's maintain her cover and not tell anyone her real job. I want control over this." She then smiled at Sally — her eyes staying deadly serious — and added, "Let's hope she's soon bored out of her mind and finds nothing."

"Well," Cindy said, looking at Sam and Lester. "Like I was saying, I can only go by what they tell me, so technically, there were no complaints of a knife wound recently."

"But?" Sam suggested.

"There was one student who came in with sports-related injuries that didn't look totally right for what he told me."

"Meaning?" Lester asked.

"It sounded like one of those things jacked-up males get into, you know? Starts as a dare, one thing leads to another? Anyhow, supposedly, despite the weather, these guys challenged each other to an after-dark ball game somewhere out there." She gestured toward her office window and the frozen fields beyond the infirmary. "And one of them came in here afterward, all banged up. I guess he was at the bottom of the pile. Which was the other odd piece of it," she added. "No one else showed up with any injuries at all. He looked like he'd been hit by a truck, but he was the only one."

"Describe his wounds," Sam requested.

"Multiple facial abrasions and contusions," Cindy replied from memory. "A sore rib, for which Dr. Klein ordered an X-ray — negative — and what's probably best described as a mashed right hand, which he claimed had been stepped on by shoe cleats and cut by ice. They'd been playing a pickup rugby game," she explained, "ergo the cleats and roughness. I get injuries related to rugby a lot."

"But not like what you saw with that hand," Lester said.

Cindy looked at him. "Right. Bruises and cuts? All the time, but nothing like the slice across his right palm. There just aren't those kinds of sharp cutting edges in a rugby game. Nor have I ever seen such a cut from a piece of ice. It seemed weird to me, but" — here she gave them a hapless expression — "like I said . . ."

"You only know what they tell you," said Sam, finishing the sentence. "True or not."

"So," Lester finally asked, "who was the kid?"

"James Dunning."

CHAPTER 21

Jonathan Marotti wasted no time. Prepped by Sally the day before their meeting with Mary Mroczek, he'd had enough time for his staff to set up the school's boardroom with an impressive show-and-tell display, including easel-mounted drawings and blueprints, and even a model featuring the targeted piece of school property, including the tiny trees and parked cars architects use to personalize their projects.

"And Dunning Cottage would be the only casualty?" Vince Clemente asked.

"As you can see," Marotti replied.

Norm Ketcham, the COO, cleared his throat, uncomfortable in a roomful of millionaires. "I was asked to do a cost analysis of the proposed auditorium–black box theater–court space, in terms of what it might realistically generate via tickets sales to the public, and enhanced recruitment of prospective students. The bottom line is, there's really no downside, especially," he added with an awkward smile, "considering that the entire cost of the new building will be borne by Mr. Marotti. It is true, however, that the whole concept only works if the proposed building is integrated into the structure next to it." He indicated what he was talking about by using a laser pointer on the model. "Unfortunately," he added, struggling for the right wording, "that also means there's no other option to making it all work except by committing certain sacrifices."

In the ensuing silence, Harriet Ogleby, the board's sole woman, finally said, "We're talking about replacing Dunning Cottage. I'd like to hear how you feel about that, Willard. It was your family's homestead, after all."

Willard gave nothing away. "Since we're hearing about this for the first time, here and now," he replied formally, "I'm assuming we're not being asked to vote on the proposal's acceptance today, is that correct?"

Jonathan Marotti's reply was swift and diplomatic. "Good Lord, of course not, Willard. There are countless details to consider yet. All of this" — he indicated the props — "was merely to give everyone here a thorough and detailed first look."

Dunning appeared as if he were about to respond, but then he pressed his lips together and silently nodded.

After a momentary and awkward pause, Ogleby said, "Thank you, Willard," and the meeting proceeded.

"I say we pull him in and sweat the son of a bitch," Willy said.

Joe waited for the others to speak up, if inclined. It wasn't his preference to conduct staff meetings by conference call, even if he had been the one to propose it at their last get-together. They were awkward and less fulfilling without everyone's body language contributing. On the other hand, it didn't make sense to pull everyone in solely for a quick briefing. Vermont cops in general already spent an extraordinary percentage of most workdays in their vehicles.

"Why," Sammie finally chimed in, "other than for the pure satisfaction of it? You just want to tuck it to one of the upper class."

"Got that right, babe," Willy told her.

"Which suggests why we should wait," Joe argued, even knowing that Willy wasn't being serious. "What we've got against James Dunning barely scratches probable suspicion, much less probable cause. A nurse who *thinks* a rugby player's injury looked like a knife cut. If we leave him alone, find out if there's anything that even remotely puts him in Bellows Falls *and* in the company of Lyall Johnson, and only then submit him to Willy's rubber hose, it might make more sense."

"Yeah, yeah, yeah," Willy growled. "Play it by the rules."

"It shouldn't be too tough to get some kind of corroboration," Lester put in. "How careful could this kid've been?"

"You two are on the ground at Thorndike," Joe stated. "What do you think of him as a flight risk?"

"What he doesn't know won't scare him," Sam said. "Not to mention that he may have truly been hurt just playing ball. But to answer your question, before we left the nurse, it was clear she didn't like young Master Dunning, and was totally agreeable to keeping her mouth shut."

"So you're saying we have a little time before word leaks out," Joe suggested.

"Yeah." She laughed. "Could be a couple of days."

"Willy?" Joe asked. "You still up in BF?"

"Nope. At home with the kid right now. Working on my parenting skills."

Everyone knew Willy's schedule was eccentric, and his habit of putting in hours he never billed for was well enough established that none of his colleagues balked at the comment.

"Good for you," his boss said, "but now that we've finally got a suspect with a name and photo, see what you can find in terms of witnesses, et cetera."

"You got it."

"We'll do the same on campus," Sam said. "Quietly. I want to dig into that story about the pickup rugby game and find out why James was the only one to report for medical attention."

"The nurse said he looked like he'd been run over by a truck," Lester added.

"Go gently there," Joe cautioned, unnecessarily, he knew, given his team's skills and experience. "I don't want James spooked, just in case we're right about his having cut himself with that knife. Make sure you come up with a good cover story as to why you're asking."

"What about you, boss?" Willy asked, the faint tones of *Sesame Street* audible in the background. "Any progress on Alex Hale?"

"Still working on it. Our theory suggests James may've done in Lyall. But did he also take out Alex?"

"Gotta be drugs," Willy said flatly. "The

great common denominator."

But Joe was less sure of that. He had no argument with drugs playing a role in some way, but how and to what extent remained to be seen.

To give Willy his due, however, he decided to play that most obvious card. "All right," he said. "Let's start there. Lyall was a dealer, or at least a middleman. And unless things have changed, places like Thorndike are prime marketplaces for his trade. Let's pretend we're right about how James cut his hand. That means Lyall and he knew each other, and likely did business together. It's reasonable this wasn't their first encounter, which means James probably knew where Lyall lived. So that's where we begin: Willy works it from the BF side. Sam and Lester figure out how drugs wind up on campus. Let's see if we can identify a conduit. If James surfaces there, so much the better. Willy's ambition to refight the French Revolution against the ruling class will get a leg up.

"We are getting places, people," he said. "It's slow and frustrating — two murders and no hot leads. But we know how this works. Just keep pushing until something breaks. It'll happen."

They said their good-byes, each according

to his or her style, which meant Willy simply hung up. As for the assignment Joe had set for himself, the fate of Alex Hale, he certainly had one lead he'd been wanting to explore for a couple of days already. And it involved a bit of diplomacy.

It was Willard's kind of restaurant — small, quiet, secluded, very pricey, and serving excellent food and wine. Located in West Brattleboro, far from any downtown competitors, it was reservations only, and Willard suspected that its owner, an old friend, made exceptions for him.

James enjoyed it also, having been brought up by both competing parents to demand and expect if not the best, then at least the most expensive. His father and he dined here regularly as a result, whenever James's Thorndike schedule allowed.

"Twice in one week," he now commented to Willard, sipping from his illegal but happily served glass of pinot noir. "Mom better not find out. She'll sue for equal time."

"Please. Don't ruin a good meal by bringing her up," his father requested.

James laughed, but he'd noticed that for Willard, the mood was already tainted.

"What's up, Dad?" he asked, unusually solicitous for a young man of his cold disposition. "You seem down in the dumps."

Willard imagined that his state of mind was less a concern to his son than an unwelcome shadow being cast upon the latter's enjoyment of his filet mignon.

"That idiot Marotti pulled a fast one at the board meeting — proposed a huge monstrosity of a building. God, I hate people who rub their cash in your face. And you should see this eyesore. You know they'll call it the Marotti Building, or some damn thing. That's going to look good in the middle of Yankeeland. Marotti? Jesus. Why not Corleone while they're at it?"

James smiled at the familiar tone of his father's rant, working on another mouthful of steak. Once Willard was finished, he said, "You do realize I haven't the slightest idea what you're talking about."

Willard stopped, realizing his error. He also considered the indiscretion he'd almost committed, speaking of board business publicly, and to a member of the student body.

His smile slowly matched James's, however, although for entirely different reasons. "Man-to-man?" he inquired. "Under the laws of omertà?"

James's pleasure spread across his soft features. He and his father had used this pseudo-Mafia language before, bonding over one trivial secret or another. It was precisely the kind of private enjoyment the elder Dunning knew James's mother would find incomprehensible.

"Shoot," James requested eagerly.

"Marotti wants to give me a double screwing: shove an auditorium down my throat with his name on it *and* make sure Dunning Cottage gets paved over in the process."

"No way," James exclaimed.

Willard glanced around, heightening the theatricality, but also to make sure no one was, in fact, overhearing them. He was, after all, playing with something that could backfire, far beyond what his son could imagine.

"It's typical of the guy," Willard went on. "More to the point, it's a direct slap at our family. What better way to set yourself up as king of the hill than to simultaneously stamp your name on something the size of the *Queen Mary* and take the wrecking ball to the most iconic building on campus? That cottage is the last visible vestige of the Dunnings' contribution to Thorndike's founding."

James, who'd never considered Dunning Cottage an icon, and actually saw the logic of replacing it with something more useful, nevertheless understood his father's passion. Willard had always held James's great-grandfather, who'd sold the property, in high esteem, and had forever referred to the modest farmhouse as most Mormons do to Joseph Smith's birthplace. For his own part, James might have greeted the destruction of Dunning Cottage as little more than the price of progress. Today, it was used for receptions and to put up visiting artists and dignitaries — hardly an asset to the school's betterment or prestige, which, by contrast, truly needed a multifunctional building of the type Marotti was proposing.

But James had been increasingly seduced by Willard's influence over the past few years, and had developed a growing distaste for his cloying, shrill, and grandstanding mother. He was therefore happy to support the elder Dunning's outrage at this threat to the family shrine, even though he knew for a fact that Willard had never called it home, or even spent a night in it.

What caught him unawares, however — although not out of any political correctness — was the seething and xenophobic portrayal of Jonathan Marotti.

"I didn't know Marotti was such a creep," he commented.

Willard took a swig of his wine. "You know he has somebody he pays to keep his name in the papers?" he said, wiping his mouth with the back of his hand. "You can't go a week without falling over him somewhere."

James nodded, unaware of any of this. "Is it going ahead anyhow?" he asked.

"Over my dead body," Willard said darkly, pushing his half-full plate aside. "I've had enough of this guy and his type. First coeducation, then shit like this. Next, the dress code'll go, and who knows what else? Might as well be one of those pointy-headed schools for dope-happy nerds. That'll guarantee Thorndike going down the tubes: We won't be groovy enough, and we will've sacrificed our principles in the process."

James might have disagreed under better circumstances. He liked the coeds, and even better that they had access to birth control. The dress code, he could take or leave. His plans were to enter law school and end up in either New York or Boston, where people expected you to sleep in a suit. And as for other schools in the area? He didn't begrudge them their doper appetites — he'd made some good pocket money supplying his fellow students in that line. He was no one to dis a capitalist marketplace.

But he knew enough to keep his mouth shut on all of it.

Instead, he asked half-jokingly, "What're you going to do? Stage an overthrow?"

Unexpectedly, his father shifted in his chair, crossed his legs, and eyed him thoughtfully. "That's the basic idea, but it's not going to be easy, and I may need your help as a go-between."

Rachel was standing on a ladder, swaying slightly, hoping for an unusual angle of a man using an electric chain saw to sculpt a ten-foot ice statue of an angel. They were in Pliny Park, in central Brattleboro, surrounded by a crowd of admiring onlookers. The sun had come out for a while, the ice was beautifully translucent, and the addition of glittering shards flying over the artist's head in an arc supplied the final needed touch.

Straightening after her last shot, she suddenly felt the ladder stabilize beneath her.

"Thanks." She smiled, looking down.

Joe Gunther was below her, hands gripping the ladder. He did not look happy.

That was unusual, and caused her immediate concern.

"What's up?" she asked tentatively, climbing down while keeping her gear from swinging wildly.

"We need to talk."

It didn't sound encouraging. A solicitous man by nature, Joe was given to routine qualifiers like "if that works for you" or "if you're not too busy." The omission was foreboding, as she was sure was his point.

"Okay," she said, checking her watch, an hourly habit lately. "I've got thirty minutes."

"My car's over there." He pointed. "You need to do anything with your ladder?"

Rachel smiled. "No. That's his." She gave the sculptor a thumbs-up and a wave as he paused to look at her, then followed Joe to his unmarked car, stuffing her camera into her shoulder bag as she went.

Once inside, she decided to beat him to it. "I'm in trouble. At least that's how it feels."

"I am a little unhappy," he allowed. "You chose not to tell me that you'd spoken to Carol Wilcox, after we'd clearly discussed the need to respect the boundaries between us."

She didn't answer, feeling her face redden.

"Why was that?" he asked. "I found out as I was speaking to her about her son's murder, having coffee in her kitchen, trying to be supportive and inquisitive at the same time. Finding your business card there was a surprise I didn't need."

"It's not like she told me anything," Rachel said, regretting the words as soon as they were out. "She almost slammed the door in my face."

He had been gazing out the windshield at the cars and pedestrian foot traffic, always busy in the middle of Brattleboro. Now he turned toward her. "That almost makes it worse. To repeat the obvious, I'm conducting a multiple homicide investigation. You are also doing your job. I get that. But to talk to me as you did outside Alex's apartment, where we were mostly speaking as friends, and for you to hand over a tidbit about Alex's interest in Thorndike but omit that you'd talked with his mother makes me wonder what game you're playing. And the fact you got nothing out of her doesn't improve things. Our jobs may pit us against each other professionally, but in this tight-knit rural society, our trust in each other should be solid. As mine was when I respected your not giving me your source for the information about Alex."

Rachel felt trapped. She'd watched scenes like this on TV, where her character always had a sharp comeback, but her brain was filled only with anger, embarrassment, resentment, and guilt.

"I'm sorry," she muttered.

"Beginner's error," he said evenly. "It happens. Which I do not mean condescendingly. Most of my colleagues treat reporters stupidly, to no purpose. I hope I've never done that. I try not to anyhow."

His voice lightened as he shifted gears. "Now, would you like to know what I got from Carol — off the record?"

"You'll tell me that?" she asked, caught off-balance.

"Within reason, yes. That's my point. I'll always give you what I can. I did it with Katz, even when he was driving me crazy; I'll do it with you. I may not tell you everything, but I'll try to help whenever possible. Quid pro quo. There are times when you'll discover things that could help me, too, like when you told me of Alex's latest target. I need that. I'm willing to pay for it with reasonable cooperation. It's that easy."

"I am sorry, Joe," she repeated, her emotions settling back down. "Thanks for letting me know."

"Don't worry about it. We talked. We're good. For what it's worth, Carol didn't know about Alex's targets. She never asked, because she didn't want to encourage him.

She was resigned to his probably doing bad things, but she didn't want to play a part in it. It was a terrible but loving dynamic, right up to the edge of the cliff he fell over."

"Was pushed over," she said in a half whisper.

"Only because he put himself there," Joe corrected her. "Like so many others we deal with."

"Was she nice?" Rachel asked him. "She was pretty hostile to me." She was grateful for Joe's typical gentleness and understanding. In a few minutes, he'd chastised her, treated her like an ally, and was now being solicitous of her feelings. No mean feat, and very true to character.

"I liked her," he replied. "She was fatalistic and heartbroken at the same time. Ours was a conversation she knew she'd have eventually, even if it ran against everything in her prayers."

Rachel sighed. "I really liked him. He had such . . . energy. And brains."

"I bet," Joe said, suddenly struck by a thought. "You once told me you first heard about him from a source at the Bratt PD. Without telling me who that was, did you get a feeling they had an actual file on him?"

"I don't know," she answered. "My guy just told me to interview a woman named

Angie Hogencamp, who was one of his victims, but I don't even know if they *had* a name, much less a file on Alex. Most likely not."

She then added with an apologetic smile, "And my contact was Sergeant Tyler Wolfson."

Joe laughed softly, reached out, and squeezed her hand, already knowing exactly whom to interview at the PD. And it wasn't Sergeant Wolfson, whom he'd never met.

"Thanks, Rachel. We good?"

She leaned in and kissed his cheek. "I'd never want it otherwise."

CHAPTER 22

Ron Klecszewski's boyish face lit up as Joe appeared at his office in the newly transplanted Brattleboro Police Department, now awkwardly under the same roof as the *Reformer.*

"Boss!" he exclaimed, rising and circling his desk, hand extended in greeting. "My God. I haven't seen you in a dog's age."

"You're the boss now," Joe said, shaking hands, well used to Ron's self-effacing style. "How're you holding up?"

Ron shoved two of his guest chairs around, motioned Joe to one and sat in the other. He was dressed, as always, more like a high school English teacher than a cop, an appearance and even a manner that stood him in good stead with people who erroneously took him for a pushover.

That, he'd never been.

"Great, great," he said. "An almost full complement of officers, the town hasn't had a riot, a flash flood, or any visitors from outer space in years, and have you checked out the new digs? Spacious, modern, clean, heating and cooling that work, and cells that don't look like they're from *The Man in the Iron Mask*. Who's to complain?"

All that was true enough. The PD's new quarters had been designed and built, for the first time in the department's history, to its specifications, instead of being shoehorned into the confines of whatever ancient edifice had available space. Ron's lasting giddiness over the change was understandable.

"And the family?"

"Everyone's healthy and happy, or maybe just successfully keeping me in the dark. How 'bout you? You and the medical examiner still an item? I heard her daughter had signed on to the *Reformer*. Word's already out that if you're not careful, she'll duck under the police tape and grab shots you don't want her to have."

"Yeah," Joe agreed. "Rachel. Her enthusiasm wears me out just looking at it. It's actually one of the reasons I dropped by."

Klecszewski laughed. "Ah, smooth segue. You were always good at those. God, you taught me a lot."

The outburst made Joe laugh, bringing

back the days when Klecszewski, Sam, and Willy had all worked under Joe for this department, many years ago — and in those already-referenced far humbler quarters. Only Ron had opted to stay behind when the VBI was born, and Joe had always credited him with being inspired on that score. A solid cop and an outstanding human being, if a little "golly-gee," in Willy's words, Ron had recognized what staying put could do for him professionally. And indeed, with the promotion to lieutenant in charge of criminal investigations — an unlikely possibility when they'd all been there — had come respect, better pay, and a degree of self-confidence that Joe had always wished for him but never was able to instill.

"Okay," Joe began. "One of the uniformed crew mentioned to Rachel that if she wanted a good human-interest story, she should interview the victim of a particularly complicated burglary, assuming the victim was willing to talk. That got the ball rolling, the article began expanding in Rachel's head, until it came to a screeching halt with the murder of the burglar in question."

Ron's face showed surprise. "Alex Hale?"

"Yup. Found dead in the Connecticut River."

"I heard you guys had gotten that signed

over from New Hampshire. How's it going?"

Joe shook his head. Wolfson, Rachel's source, might have known about Angie Hogencamp, but it was Ron's job to see the world in broader terms. "I need help. I'm hoping Hale was so unusual in his methods that you have a special file on him, based less on actual evidence or sightings — or even a name — and more on MO. Rachel certainly made it sound as if the guy had earned a special place in your minds, if not your hearts. This would be the kind of information that doesn't fit on a computer database but still gets cataloged somewhere for future reference."

Ron crossed to his desk, saying, "Ah, old habits dying hard. Of course, you're right. I'm big on computers, but there's always stuff nobody knows what to do with, which is probably why so many people just throw it out."

He returned with a business card. "That's the contact info of a state police sergeant out of the new Westminster barracks. Along with the sheriff's office, we've been building a countywide file on open cases without obvious suspects as part of our intel sharing. Vandalisms, burglaries, vehicular complaints, you name it, if it fits the category of 'too vague to go anywhere else,' it's put into his folder, just in case it might prove useful. It's actually come in handy now and then, which makes us feel a little less like pack rats who can't throw anything out. Maybe you and he can match something to Hale and find out what the kid was up to. That what you were after?"

Joe placed the card into his breast pocket. "Even better."

"Hey," Sally said as Rachel opened her apartment door.

"Hey yourself," Rachel replied, stepping back. "Want something to drink? Or eat, for that matter? I was about to have a bowl of soup."

Sally opened her mouth to turn down the offer, before realizing that she, too, had forgotten about dinner, despite that it was nearing midnight.

"Sure. Thanks. How's the digging into Alex going?" she asked, following Rachel toward the kitchen corner of the apartment and settling onto a stool by the counter.

"Frustrating," Rachel replied, fetching another bowl. "I guess it's no surprise that a guy avoiding capture is hard to track, but my day job keeps getting in the way, too." She turned to add with a smile, "Not to mention that the cops are getting fidgety about my hovering too close to their case."

Sally rolled her eyes. "Welcome to my world."

"Speaking of which," Rachel transitioned. "You still working at the school?"

"Off the record?" she asked cautiously.

Rachel laughed, ladling up the heated canned soup. "You kidding? After what we've been through so far? You bet. Totally off."

"Then yeah." Sally smiled. "I'm mostly just mopping up by now, but still there."

Rachel put a bowl before Sally, along with a box of crackers and a spoon, then sat opposite her. "You haven't run across any historical records, have you?"

"Historical? Like what?"

"Having to do with how the place was founded," Rachel explained, beginning to eat.

Sally had already started, hungrier than she'd thought. "Sure," she said between mouthfuls. "They've got a shelf of the stuff in the office vault. Why?"

"I'm starting to think Alex was after something to do with the school's ancient history."

Sally paused, spoon halfway to her mouth, wondering if this might relate to her being kept on after exposing Barry Rice's appetite for the company's cash.

"Really," she said suggestively, instinctively keeping those cards to herself. "Do tell."

"It was something Alex told me when we met in the warehouse. He talked about people protecting things 'older than the computers and cell phones they use to hide it,' and that they'd be better off using wall safes. It was a weird phrase, and I didn't know who or what he meant, but it came back to me when I was getting a crash course on local history and Thorndike at the library."

Her soup now ignored, Rachel's enthusiasm grew as she traced her latest thinking. "We know the common denominator with Alex was his attraction to valuables. Whatever it was, from purses to cars to electronics, it had to be worth something. Romanticism aside, the man was a thief."

That resonated with Sally, who'd been mentored by a man with similar techniques, if a far more morally complicated set of motivations. "Okay," she said encouragingly.

"So," Rachel continued, "What was it about that damned school that was both valuable and older than computers and cell phones? It struck me that maybe it dated back to Thorndike's founding, even involving something of great worth. It was supposedly a big-money deal. I'm wondering if money wasn't the only bargaining chip."

That off her chest, she returned to her meal with energy.

Sally stared at her. "The founding? That was what? Eighty years ago, more or less? It's not like they cast a commemorative bell out of solid gold and buried it somewhere. I would've heard about that. It was just a business deal. What exactly are you thinking?"

Rachel remained undaunted. Smiling broadly, she simply said, "That's the point. Alex had a complicated brain. Let's try thinking like he did. Can you get me into that vault?"

Sally looked at her a moment in silence before smiling slightly and conceding, "Sure. What the hell."

"That him?" Lester asked.

Sam double-checked the document she was holding on her lap, using her hand to cut down the flashlight's glare. "It's his vehicle."

Lester put the car into gear and discreetly swung in behind the new New Jersey–plated SUV of interest. This belonged to Michael Purcell, a classmate of James Dunning's, a fellow rugby player, and — according to Lester's old friend, the school nurse Cindy Puza — a reliably rumored campus supplier of illicit drugs, second only to James himself, whom Cindy had called "a snarky, stuck-up, rich bitch loser."

Fortunately for Purcell's part-time occupation, he was a senior, with driving privileges and his own car, which had apparently improved his standing in the Thorndike community this year. Lester and Sam were hoping the enhanced status had also stimulated his greed, along with a need common to most males to be indispensable to one's companions in their perceived times of want.

Following that thought, Lester commented, "Let's hope he's not just making a Twinkies run." The small convoy was approaching the southern end of Brattleboro, parallel to the frozen Connecticut River. It was by now late enough in the winter that the river was locked up solid along this section, aside from a narrow channel on the New Hampshire side, making most of the slab reflect the moonlight like a pouring of fresh blue-tinged concrete.

Purcell veered left onto Cotton Mill Hill, leaving the river and Route 142 behind, headed toward the lower reaches of South

Main Street.

"Good neighborhood if he's going for dope," said Sam as Lester allowed more space between the two cars.

"Should we give a heads-up to the local PD?" Lester asked, happy again to be pulling a detail with Sam. Willy's assignment to Bellows Falls had worked to Lester's advantage, exposing him once more to her reassuring and dependable style in the field.

"We should," she replied, "but I don't want to. Let's keep our options open till we see what's going on."

They saw Purcell's brake lights come on as he slowed at the three-way stop sign at the top of the hill, where there was an awkwardly designed sharp turn, laid out to force motorists to heed the signs.

Purcell turned right, down South Main, which meant he was either headed to some nearby dealer's place, of which there were several to choose from, or straight into downtown, for reasons less clear.

In the interest of time and efficiency, however, the two cops were hoping for the former. Their young suspect did not let them down.

His car rolled to a stop a quarter mile along the street, not quite to the vast cemetery on the right, occupying a hillside that fell off toward the iced-over river below and exposed a broad, if dark, view of Mount Wantastiquet in New Hampshire beyond. Lester killed his lights and hid behind a parked car, which still allowed them to see what would happen next.

"We go or wait?" Lester asked as Purcell entered a house.

"My vote is we wait," Sam recommended. "We don't want his dealer; we want this guy caught holding."

Lester was good with that. They had no knowledge about the address in any case, and therefore no reason to do anything beyond watch.

It didn't take long. Some two minutes after Michael Purcell had stepped inside, he was back, shoving a small bag into his pocket as he circled his car.

Lester eased into gear, preparing to pull out once Purcell finished his three-point U-turn in the bulky SUV. But just as the young man was picking up speed and heading back where he'd come from — and Les and Sam were about to duck to avoid being seen — there was a loud, repetitive, and startling pounding on their hood, accompanied by the blinding beam of a flashlight.

"Who the fuck are you?" an angry voice called out, belonging to a dirty-faced fat man in a greasy down coat and a torn watch cap. "You cops? Get the fuck offa my street."

The timing couldn't have been worse. Just as this occurred, Purcell drew abreast, his headlights illuminating the scene, and Sam saw the whites of his eyes as he stared, alarmed, at the two of them being rousted.

"Great," Lester said, ignoring the angry protester and hitting his accelerator as Purcell's wheels squealed and slithered against the sudden uptick in speed.

"He's running," Sammie said unnecessarily.

Lester spun their car around, slipping on the snow-packed pavement, as the burly protester leaped out of the way, his mouth open.

Sammie hit the car's hidden strobes, igniting the surrounding trees, cars, and houses in a pulsing, blinding blue rhythm. Ahead of them, Purcell realized the challenge of the tight intersection with Cotton Mill Hill and blasted straight through instead.

"Perfect," Sam said. "Cut him off on the right."

Lester understood her meaning. If Purcell left South Main and took the right fork onto Fairground Road, he'd have a chance of reaching Canal Street and even the interstate beyond. If he took the easier option of staying straight, he'd enter what became a dead end road a mile later.

Lester helped him decide by abandoning his usual caution and lightly tapping Purcell's right rear bumper.

"Nice." Sammie laughed nervously, the two vehicles rocketing down the narrow, dark road, suddenly beyond any homes or parked cars.

Lester eased off slightly then, knowing what lay ahead. Purcell, by contrast, kept his pace, rounding a final corner and discovering the closed heavy wooden gate barring the entrance to Fort Dummer State Park.

From behind, Lester and Sam saw him pirouette as he lost control, slamming into one snowbank, bouncing against the one opposite, and finally coming violently to rest against several large rocks buried in the snow by the side of the gate.

"Ready?" Lester asked his partner.

"Go," she said, opening her door before their car had come to a full stop.

The two cops split up, guns drawn, and approached Purcell's silent vehicle from different angles. Arriving at the driver's door first, Sam yanked it open, reached inside, and dragged the young man out onto the road.

"You do not move," she ordered in a clear,

loud voice as Lester checked the rest of the car's interior. "Do you understand?"

Purcell was struggling, facedown on the ground.

"Do you understand?" Sam repeated, nudging him with her foot for emphasis.

"Yes."

"Then stop moving, butthead."

The boy lay still.

"We're good," Lester reported, holstering his weapon.

Sam stood to one side, gun still out, while Lester cuffed and frisked Purcell from top to bottom, none too gently, emptying his pockets and throwing their contents into a small pile. The small plastic bag they'd seen him secure as he'd left the house earlier was prominent among them.

Lester held it up so Purcell could see what they'd found. "Bad boy, Michael," he said.

"I've never seen —"

Moving fast, Sam dropped to her knees and shoved her face next to Purcell's. *"Don't,"* she ordered. "I don't wanna hear it."

Lester rolled their captive over onto his back. "Would you like to sit someplace warmer and more comfortable?"

"He's fine where he is," Sam said darkly.

Lester tapped Michael on the forehead

and repeated, "Would you?"

Purcell eyed Sam warily before nodding silently.

"Good," Lester said quietly, helping him to his feet.

They walked him to their car, where Lester joined him in the backseat. Sam returned to the SUV for a more thorough look.

"She gonna find something else?" Lester asked the boy.

His hesitation was more eloquent than anything he might've said.

Lester spoke in a pleasant voice, "Thought so. Things are not improving here, Michael."

"Do you know who my father is?" Purcell challenged him, trying to recover his poise.

"Probably someone who wouldn't be too impressed by his son's stupidity right now," Lester replied, having already taken in the young man's heavy white sweater, hand-made loafers, and trendy, if impractical, lack of socks. "How many times has he bailed you out of trouble?"

No answer.

"You want to spare him ever knowing about this?" Lester asked.

Purcell scowled. "What? What do you mean? Money?"

Lester laughed outright. "You can't help

yourself, can you? Don't you ever watch TV?"

"Sure," he said, but the response was slow and doubtful.

"This is where we discuss what you can trade to make this disappear."

"I'm not a rat."

Lester laughed again, patting the kid on his shoulder. "See? I knew you'd watched TV." He took hold of Purcell's thick leather jacket and twisted him around slightly, reaching for the cuffs, adding, "Let's take these off."

That done, he slipped them into his pocket, saying, "Of course you're a rat. I would be, too. You'd screw your best pal in a heartbeat if the asking price would get you laid, or land you something you were hankering for. It's human nature, and the crowd you run with would do it to you without a second thought. Tell me I'm wrong."

"What do you want?" Purcell's voice had a hint of pleading behind it. He was slowly losing his footing.

Lester dangled the Baggie before him. "You made some bad choices tonight, Mike. I want you to turn back the clock. You help me; I help you. Easy."

"How?"

"Who else brings drugs onto campus? And," Lester added, stopping him before he could protest, "keep in mind that this is not court, there's no prosecutor here, and if you play it right, this conversation never took place. We give you back your cell phone, you call Triple A for your car, and tell Dad you're sorry for losing your way back from the movies and having an accident."

Purcell stared at the floorboards for a few moments, considering his options. Lester didn't know the true father–son dynamics he'd invoked, but he could tell that he hadn't been far off.

"No strings?"

"Not if you're straight," Lester confirmed. "What you say has to check out. I find you fucked me over, all this" — Lester waved his hand around — "comes back to crush you."

Michael Purcell nodded once, his lips compressed, before saying, "Okay."

CHAPTER 23

Joe got back behind the wheel and finished the remains of his lukewarm coffee. He was frustrated, tired, and a lot less hopeful than when he'd set out tracing Alex Hale's suspected escapades through past police reports. After leaving Ron Klecszewski's office, he'd thought the idea simple enough. He only had to drive up to the Westminster state police barracks and read through the intelligence files Ron had mentioned were there, looking for any of Hale's unusual antics.

So much for that plan. Now, after hours of fruitless searching, he was in Windsor, Beverly's new alternate hometown, and about as far up the interstate as he intended to go. Driven by frustration more than any worthwhile evidence, he was here because of a mention of broken glass. In one of the cases he'd read, the Windsor police had referenced shattered tinted automotive glass, found near the Windsor Station restaurant. There had been no vehicle connected to it, no complaint registered with the PD, and no witness reports of anything amiss during the previous night. A dog walker outside the restaurant had merely spotted the debris and called it in as a hazard.

Acting on impulse and a finely honed instinct, Joe had begun by making a phone call. The sergeant he'd spoken to remembered the glass. It had apparently come from a broken side window, was factory-tinted, which to him had implied an expensive car, and had been broken overnight in the middle of winter. The cop had thought it peculiar that no one had reported it.

Joe agreed. It was a small, virtually unnoticeable black hole in the fabric of everyday life. Exactly the kind of aberration he was looking for.

He reached behind him, shoved the empty coffee cup into a trash bag he kept on the floor, adjusted his trusty fishing hat, and prepared to sally forth once more. He'd already checked four businesses around the irregularly shaped parking lot, without finding anyone with knowledge of a break-in or any vandalism to a car.

Joe had no idea if the vehicle owner of

interest had been a train user, a restaurant diner, or just a local in need of a parking spot, but given the growing ubiquity of closed-circuit cameras, he was hoping if not for a witness, then some footage that might show that glass being broken.

His focus on the task, already based on so little, was further blunted by the weather. Clear skies had clouded over, and a slight warming trend had commingled perfectly with overhead atmospherics to produce a mixture of rain, snow, and wind that ranked near the bottom of tolerable conditions, even for a dyed-in-the-wool native like Gunther.

This was an ingrained, poorly reported fact about living in northern New England: Winter amounted to an endless list of obstacles and obligations, ranging from heating and clothing needs, power outages, and snow removal to falling on ice or having pipes freeze, and uncountable others in between. New Englanders began and ended every day contending with a staggering number of weather-related stumbling blocks, most of them taken in stride, virtually without notice.

But it could be wearisome. For Joe, this last business he was about to visit would be the final one he called upon.

■ ■ ■ ■

"Did you read this?"

Sally was removing her coat as Emily came striding down the broad hallway that harbored their two desks as a canal might have two berthed barges. She was holding a copy of the *Reformer* in her hand.

"It's Jonathan Marotti," she reported. "He's been accused of sexual harassment."

Sally hung up her coat and reached for the paper. Her brain was alive with questions, possibilities, anger, and a strong impulse to grab the phone.

But she was still undercover, and needed to play the role.

"Who?"

"Jonathan Marotti. You know," Emily stressed. "He's on our board. You've seen him around. An older man, always wears a coat and tie. Full head of white hair."

Sally was nodding. "Right, right. I remember. Nice."

"*Really* nice," Emily repeated with emphasis. "Like everybody's idea of the perfect grandfather. There's no way he did this."

Sally didn't respond, trying to read the article.

Emily perched on the edge of Sally's desk,

continuing. "Of course, maybe that's the whole point. Lure younger women into thinking they're safe, and then the next thing you know . . ."

"Who's Wilva Sargent?" Sally asked.

Emily effortlessly changed tack. "Amazing, right? Billie? I mean, I never would have put the two of them together. Of course, she does have that perpetual teenager look that men like. All the peekaboo clothes and tomboy-in-skirts shtick. I know for a fact she doesn't wear a bra."

Sally shook the paper slightly. "It says she works here."

"Art department," Emily informed her. She tilted her head back to take in the ceiling — a contemplative pose. "I always wondered what she did with her spare time."

"Not married?"

"Oh, no. No kids, either. That's what I mean. Kind of footloose, if you get my meaning."

Sally smiled vaguely, not getting her meaning at all, and resisting the urge to remind her of her own marital and maternal status.

Sally glanced at the wall clock so Emily would catch the gesture. The latter slid off the desk, her eyes wide, and said, "Oh, right. You'd better go in and see Mary. You two are gonna have a busy day, I bet."

Sally smiled. "Unlike you, right?"

That made Emily laugh. "Yeah. The secretary with no boss. That's me. I'm going to enjoy it for as long as it lasts. Rumor has it they'll have a financial hotshot in here by this afternoon or tomorrow to sort out Barry's mess. Then I'll be wishing I were you."

She began retreating down the hall, adding, "This whole place is suddenly turning into the *Titanic*."

Mary was, in fact, at her desk, reading the same paper, when Sally entered.

"You heard," Sally stated, sitting across from her.

Mary looked up. "Last night. Jonathan called me. He's befuddled and clueless, of course."

Sally gave a half shrug. "He was the one who wanted me kept on. He seems to have had his reasons."

Mary rose to stand by the window, shaken and distracted. She spoke as she looked out. "You think he saw this coming?"

"You were there," Sally reminded her. "I don't know if he knew what was coming, or was just suspicious that something might be."

Mary turned. "But this. It's so . . . unlikely.

He told me he wasn't sure he'd even met Billie Sargent."

"It is topical, though. And given the number of prominent male bodies lying by the side of the road to bad PR, it's not like a woman needs proof these days. He said/she said has become she said/he protests to no effect. Not," Sally added, "that I have the slightest problem with that. About time the scales tipped in our favor. But is this credible?"

Mary looked crestfallen. "I don't argue with that emotionally. And most powerful men fit the profile. But Jonathan Marotti is like a small-town, local version of Warren Buffett — all kindness, wisdom, and generosity."

"You know Buffett?" Sally asked pointedly.

"No," Mary admitted. "But you get what I'm saying. Neither one of them's ever had the slightest reproach put against them, and they've been under the microscope. Politics, sure, but not something like this."

"Okay," Sally conceded. "Then let's go conventional: innocent till proven guilty. Tell me about the accuser."

"Wilva Sargent, nicknamed 'Billie.' Been an art teacher for eight years. Unmarried, which is unusual around here, well liked, volunteers a lot on campus and in the community — Big Sisters, coaches softball. She's a dorm mother. Does a good job."

"She gay or straight?" Sally asked bluntly.

Mary pointed to the paper. "Given those headlines, I'd say you got your answer."

Sally pressed her point. "Most of your faculty members are married. Have there been any rumors about her, considering most men's fantasies?"

Mary hesitated.

"Emily already told me what she thought of the woman," Sally said.

Mary sighed. "For God's sake. People. Okay, maybe she does get talked about a little. I have heard that her manner of dress can entice the senior boys — or all the boys, for that matter — and that her extracurricular classes are disproportionately popular among males. But I have *never* caught wind of anything inappropriate, and I think I would have."

She turned back to studying the view. Reading the rigid set of her shoulders prompted Sally to ask, "What else? There's something on your mind. I need it all to get behind this."

Mary faced her. "It's nothing sexual. It's more her . . . I don't know . . . Call it level of maturity. She's like a kid in some ways.

That's probably why the clothes. But she's also insecure, and easy to push around. I've never had complaints about her serious enough to warrant action, but concerns? Sure."

She sat back down, frowning at the newspaper on her desk. "Guess we'll find out now."

Sally considered what they might be facing before asking, "Did you and Jonathan talk about the building project?"

"What? Why?"

Like her father, Sally had a calculating mind, not easily derailed by emotion. "I realized it hasn't been released to the public yet, but I'm surprised one of the board members hasn't leaked it already. People talk. You know how it is."

"No," the school head admitted softly. "We didn't discuss it — not in relation to this."

"You should," Sally recommended. "A thing like this catches fire fast, especially on the heels of a proposal that size. The two of you had better break out the sand and water buckets if you want to keep in front of it. The press, the alums, and your own board are all going to be talking at once, and it won't be long before somebody asks for Marotti's head. It's probably already started."

401

Mary looked at Sally unhappily. "What are you going to do in the meantime?"

"Keep at it."

Joe was wedged into one of the smallest, most claustrophobic offices he'd visited in a while — a virtual closet. Before him, almost close enough to make his eyes cross, was a modern, all-digital, closed-circuit recording machine displaying a monotonous, un-changing string of snapshots, all showing the parking lot between the building he was in — a Realtor's — and the erstwhile Windsor train station across the way. The surveillance footage, from a camera dis-guised as part of the mailbox, had been aimed to watch the rear door of the com-pany; the fact that the lens also caught the lot beyond had turned out simply to be Joe's good fortune.

But lively viewing it was not. Shot by shot, the same picture twitched onto the screen, sometimes with a car or person in its frame, sometimes with nothing for long stretches at a time. It was a mixed blessing that the owners of the camera had programmed it to shoot every few seconds only, and not continually. On one hand, it speeded up the overall span of time Joe had to review; on the other, the rhythm of watching an endless slide show was becoming almost twice as grating.

He was therefore delighted by his phone going off — one electronic device distracting him from another, like quarrelsome children. He placed it on his lap, hit the speaker function, and kept his eye on the footage before him.

"Gunther."

"Joe?" Sam said. "You sound funny."

"Just watching surveillance footage, hoping to catch Alex in the act. . . . Any act."

"Where are you?"

"Windsor. Too boring to go into. I'll tell you later, unless I get lucky, which I'm seriously beginning to doubt. What's up?"

"You haven't heard the news about Marotti, then? It was in the paper."

"Missed it this morning. What happened?"

"He's been accused of sexual shenanigans with a teacher at the school."

Joe glanced at the phone's screen, as if his show of surprise would somehow register there. "Is it credible?"

"Nowadays?" Sam replied. "Who cares? The accusation alone is enough to mess him up."

Joe took her point. "Do *we* care?" he asked. "Does it touch on anything we're digging into?"

"Not that we know of, but it's barely warming up, and the coincidence is too good to ignore. I'm here with Lester, by the way, and Willy's on the other line."

"Good," Joe said. "What've you got?"

"Ask the two of them," Willy said. "I'm still beating the bushes in BF, getting nowhere fast."

They'd all been in that spot, as Joe was feeling now. "Okay," he said, encouraging Sam to keep going.

"You read in our report that Les and I grabbed this kid Michael Purcell late last night, didn't you?"

"That, I did get," Joe confirmed. "Did you flip him like you were hoping?"

"Once we convinced him Daddy dearest and his school buddies would never know he squealed," Lester said.

"The bottom line," Sam told him, "is that we got him to open up about James Dunning without planting the name in his head. He came up with it first."

"How'd you do that?" Joe asked.

"The staged rugby game," Lester said. "We started there, since we weren't even sure it took place. Turns out it did, but Purcell was totally confused about why. Dunning's role in it and afterward followed naturally."

404

"What *was* that all about?" Joe asked, still watching empty pictures flipping by.

"Like we thought," Sam explained. "Or suspected. Dunning set it up, got everyone excited about a pickup game at night on a frozen field. There was some wagering involved as well, to up the ante."

"Along with the requisite booze," Lester interjected.

"But when they finally got out there," Sam continued, "Purcell said Dunning turned into a kamikaze, literally throwing himself under their feet and getting torn up. Apparently, they tried to stop it, because of what he was doing, so he picked a fight with one of them, and let the kid punch him in the face, without protecting himself. That's when they quit and walked away. None of it made sense."

"Purcell said the most confusing thing was that Dunning started laughing, bleeding from the nose, and thanked them all as they left."

"From that point on, we couldn't get him to stop talking about Dunning," Sam said.

"And from throwing him under the bus," Lester added. "He said Dunning's drug dealing makes his own look like an amateur's. Of course, he went on and on about how little he did of that anyhow — how this was only his second time scoring, and blah, blah, blah. Not that we cared, since we weren't busting him anyway."

"More to the point," Joe asked, "did he say where Dunning bought his supply?"

"Yes," Sam said, her pleasure clear over the phone. "Bellows Falls. Purcell didn't have any names, since Dunning doesn't share his sources — no surprise — but apparently he did let that much slip once. Lucky for us, boys can't resist bragging."

"Did he cough up any students' names?" Joe asked. "People we can lean on later for corroboration?"

"Yup," Lester said.

"One other point," Sam added. "We asked if Dunning had any injuries before the rugby game, and Purcell said he had a bad cut on his right hand, and that he tore the bandage off it partway through the game."

Joe congratulated them. "Nice work. Willy, you going to be able to line up witnesses to young Dunning buying dope in BF?"

"Should be," Willy said. "Soon as someone sends me a picture of him —"

"Hang on," Joe interrupted him, his eyes glued to the monitor. "I'm just getting footage of somebody doing a smash and grab on a high-end car in Windsor's Amtrak parking lot, about a week ago. Any of you near a computer? I need a plate number run."

"We are," Lester said.

Joe froze the best image he had and manipulated the close-up feature. The car's registration was slightly blurry, but easy enough for him to repeat over the phone.

It took Lester under a minute to respond. "You're kidding."

"What?" Willy asked.

"It comes back to Willard Dunning," Lester said. "Tell me *that's* a complete coincidence."

Joe's eyes were fixed on the screen. "And try convincing *me*," he said, "that the guy breaking its window — disguised or not — isn't the late, lamented Alex Hale."

Chapter 24

Rachel stepped through the fire escape door Sally was holding open and gazed around like a kid trespassing in a grown-up's room. Maintenance lights created pale pools along the dark, long row of offices and desks that stretched to the far end of Thorndike's administration building.

"This is where you work?" she asked, feeling foolish as the words left her mouth.

But Sally only smiled as she played along. "That's me — Sally Secretary. Little do they suspect my secret powers."

Rachel was taking in the suite's carefully fabricated corporate appearance, from the beige colors to the hardwood veneer and brass lamps to the thick Oriental rugs here and there, laid over wall-to-wall carpeting.

"God," she finally declared. "It looks like the world's most expensive bowl of oatmeal."

Sally laughed. "I guess it does. Making

me a raisin, I guess?"

Rachel joined her before asking, not for the first time, "Are we okay here? I mean, kidding aside, I don't want to get you fired."

"No risk of that. The head of school actually knows what I am, and people here work late now and then anyhow. If anyone asks, you're just a friend who dropped by."

Rachel considered pursuing the comment about the head of school. Sally had never detailed her reasons for being here. But she knew better than to ask. Rachel was pleased and flattered by Sally's inclusion and generosity. She wasn't about to press her luck by possibly crossing an unmarked line.

Compounding that sensitivity was Rachel's realization that for the first time since her early college years, she was on the edge of what she hoped would become a genuine friendship.

But one step at a time, she counseled herself, and watch how you go. With someone of Sally's apparent predisposition, respect in regard to familiarity was key. Rachel knew she shouldn't rush things if she wanted her fondness to be reciprocated.

All this ran through her mind as she followed Sally's lead into an adjacent storage room, the back wall of which was blocked by a heavy fireproof door.

"The vault," her guide announced, pulling out a set of keys and working the lock.

Rachel stood before its yawning mouth for a moment, almost poised for something wondrous. But, other than complete darkness and the odor of stale air, there was nothing to perceive.

Sally hit the lights, turning the mystery into a bland dead-end room full of shelves stacked with plastic bins and file boxes.

"There's a mood killer," Sally commented. "Boring, huh?"

Rachel had to admit she'd reached the same conclusion. "I guess. You said you'd seen what I'm after?"

Sally once more led the way, pivoting left near the back to face a shelf about chest-high. "Here."

It was a semitransparent Rubbermaid box filled with documents. As Rachel reached for it, she glanced at Sally and asked, "Is this going to help your assignment here, too? If that isn't prying?"

Sally's response, to Rachel's relief, was immediate. "I'm hoping it can only help. I'm not exactly sure what I am looking for. With luck, this can only be a win-win. It helps you, and it sure can't hurt me."

Rachel smiled with pleasure. "Cool."

They moved the box to a table pushed up

against the end wall and began sorting through its contents.

Despite the brusque image he put forth, Willy Kunkle could be a patient man. As a combat sniper, he'd been known to stay in position — unmoving, silent, and invisible — for hours. Similarly, as now, he could work a detail, like prowling the streets of Bellows Falls, quietly trying to identify the right people to interview, for days without encouragement.

It had much to do with self-awareness, he believed. Biased as he was against other people's learning curves, obdurateness, or rank stupidity, he distrusted his own predisposition to dismiss people prematurely. It riled him to ever appear predictable — a sniper's crucial error. So a show of composure — interpretable as calmness, stoicism, or even understanding — he saw as valuable. It confused those who thought they knew him.

Along these lines, he often avoided the eager snitches police sometimes passed among themselves. They had their place for facts often just barely out of sight, but they could be seduced by their proximity to cops to invent things they thought might be appetizing — not to mention profitable.

411

Willy preferred sources of a less likely nature — observant people working out in the open, or within proximity of windows or lots of conversation. They could be barbers or waitresses or trash collectors or meter maids, all often rendered near invisible by the nature of their jobs. These folks were often flattered and therefore more helpful when someone like him approached to ask a question, especially when he played up the presence of his disabled left arm, which he often did for the sympathy it aroused.

He didn't do this every time he needed a witness, of course. He, too, had his regular informants, and there was the wider network of people who might be willing for one reason or another to dole out information, all of whom were useful often enough to move a case forward.

But therein lay an important difference between Willy and many of his colleagues. Going back to his patience, his perseverance, his attention to detail and need to complete each mission, the hunter in him insisted that upon meeting disappointment, the reasonable next move was not to give up, but to search out an alternate approach.

And so it had been with his assignment in Bellows Falls. In his heart, he knew the key to Lyall's death was within reach. The person who had hidden it, whether willfully or unwittingly, had simply been lucky so far. Of that, Willy was convinced. The trick was to become as lucky in turn, if helped by just a bit of tenacity.

The source of his interest at the moment was the driver of a water-delivery truck, whom he'd seen several times trundling around town, exchanging large pale blue plastic jugs of water for their empty equivalents at various banks, libraries, lawyers' offices, and other businesses where people had come to expect or demand something other than what came out of a tap.

To Willy, who'd been reduced in combat to drinking from puddles and fetid pools, the desire for bottled water was an indulgence he didn't share. But the man delivering it here had struck him as perhaps just his type of guy. Affable, friendly, chatty, and constantly calling people by name — including those he passed while rolling his handcart across the sidewalk — the water truck driver was obviously plugged into who was who in town, and had a memory for faces and names.

Willy chose his moment carefully, waiting until the man had racked his cart to the back of the truck, swung up into the cab behind the wheel, and was consulting his deliveries sheet. Only then did Willy open the passenger door and join him, slamming the door behind him.

"Whoa, mister," said the startled man, almost dropping his clipboard. "You can't be in here."

Willy showed him his badge. "Willy Kunkle. VBI. Didn't mean to frighten you. Sorry," he said, smiling apologetically.

The driver was nonplussed. "Okay," he said carefully. "What do the police want with me?"

Willy's approach was charm personified. "Just your help. What's your name?"

"Phil Ryder."

"I noticed, Phil," Willy went on, "that you're supergood with people, and that you pay attention to what's going on around you."

"I get along with most folks," Ryder agreed. "Never saw the point in doin' otherwise."

"That's what I figured," Willy said. "What I'm hoping is that in your driving around town, maybe you noticed somebody I want to talk with."

"This for the murder everybody's talking about?" Phil asked.

"It's more like one of those 'guy who

414

knows a guy' things," Willy said cheerfully, ignoring the bait. "I'm thinking the man I'm after saw something I'm interested in. Sounds a little crazy, I know, but I'm sort of desperate by now."

The pleading undertone in Willy's voice did the trick. Phil's expression softened. "Sure, I'll help if I can," he said.

Willy produced a photo of James Dunning, captured from the school's Facebook. "Cool. It's this squared-away-looking young man."

Ryder studied the picture, giving Willy a moment's hope, before he shook his head mournfully and said, "Nah. Can't say I've seen anybody looking like that. He's like a wannabe lawyer or politician."

He returned the photo and gazed out the windshield, watching the people circulating before them. His tone was philosophical. "It is funny, though, you showing up out of the blue like this. They say coincidence is like that — a knock on the head that makes no sense. Doesn't make it any less surprising every time it happens, though, does it?"

Willy was looking at him, his smile still in place, but privately wondering what he'd picked out of the crowd. "Sure," he said vaguely, adding, only because his true nature demanded it of him, "What the hell you talking about?"

Phil laughed. "Right. That didn't make much sense. Sorry." He reached for the folded newspaper resting between them and held it up. "Today's headline. Some rich guy accused of carrying on with a woman. You read that?"

"Sure."

"Well, that's what I mean. I don't know her, never met her." He paused to open the paper and check the caption under the two pictures showing accused and accuser. "Wilva Sargent. Never even heard the name before, which you'd remember, since it's so unusual."

He replaced the paper and looked at his impromptu guest. "But then here you are all of a sudden, showing me a picture and asking if I ever saw a guy. It's kind of crazy. Not out-of-this-world crazy, of course," he added quickly, "but weird."

Willy resisted the urge to simply get out of the truck without a further word, and said instead, "I don't guess I'm following."

Phil patted the paper with his broad, meaty hand. "Wilva. Like I said, don't know her from the man in the moon, but I see her picture here, like you showed me your guy's just now, and boom, I knew I'd seen her, just like you wish I'd seen your fellow.

Freaky, huh?"

Willy rubbed his forehead quickly, putting together what he'd just been told. Maintaining his composure, he asked, "You saw Wilva? Around here?"

"That's what I'm saying. I wish it coulda been him" — he pointed at the picture in Willy's lap — "but instead, it was her. Random."

"That's okay," Willy said soothingly. "I want to talk to her, too, given all the publicity. Before it's all said and done, I may even be called on to look into it. Who knows? Where did you see her? I mean, what was she doing?"

Phil Ryder scratched his cheek thoughtfully. "That's part of it. It was a long time ago — months. Before the snow started flying. I don't know that she was doing anything in particular. She was just getting out of that crazy thing she drives. That's why I noticed her."

Willy couldn't resist smiling. "Describe it."

Ryder chuckled. "One of those old-timey buses. A Volkswagen, all painted up and everything. It was rusty and pretty beat-up, but it was like some UFO had beamed it down from the sixties, you know?"

"I sure do," Willy said.

■ ■ ■ ■

James Dunning was openly surprised to see his father standing in the dorm hallway. "Dad," he said, stepping back to let him in. "You never come here. Now I'm seeing you every other day."

Willard was in a good mood, rare for him, especially recently. He entered his son's room and looked around appraisingly, like an exterminator evaluating a job.

"You complaining?" he asked. "You aren't the first Dunning to live in one of these rat holes. Course back in the day, I thought I was pretty hot stuff, having a single to myself. You care that it looks like this?"

James was slightly offended. He prided himself on having taste, and thought that he'd actually done the room proud. The bed was unmade, however, so he hung his father's distaste on that.

"You happy with the headlines?" he asked, moving off the subject.

Willard settled onto a corner of James's desk. "I am. Marotti's going to have his hands full explaining that away."

"Billie going to stand up to the scrutiny?" James asked, using Wilva's nickname.

Willard eyed him closely. "You know

418

something I don't?"

James barely resisted rolling his eyes. "Dad, you know my low opinion of her. That's why you used me to lean on her instead of asking her yourself — no more Mr. Nice Guy."

"You gave her the money, didn't you?"

"Of course I did. That's not what I meant. And I think the money was a mistake, like I already said. It'll probably go straight up her nose, or wherever the hell she puts it, and it undermined my threatening to expose her to the school brass. But it's done. I was asking if she's got the backbone not to cave under the attention she's about to get."

Willard laughed dismissively. "You're talking like a city kid, James. This is Vermont. It ain't the big leagues. Billie'll have to do a few interviews, issue a couple of statements, but for the most part, she just has to hide behind the lawyer I got her and keep her mouth shut. That's why the money, son — to let her taste what playing ball with us will bring."

"Whether it's true or not?" James asked cynically.

He wasn't wrong. His like-minded father smiled as he replied, "We'll cross that bridge when we come to it."

CHAPTER 25

"You know, it probably sounds funny, given how I'm paid to poke my nose into people's business," Sally said, "but I almost never come here."

Rachel laughed, also sitting at the table dominating the library's local history room. "That's probably because you deal with real live people."

"It's a neat place, though," Sally continued. "I didn't remember it being so inviting. And I like that it has rooms like this, where you can get away from the chitchat and noise."

"You didn't use it when you were in high school?" Rachel asked. "In Burlington, we used to call the local library 'a home away from home.' Not that we actually did any work there. It was just a cool place to hang out with friends."

Sally didn't tell her that her father had sent her to Deerfield Academy, in Massachusetts, instead of to Brattleboro's high school. Along with the education she'd received there, she'd also learned how to interact with society's elite on an equal plane — no doubt part of Dan's grand plan. But it still wasn't something she tended to advertise. Her apparently plebeian upbringing trumped bragging about where she'd acquired so much of her book smarts and self-confidence.

"I didn't go to school here," she said briefly, then asked, "So who's this guy we're supposed to be meeting?"

"Topher Pluff," Rachel told her, taking the hint and moving on. She checked her watch. "Running late, I guess."

"That him?" Sally asked.

Rachel glanced up and saw Topher wending his way past the mezzanine stacks toward them, looking slightly addled, like an elderly man about to miss church, although he probably wasn't beyond his fifties.

As he opened the door and swept in, a broad smile creased his face. "Ms. Reiling. And you've brought a friend."

Rachel rose and opened her mouth to make introductions, but Sally cut her off by sticking her hand out and saying, "Hi — Sally," and no more. Rachel took the cue and turned her gesture into a wave of the hand toward a chair nearest the door.

"Have a seat, Topher, and thanks for agreeing to meet."

"Not at all," the librarian said, settling down and adjusting his half-glasses. "Still at work on Thorndike Academy?"

"Good memory," Rachel said, complimenting him. "I am, but focusing more on the Dunning family you mentioned — on how they transferred their land to the school. I'm wondering if that was more than just a straight-out real estate deal."

Topher raised his white eyebrows questioningly, prompting Rachel to add, "Something beyond cash for land. Less so now, I suppose, but I always thought people were inclined to add things of value to a deal, to bring it up to scratch."

He laughed. "Like slaves? Or livestock?"

Rachel tried to hide her frustration. She only felt she might be onto something here, but putting it into words was getting her nowhere.

Topher appeared sensitive to her plight, however, and got her off the hook. "Ah. People. You're right, of course. They'll do almost anything to get ahead. That's why they're my favorite topic. I like it all, of course — towns, businesses, eras, times of famine and plenty. I'd better, given my job. But people are my favorite."

He rose and crossed to where several closely packed, freestanding shelf units and a couple of computers had been placed, and began scanning the titles of the books before him.

"I can't answer you directly, Rachel," he said. "I just don't know. But let's begin from the outside in, with the town of Vernon, before burrowing toward the Dunnings themselves, just to keep everything organized. That work for you two?"

Sally weighed her options. This wasn't what she considered a hard lead — going along with Rachel's notion that Alex's latest pursuit of riches somehow lay in Thorndike's creation. On the other hand, they had found something in the school vault that had encouraged them to consult Topher Pluff. The school had indeed been built on Dunning land because of a transaction between Arvid Dunning and a consortium of out-of-staters.

But there had been a hitch of some kind.

The paperwork stored in Thorndike's vault had revealed the barest outlines of a breakdown in negotiations. Nothing fatal, obviously, but intriguing nevertheless to both Rachel and Sally, if for different reasons.

Rachel had been more excited than Sally by the find, which made sense. She'd been hoping to validate her ancient history theory, and here was a satisfying teaser. Sally, by contrast, was having a far tougher time connecting the dots between a minor hitch in an old business deal, her assignment to ferret out any lingering embarrassments at Thorndike, and her benefactor's being sucked into a sex scandal immediately after laying out his dream of a building project before the board.

Still, she kept telling herself as one hour stretched into two, What could be the harm?

And it was interesting, especially led by someone like Topher Pluff, whose delight in his trove of books, charts, maps, and census reports became infectious. The young women were soon paging through volumes on their own under his direction, homing in like bloodhounds on the events that had led up to, and resulted from, the transaction and players under scrutiny.

They all paused upon the discovery of a single loose photograph, however, that Topher extracted from the leaves of a timeworn album showing purported SCENES OF OLD VERNON.

"Huh," he said, placing it on the broad table, which by now had been covered with artifacts of their labor. "This might be useful."

The three of them studied the photo. It showed an older version of what was now called Dunning Cottage, with a long-gone porch, populated by a disparate collection of people posing for the camera. Helpfully, someone had carefully inked in names above the subjects.

"Meet Arvid Dunning," Topher said, tapping his finger on a man at the far end of the porch, "who, we know from the census, was better known as Butch."

Sally leaned forward to get a closer look, commenting, "Not a nickname you'd associate nowadays with the likes of Willard and James. And here's Peter, Willard's dad, as a newborn; I guess Marge is his mother, not that she looks too motherly holding him. And too old, maybe. Butch sure doesn't present like any Dunning does now, does he? What you can see of him under the ratty beard."

"Pretty rough," Topher agreed. "Reflective of the times, I'd say. Even the building shows it. See the peeling paint behind them, the rotting clapboards here, and the shutters half in pieces?"

"Does look better now," Sally said.

"So who're these?" Rachel asked, drawing a circle with her fingertip around a cluster of four, sitting close together on the uneven porch steps, below the others.

Only one of them, a wan and tired-looking teenage girl, her gaze off to the side, had a label above her, which read cherie. The rest of this small subgroup — a couple and one other, younger girl — were anonymous.

From their lost expressions, in more ways than one.

Topher was consulting another document as Sally turned the photo over to see if anything was written on its back, which turned out to be blank. For all her support of Rachel, not to mention the intellectual benefits of this line of inquiry, she was beginning to question its worth.

"According to the census," Topher said, interpreting what he'd read, "I had it wrong — Marge was a so-called domestic. And you were right — she's listed as being sixty-three. Evelyn is Butch's — or Arvid's — wife."

"She's not in the picture," Sally said, looking at the front again.

"There?" Rachel asked, pointing to the window farthest from Butch.

The three of them peered carefully as

Sally held the image up to the room's overhead lighting. There was a barely discernible paleness, framed by one of the panes, the size and shape of a human face.

"Could be," Topher said uncertainly. "I guess she was camera-shy. Of all those who appear in the census, only Evelyn is missing from the porch. And the couple with the two girls don't appear at all."

"They could be anybody," Rachel commented, "Even neighbors who were visiting when the photographer dropped by. It does remind you of one of those WPA shots, like Dorothea Lange was taking out west, during the Depression."

The reference triggered a thought in Topher's memory. "Hang on," he said, stepping back between two shelf units before returning with a leather-bound book. "Maybe this'll tell us."

"What is it?" Rachel asked.

"What I call a reminiscence," he explained, opening it and scanning its contents. "They were common a long time ago, mostly written by women. A sort of free-form regional narrative about people, places, and events — what someone might write to a friend in a letter, but longer, and spanning a greater time period. They weren't strictly histories, and they weren't really organized. They tended to read almost like diaries, but of an area, rather than a person or single family. This" — he hefted the book — "was done by Virginia Oliphant about Vernon, which is why we have it. I think it's an only copy. That's another thing that would happen: Some relative or another would transcribe a collection of family letters and/or journal entries to make something thematic."

He paused for a few minutes, reading and flipping through pages, looking for something he'd obviously stored far in the back of his mind.

"Here," he said finally. "Unbelievable. I can't imagine how I remembered this. There's a mention of the Dunnings. The Oliphants lived some three miles away, but you never know when or why someone will appear in something like this." He chuckled, adding, "Of course, it's often for some scandal."

He cleared his throat and read, " 'More happenings at Westview Acres again. The Dunnings are certainly a spirited lot, and never at a loss for supplying the rest of us with things to talk about.

" 'Of course, Butch is the true troublemaker there. No one around here can fathom how Evelyn makes do. But she does, showing up at church every Sunday, regardless of weather or circumstance, her jaw firm and her gaze steady. She, more than any woman I know, embodies the strength and determination that will see this nation through its hard times and travails.

" 'She will need all of that and more, rumor has it, if she's to steer her family ship safely by the shoals while her husband, the purported admiral of the fleet, stands before her, blocking her view, doing his best to talk his way past his own misdeeds and the fruits they have generated.' "

"Wow," Rachel said when Topher stopped. "That's some purple prose."

The librarian laughed. "Bit of a throwback, even then. And talk about mixed metaphors. But Ginny Oliphant was nothing if not a closet Jane Austen or something. She'd attended school in Boston before she moved up here and married, and was well known for flaunting her literary flair. I've interviewed a couple of her descendants — she died in the sixties — and the picture I got was that she might have been almost as obnoxious in her own way as she paints Butch Dunning. I was told they were the proverbial cat and dog, constantly mixing it up within Vernon's all-too-small community."

"But what's she saying?" Sally asked, her interest revived. "She seems to be dancing around something."

"Well, of course," Topher agreed. "Even for someone of Ginny's self-proclaimed sophistication — or maybe because of it — she wasn't about to lay it out on paper. More than libel, people in the thirties still clung to what was proper. Not only that but she wasn't writing for *The New York Times*." He displayed the book again. "These things were intended first and foremost for locals. Sometimes family only. Their audiences were more interested in having their memories revived by passages like this — or amused or titillated — than being informed by them. And if a reader or listener couldn't make sense of it — like us right now — there was someone within earshot to explain what wasn't being written down."

"Okay," Sally agreed. "I'll bite. You're the closest we're gonna get to an inside source. What's the writer not quite telling us?"

Topher put the book down, his eyes bright. "That's the fun part: interpreting the language and its nuances, and then superimposing it over whatever time frame and facts we have available. It's like building a house, beginning with the beams and working out to the finished walls."

430

"What time frame?" Rachel asked.

He laughed with satisfaction. "We'll get to that. First, to the possible meanings behind Ginny's snarky comments, which bear mostly on Butch's unmentioned behavior."

"The 'admiral of the fleet,' " Sally echoed.

Topher held up his finger in protest. "Not actually. The emphasis is on the word 'purported.' My interpretation is that Ginny was talking less about his bluster and more about those so-called fruits he generated."

Both women stared at him before Rachel quietly suggested, "Cherie?"

"That's what I'm thinking," Topher concurred. "At least in terms of where the fruit came from."

Sally shook her head, picking up the photograph again and studying it, especially the young woman of interest, whose aura of pathos seemed ironically in contrast to the small heart-shaped pendant hanging from her neck. "Old Butch — you dirty dog."

Rachel peered over her shoulder. "So, based on not much more than pure conjecture, we're saying Butch had sex with Cherie and begat Peter?"

"The person who became Peter," Topher said, correcting her. "I would suggest — and I agree with you about how provable any of it is — that Cherie's baby was simply added to the Dunning family tree, and ascribed to Evelyn, who never said otherwise. Birth certificates weren't what they are now, home births were common, especially at some social strata, and a little technical fudging and swallowing of pride was far preferable to the scandal attending an out-of-wedlock birth."

"And look at her," Sally added. "She's maybe fifteen."

Topher shrugged. "Less of an obstacle in those days, but you're right. It wouldn't have helped."

"I wonder what became of them," Rachel said wistfully.

"Shipped off, I wouldn't doubt," Topher suggested. "My guess is that if you had the resources and the interest, you might be able to find a record of this family entering Canada at about this time."

"To remove the social blight?" Sally asked him.

"Yes, although everyone local knew about that, as Ginny's book makes clear. But," Topher continued thoughtfully, "I think it runs more to money than reputation. You told me the land sale to the school founders hit a temporary stumbling block." He pointed at the photo. "What I'm saying is that if Butch sold them on Peter's being Evelyn's child, and then got rid of Cherie's family, that would probably have been enough laundry cleaning to allow the deal to go through. That's what I meant earlier by our time frame, the evidence for which is right there: the family photo, showing Cherie, baby Peter, and a humiliated Evelyn Dunning at the window; the census, which is date-stamped — presumably after the photo was taken — showing Marge as the only non-relative living at the farm; and, finally, the pot of gold at the end — the sale, again date-stamped, right after the census — making it all a neat and tidy package."

"In our fantasies," Sally said pragmatically. "We don't have anything to back it up."

Rachel gave her a pensive look. "We might have something. Not big, but a start." She shifted her attention to Topher. "Am I remembering right? When I went through the *Reformer*'s old files, I thought I saw some of those neighborly notices, where so-and-so says that her great-aunt Alice is up visiting from Boston, or something."

Pluff didn't need any more prompting. He was moving toward one of the computer terminals before she'd finished speaking, saying, "That would be just the right thing to do. Put one of those in the paper to let everyone know you'd cleaned up your mess."

He sat before the screen and summoned back files of the paper from the 1930s and began narrowing his search. Considering his background and experience, it was a matter of mere minutes before he sat back and indicated the shot before him.

"There you go."

Sally and Rachel approached to read the notice: "The Aucoins pulled up stakes last week to return to Canada, thanking their hosts, the Dunning family of Westview Acres, for their support and help during challenging times. Dear friends must occasionally ride the waves of change in order to make ends meet, and parting is such sweet sorrow. Best of futures to all four of the Aucoins, and thank you for your company."

Topher snorted. "I bet that last line was a hit with Evelyn."

"God, what a legacy," Rachel said.

"If any of it's true," Sally stressed, back in her familiar territory of human depravity. "We like what we put together. All the pieces fit. But it's like a shape-changing riddle, where there's more than one possible meaning. If someone walked in right now and suggested a few credible alternatives, we might be forced to reconsider all this. And where does Alex fit in?"

"She's right," Topher said. "It is a lot of conjecture."

"Can we do anything to narrow it down?" Rachel asked.

"The irony," Sally answered her, "is that even if we hooked Willard up to a lie detector, chances are good he wouldn't know where his father came from. Could be even Peter himself didn't know." She indicated the photograph again. "Look at them. Arvid, Marge, Evelyn. They're all dead. And if Cherie's not, too, then she's long gone. I'll almost guarantee you that. If you wanted to pull something off like we're thinking they did, you'd make sure the people who know about it are few and sworn to secrecy."

"And that eventually they take it to the grave," Topher added.

Rachel backed away, feeling hamstrung, and began pacing the room. "Damn it. Okay. So maybe we are right, and maybe it doesn't matter. But for whatever it's worth, it's the one piece of evidence we have, and maybe it got Alex Hale killed. There's got to be something about this we're missing."

Sally laid a hand on her shoulder, back on track. She looked her friend in the eye and said, "Welcome to how these things work.

435

Could be we just found where to start digging."

CHAPTER 26

Lester and Sam chose their timing carefully. A court-ordered search, in the best of circumstances, should happen after daybreak, in good weather, during a weekday — in case someone official needs to be reached by phone — and without the lawful occupant in residence. It is handy, however, to know where that person is, in case he or she ends up qualifying for a pair of handcuffs.

In this situation, the location was James Dunning's dorm room, and for thoroughness, competence, and company, they'd invited the state's crime-scene search team to join them. As for Dunning, they had a couple of extra agents keeping him in sight as he followed his usual routine on campus, starting with classes, then moving on to lunch and afternoon sports.

The search process takes hours, if done properly. It is slow, meticulous, preplanned, obsessively documented, and punctuated by endless pauses in order to cross-communicate. Everybody knows what everybody else is doing. There's even a prosecutor available by phone throughout.

This is what television shows love to portray, because of the white Tyvek suits worn by the techs, but what they always gloss over because of the time requirements, even of searching a single room.

Nevertheless, it has its rewards, as it was having here, starting with James's drug stash.

"Wow," said the search team's leader, a no-nonsense woman rarely given to being impressed. Tellingly, her smile was sardonic. She pointed to the ventilator grille mounted near the ceiling. "Think that's a clue?"

Even from the middle of the room, everyone could see the faint smudge of fingerprints surrounding the grille's two screws, presumably left there over multiple visits.

Photos were taken and the precise location recorded before the grille was carefully removed, revealing a thick wad of small waxy bags, bundled together and bearing the Pinocchio stamp Lyall Johnson favored for his product.

"Ah," Lester commented, "to think how

much time I wasted in school drinking coffee."

Sammie pulled out her smartphone to compare this with what she'd photographed in Lyall's apartment. "They obviously need to be analyzed, but they sure look the same," she said.

"So," Lester mused, "either Lyall lied to Brandon about not having any dope around or this batch predates the murder."

"Or explains why Lyall was short of product," Sammie suggested. "Could be he sold all this to James a couple of days before."

"I hit a gold mine here," another of the techs announced from near the one bed.

He'd pulled back the covers to reveal sheets stained with both blood and what appeared to be seminal fluid.

"We are gonna keep the chem people busy," Lester said.

And so it continued. They eventually discovered how James himself had collected evidence of his drug sales to other students for blackmail purposes later, video-recorded his trysts with coeds for sale on the internet, and, it seemed, enriched himself by simply stealing everything from wallets to laptops, watches to jewelry. He'd taken the adage that a man's home is his castle to mean that it was therefore safe to store everything incriminating about oneself within its walls — as long as you locked the door.

"Christ," one team member finally said, "you close this guy down, the on-campus crime rate should drop to zero."

This was looking to be prescient. Six hours into the search, there was no longer any question about having probable cause to arrest young Mr. Dunning.

The prize reward for the two VBI investigators, however, was none of those flashier trophies. During the careful and progressive disassembling of the room, an old-fashioned black-and-white notebook was located in the desk's one drawer, and put aside. Sam, however, recalling Willy's on-going Bellows Falls research, was drawn to examine it before it either got bagged or simply forgotten.

"What d'you have?" Lester asked, seeing her leafing through it with gloved hands.

"The proverbial smoking gun," she replied. "We'll need it corroborated, probably by his daughter, but I think it's Homer Nelson's missing notebook, the one he kept by the window."

"The neighborhood watcher," Lester said, remembering his name.

Sammie turned to the day that she and Joe had stood in Lyall's apartment, wondering who might have killed him, and read the entries there. Grunting softly, she showed the page to Lester.

"It's cryptic, but I'm betting this is James."

Les looked over her shoulder, quoting, " 'Lyall prowling, like always. Tailed by boy, tr'ng not to be seen. Dirty doings.' "

Sam looked up at him. "What do you want to bet Dunning saw the old man looking out, complete with field glasses?"

As if in confirmation, one of their Tyvek-dressed colleagues stepped out of the room's closet, holding a black balaclava with red stitching.

"This guy do any bank robberies?" he asked them.

"We're thinking a lot worse than that," Sam told him.

"He say anything?" Joe asked.

Sam shook her head. "We grabbed him fresh off the cross-country course and he lawyered up as if on autopilot."

Joe draped his coat across the back of his office chair before sitting down, saying wearily, "Unbelievable. And you're feeling solid about this? You know we'll be facing a legal team six people deep out of Boston within hours."

"Never felt better," Sam assured him, feeling pleased. "The cocky bastard basically handed us everything we needed. It was just lying around."

"You want a for-instance?" Willy asked rhetorically. "The two drivers I interviewed said their so-called Spider-Man never took his gloves off when he helped them inside with Nelson, implying that he still had 'em on when he killed the old man and stole the book. But when we collected it, the book was covered with his prints — the dumb bastard obviously couldn't have cared less after he got back to his dorm room. Same with securing his ski mask, hiding his dope, or any of the other garbage we're using against him. Arrogant prick."

Willy suddenly straightened in his chair as Joe was about to speak and added, "And you remember Shelly Ayotte? The sole witness to Lyall meeting the mystery woman with the VW minibus? I found her."

"How?"

Willy waved that off. "Doesn't matter. Point is, I traced her to an aunt living outside Buffalo, and risked phoning her instead of trying to get out there. I got lucky. She was a regular chatterbox. Barely had to prompt her before she told me some

young rich punk had paid her five thousand
bucks to give us that story and then disappear, promising her another five if she
stayed where she was for six months. All I
had to do was tell her we'd just ruined her
deal by busting him, and she spilled. Her
description fits James to a tee, and she said
she'd tell a judge the same thing, if we made
it worth her while, which I let her believe
we would, without actually saying it."

That made Lester laugh and comment,
"Good old Willy."

"But what was the point?" Sam asked
from her desk, the perpetual detail person.
"Why go to the trouble of pointing us at the
van and the woman when it was guaranteed
to end up as a dead end? If you hadn't
found the water truck driver, we never
would've connected Wilva Sargent to the
VW, and even then, that's where it stops:
There's nothing connecting her to Lyall's
death."

"He's a kid," Lester said. "He thinks like
a kid."

Willy conceded Lester's point, happy to
acknowledge the careless hubris of youth,
but he agreed with Sam's need for a better
explanation. There was something behind
James's rashness, impulsive as it seemed,
that ran to a deeper truth.

443

Joe appeared to share that view. "Let's step back," he recommended. "We're finally getting places here, but we're a long way from filling in the details: Who killed Alex Hale? And why? With James surrounded by legal wolfhounds, we're left to doing the spadework on our own, and I doubt it's going to be easy."

"Maybe another 'why' question should be, Why did James kill Lyall?" Lester mused. "He was on top of the world before then. A senior, wealthy, big man on campus, getting laid and building a little black book for later contacts and/or blackmail deals. He seems to've been the perfect heartless carnivore. Why mess it up by knifing a loser dirtbag druggie?"

"Hey," Willy protested. "I'll take ten Lyalls over a James Dunning any day."

"Granted," Joe agreed, "but the point's a good one. What did happen between those two? We know James was hiding in Lyall's apartment — maybe to spy only — and that he then grabbed a weapon of opportunity, implying the attack was unplanned." He paused to look at Sam. "Did the lab get back to you on matching James's Pinocchios to Lyall's empty Baggies?"

"They did and they do," she said.

"So," Joe resumed, "does that mean James

ripped him off after killing him, or that he bought that supply from Lyall earlier and killed him for something he overheard while in the closet?"

"The second makes more sense," Lester suggested. "Otherwise, why would Brandon go out to buy dope if he thought they had some at home?"

"And how and why does Wilva fit into it?" Willy asked, not wanting to let his own small mystery slip from view.

Joe looked at him. "That's good, too. 'Cause let's not forget: She's also the one pointing the finger at Jonathan Marotti. That's not a coincidence I want to let slide."

"Another coincidence," Willy continued, "is that — with all due respect to the village — someone with her habits probably wasn't visiting BF for the sights. That would make drugs a crossover to why James was there, and what Lyall did for a living. Lyall may be dead now, but I think we ought to ask Brandon Leggatt if he ever saw Wilva come by to score product. He's been released, hasn't he?"

"Yes," Lester said after a moment's consultation with his computer.

Joe nodded. "Good. Do that."

"What about fitting James with Alex's murder?" Sam asked. "Can we do that?"

Joe looked thoughtful, locking his hands behind his neck. "Willard owned the car Alex broke into, and from what I could see, Alex then followed his MO and stole the garage door opener and registration, so he could enter Willard's house."

"How 'bout if James had borrowed the car that night, and what you saw Alex steal was something belonging to him? Are you sure it was the opener?"

"No. It was small, but it could have been anything."

"It makes for a nice story," Willy stated. "If we can make it work somehow, then James is dirty for everything."

"Let's not get overly attached to that," Joe cautioned them. "There are too many unanswered questions. Too many loose ends. If we shove all our problems onto one suspect without due diligence, we'll deserve whatever his legal team throws at us. Let's concentrate on the oddities: What motivated James? What does Brandon know that we haven't asked? Why's Wilva in the mix? Why didn't Willard report the vandalism to his car, was there a break-in at his home, and how in God's name does the school fit into everything?"

Sally Kravitz was also wondering about

Wilva Sargent, and sitting at that moment in Marotti's expensively appointed living room, surrounded by custom-made hardwood furniture, oversize lamps, and buttersoft leather-upholstered seating. Suitably theatrical, a large blaze was crackling in an enormous fireplace.

"Did you know her?" she asked.

Marotti was walking back and forth before her, a human metronome regularly cutting across her view of the flames. "I met her," he replied. "I didn't know her. I don't even remember the circumstances, except that it must have been at an official function — a meet and greet, or one of those artist-in-residence affairs they hold at Dunning Cottage."

"How do you know you met her, then?"

"It was the phenomenon more than the woman. She was pretty flamboyant, especially given the setting. Thorndike isn't given to displays of that kind."

"Makes her sound like a stripper invited to an old folks' home," Sally said.

Despite his serious mood, Marotti laughed. "I suppose it does. I guess I'm a little angry about all this. Let's just say she was a peacock among the chickens, if that's not biologically incorrect."

"I get the idea," Sally said. "Did she say

anything to you at the time?"

Marotti stopped in mid-stride and looked at her. "Hello?" he suggested. "Seriously, it was that kind of situation. I remember seeing her because of the clothes and hair and the manner, which were all sort of a throwback to Greenwich Village — and I know someone pointed her out to me as a result — but I'm not sure we even shook hands."

"All right," Sally said, moving on. "Then it's a tactical move. Something to embarrass you, or throw you off the rails. The drums are certainly beginning to beat."

"The building project?" he asked. "I'm not so naïve as to think that everyone loves the idea, but a sexual harassment charge? Whatever happened to a simple thumbs-down?"

Sally spared him her hard-earned knowledge of how issues of the sort had been losing their gentler, more civilized character for years. Instead, she said, "People want to change your mind or get a clarification, they debate you; they want to stop you dead in your tracks, they blow your wheels off. Unless we disprove this allegation, do you really think you'll be allowed to concentrate full-time on a fifteen-million-dollar project — in this political climate?"

"I see your point," he said.

"Let's start with the obvious," she suggested. "When you made your pitch to the board, who dug in their heels the most?"

"At the time?" he replied. "No one. But I'd be an idiot not to suspect Willard Dunning is somehow involved in this."

"Why?"

"The cottage, for starters. To integrate seamlessly with the rest of the campus architecture, my project requires its demolition. That's his family home, the only structure left from when the school was created."

"He's that sentimental?"

Marotti finally settled into an armchair next to hers, crossing his legs and staring at the rug before him. "Good point," he said. "I don't think so. I've seen him play hardball in the past, in labor disputes and contract negotiations. He's ruthless when he's inspired — driven to win. We had a lawsuit pending once from a family whose child was injured on campus, and Willard made a motion to hire someone of your profession to get dirt on them and force them to back down — essentially a blackmail scheme."

Sally let slide the presumption that someone of her profession would always be open to being party to extortion. She was used to those kinds of comments.

"And what about his views on the fate of the old cottage? Has he been historically hyperprotective of it?"

Marotti had to think about that. "The subject of destroying it had never come up before. Most of the time, we discussed how to use it." He paused, scratching his cheek, before saying, "No. That's incorrect. There was a proposal years ago about turning it into a dorm. He was dead set against that."

"Why? It's a guesthouse now."

"It was a gradual thing," Marotti recalled. "He seemed receptive at first, but you know how such proposals expand in scope. Once the need for engineering studies were mentioned, Willard came down hard. He said it was one thing to put in a bathroom or two, or add a fire escape, but he was dead set against shifting the foundation or doing anything of that magnitude."

Sally frowned. "Shifting the foundation? Is that what you were looking to do?"

"Not at all," Marotti stressed. "It was a gross overstatement. We would have had to ensure the building's different code compliance were we to put students in it, but nothing was supposed to change from the outside. The whole point was to preserve the place's charm. Such as it is."

"You're not in love with it?"

"Ah," he said dismissively. "It's not a gem architecturally. It's an old clapboard building. We've made it pretty enough, with a nice roof and paint scheme, but let's face it, it wasn't going to last forever. But it goes to show how worked up Willard can get." Marotti hesitated before admitting, "I also think he doesn't like me personally."

"Why?"

"It's too petty to mention, and may be just my thin skin."

Sally thought that being thin-skinned was one attribute she'd never heard lodged against her patron.

She twisted in her chair to better make her point. "Jonathan, I hope you understand the seriousness of what you're facing. People get fired in these she said–he said situations, sometimes without any proof on the table. This could get you in very hot water, and cost you a fortune in the process, not to mention your building donation, along with your good name. It's no time to be gentlemanly about the man you think may be pulling the strings here."

"But that's just it," he countered. "We have no clue who's doing what. This young woman may be acting on her own for reasons we know nothing about. She could just be crazy. Willard's feelings about me might have nothing to do with it."

"And what are those feelings?" she pressed him.

He blew out a sigh through pursed lips before explaining. "He was unlucky in 2008, lost a bundle on the market, along with so many other speculators. I didn't. I played it safe, even saw it coming, and stepped out before the floor fell through. That's when I started noticing what I interpret to be resentment or envy or anger of some sort. I also think my Italian heritage rubs him the wrong way." He stood up and resumed his pacing, adding, "It's just too stupid to talk about, and I have nothing to base it on."

He stopped to stare at her, almost pleadingly. "Haven't we discussed this enough? I'm afraid I'm wearing out."

Sally rose as well and headed toward the library's door. "It's been very helpful to me. I'll be getting back to you soon. You're one of the few people I've met with integrity, Jonathan. Please don't let this wear you down."

He smiled ruefully. "I'll do my best."

CHAPTER 27

Joe slowed his car to get a feel for the neighborhood. He was on a back road in Vernon, not far from Thorndike. The snow was rounded, dazzling, and postcard pretty in the morning sun, like a Christmastime display placed in the middle of dollops of meringue-smooth icing.

The houses weren't arranged as in a traditional suburban setting. The yards were larger here, where the population was sparser and land prices cheaper than south of the border. So, rather than a cheek-by-jowl arrangement, the properties were situated farther apart from one another — within sight, but not so close that you could peer through anyone's windows and see what was going on.

Joe stopped at the bottom of Willard Dunning's driveway, getting a feel for the sight lines, before continuing next door, to a split-level log structure at once vast and self-effacing.

This was not a part of town for the meek of income.

The drive was paved, gracefully curved, and had been cleared by a snowblower, as opposed to a plow truck — as Dunning's had been — rendering its edges sharp and chiseled, as if cut with a blade. The ethos of snow removal in rural areas like Vermont was pretty much restricted to those two options and a shovel, although the latter routinely came into play at some point regardless. But as in all such choices, debate dogged its heels, and often stern, reserved, usually unspoken opinion accompanied users of plows versus those of snowblowers.

Joe was privately pleased to see that Dunning and his neighbor favored opposite stances on the subject. It boded well that they might disagree on other things, as well.

The design of the driveway served to make the house look smaller from the street than it was when he reached its immaculately cleared parking area, capable of storing six vehicles. The ornate front door continued the illusion, looking stolen from a wooden castle.

The man who answered the bell, however, ran comfortably at odds with the setting, being dressed in jeans, moccasins, and an old checkered shirt. He was a barrel-chested, white-haired extrovert who greeted Joe with a crushing handshake before his visitor had even introduced himself.

"Hey there," he said. "Leslie Edwards. People call me Stew, from my middle name."

He half dragged Joe across the threshold and slammed the enormous door.

"Joe Gunther. I'm from the police." Joe kept the reference vague on purpose.

"Really?" was the man's guileless response. "To what do we owe the pleasure? Can I take your coat?"

Joe complied, removing it so his host could then hang it on an already laden coat-tree. "It's probably nothing," he began. "I'm just following up on a report that may have no basis in fact."

"Come on in," Edwards said, turning on his heel and leading the way through the entryway into a long, low living room with a sweeping view of snow-dusted trees in the distance.

"Take a seat," he continued, grabbing an armchair for himself. "You want some coffee?"

"Not for me, thanks," Joe said, perching on the edge of a sofa long enough for ten people.

"Tell me about your report," Edwards prompted him, giving Joe a small glimpse into the man behind the manners. Joe would look into his background later, as he did out of habit, but he suspected he'd find a restlessly retired so-called captain of industry in Leslie "Stew" Edwards, still accustomed to giving orders and expecting results.

"We're following up on a person of interest who supposedly has been targeting houses in the general vicinity."

"Any of my neighbors?" Edwards asked bluntly. " 'Cause I haven't had any problems."

"That's the catch," Joe said apologetically. "We can't be sure. It turns out that — as with so many fender benders — people are reluctant to call either the police or their insurance companies if they think the rate increase will exceed their loss."

"I know the feeling," Edwards replied. "Can't say I fault them. I'm still not sure how I can help you, though. I haven't heard of any break-ins, or even of anything strange going on."

"You might want to interview Willard Dunning," said a female voice from the doorway. Both men turned toward it, Joe rising from his seat.

456

A dark-haired woman in jeans, turquoise cowboy boots, and what looked like a chamois button-down shirt entered.

"Hey, honey," said Edwards from his seat. "It's the police."

"So I heard," she said, crossing to shake Joe's hand and motioning him to sit back down. "Clarissa Edwards. Nice to meet you."

She joined him at the other end of the sofa, striking the pose of someone used to having her photograph taken. "Why did you recommend I talk with Dunning?" Joe asked her.

"He had a security installation outfit drop by his house not long ago. I walked down to talk with them, just to be nosy. Willard wasn't in — just as well — but the man told me he was getting the whole package, whatever that meant. Sounded expensive, not that Mr. High-and-Mighty would care."

"When was this?" Joe asked.

She gave him the date, which was right after Alex's assault on Willard's car.

"I'm sensing no great affection between you two," he said.

"Not on my part," she confirmed. "I frankly don't care what he thinks of me."

Edwards chuckled. "Don't get her going. You've been warned."

"When you spoke with the security guy," Joe continued, "did you get a sense why he'd been called?"

"He didn't say," Clarissa said. "And I didn't ask, but like Stew was saying, we haven't heard of anything going on locally. It's been very quiet that way."

"If it isn't asking too much," Joe said, "could you tell me what your problem is with Willard?"

She didn't hesitate. "He's an arrogant, stuck-up, pompous little jackass. And he's a local boy, too. Born and bred in this town. Acts like he's Manhattan high society, which, by the way, would eat him up and spit him out in two seconds flat, not to mention his ditzy girlfriend. Course, she wouldn't have the brains to know how to drive that far."

"So you see each other out and about, so that you know who his girlfriend is?"

Clarissa laughed scornfully. "*Know her?* She crashed into my car. You did see where we live, right? How complicated do you think it is to pull out of your driveway around here?"

Edwards rose and headed toward the door, announcing, "I'm going for some coffee. Still no takers?"

His wife didn't answer, and Joe couldn't

get a word in.

"I was heading for town. Beautiful day, sunny weather, no snowbanks — this was months ago. You could see a quarter of a mile, if you looked. That stupid bitch comes screaming backward out of Willard's driveway like a bat outta hell, doesn't even pause when she reaches the street, and T-bones me like I was some frigging squirrel. I'm driving a tank, mind you. A Navigator with all the fixings. Goddamn thing needs a ladder just to get behind the wheel. But does she see it? Nope. She takes me out at thirty miles an hour. Never even touches the brakes. What an idiot."

She paused to breathe, allowing Joe to ask, "Was she alone?"

"She was, in the car. But at the sound of the crash, the lord of the manor comes tearing out, worked up like he was in heat, I swear, and tries to lay the whole thing on me."

By this time, her outrage had pushed her to the edge of her seat. Joe tried to head her off by asking, "Who was this woman?"

But she rose to her full height and spread her arms wide. "You'd think that would be the first order of business, wouldn't you? Crash into somebody, first thing you do, after saying you're sorry and asking if everyone is okay, is exchange names. You're a cop. That's right, isn't it?"

"Generally."

"Well, not this babe. And ol' Willard is having none of it. Because of her stupidity, this cow obviously blew his cover, 'cause he's doin' everything he can not to let me know they're bangin' boots."

"You gotta love this," her husband said, returning with a mug in his hand and leaning against the door frame. "He gave her cash for the repairs — a lot of it."

"Fifteen thousand dollars," Clarissa said. "Can you believe that? I had six left over after the bodywork. I sure as hell put that to good use, I can tell you."

"Odd, but it does sound generous," Joe said quietly. "I'm assuming he wasn't overly gracious?"

Clarissa sat back down, glaring. "You got that right. Called me names for almost killing his friend. *Friend.* Might as well be screwing his daughter. That's how young she was."

"You tell him, hon," Leslie chimed in, smiling before taking a sip.

She gave him an angry stare, but the steam had gone out of her. "You can laugh. I have my pride, damn it. Accidents happen, and old men sleep with young girls if

460

they can, but I'm not gonna be the bad guy because of it. That's all I'm saying. He was caught out and got embarrassed. Fine. But then to let me have it for being in the wrong place at the wrong time? That's bullshit."

"Totally understandable," Joe said, trying to appease her.

He let her take a deep breath before adding, "All that aside, though, you never did get the woman's name?"

Unexpectedly, she smiled broadly at him. "Not from her license, I didn't. Willard did everything except throw his body on that grenade, but then the dummy blew it by saying her name when he sent her back into the house to get her away from me."

Clarissa sat back, getting comfortable once more. "It's only a first name, of course, and not anything I could do anything with — not that I care anymore, what with the damage paid for. But he called her Billie. That I remember, clear as day."

The penalty at the end of a bright, sunny, cloudless winter day in Vermont is called radiational cooling — a well-known phenomenon. Essentially, the same overhead clarity that delivers a day to heighten the spirits then allows the residual warmth to be displaced by arctic cold, dropped unim-

461

peded from the glacial atmosphere like a bone-numbing blanket. The compensation, however — so often true in a state plagued by lethal weather — is an inspiring beauty: a star-packed black sky, awash with crystals.

That kind of cold was what Sally's car heater was combating as she drove through the gloom of New Hampshire's Route 9, heading toward Keene.

Far ahead of her was the vehicle she and her passenger had seen Wilva Sargent use to leave the Thorndike campus, the venerable, now slightly infamous Horse with No Name.

"Do you ever lose sight of who you're following?" Rachel asked, cradling her camera.

Sally glanced at her, smiling. "In other words, would I please close the gap, 'cause it's driving you nuts?"

"No," Rachel protested. "I know you're a pro. I was really just wondering."

"You can," Sally replied, not quite believing her. "It's a balancing act. In the movies, the driver in front always picks out the tail six seconds into it. That's baloney, in my experience. People are clueless, even the paranoid ones. Particularly in traffic like this. Put us on an empty country road somewhere, it gets dicier. So, yes, I have lost a few. But generally, I have an idea

462

where they're going, or at least who they're planning to see, and I catch up to them later. The biggest problem with these tails isn't being spotted; it's having enough gas. At least more than the other guy. I remember once having to pass the suspect car, drive like hell to the next gas station I could see from the road, and then fill up until I saw the car come into view."

"Did it work?"

"Luckily," Sally said cheerfully. "Surprised the hell out of me, and made me a believer in having a full tank ever since."

She indicated the VW ahead with her chin, keeping both hands on the wheel. "This is not really a challenge. Its back end is so distinctive, I'd have to be blind to lose it in all but the worst traffic, which is hardly the case now."

She was right, of course. It was near midnight. To Rachel's surprise and delight, Sally had phoned her without excuse forty-five minutes earlier and told her to be standing in the driveway of the old, abandoned Friendly's restaurant, just shy of the bridge leading into New Hampshire from Brattleboro, in exactly ten minutes. She hadn't said why, and Rachel hadn't asked.

But she did now. "You know who Wilva's planning to see?"

"Not really," Sally told her. "I was just sitting on her, hoping I'd get lucky. Could be a dealer, since I'm pretty sure she uses. Could be a different player entirely — maybe somebody who's paying her or forcing her to smear Jonathan Marotti. Or maybe she just prefers Market Basket in Keene. I don't know."

"But you called me," Rachel said. "You must've suspected something."

"I suspected something when she became headline news," Sally replied.

"You're that sure Marotti's innocent?" Rachel asked. "Not very trendy of you."

Sally laughed. "I know, right? And a girl, too. That should tell you just how sure I am. I look at most men and think they're up to something nasty. I absolutely know when they're checking me out. But Marotti? It may sound corny, but he's the real deal when it comes to decency. I've never known him to stumble. Plus, the whole story sounds cooked up to me, and way too convenient, given other things I know about."

"Like what?"

"Gently, Ms. Ace Reporter," Sally cautioned her. "I still have my ethical standards to observe."

"Which you've got to be bending right

now, having me in the car," Rachel shot back.

Sally smiled broadly and decided to bend those standards even more, here and now. "Yes and no. I'm hoping this'll turn into a little mutual back-scratching. I give you a story, and you get my client off the hot seat. All for simply exposing the truth. You good with that?"

Rachel nodded. "Totally."

"Then you should be apprised of a little detail my dad told me is already heating up the virtual text-messaging wires: This little embarrassment to Marotti popped up right after he'd announced his decision to the school board, at a closed meeting, to underwrite a fifteen-million-dollar building project. There was no opposition at the time, but I suspect that it and what we're checking out right now are connected."

Sally let Rachel absorb that for a couple of seconds before adding, "But I'd like you to sit on it for just a bit. You can tell Katz, so you don't get in trouble. I only want a few hours' headway, maybe a day, to allow the truth to come out before this hits the fan with guesswork and innuendo."

To Sally's profound happiness, Rachel merely nodded before saying, "You got it."

Wilva's next move struck a familiar chord

with Sally. As they came within view of Keene's city lights, and the shopping complex on its western edge, the multihued VW turned into a motel parking lot, bringing Sally back to the last time she was in such a setting, and ended up calling the cops to put things right.

She hoped that wasn't going to be the case this time.

They drove by the motel before completing a U-turn at the first opportunity, and entering the lot from the opposite direction. Wilva's car was parked near the entrance, and they could see her crossing the lobby through the double glass doors. Sally slowed to see that she didn't pause at the reception desk, apparently knowing her destination.

"Get out and keep with her," Sally ordered Rachel. "I want to know what room she's going to. Just the number. Nothing fancy."

Without comment, Rachel swung out of the car, slipping her ever-present camera over her shoulder.

Only as she was jogging to catch up did it occur to her that Wilva might take the elevator.

Which she did.

Rachel chose to go for it. "Hold on," she requested loudly, closing the gap and reaching the elevator doors just as Wilva punched the button for the third floor.

"Thanks," Rachel said to her, quickly adding, "Three, please. Oh. Sorry. Didn't realize you'd hit it."

As most people do in elevators, Wilva avoided looking at her fellow traveler, allowing Rachel to study her. In contrast to Rachel's expectations — based on little beside the hype her own paper had given this woman — Wilva appeared worn and frightened, fidgety, her hair unkempt, and with dark smudges under bloodshot eyes. Rachel wondered if one of Sally's scenarios had perhaps been accurate and Wilva was here for a fix.

The doors opened, Rachel stepped back to let Wilva out first, and as she turned left, Rachel went right, moving slowly and pretending to dig into her coat pocket for her key. Wilva proceeded hurriedly, by contrast, reading the numbers on the doors as she went. About halfway down the corridor, she stopped, knocked, and shortly thereafter disappeared, allowing Rachel to sprint back silently, take note of the number, and continue to the stairway, where she double-stepped down and returned to the parking lot. She found Sally parked facing both front and side entrances, the car dark but running, its heater still on.

"You see who she's visiting?" she asked as Rachel closed the door.

"Not that lucky. It's room three twenty. She looks terrible. Really stressed."

Sally wasn't overly sympathetic. "Yeah. Well, goes with the turf."

Unconsciously, each prepared for a long wait, Rachel anticipating an hour at least, Sally, the veteran of such stakeouts, ready to spend the night, complete with a comforter that she pulled from the back and draped across both of them. As a result, the two of them were caught off guard when, only ten minutes later, the motel's side door opened with a bang. First out was a man wearing a long tailored coat and putting a fur Russian ushanka on his head with both hands, in the process obscuring his face. After him came Wilva, with no hat, coat open, and her gloves now missing.

"Look at the getup," Sally growled as Rachel began taking photographs with her long lens. "Without even seeing his face, I'd know that foofy hat anywhere."

The man turned to address his distraught companion, who was clinging to his arm. It was Willard Dunning. He looked impatient as he faked comforting Wilva, buttoning her coat and patting her shoulder.

Sally kept up her commentary. " 'There,

there. Let me show you how I'm not stabbing you in the back.' "

Rachel documented their progress over to the VW bus, where Dunning opened Wilva's unlocked door and steered her toward its embrace, just shy of pushing her in.

There, she threw her arms around his neck and kissed him, allowing Rachel to unleash one last flurry of shots.

"Money shot," Sally commented, admiring her friend's easy skill with the camera, as Willard stepped back and Wilva, now crying, folded in behind her steering wheel.

They stayed put when Wilva drove off, followed later by Dunning, whose expensive ride had been parked across the way.

After that, Sally hit the overhead light and handed Rachel a laptop computer, into which Rachel plugged the memory card from her camera, all without comment — a well-oiled team. Moments later, they were both admiring Rachel's shots on the screen.

"You oughta do this for a living," Sally kidded her as they clicked through the images.

"They look better than I thought they would," Rachel said, "especially given the sketchy lighting."

Sally straightened after the slide show concluded. "You do realize your boss will never print them."

Rachel returned the card to her camera and closed it up as Sally stowed away her laptop. "Yeah. Not that kind of paper. Maybe useful to have on file, though."

Sally revealed the patience, even reticence, born of a lifetime of witnessing other people's misery. "Honestly? I hope they never see the light of day."

Rachel was curious. This was, after all, a person she'd come to increasingly respect on an almost daily basis. "No argument from me, but how come?"

Despite her critical comments earlier, Sally said, "You said she was looking terrible, and we just saw how that slimeball treated her. My gut tells me she's been caught between a rock and a hard place, lying about Marotti to keep Dunning from dumping her. Maybe he pays for her habit; maybe it's true love on her part. I don't really care. But I'd hate for us to victimize her along with everybody else."

Rachel was thoughtful. "What're you going to do with your copies?" she asked.

"Simple," Sally said, turning on her headlights and aiming for the parking lot exit. "I'll give them to Marotti. He's the customer. My guess is that once he's done showing them to the right people, his problems will go away."

They pulled into what traffic there was and began returning to Vermont.

After a few minutes, Rachel asked, "So, why did you invite me on this? You could've taken your own pictures."

Sally glanced at her and smiled, giving in to feelings she rarely aired. "I wanted your company."

Rachel laughed and quickly squeezed her friend's forearm. "Yeah. Me, too. Thanks."

They left it at that, enjoying the aftereffect. Sally soon followed up with her own question. "Are you going to show those shots to Katz?"

"In a way, I have to," Rachel replied, "but with a your-eyes-only memo covering everything we've learned about Dunning and the cottage and how Marotti's project seems to have been the incentive for it all." She hesitated before adding, "I was also wondering if Joe Gunther might be interested in them, too."

CHAPTER 28

Vermont's newest state prison, in Springfield, had been a long time in the making. Initial obstacles were predictable, fitting the not-in-my-backyard category. Later, they'd become quirkier, as when a local stargazing club had protested the threat of light pollution.

But money had won out, along with a few concessions and compromises, and what became the Southern State Correctional Facility, or SSCF, had moved onto the completely tree-screened and decapitated top of a hill right off I-91's Exit 7 — invisible to all except those who scaled its steep, curvilinear driveway, to be greeted by the forbidding facade that only a prison can provide.

Willard Dunning made this trip on the first day he was permitted by law and circumstances to visit his son.

Willard was a man who prided himself on

his self-perceived hardiness. When seeing his image in reflections or photographs, he liked what he saw, and naturally imagined others did, too. He was handsome, manly, decisive, attractive, eloquent, gifted, clever, very bright, wealthy, and a textbook father. The fact that few of these attributes actually applied to him didn't register.

He was, as a result, virtually at sea about James's fate, without precedence or guidance to help him navigate the future.

He'd read the charges, running from drug dealing to murder, although those were not among his primary objections. They weren't good, of course, but their biggest offense, in Willard's mind, was how they reflected poorly on him and the family name. He simply couldn't believe his son had let himself be caught.

Proceeding from the prison's predictably austere lobby to the long, narrow visitors' room at the end, Willard progressively surrendered his driver's license, Gucci wallet, change, keys, Mont Blanc pen, cashmere coat, cell phone, custom-made shoes, and belt at the metal detector. Finally, he was sniffed at by a dog with a handler, who also looked like he was smelling something unpleasant.

Finally, his body and dignity threadbare,

just shy of the room's entrance, he was subjected to a monotone recitation from an imposing shaved-head officer with jangling keys, who said, without break, "Physical contact between inmate and visitors is prohibited. Visitors must be seated when the inmate arrives. Inmates and visitors must keep their hands on the table at all times. No items may be passed between inmate and visitor. Inmates and visitors must keep their feet on the floor at all times. No disruptive behavior or loud voices are allowed. Visitors may use the restrooms before the visit. If a visitor must use the restroom after the visit has started, the visit will end. If there are any violations of these rules as I have recited them, the visit will end. Is everything I have just told you clear and understood?"

Willard nodded dumbly, finally humbled at least a notch, and was led through the door into a surprisingly pleasant, brightly lit room, where he was taken to a wooden seat facing a long table split down the middle by a barricade the size of a Ping-Pong table's net and told to wait.

A few minutes later, James entered from an opposite door, dressed in prison garb, disheveled and in need of a shave. Like his father, he was escorted to his seat, after which the corrections officer retreated to a far wall and stood with his hands clasped before him, presumably ready to pounce at a moment's notice.

"When're you getting me out?" James demanded sullenly.

Willard's expression was mystified. "What? What happened to your lawyer? That's supposed to be in the works. I called him as soon as I heard about this."

James scowled. "He's full of crap. At arraignment, the judge ordered me held without bail. It's totally not fair, and your loser lawyer did fuck all to stop it."

"They found a lot of evidence against you," Willard said lamely, still struggling to see his son in this context. "Blood and fingerprints and drugs and testimony from your friends."

"Friends?" James burst out, stimulating a sharp tap on the wall by the officer, who said sternly, "First and last warning. Keep it under control."

James fell into glowering silence.

Willard searched his brain, hoping to find something close to the common ground he thought he occupied with his son. Unusually for him, he opted for honesty. "I'm sorry, James," he said. "I don't know what to say. I'd do anything for you. I hope I've proved that. But I'm lost here."

Momentarily, James seemed to get beyond his own bitterness to resume eye contact and say, "I know, Dad. Sorry I screwed up."

Willard dropped his voice so the man against the wall couldn't hear him. "What really happened?"

James gave him a lopsided smile. "I got caught."

True to type, Willard laughed softly. "I thought I taught you better. We could've pulled it off together, you know, if you'd let me in."

James shrugged. "Now you tell me."

Willard raised a hand, as if to reach out and offer comfort, before he saw the officer's baleful eye over James's shoulder and replaced his palm flat on the table.

His voice kept low, he now said, "Don't worry about all this, son. They're looking strong now, but I'll make it go away. Part of the price of doing business."

"I know," James replied, sounding less than convinced. He had the benefit, after all, of firsthand knowledge of the crimes he'd committed, a distinction both men felt as keenly as the low barrier now stretched between them.

In an effort to breach what he could, Willard leaned forward in his chair, whispering by now, and asked, "How deep in are you, James? It would be useful to know, so I can rally the right people."

Adherent as he was to the family's narcissistic and self-serving code of ethics, James didn't hesitate to emulate his father's body language and whisper back, "I did it more for you than me, Dad."

Willard's eyes widened. "What?"

"Lyall Johnson. And your big squeeze, Billie. You *knew.*"

"Knew what?" Willard pressed him, almost rising out of his chair.

"He was her supplier. Hell, he was *my* supplier. But at least I wasn't fucking him."

That put Willard back in his seat. He stared at his son, speechless, his ego battling with what he was hearing.

James continued, driven to justify his actions to the one man he wanted to understand them. "Why do you think I helped you frame that upstart dago, Marotti?" he demanded. "You know what they say about the shoe fitting. I didn't think it would be a big stretch, adding another notch to her bedpost, even if this one wasn't true."

Willard was still processing this. "Are you sure?"

"From the horse's mouth. Did you think I didn't know you were doing her? Jesus. She was *so* beneath you. Everybody I know's given her a ride, or tried to. And she loves it. Running around like she does, doing dope and hanging out with students."

James's expression intensified as he reemphasized, "That's why I did all this, Dad. For you. At first, I was just gonna frame Billie for buying dope — spread the word about her supply trips to Bellows Falls. I even paid a fake witness. I hated that she was using you, taking your money and cheating on you behind your back. That's why when I heard Lyall bragging about how she was paying him with sex, I lost it and confronted him. It just wasn't right."

Willard recoiled, shifting his chair. In the same gesture, he wiped his face with his open palm, hoping to clear his mind.

Keep it logical, he thought. The kid's in trouble, he messed up, and he's scrambling for what dignity he can find. That includes exaggeration, excuses, maybe even a little payback for my having asked for help in compromising Billie and Marotti. That's even fair, Willard reasoned. A father shouldn't put his child in that kind of position. Of course he would cook up a story about her being loose.

Perfectly understandable.

Satisfied, he leaned forward again. "I'm

sorry I put you in a tough spot, son. I'll make it up to you once this is all history. If it helps, I think it's done between Billie and me anyhow. She's gotten way too worked up about this." He paused a moment, as if figuring out a math problem, and then asked, "But what about the old man they're talking about? The homebound invalid?"

James looked disgusted. "Asshole. I didn't anticipate that. He saw me. The stupid bastard sat at his window and snooped, day and night. How the hell did I know? He had me right in his binoculars when I looked straight at him. It would've ruined everything. I went back later and dealt with him. He was almost dead anyhow. I don't get what they're worked up about, to be honest."

Given his own values, Willard saw his point. The regret was that James hadn't been more clever. There were ways of doing these things. The real question was now one of evidence, and the ability of prosecutors to present it in court. From this point forward, since Marotti had been successfully stopped, that's where Willard was putting his efforts, and his money — on the best lawyers available.

They chatted some more, Willard asking conventional questions about James's welfare and needs. At the end, he asked, as if in passing, "You hear from your mother?"

James rolled his eyes. "She's coming up."

"Really," Willard replied. "I'm impressed. She's not gonna approve of the décor."

James laughed. "She won't get the chance. I'm not putting her on my visitors' list."

Willard was delighted. "No kidding? That's harsh."

James gave him a pitying look. "Dad. Give me a break. Can you really see her in here? Obeying the rules, keeping it under forty decibels? And where would she stay? There's no hotel fancy enough, probably not in the whole state."

Willard was laughing by now, but was interrupted by a woman with a small child entering the room after receiving the same monotone lecture.

With a nod to their own corrections officer, Willard stood and said to his son, "I'll take that as my cue. Stay strong, James. We'll get you out. Don't worry about that."

James tried to smile and made his way toward the inner door as Willard headed out, reequipping himself with his armor of status symbols as he went.

Following their departure, Joe Gunther stepped from a small back room and addressed the officer who sat at the one-way glass overlooking the room. The man was finishing downloading the recording he'd made of the Dunnings' complete conversation from a microphone Joe had placed earlier near their spot.

"You get it all, Robert?" he asked.

The man nodded. "Yeah. Good mic. Even when they were whispering. This kind of stuff work in court?"

"Probably not," Joe conceded. "But nice to have anyway. Thanks for the heads-up about the father scheduling a visit."

"Sure thing, Joe. I was hoping it would help. I knew Homer Nelson when I was a kid. He didn't deserve that."

Joe patted him on the shoulder as he received the thumb drive Robert handed him. "You're a good man. Say hi to your mom for me."

"Damn," Stan Katz said, studying the photo of Willard Dunning kissing Wilva Sargent. "I've unleashed a monster." He glanced uneasily at the closed glass door overlooking the diminutive newsroom, torn between caution and delight.

"I know you can't print it," Rachel told him. "I just wanted you to see where your money was going. The point isn't so much that Wilva has two guys supposedly on the

481

hook. It's that both men are on the board at Thorndike, and, according to my source, Dunning is hell-bent on stopping Marotti from building the fancy auditorium I wrote to you about in that memo, obliterating Dunning Cottage."

Katz kept studying the image, his brain working overtime.

"I figured it has to be relevant to the charge against Marotti," Rachel said without much conviction.

"I'd think so," Katz agreed, returning the print. "But not by itself." He tilted his chair back and placed a foot against the edge of his desk. "Plus, like you said, we wouldn't publish the picture anyhow. The way I see it, you've got two options: You either run it by Willard or confront his girlfriend."

He paused, obviously challenging Rachel. She rose to the bait. "I choose the girlfriend. She made the accusation, she's the weak link in this chain, and, the way she looked last night, I'd say she's the most likely to spill the beans."

Katz stood up, banging his chair legs on the floor. "Done. Go out and slay the dragon. If you succeed, what you got becomes hard news. That, I'll print any day."

He smiled to himself as she left, pleased that his investment in her was paying off.

■ ■ ■ ■

It took some doing to find Wilva Sargent. Sally had given Rachel an idea of the school's layout, including Sargent's apartment and classroom, but the art teacher had also been allotted a studio of her own, which, it turned out, only a few knew about.

It was in the basement of the same building as the classroom, but down a long, poorly lit hall primarily designed for storage rooms and utility clusters — furnaces, massive water heaters, electrical panels, and the like. When she finally reached the door she'd been directed to, she eased it open, slowly spilling the light within onto the floor around her feet, unsure of what she'd find.

There was a narrow corridor carved among the partly constructed sculptures, half-finished canvases, and assorted piles of lumber, metal, junk, and stacked supplies. This, Rachel tentatively followed to its end. It delivered her to a curious mixture of workroom and human nest, with a muddled combination of a potter's wheel, two easels, a workbench, and an enormous, ancient, very stained couch, heaped with pillows and a curled-up, sobbing woman in its far corner.

Acting on instinct, Rachel approached the woman, maybe ten years Rachel's senior, and quietly sat beside her. Wilva Sargent looked up, her face damp and eyes red. Rachel wondered, given those eyes, if she wasn't also on something pharmaceutical in nature.

"Who are you?" Sargent asked.

"Rachel."

"Do I know you?"

Yes, Rachel thought, from the elevator last night, when, thank God, you were too distracted to notice me. "Not yet," she said. "I was hoping to change that."

"Why?"

Rachel did some quick thinking, "Because I believe you've been royally screwed by a toad who should be held accountable."

Sargent stared at her in astonishment before shifting in her seat and burying her face against Rachel's chest, her sobbing reaching a crescendo.

Trying not to disturb this momentary and unexpected bond, Rachel awkwardly worked her arm around and draped it across Wilva's shoulder to comfort her.

They sat there for a while as Wilva settled back down, almost dozing off momentarily. Rachel looked around as best she could, hoping to gain some insight into this woman's life. The primary evidence told of chaos and upheaval, but Rachel also sensed an underlying aimlessness and perhaps a search for purpose or identity. As an artist, Sargent was clearly accomplished. She had an eye, but her biggest challenge seemed to be finishing anything. Wilva struck Rachel as a person to whom life happened, before dropping her in its wake.

Like now.

Eventually, Wilva stirred, rubbing her face before looking up into Rachel's eyes, her expression wondering. "Where did you come from?" she asked.

"I heard you were in trouble," Rachel replied disingenuously. "I figured you'd been put in a jam by people who didn't care about you."

"Story of my life," Wilva muttered.

"Tough childhood?" Rachel asked.

"No childhood," Wilva countered. "Not the kind you read about. We were all too busy chasing things — drugs, booze, people, dreams, money."

"Your parents?"

"Biologically, yeah. But the three of us were just kids, parents and me. We traveled around like three golf balls in an empty box, until, one by one, we fell out."

"I'm sorry," Rachel said.

Wilva was slowly resurfacing. She straightened to free herself of Rachel's embrace and wiped her nose on her sweatshirt's sleeve. "I really don't know you? You look familiar."

"No," Rachel maintained, bracing herself. "But I'd like to be the one to help you set things straight."

Wilva smiled sadly — clearly a woman without friends. "Good luck. How?"

"I'm a writer for the *Reformer,*" Rachel explained. "And I want to describe how you were used and dumped."

She waited for the predictable accusations of invasion of privacy and meddling in other people's business. But Wilva merely absorbed the news, staring at her hands, and stayed silent.

"I know about Willard Dunning," Rachel added.

Wilva looked back up, the tears returning, but without any outburst of emotion. "I thought I'd gotten lucky with him," she said.

"What happened?"

"What always happens. The outside breaks in. The walls never last. Mostly, that shitty kid of his happened."

"James?"

"Yeah. Perfect name, right? 'Never Call Me Jim.' That was my nickname for him. He should be the poster child for this school: spoiled, rich, selfish, totally without feeling. I guess I found out he got it all from his father." She thumped her forehead gently with the heel of her hand several times. "You'd think I'd learn."

"Tell me," Rachel urged her, pretending not to know.

"What's to tell? I was stupid — again. I glommed on to Willard and never looked back, or even around. The warning signs were there. His lack of commitment, his secrecy about us — like he was embarrassed — his always having somewhere else to go. But when he was on, it was like being caught in a bright light. I couldn't see anything else. He really knew how to lay it on."

"Why or how did you get involved with Jonathan Marotti?" Rachel asked.

Wilva's eyes widened. "I didn't. I met him at a function once. That's it. It was all made up. Willard sent his lousy kid to seal the deal, told me his dad was in real trouble, and too embarrassed to come to me himself. James pretended to be the doting son, desperate to give back a little to the father who'd done everything for him."

She suddenly straightened with outrage before adding, "And then he paid me. Can you believe that? These fucking rich people;

always about the money. Paid me five thousand bucks."

"Did he explain why?"

Wilva smiled knowingly. "I could tell he was lying. He said it was his own money, because he knew I didn't like him — that I'd do a favor for Willard but not for him, so the money was to compensate, or some damn thing." She paused and then conceded, "Of course I went along with it. That's what I do. I cave in. Even when I smell a rat."

"What were you supposed to do?"

"You should know," she burst out. "You people printed it. That was the whole point. I just said Marotti harassed me, and it was stand-back-and-let-the-dam-break time. Pathetic."

"But why?" Rachel pressed her.

"Some dumb building project. That's what James said. Called Marotti 'an upstart dago' who wanted to pull down the old family home, or something. I don't know. He actually cried when he told me. Said his dad was next to crazy about it."

"Did James know about you and Willard?"

"That we were seeing each other? Yes, but he told me Willard still thought we were a deep, dark secret. Why, I don't know, not that it matters anymore."

488

Rachel was thinking overtime by now. "Do you still have the money?"

"Most of it. I put it in my account. It was too much cash."

"You have a deposit slip?"

Wilva frowned. "You don't believe me?"

"I'm asking because I do. It's proof of what you're telling me."

Wilva processed that before rising and pawing through a woven bag she used as a purse. She sat back down, giving Rachel a crumpled slip of paper. "There. Have at it."

Rachel double-checked its contents and nodded. "I will. So, why're you telling me all this? You love Willard, you got paid, and you went along and framed Marotti. Why the change?"

Wilva didn't answer at first, staring at her hands. "Willard and I met last night," she said, not looking up. "I told him I was having second thoughts, that I wanted to talk. As usual, he said it had to be somewhere out of sight." She finally made eye contact. "I just wanted to hear him say it was okay between us, that what I'd done was for the right reasons. I wanted my suspicions to be wrong — that I hadn't fucked up again, and been had by another man."

She sighed. "But of course I had been. He was all pissed off, not grateful at all, didn't want to listen to how stressed out I was about lying in public and screwing up another's person's life. I'm not stupid. I know what I did."

Hesitating, she then said, "Worse than that, I fucked over every woman who's ever told the truth. That's why I'm talking to you. I messed up. I want people to know that. Mr. Marotti never touched me, but there are other ways a woman can get assaulted by a man. Willard and his loser son did that, and I let them, and that makes me a traitor to women everywhere. If I'm gonna live with that, I want people to know why. I admit it; I want those two bastards to admit to it, too."

An hour later, the details of Wilva Sargent's story collected and organized in her head, Rachel stepped out of the art building and into the cold fresh air, feeling at once resolved and purposeful. Working for Stan Katz, meeting Sally Kravitz, and having Joe Gunther and her mom as indirect, even unintentional mentors had all combined to create in Rachel an intellectual and moral progression she might have otherwise ignored. From someone who in college had recorded facts and images, received instruction, and generally watched the world from the outside, she had — largely thanks to those people — recognized and embarked upon a sense of mission to do more.

With Wilva's voice in her ears, the loss of Alex Hale still paining her, she felt fueled by a resurgent resolve.

She took out her phone, dialed, and, once Joe had picked up, said, "I'm about to write an article, but I won't submit it until twenty-four hours after I give you all the details. In exchange, I'm asking you to give me first crack at what you do with it. Do we have a deal?"

His answer was simple and predictably direct. "We do."

CHAPTER 29

"Hi. Topher?"

Topher Pluff adjusted his glasses as he pressed the phone against his ear, trying to hear the older woman's soft voice. "Yes, speaking."

"This is Dorothy Robbins, from the Vernon Historical Society. I am responding to your inquiry about anything having to do with the Dunning family and what was once called Westview Acres, their farm."

"Dot," Topher exclaimed, finally making the connection. "Right, of course. Wow, that was fast. Aren't you kind. Were you able to find anything?"

"Well," she said, "indirectly. We do have some material, as you'd expect, but it's mostly statistical stuff, like they'd put in an assessor's ledger or an annual town report, and it's pretty dry and uninformative. My understanding was that you wanted more than that."

"Correct," he replied. "You got that right, Dot. Letters, diaries, journals, things like that."

"Yes, yes. Well, what I've found is similar. It's a work log, I guess you'd call it — kind of a contractor's progress diary — written by Mack Morse, who was a contractor hired by the people who bought the Dunning place and converted it to the school."

"You don't say?" Topher responded, his interest piqued. "That sounds fascinating. Just the kind of thing I was after."

"Not sure 'fascinating' is the word," Dorothy cautioned him. "It's not much to read. But at least it's better than a list of figures. I'll give you that."

Topher laughed. "Well, I appreciate it, Dot. I'll be right down to pick it up. Thanks so much. I know a young woman who will be very happy to hear about this."

Still smiling as he hung up, Topher studied the screen of his smartphone, locating Rachel Reiling's number.

Two hours later, Rachel was at Thorndike Academy's administrative offices, standing before Sally's desk, pleased, as always lately, to be working with her.

"Hey, pal," Sally said. "You look like you just won the lotto."

493

Rachel smiled broadly and brandished an old, worn, much-stained canvas-backed record book, about the size of a slim hardback. "Maybe. You need to look at this."

Like coconspirators, and with Rachel giving a quick wave to Emily down the hall, the two of them retired to the vault, where the old documents were kept, and which by now had acquired the feel of a private clubhouse.

"Topher called me," Rachel explained. "He kept digging after we left, and contacted the Vernon Historical Society, one of whose members produced this." She laid the book on the edge of a shelf and opened it. "It's a kind of work diary, I guess so the customer could account for time and labor costs. It belonged to Mack Morse, who was a contractor hired to convert the original Dunning Cottage into the first official Thorndike Academy building."

She flipped it to a page near the middle. "Here's the part I think's interesting. 'Cellar: dirt floor, unmortised granite walls, headspace mostly sixty-eight inches. Beams sound, plumbing okay, wiring needs replacing. Reeks. Source: unkn. animal carcass? Question: Find source or let it air out?'" Rachel stabbed the page with her finger. "Right there. There it is."

Sally straightened and looked at her incredulously. "What? An animal carcass?"

"If that's what it was," Rachel replied with a smile.

Sally tilted her chin up a fraction, sensing her friend's meaning intuitively. Instead of challenging it, she asked, "Did he find the source?"

Rachel's eyes were gleaming. "Nope. There was time to spare. They had a lot of other things to do, so they let it air out. There's a note later about nature's having taken care of it. It never comes up again, and there's even a reference to the cellar near the end, where some rewiring is mentioned. No more talk of an odor."

Sally didn't need to be persuaded. She checked her watch, grabbed Rachel's elbow, and said, "Come on, girlfriend, let's go see the boss. She doesn't leave for an hour yet."

She paused at the door, nevertheless, to add, "I'm going to say you're an operative of mine, okay? Not a journalist. They're not much into subtle distinctions around here, and you being from the *Reformer* would flip them out."

They found Mary Mroczek at her desk, editing remarks she was scheduled to make for a local press interview later on.

"Okay," she said after Sally had introduced

Rachel. "What've you been up to? It better not be bad news."

Sally took the lead, placing Mack Morse's book before her. "These are progress notes recorded when Dunning Cottage changed hands and got converted into Thorndike. We're doing a bunch of reading between the lines here, but there's a chance we found mention of a body in the cellar."

Mroczek sat up. "Are you kidding me?"

"No, but it takes some telling, if you got a few minutes."

"I do now."

Taking turns, the two young women brought her up to date.

At the end of it, her writing forgotten, Mroczek rose and took her place by the window. "You think the odor Morse noticed might have come from Cherie Aucoin's body?" She didn't mask her incredulity.

"What we think doesn't matter," Sally countered, more used to pushback than Rachel at this point. "What we know is that the school's reputation is in the balance, its primary benefactor has been tarred and feathered, and the son of Willard Dunning is in jail, facing homicide charges. What can it hurt to check this out?"

Mroczek rubbed her forehead. "By digging up the cellar?"

"Not necessarily," Sally argued. "I know Norm Ketcham's grounds crew has a metal detector. They use it to trace old piping underground and to find metal in the logs they saw up at the school mill. I've processed the bills."

"It won't work on bone," Rachel said reluctantly, not wanting to oppose her comrade in arms in mid-negotiation.

But Sally was undeterred. "Which only matters if the body was naked. If it was buried wearing clothes, a metal detector should pick up a belt buckle or a zipper. Who knows? It's got to be worth a try, especially given the chaos that's already swirling around. If we don't find anything, no one'll be the wiser. If we do, it could change the game completely."

Mroczek was in no mood to argue. She reached for her phone and said, "I'll tell Norm to give you whatever you need."

Joe reached out and hit the Off button on the recorder he'd been playing. The rest of his squad, whether audibly or not, seemed to let out a collective sigh of released tension.

"I love people," Willy commented first. "They're so consistently inclined to shoot themselves in the foot."

"As you are fond of saying," Sammie replied.

Lester asked his boss, "Can we use that? I mean, I know it was the prison's visiting room, which is nobody's private space, but couldn't some lawyer raise a stink?"

Willy started laughing as Joe responded more constructively, "They could try to, and they might keep it out of a courtroom, but I ordered it for investigative reasons, and ran it by Tausha beforehand. We're good to try using it any way we can."

"Ask forgiveness instead of permission?" Willy suggested.

Joe had never liked the expression, but he couldn't argue with it here. "Something like that," he conceded.

"The interesting thing about it," Sam observed, "is that while it puts James in more hot water, with his own words, it still leaves Willard beyond reach. He seemed to have no idea what his kid was doing, and neither one said a word about Alex."

"Even if you add what Joe found out about Alex probably ripping Willard off, we got nothin'," Lester agreed, referring to the Windsor footage and Clarissa Edwards's statement about Willard's hiring a firm to tighten his home security.

"I did interview the installer, like you

498

asked," Sam said. "According to him, Willard might as well've been a doorpost. Didn't say a word about why he was ordering the premium package. The guy even suggested cheaper options. Willard wasn't interested."

"We do have him on the Marotti blackmail," Joe mused, glancing at the picture of Willard and Wilva kissing that he'd printed from Rachel's email attachment to him, accompanied by a synopsis of her interview with Wilva.

"So what?" Willy asked bluntly. "It's one millionaire screwing another. I doubt even the Bratt PD would be interested."

"I am, though," Joe replied. "It's too tight a circle not to be connected. Too coincidental."

"There are three coincidences, as I see it," Lester contributed. "James and Willard are father and son, both are associated with the school, and both seem to be natural-born sociopaths — like it's a family trait."

"That frigging school," Joe said, half to himself. "Always comes back to that."

"It's creepy enough, I'll give you that much," Rachel said, looking around at the dusty, dark, cobwebbed ceiling joists almost touching the crown of her head.

Sally was running the metal detector, her eyes down, following the beam from the light encircling her head as it bobbed across the cellar's dirt floor, methodically tracking the detector's dishlike receiver.

The cellar was smaller than the building's overall footprint, reflecting Dunning Cottage's origins rather than how it had ended up, including a couple of building wings. But the cellar had been overlooked historically in other ways, too, being as gloomy as a dungeon and clearly not used for much anymore. Most modern-day equipment, like furnaces and water heaters, had long ago been situated elsewhere in the building for easier access and service.

The result was somber, slightly damp, very quiet, and, for Rachel, spooky.

The good news for Sally, unaffected by this aura, was that not much had been altered down here, probably since it had been built. Aside from the anemic lightbulb near the ladderlike staircase, and the presence of some overhead wires and water pipes, there was little representing the past seventy-five years.

Sally, who was also wearing headphones, suddenly stopped and straightened, although not for the first time. They'd so far uncovered a small collection of nails, canning tops, scraps of rusty metal, a spoon, and what appeared to be the remains of an old broken flashlight.

She slipped off the phones and tapped the ground lightly with the detector head.

"Big or small?" Rachel asked, readying her shovel, as she'd been doing for over the past hour.

"Small again," Sally replied.

Rachel scratched at the ground's surface with her blade and then began digging in earnest, pausing now and then to sweep with her own headlight across the growing hole for any reflections or signs of foreign objects.

"How far down is it?" she asked after a few minutes, grateful that the soil, unlike that in most of Vermont, was relatively free of large rocks.

Sally checked the screen on the detector again. "About three feet."

"You're kidding me," Rachel protested, spoiled by how shallow their previous finds had been. She was already stripped down to a tank top and jeans.

Sally shrugged. "Maybe that's good news. Want me to spell you?"

Rachel went back to it. "No. I'm good for a little more. Give it another reading, though. To make sure I'm over it."

Sally followed suit, then gave her a nod. "Right on. About another foot and a half."

The soil had changed in nature, making Rachel's efforts easier, a discovery that played at the back of her mind, and made her dig with less aggression, along with a growing apprehension. In the end, she dropped to her knees and exchanged her shovel for a garden trowel they'd also been given by Norm Ketcham.

Instinctively, Sally put aside her detector and joined her, combining her light's halo with Rachel's over the hole.

Sensing more than seeing something, Rachel finally stopped working with any tools and resorted to clawing away the dirt, slowly and carefully, as if anticipating an archaeologist's long-awaited reward.

She wasn't disappointed. In the end, she rocked back onto her heels, Sally tight beside her, a small metallic object cupped in the palm of her dirty hand, found deep enough that it couldn't have simply been dropped.

"Oh damn," she said.

Caught in the light was an encrusted small pendant, unmistakably shaped like a heart.

CHAPTER 30

"Make yourself comfortable, Mr. Dunning," Joe said. "Would you like some coffee? I know it's late."

Willard looked around. In the time since the Brattleboro PD had abandoned the downtown municipal building, the VBI had been allowed to set up one small room within the old detective enclave as an interview area — the same office in which Joe and most of his squad had worked years ago as cops.

It looked radically different now, of course, less stark and task-oriented and more conducive to conversation, if in a more severe way than the average living room. Nevertheless, there was a sofa, a couple of chairs, and a table on which documents could be spread out.

Joe casually but pointedly waved his guest to a seat at the table, which Willard accepted while replying, "No thanks. I'm all set. I try to avoid coffee this close to bedtime."

Joe sat opposite him, a file folder by his elbow.

"Okay," he began. "Then let me start by thanking you for coming by. I know you were under no obligation to do so, and I appreciate it."

Willard checked his watch. "You said you had something you wanted to discuss."

"Well, yes," Joe replied affably. "As you can imagine. Not to overstate the obvious, but the Dunning name has been in the news lately. It seemed only reasonable that you and I should touch base."

He was only half-stating what he knew, since Rachel's article outing Willard's use of Wilva to compromise Marotti was slated to appear in the *Reformer*'s morning issue.

"Without lawyers?" Willard commented with a wry smile and a raised eyebrow.

Joe laughed, relying on his self-deprecating style to encourage Willard's ingrown arrogance. "Hey, I asked you about that, Mr. Dunning. This is just a conversation, but if you want a lawyer or to walk out the door, that's up to you."

Willard held up his palm. "No, no. You've got me interested. Please carry on. I can't imagine what you want to know from me, or what I can contribute, to be honest."

"There is your son," Joe said.

Willard looked at him pityingly. "Surely, Agent Gunther. You don't expect me to squeal on my own child."

"No, hardly," Joe agreed, while hopeful that might soon change. "Since you bring it up, though," he added, "I couldn't help noting how strong your sense of family is. Your devotion to the school founded by your ancestors, your own enrollment there and that of your son, following in your footsteps. Even your opposition to razing Dunning Cottage in favor of an auditorium and sports center, despite how it would surely benefit the school."

Willard reacted sharply. "That has nothing to do with my family. It's a nice gesture, and of course appreciated, but it was proposed without consultation or consideration of other factors. I'm only against how it was presented, as if it were a done deal. That was overly aggressive and unnecessary."

"Especially from an upstart dago like Jonathan Marotti?" Joe asked.

"I would never use such language. Mr. Marotti's heritage is irrelevant to me."

Joe put on a mildly surprised expression. "Really? According to Wilva Sargent, it's not."

Willard let slip a telling hesitation before

he asked, "Who?"

"You don't read the paper?" Joe asked.

Dunning feigned surprise. "Oh. Marotti's reluctant girlfriend. I didn't know he had it in him. Never struck me as the playful type. She called him an upstart dago?"

"Your son did. He paid her five thousand dollars to claim Marotti harassed her, when, in fact, she barely knew the man."

"You don't know what you're talking about."

Joe extracted Wilva's bank deposit slip from his file and slid it over so Dunning could read it. "We have her sworn testimony," he said. "She'll be issuing a formal retraction in the morning, clearing Marotti's name."

Dunning pressed his lips together, thinking hard and fast. "Maybe I will have that coffee. Hard to keep awake." He tried to sound bored.

Joe rose and poured him a mug from the counter near the door. As he placed it before Dunning, the latter asked, "Why is the VBI interested in a he said–she said civil case anyway? That's not your deal."

"By itself, you'd be right, but putting your son in the middle of your shenanigans with Marotti made you a person of interest in James's murder case."

"Which is another fabrication. My son's no more a murderer than I am, for Christ's sake."

Joe found that an interesting choice of comparisons. He was grateful that the man's self-importance had encouraged him to make it, however.

"James's legal problems are for others to debate," Joe said carefully. "I will say, though, that in the course of filing charges against him, we found a couple of instances where we were thinking you could help him out."

Willard showed genuine surprise. "Oh?"

Joe opened his file again and removed a still from the Windsor train station surveillance footage. He slid it across the table. "This is a photograph of your car, where you parked it overnight, on the day you traveled to New York City."

A stillness settled on Willard's features as he glanced at the picture. "Okay . . ."

Joe added a second shot, this one of the vehicle vandalized. "And this is what happened to it while you were away. It is your car, isn't it?"

Again, the slight reflective pause. "Of course it is. You can see the license plate."

"True enough," Joe said conversationally, sliding an invoice across the table. "And, in fact, here's a copy of the repair bill you got from the body shop for fixing the damage to that window."

"Right," Dunning replied. "I got broken into."

"Did they steal anything?"

"No. I guess they were interrupted. It pissed me off, though. It made a mess of the interior."

"Is that why you didn't report it?" Joe asked. "Even to your insurance company?"

"Right. I didn't want my rates jacked up." Willard tried on his tough-executive face as he then demanded, "What the hell does my getting a broken window have to do with my son?"

"At first, we thought he might have borrowed the car that night, and had an accident," Joe told him. "Possibly explaining why you didn't report the damage or the theft."

Willard appeared baffled, before latching on to Joe's last word. "What theft? I told you nothing was stolen."

"Right." Joe looked apologetic. "I should've shown you this." He displayed a third shot from the Windsor site, showing a man in black clearly removing a couple of small items from the car.

"It's not much, but important: your registration and garage door opener, with which this man then located your home and broke into it."

"That's crap."

Joe delivered a second invoice. "You hired a security firm the next day to install their most expensive system."

"So what? The broken window made me nervous. Nobody actually stole anything."

"Did you enjoy your trip to New York?"

Dunning scowled. "What's it to you?"

"I just wondered. You had company. I was hoping you had a good time."

"Who said I had company?"

Joe presented a copy of the image of Willard kissing Wilva outside the Keene motel. "She did," he stated simply. "The girl you seem to consider less than your social equal. Maybe even an embarrassment?"

Dunning was quiet, his eyes moving from the picture to Gunther's face. "What do you want?"

"Not much," Joe said. "Most of what's troubling me is how far you involved your son, 'cause I think we can both agree, he's got enough on his plate as it is."

"James has nothing to do with this," Willard said.

Joe suppressed his pleasure at this first

crack in Willard's armor. Instead, he reached out and tapped Wilva's bank deposit slip with his fingertip. "That tells me otherwise. Why would you have used him as your go-between if he wasn't fully aware of your affairs? It's simply not credible that you sought his help with this but left him in the dark about Alex Hale."

"Who?" Willard said, trying again to appear clueless.

Joe frowned. "Haven't we moved beyond that?" He extracted from the file what he hoped was his trump card and placed it faceup between them, on top of what was becoming a damning pile of evidence.

"That's a photograph from one of those traffic trailers you see by the side of the road. You know the ones? They flash your speed if you're going too fast?"

Dunning didn't respond.

"The fancy ones," Joe continued, "can be outfitted with cameras. Of course, few of them are, since no one wants to do the paperwork. But the PD in Charlestown, New Hampshire, just purchased one with a grant, and they thought they'd give the camera option a go for a while, to see for themselves."

Joe indicated the picture. "That's Alex Hale, heading for his rendezvous with you

510

by the river."

Willard shook his head, forcing a smile. "You're full of it."

Joe produced a second picture. "And that's you, right behind him. In fact, in the first shot, you can even see a section of your car in the background, just before you earn your own close-up. It sort of puts you both in the same frame."

"It doesn't prove anything."

"It does tell me you've been lying since we sat down," Joe countered. "My question is, why?"

Willard was red-faced. "Because it's all nonsense. You might as well be making it all up. None of it holds water, and you know it."

Joe was already waving his hand back and forth. "No, no, no. That's not what I meant. There's no doubt you killed Alex Hale. The poor bastard did what he'd been doing for years: He stole your opener from your car as you headed out of town by train, broke into your house that night, and stole a laptop — all as he was prone to do by habit. Except this time, he hit the jackpot. That computer had the goods on you, and the family secret that would destroy everything you hold dear if it got out."

Dunning started to respond, but Joe cut

him off. The timing of his sleight of hand was crucial, seeing how slim was the evidence that had brought him to this point.

"Here's my biggest worry, Willard," he stressed, slapping the table gently with his hand. "Like I said before, you love your son; your family name is everything to you — to both of you, in fact. I understand that. James was your torchbearer, your light into the future. Until he messed up. Out of love for you. Why do you think he killed his own supplier in Bellows Falls, and the old man who saw him in town that day from his window and recorded the fact in his version of a birdwatcher's book?"

"He didn't —"

Joe stopped him cold. "It was because James overheard Lyall Johnson bragging how part of his dealings with Wilva Sargent involved sex. James already thought Wilva was beneath you. That she was cheating on you with a dirtbag like Lyall was more than he could stomach. James flipped out. Killing Lyall was merely a way for your son to correct the social order."

Joe leaned forward for emphasis. "Let's face it, Willard. Didn't you feel much the same way about Wilva? Fun to play with, but eventually better as a means to an end? Like in blackmailing Jonathan Marotti?"

Dunning pushed his chair away and stood up. He wiped his mouth with the back of his hand. "None of this is true. You're making it up."

"Don't you wish," Joe corrected him. "James thought so little of Wilva that he planted a fake story about her driving around Bellows Falls scoring drug deals. He *told* you that. He did it to expose her, humiliate you, and break the two of you up. The irony is that his blind prejudice drew our attention to you."

Joe removed one last document from his folder and held it in the air, standing also. "We know about the Aucoin family, Willard," he said, showing him the same photograph that Topher Pluff had located for Rachel and Sally at the library. "We found their remains in Dunning Cottage's cellar earlier today. All four of them, including your grandmother Cherie. We're running DNA tests on Cherie's remains, which you and I both know will prove your true lineage. We also have evidence-recovery teams at your home and office right now, collecting everything we need to lock you up. You killed Alex Hale for trying to blackmail you with this: exposing you as the bastard grandchild of Butch Dunning and his underage rape victim. At first, I doubted that you or even your father, Peter, knew anything about Cherie, but I was wrong. From father to son, the curse of the Dunnings is that knowing about the burial site had to be passed along, to guarantee its being left alone."

Willard actually clapped his hands over his ears, as melodramatic as a starlet getting bad news in a movie. Except, Joe knew, his horror of the truth was real, and as unacceptable to him as seeing his family's reputation swirling down the drain, a victim of three generations of Dunning male egotism.

Joe was silent until Willard regained his composure, dropping his arms and standing with his eyes downcast and his shoulders slumped.

Joe saw what he hoped was his chance, for, in fact, he had purposefully overstated his case. They had been acquiring evidence, most of it circumstantial. A confession was going to be the key.

"Talk to me, Willard. This has been eating at you for decades. The skeleton in the closet in all senses of the phrase. When did you find out?"

Willard sighed. "Oh hell. I don't even remember. Somebody had to know. You were right, to make sure the house was never disturbed, or at least the basement. I

514

was the one."

"Not James, too?"

"Not yet. I would have told him, when the time came."

"Was it Butch who did it?"

Willard nodded.

That wasn't good enough for Joe. "Butch killed them all? The whole family?"

"Yes," he said, his voice barely audible.

"Why?" Joe couldn't hide his incredulity. "Because he'd gotten randy with Cherie?"

Willard looked up, stung, and Joe feared for a moment that he'd shown too much revulsion. *"No,"* Dunning stressed, apparently not the least bit offended. "It was the sale. Those were different times. The buyers were sensitive to bad publicity. There were rumors already about my grandfather and the Aucoin girl. And my father's birth was almost the last straw, until the Aucoins disappeared, supposedly back to Canada, and my grandmother told the world how happy she was to have given birth one last time, as unlikely as that was."

"No one questioned it?"

"No one wanted to. Appearances were everything. Not facts."

"And your grandmother went along with it."

"Things for her improved immeasurably

after Peter was born," Willard said bitterly. "Obviously helped by the cash from the sale." He tilted his head back and stared at the ceiling briefly, admitting, "They did for all of us, for God's sake. That was when the Dunnings became something."

Something pretty unappealing, Joe thought. He said instead, in pursuit of his own ends, "So the whole con game against Marotti was to derail his project and save the cottage?"

"For the time being. It was a stopgap measure, until I came up with something permanent, like maybe hiring my own crew to pour a concrete swimming pool or some damn thing. Marotti just sprang this on us, like a surprise birthday party. My plan would've worked, too, if stupid Wilva had kept it under control. I was *so* going to make it a good payday for her."

Looking back, Joe figured that Wilva Sargent had been the least of Willard's problems. He resisted pointing out how a little love and respect might have completely changed the outcome.

But those were quite obviously missing from the family gene pool.

"Tell me how you killed Alex Hale."

Willard was dismissive. "He was an idiot. You know how sometimes you don't think of trying something, because even a moron would see through it? But then you figure, What the hell? That was how it was with Hale. I told him to meet me one place, then changed it to another at the last second, out of the way, and to bring the computer, and he did." Willard stared at Joe, round-eyed with amazement. "You should've seen his face when I walked up and shot him through the head. Bam. Like that. Not a word said. As soon as I saw the laptop lying next to him, he was dead."

He laughed abruptly, adding, "And you know what the kicker was? He'd implied he had a backup drive, as insurance, which did concern me a little. I found the goddamned thing on him. No wonder he was a thief. Probably couldn't qualify to flip burgers."

Joe was tempted to ask who was calling the kettle black. Instead, he said, "Still, seemed like you weren't able to get into the toolbox."

Willard waved that away. "I got what I needed. I was just trying to be thorough. Who knew what else the little rat had on me? I was pissed off he'd hidden the key. Who the hell does that, for Christ's sake? Fucking squirrel."

Joe let that go and asked instead, "What did you do with the gun?"

He received his answer, in an uncanny reflection of the scorn Willard had just directed at Alex. The other man looked at him, baffled. "I kept it, of course. It's a Colt Python. Those are collectors' pieces."

ABOUT THE AUTHOR

Archer Mayor, in addition to writing the *New York Times* bestselling Joe Gunther series, is a death investigator for the state medical examiner and has twenty-five years of experience as a firefighter/EMT. He lives near Brattleboro, Vermont.